WITHD

SAVED

Also by Jack Falla

Home Ice

Sports Illustrated Hockey: Learn to Play the Modern Way

Quest for the Cup
(with Jack Batten, Lance Hornby,
George Johnson, and Steve Milton)

SAVED

Jack Falla

R.I.P. 9/14/2008

Thomas Dunne Books
St. Martin's Press ❧ New York

This is a work of fiction. All of the characters, organizations, and events portrayed in this novel are either products of the author's imagination or are used fictitiously.

THOMAS DUNNE BOOKS.
An imprint of St. Martin's Press.

www.thomasdunnebooks.com
www.stmartins.com

ISBN-13: 978-0-312-36826-5
ISBN-10: 0-312-36826-7

First Edition: January 2008

10 9 8 7 6 5 4 3 2 1

To Barbara,
a.k.a. the Franchise

Acknowledgments

An assist is as good as a goal, or so goes an old hockey saying. Thus, I want to acknowledge—indeed, celebrate—the assistance of several people who helped with this book.

Thanks to my Canadian writer friends Steve Dryden, Eric Duhatschek, and Frank Orr for their support and encouragement during the early stages of the work. And likewise my gratitude goes to my American writer friends Michelle Seaton and Mark Leccese for coming up big when it counted most.

Sportswriter Justin Pelletier of *The Lewiston Sun-Journal* and his mother Marguerite Pelletier of Lewiston, Maine, helped me with their knowledge of Franco-American culture. Marc Jacques of the Boston office of the Consulate General of Canada was helpful with his knowledge of French-Canadian culture.

My friend Larry Bean supplied me with technical specifications and background on the Ferrari 612 Scaglietti Supercoupe and, wisely, didn't let me drive one.

Dr. Lisa Cogliano explained to me some of the workings of medical education and the internship process.

Tom (Chico) Adrahtas, director of the Midwest Goalie School, was generous with his knowledge of that position. Rock musicians Chris McManus and Gerry Hailer helped me with some of the music trivia. And nephew Michael Reynolds bailed me out when my computer was on the disabled list.

My son Brian and daughter Tracey were helpful and encouraging as they have always been.

Additional assists in the form of friendship, encouragement, and information were dished out by Ken Holmes, Micha Sabovik, Theresa Spisak, Heidi Holland, and Elizabeth Shinzawa.

Special thanks to my agent Mollie Glick of the Jean V. Nagger Literary Agency for taking care of the numbers so I could take care of the words. Upraised hockey stick salutes go to copy editor Adam Goldberger (third man in during my battles with syntax and punctuation) and editor Peter Wolverton who may have saved *Saved*.

And a celebratory hug to my wife, the former Barbara Spelman Baldwin of Northampton, Massachusetts, who can still skate into life's corners and come out with the puck, a trail of bodies in her wake.

—Jack Falla
Natick, Massachusetts
July 3, 2007

The first rule of life, love, and hockey is the same rule—
you've got to play hurt.

SAVED

The Skating Pond

I remember the day I became a goalie.

I was playing pond hockey with the twins, Paul and Andre LeBlanc, on a little thumb-shaped cove on what we called the Skating Pond in Lewiston, Maine. The LeBlancs and I were second-graders at St. Ursula's, "the Sisters' School" we called it. We were playing against a couple of other second-graders from the public school and Russell White, a third-grader from a private school. Russell was the only kid on the pond wearing a complete hockey uniform and a knit hat that said Parkhurst Country Day. Russell White was a preppy twit but he was also the best skater in our game. We were playing five goals wins, and Russell and his friends had beaten us three or four straight. Not that Russell needed teammates, seeing as how he passed the puck about as often as I passed arithmetic.

"Next goal wins!" yelled Russell, who somehow got to decide everything.

"Your turn in goal, Jean Pierre," Paul LeBlanc said to me. I knew it was Paul's turn not mine and I was only being put in goal because I didn't skate or play as well as the other kids. My mother bought my skates at a secondhand sporting-goods store called On the Rebound. She deliberately bought them one size too large so I could "grow into them" and they'd last two years. But even my thick woolen socks didn't make the skates fit, and instead of gliding across the ice I clip-clopped

along with a stride that more closely resembled running than skating.

I took my place between the two boots that marked our goal. I held my hockey stick in my right hand, tapped it against my shin pads, which were really Andre LeBlanc's old pads tied to my legs with frayed skate laces. I put my stick on the ice and bent into a deep crouch as I'd seen goalies do on TV. Off to my left on the best ice in the middle of the pond there was a bigger game played by high school kids. Their skates tore the ice with a scrunch . . . scrunch . . . scrunch . . . as they crosscut on turns, their bodies extended at what looked like impossible angles, their heads up and the puck seemingly stuck to their stick blades. God I wished I could skate like that. On the edge of that game three girls wearing white figure skates glided backward in unison. "What are they doing?" I asked Andre LeBlanc.

"They call it sympathized skating," Andre said. Andre knew everything.

It was our turn to bring the puck up ice. Paul LeBlanc started up the right side, drew Russell White toward him, then passed left to Andre. But the pass was in Andre's skates, giving Russell time to recover. Andre shot just as Russell hooked him. The puck bounced off the boot marking the left goal post and skittered back toward White, who corralled it with his stick, whirled, and started up ice, leaving his teammates and the LeBlancs behind. Russell had scored a bunch of goals on me that day and always by doing the same thing—faking to his forehand, then drawing the puck to his backhand and tapping it into the goal, after which he lifted his stick in the air like he'd just won the Stanley Cup. This time, instead of waiting in my goal for trouble to arrive, I moved out toward the streaking White. When White dropped his head to see where the puck was I hit the ice and slid directly at him, my body in the shape of a V, a box canyon from which Russell White had no escape.

"Ah, shit!" he yelled as he crashed into my shin pads and flew—headfirst and puckless—toward our goal.

I hopped to my feet and passed the puck up to Paul, who passed to Andre, who scored with a long shot that slid between the boots and into the frozen marsh grass beyond. Paul and Andre, their sticks in the air, skated back toward me, where we pounded one another and fell to the ice in a pig pile, our gray hooded sweatshirts reeking of sweat and melted pond water. At least we'd won one game.

"That was trippin'," Russell White said as he hauled himself to his feet, his game shirt covered with ice chips, his knit hat askew.

Andre looked up from the pig pile. "Hey, Russell, quit whinin' like a bitch," he said. I didn't know exactly what that meant but it sounded funny so I laughed. The LeBlancs and I skated over to a fallen tree we used as a bench to take off our skates. Russell White picked up his boots and headed for the far side of the pond, where his father had just arrived and was flashing the lights on his Jeep.

"Great save, JP," Andre said to me. "I'm gonna use that move tomorrow."

"That's right. It's your turn to play goal," Paul said.

"Shit. I hate playing goal," Andre said.

"Don't you guys have a goalie?" I asked.

"Had one but he quit. Now the coaches make us take turns. Sucks," Andre said.

"I'd play if I had the pads and stuff," I said, still flushed with the feeling of having stopped Russell White.

"The coach gives you all the stuff. You wanna play?" Andre said.

"I'll ask my mother," I said.

We ran the shafts of our hockey sticks between the boots and blades of our skates, put the sticks over our shoulders, and headed through the trees toward the streetlights, which had just blinked on. When we got to the street the LeBlancs turned right toward their house and I continued across the street and down a side street toward my grandmother's house, which is where my

*mother and I had lived in the two years since my father did his
Barry Bonds and took a walk.*

*I was cold, wet, tired, and content. I liked playing hockey. It
made me feel like I belonged. And I had liked playing goal. It
made me feel important.*

*I climbed the stairs to my grandmother's house. It was Satur-
day night and I could smell the homemade baked beans we'd be
having with franks and brown bread. As I opened the door I
glanced back up the street and saw one of the older boys from
the game in the middle of the pond. He was walking with one of
the figure skaters. He carried her white skates on his hockey
stick. I wondered why any boy would walk with a sympathized
skater. Or a girl. But this was a long time ago and there were a
lot of things I had to learn.*

One

A Ferrari is foreplay on wheels. Lisa would have hated the car. And was the reason I'd bought it.

It was a 612 Scaglietti—Boss Scags I called it—a bluish gray hardtop four-seater with a six-speed gearbox and scooped-out sides like the Ferrari Italian film director Roberto Rossellini had custom-made for Ingrid Bergman in 1954. I don't know what was on Rossellini's mind but I'll guess it was the same thing that was on mine. Ferraris are about sex first and speed second.

The Boss carried a 540-horse, twelve-cylinder, all-aluminum engine and could pretty much suck the headlights out of anything on the road. But it didn't, because I drove it at the speed limit or maybe five miles per hour over, which made cops and other drivers crazy—the cops because they couldn't pull me over and the drivers because I wouldn't race them. I drive the Ferrari the way I play goal: patiently, letting the others come to me, then denying them and sending them away and, by that, changing the game. Then I wait for the game to come to me again. Lisa used to say I'm passive-aggressive.

I'm Jean Pierre Lucien Savard, thirty-one, and I could be a stunt double for Ichabod Crane. I've got big ears, long arms and legs, floppy blond hair, and a big hooked French nose that isn't good for much of anything except hanging over the rim of a wineglass . . . well, that and breathing. I'm six feet and 170 pounds. I dropped out of college and I don't know much about anything except my job. But I make $2.7 million a year, which is serious money even in pro sports. I do this by playing goal for the Boston Bruins of the National Hockey League. I think the money, the job, and Boss Scags were what appealed to the women I dated in the years after Lisa.

Now that you think I'm one of these obnoxious nouveau riche pro athletes we're all tired of reading about, I should explain that I'm a widower. I hate that old-fashioned word—*widower*. It makes me think of the nodders and droolers you see slumped in wheelchairs in nursing home parlors. But I don't know what else to call myself. Lisa was twenty-eight—two years older than I—when small-cell lung cancer ripped through her like fire through a three-decker. Took her down seven months after a self-congratulatory surgeon came out of the operating room at St. Elizabeth's and told me, "We did it. Got it all." Doctors always say they won. The operation is always "a success." Must be nice to be the one who gets to decide. None of Lisa's doctors showed up at her funeral. Four of her nurses did.

Lisa was a registered nurse. She gave me the skinny on male doctors. Maybe there are a few saintly ones at inner-city clinics and a handful of medical missionaries working in a jungle somewhere, but they're the minority. Ask any young female nurse and you'll find out that a lot of male physicians are as vain, arrogant, and horny as an NHL owner. Some docs will hit on your wife or girlfriend as fast as they'll take swag from a drug company. Lisa liked her job as an oncology ward nurse and she worked part-time even after we got married. But I think she took more hits from doctors than I take in an NHL season. Unlike me, Lisa never got scored on. "One more dinner invitation and I tell your wife, your girlfriend, or Cam Carter," Lisa would say in a voice serious enough to keep the doc off balance.

Forced to choose from Lisa's list I doubt any of the doctors would've picked Cam Carter, my teammate, friend, fishing buddy, confidant, onetime best man, investments adviser, and part-time bodyguard. Maybe you were watching the playoff game two seasons ago when we were hammering Philly 5–1 in the third period and Serge "the Weasel" Balon of the Flyers jumped on me and cross-checked me on the back of the neck after I'd fallen on a loose puck. That was Cam you saw dropping his right glove, putting two fingers in Balon's nostrils, lifting him up about a foot, then using a gloved left hand to fetch Serge a clout on the ear that dropped the Weasel like a sack of cow manure. Cam would've hit Serge with a bare fist if we weren't all such good friends.

The ref gave Cam a five-minute penalty, which didn't matter because we won the game anyway. The best part was when that smarmy Channel 8 TV reporter Alvin "Captain Baritone" Crouch asked Cam on a live-from-the-dressing-room interview after the game: "How can you explain that kind of violence?"

"It wasn't violence. It was justice," Cam said.

I think even Balon agreed. Two nights later, after we eliminated Philly, we went through the postgame handshake line and no one was chirpier than Serge. "Good series, JP," he said, shaking my hand and giving me a squeeze on the neck he'd tried to chop off. "You're in my golf tournament in July, right?"

"If I get the same pole dancer who caddied for me last year," I said.

"She could really tend your pin, eh?"

"Good luck against Montreal," I heard Balon say to Cam, who was two players behind me in line.

What Captain Baritone and a lot of reporters and fans don't know about the culture of professional hockey is well worth knowing. As Robert Duvall said in *The Godfather*, "It's business, not personal." Balon is what players call "a shit disturber" and management calls "an energy guy." Every good team has one. Serge's job is to get under our skin, get us off of our game. He's the best at what he does.

Cam, a six-foot-four, 230-pound defenseman, is one of our enforcers. Part of his job is to cancel out guys like Balon, to balance the game and to make our smaller players—and me—feel comfortable. It's all part of an unwritten code we've known since we were kids playing on ponds and backyard rinks. Justice was built into our game, not tacked on by a rule book that's grown bigger than the Yellow Pages.

Serge's good wishes notwithstanding we lost to Montreal in the next round. The Canadiens threw their speed at us and we had no answer for it. We planned to hit them but you can't hit what you can't catch. Every time I looked up, Montreal was on an odd-man rush: three on two, two on one. To make it worse, I helped cost us the series by giving up a couple of soft goals, including the first goal in Game 1 in Boston, a seventy-foot roller that hit a gouge in the ice and hopped over my stick and between my legs. We lost that game 5–4, and were swept 4–0 in the series. And don't think that a gouge in the ice absolves me. It doesn't. My high school coach, Hartley Lennon at St. Dominic's in Maine, told me, "In sports there's reality and there's *ultimate* reality." In this case the reality was that the puck took a quirky and unpredictable bounce. Ultimate reality is that it ended up in the net and we lost by one goal. "In sports, ultimate reality is the only reality that counts," Coach said.

We were two games into the Montreal series when the league announced it was fining Cam $5,000 for arguing with and bumping into the ref after the Balon incident. But that's beer money to Cam, not because he's pulling down $2.3 million a year but because Cameron Cabot Carter III is the grandson of the founder of Carter & Peabody, the private Boston-based mutual fund company. Cam is the only guy in the NHL who could make more money in the family business than he can playing hockey. Four years ago I asked him why he keeps playing. "You ever been to a business meeting?" he said. "It's five minutes, max, before someone says 'synergy' and your eyes glaze over. The over-under on 'paradigm' is seven minutes, and I'd bet the under. Besides, my family built the business. I made it in hockey on my own. Hockey's mine. A game belongs to the people who play it."

"Try telling that to an owner," I said. "They're the ones the game really belongs to. What do you do if the club trades your aging butt to Buffalo?"

"Son, say hello to the newest senior partner of Carter & Peabody," he said. "And, Mr. Savard, I think it's time we rebalanced your portfolio."

Last season—the season that changed our lives forever—I felt Cam was close to calling it a career. I had to envy the Camster, an All-Star who had serious money waiting for him no matter what happened on the ice. Not that I have to worry about where next month's condo payment is coming from. After I'd signed that last five-year deal with Boston I figured I'd need only one more contract to retire with enough money so that I wouldn't have to become a scout, a goalie coach, or, worse, one of those front-office coat holders. But I mostly wanted to keep playing because goaltending is the only job I know. And it's a good life. Except for the games.

The problem with being a goalie is that you can't win a game, you can only not lose it. You try to lose as few as you can before you get hurt or old or lose your job to someone younger and better. Goaltending, like life, is only a question of how much you eventually lose by.

Like a lot of goalies I'm a worrier, which means I spend most of the eight to nine months of the season—depending on how deep we go in the playoffs—in varying states of anxiety ranging from mild apprehension the day before a game to throwing-up scared forty-five minutes before face-off. That's one of the reasons Cam and I cooked up our little end-of-summer fishing trip. It's a chance to relax before life disintegrates into the chaos of a hockey season. We go to his parents' waterfront house in Falmouth on Cape Cod. It's a seven-bedroom gray-shingled Colonial with its own dock and a twin-inboard fishing boat.

It's always just Cam and me. Cam's wife, Tamara, stays home

with their daughters—Lindsey, eight, and Caitlin, five. Cam's parents spend most of September in France. And the women I was going out with would've rated a fishing trip lower than a product recall on lip gloss.

It's the same routine every year. We spend the afternoon jigging for bluefish, come back to the house about six o'clock, clean one blue for dinner and two or three for the freezer, hit the shower, fire up the grill.

We eat on the back porch, which faces south overlooking Nantucket Sound and the distant shore of Martha's Vineyard. I like September. Days grow shorter and nights cooler. It's a meteorological overture to the hockey season. Cam says F. Scott Fitzgerald had it right: "Life starts all over again when it gets crisp in the fall."

And I like training camp. I'm not fighting for a job, preseason games don't mean anything, and I haven't begun to accumulate the welts, strains, and bruises that by midseason can erode my will to put my body in front of another frozen puck. I like getting back on the ice, catching up with friends and teammates. I even like breaking in new pads and gloves, especially a catch glove, although there's an irony to a catch glove in that the more flexible it becomes the less it protects my hand. But there's no such thing as pain-free goaltending, so I trade protection for saves and count it a good deal.

The way I feel after Labor Day makes me sorry for some of the summer people going home to boring jobs and to lives they feel trapped in. Or that they trapped themselves in because at some point they gave in to fear and did what they knew they could do—play it safe—instead of taking a chance on doing what they truly wanted to do. They call that "being realistic." Hockey scares me, but I'd rather be scared than bored.

After dinner Cam breaks out the Cognac and we sit and watch the lights of the boats on Nantucket Sound. When we're fishing we keep the conversation light. We talk about the fish, the coming season, the rookies who'll be after our jobs, the schedule. We save the heavy stuff for after dinner. It was on the back porch three years ago that Cam and I first talked about Lisa's death.

Lisa and I were married four years. No kids. But we were planning to start a family at the end of the season when I knew I'd be signing another long-term deal. In March of that year Lisa went for a chest X-ray. She had a cough that had been bothering her for months. That's when they found the cancer. Lisa didn't smoke. But more than 15 percent of the people who get lung cancer don't smoke. Most of them are women.

By August the cancer was on the power play. One of the last times I saw Lisa was a Thursday night. She was sitting up in her hospital bed, alert and breathing oxygen through a plastic tube. We were half watching an early-season Thursday-night NFL game. Lisa's father had played football at Boston College and Lisa loved the game. On a first-and-goal from the eight-yard line the San Diego quarterback took the snap and spun to his left where he was supposed to hand the ball to the tailback. But the tailback ran the wrong play and sprinted out for a pass. "Busted play!" yelled the TV play-by-play guy.

The quarterback scrambled around, ducked under the grasp of a defensive end, sidestepped a linebacker, and, while on the run, threw across his body to a receiver in the back left corner of the end zone. Touchdown.

"And the Chargers made something out of a busted play, Gene," the TV analyst said as if he were giving us an insight into quantum theory. That's when Lisa delivered the best sports metaphor I've ever heard.

"Life is a busted play," she said.

A week later she was gone.

Lisa was right. Life *is* a busted play. Love too.

. . .

I met Lisa early in my junior year at the University of Vermont, where Cam and I played college hockey. The team was doing one of those end-of-practice skating drills that are tough for goalies because of the weight of our equipment. I'd put my gloves, stick, and mask on the back of the net to lighten my load. But an assistant coach, screwing around, dinged a slapshot off the post and into my left cheekbone and nose. Blood all over the place. I held a towel to the cut and skated to the dressing room, where Bobby Breyer, our trainer, undid my leg pads and skates. I was still wearing my "Vermont Hockey" practice shirt and pressing a bloody towel to my cheek when Bobby and I walked into the emergency room at Lake Champlain Medical Center. Lisa stood near the desk. The name on her uniform read "Lisa M. Quinn, R.N.—Oncology." I didn't know what "oncology" meant. I found out later she was only working the ER to sub for a friend. Lisa was a cute kid with short black hair, an upturned nose, and big brown eyes. Midtwenties. Perky cheerleader type.

"What happened?" Lisa asked.

"Stopped a puck," I said.

"Hey, that's more than you did against Harvard," she said, laughing and holding out her hand. "You're J. P. Savard, right? I'm Lisa Quinn. And I'm kidding. I've seen you guys play. You've got a good team. But not last Saturday. What happened?"

"Couldn't handle Harvard's power play," I said, and explained that Harvard used an unbrella power play, where one defenseman plays back near the blue line like a basketball point guard. "Then they put two forwards at the top of the circles and two more down low near the net. Guy at the top had a cannon. He'd blast it at me and the little guys down low would go for the tip-in or rebound. Seems every time we hit a guy near the net we got called for interference. They scored five goals on the power play, two of them during five-on-threes. Of course I didn't do anything that would remind anyone of a goaltender."

Lisa laughed and hustled me into the ER. She stayed with me while a lady doctor put in the stitches, and then Lisa worked some administrative magic to get us to the front of the X-ray-room line so we could see if the cheekbone was broken. It wasn't. "Bad news. Not broken. Gotta face BC Saturday," she said. I liked her attitude and blunt humor.

Lisa's father was a University of Vermont season ticket holder and he often took Lisa to the games. But he and Lisa's mother were Boston College alumni, so Lisa wasn't getting her usual ticket for that Saturday's sold-out game against number-three-in-the-nation BC.

"No problem," I said. "They reserve tickets for players. I'll get you two."

"Thanks. How much?"

"Can't sell 'em. NCAA rules," I said. I only added the NCAA thing so I wouldn't seem too eager. "I'll leave them at Will Call."

"They'll rename it Won't Call if you play like last Saturday," Lisa said.

The next day I told one of our managers I wanted two tickets left for Lisa Quinn. And I wanted to know the seat locations.

I try not to look into the stands before or during a game. I don't want to be distracted. And there's nothing in the stands that can help me. But when we skated out for the BC game I took a peek at the section behind the net, third row, where I knew Lisa would be sitting. I wanted to see whom she was with. I felt relieved when I saw it was a woman. Maybe Lisa doesn't have a boyfriend, I thought.

That peek probably cost me. I let in the first shot, a fluttery seventy-footer from outside the blue line. It broke off of my catch glove. I still don't know how. Might've dipped. I could see heads drop on our bench and hear the groan from the crowd. Cam skated up to me and slapped me on the pads with his stick, and if you were in the stands, you probably thought he was saying something encouraging. But what he was doing was his Jay Leno—"You friends with that puck, JP? Saw you wave to it. Hey, only fifty-nine more minutes to go." Cam has odd ways of turning down the pressure.

This is where a goalie has to do some acting, projecting to

his teammates a confidence he doesn't feel. I whacked my stick across my pads and took up my stance at the top of the crease, crouching lower than usual, trying to strike a pose that said, "That's all, they don't draw another breath." But nothing truly sends that message like making the next save. And in goaltending, as in life, the hardest play to make is the one after the one you just screwed up. The next shot came from BC's top scorer, Paschal Fleming, on a breakaway. He opened his stick blade as if he were going to take a high shot to my stick side, but then he whirled to his backhand and tried to shove the puck inside the post. I butterflied—dropped to my knees with both legs fanned out. Fleming's shot deflected off the top edge of my left pad. I caught the puck as it bounced off the pad and before I toppled backward into the net but with my left arm held forward so as not to carry the puck over the goal line. It was a spectacular and slightly embellished save and one that got the team and me back in a game we'd go on to win 3–2 even though we were outshot 39–21. When the horn sounded I flipped up my mask and turned around to give Lisa a wave. She smiled and waved back. I looked for her in the lobby after the game but she wasn't there.

"Will you call her, for Christ's sake," Cam said about a hundred times over the next few weeks. But I didn't have the nerve to call her. In December she called me. She wanted to know if any players could stop by the hospital's pediatric oncology ward and visit patients. I told her we had a few days off before Christmas and Cam and I would come in.

"What's a pediatric oncology ward?" I asked Cam.

"Cancer," he said. "Kids with cancer. An hour in that place is going to make a torn ACL seem like a month in Paris."

Cam and I visited the Lake Champlain Medical Center three days before Christmas. We brought a bunch of plastic ministicks with "UVM" on one side and "Go, Cats, Go" on the other. Our team nickname is the Catamounts. A catamount is an eastern mountain lion. No one in Vermont has seen a live catamount in about a hundred years. Logic doesn't play a big role in the mascot business.

Cam also brought a box of three dozen green-and-gold "Vermont Hockey" hats. He tried to get the bookstore manager to donate them but when the manager said, "Well, I think I can offer you boys a discount but I have profit accountability here and . . ." Cam whipped out his wallet, peeled off three hundred-dollar bills, slapped them on the counter, and told the bookstore guy: "Discount this. And keep the change." Then Cam grabbed the box of hats and we left. "JP, there's a time, a place, and a target for fuck-you money, and that was all three," he said, tossing the box of hats into the back of his SUV.

Lisa wasn't in the ward when we arrived, so one of the other nurses—I thought she was the one sitting with Lisa at the BC game—took us into a room with two patients and introduced us. "And you have to meet Rudy Evanston," she said to me, taking my elbow and guiding me over to a boy who looked to be about ten or eleven years old. Rudy said he'd been a goalie in youth hockey before he was diagnosed with leukemia. Most of Rudy's hair had fallen out because of the chemotherapy.

He said he had some questions about goaltending. He wanted to know how to move from post to post with the play behind the net. I showed him, grateful to have something to talk about because, otherwise, I had no idea what to say to these kids. I used the legs of his bed as goalposts. I took off my shoes so I could slide on the floor as if it were ice. I was using one of the ministicks to show Rudy how to intercept passes from behind the goal line when Cam interrupted. "Don't listen to him, Rudy," Cam said. "He only has two moves. Sometimes he flips. Sometimes he flops. What the hell."

"Language . . . watch your language, please," Lisa said, entering the room just in time to see me slide into the right bed leg and collide with the side table, spilling the pitcher of water. Rudy laughed. Lisa scowled. I went into the bathroom in search of paper towels.

Lisa thanked us for coming and led us from room to room, introducing us to each kid. A lot of them were bald. Bringing those hats was a great move by Cam. We gave one to every kid, bald or not. And we had a few left over for the nurses.

"How many of these kids are going to make it?" I asked her when we were between rooms.

"You never know. Probably more than half. We treat each kid like he's going to make it. Attitude's a big deal here. And theirs can depend on ours. So pick it up, OK? Fake it if you have to," she said, flipping an elbow into my ribs.

I said I wouldn't last ten minutes working in a kids' cancer ward. "How do you face this every day?"

"By thinking I make it better," she said.

It was three o'clock when we wrapped up our visit. Lisa was working an eight-to-three shift, so she was getting out at the same time Cam and I were leaving. She said she was going to lunch, so I took a chance. "Buy you lunch if you'll give me a ride back to campus," I said.

"Deal," she said.

That's where we started. We spent an hour telling each other about our childhoods and families. She was brought up in nearby Essex. Father was in pharmaceutical sales. Mother taught middle-school English. Lisa had majored in nursing at Boston College. She'd been working for two years. She was twenty-four, two and a half years older than I was.

Lisa's life sounded like a TV sitcom to me. I was born in Montreal, where my father, Rogatien, worked on a construction crew. He did this to raise money for his real business, which was drinking. He left my mother and me when I was five. Went to work—or so he said—and never came back. I hardly remember him. I don't recall that he ever hit my mother or me but I remember him yelling a lot. Mainly, I remember our house, in the then-working-class Plateau section of east Montreal, as being a gloomy place. I think our apartment was on the north side of the building, so we didn't get much sunlight. I also remember the empty beer bottles, still smelling of their long-gone contents, that I used as toys to build forts. To this day I don't drink beer, because I don't like the feelings that smell evokes.

My mother, who'd been born in Maine, moved us back into her widowed mother's house in Lewiston, an old mill town on the Androscoggin River. My mother changed her name and mine from Lachine—my father's last name—back to Savard, her family's name. I was raised by my mother and grandmother. My mom got a job in a grocery store. She started as a cashier and ended up supervising the checkout section. We didn't have a lot of money. I never planned to be a goaltender but I kept getting picked for travel and all-star teams and eventually got a scholarship to St. Dominic's High School. St. Dom's called it a "need-based" scholarship calculated on my family's low income. My mother called it a need-based scholarship as in "we need a goalie." I started three years at St. Dom's but Vermont's Marco Indinacci was the only major-college hockey coach to offer me a full ride.

Lisa and I dated all through my junior year, when Vermont went to the NCAA semifinals and, right afterward, I got an offer from the Bruins. It wasn't a great deal, because it was a lock they'd send me to their farm team in Providence, where I'd make minor-league money. But the contract included a $200,000 signing bonus. I dropped out of school because I needed the money. Coach Indinacci understood. "Got to take it," he said. "Best I can offer you is a Ford 150 from an alumni-owned dealership and a lady tutor who likes hockey players."

I got called up to the Bruins in early November of my second season, and by March I was pushing Harry "Head Case" Harrington for the starting job, a job I got when Head Case lost three straight games to New Jersey in the playoffs and then hit the modern pro athlete trifecta—driving under the influence, re-sisting arrest, and possession with intent to distribute.

I signed a three-year one-way deal (same money whether I was in the NHL or the minors). That's when Lisa and I got married and bought a house.

It was a great marriage. While it lasted.

I didn't date in the year after Lisa died, partly because I thought it would be disrespectful to Lisa and her family (a lot of what players do ends up in the papers), but mostly because I didn't want to. The remarkable thing about that season is that I played well.

The games were the only time I could get outside of myself and feel something besides aloneness. Hockey was therapy. I started going to the rink at 3 p.m. for 7 p.m. games. I even took part in the morning skates on game day, something I hadn't done very often, ostensibly as a concession to the fact that I was start-ing more than sixty of our eighty-two regular-season games and all of the playoffs. But that excuse was a crock. I was just trying to cut down on the number of meaningless shots I had to face. Meaningless shots can hurt you just as much as game shots. Peckham "Packy" Dodd, our coach, let me get away with this for two reasons: we were winning and I was playing well. Perfor-mance is everything in the pros. Remember Jeffrey Dahmer, the serial killer and cannibal the cops found with human body parts in his freezer? If Dahmer had been a goalie with a .920 save per-centage, team management would've said he wasn't a murdering cannibal, he was a misunderstood kid with an eating disorder.

Cam and I were on the back porch of the Cape house when he asked me how I was doing. I knew he didn't mean hockey.

"First lap around the calendar is hard," I said. "Birthday. An-niversary. Christmas—"

Cam cut me off: "Hey, JP, Lisa wouldn't want you living like this. She wouldn't want you to be alone."

"Lisa doesn't want or not want anything," I said. "She's dead. Gone."

"She's not dead as long as the people who loved her remember her," Cam said, paraphrasing a Hemingway line he'd quoted at Lisa's funeral. "I don't suppose you've changed your position on the afterlife?"

"You got some game film to show me?"

"Freakin' atheist."

"I'm not an atheist. I'm an agnostic. Atheists don't believe. Agnostics doubt."

"An agnostic is just an atheist who lacks the courage of his conviction," Cam said.

"I *wish* I believed, if that's any consolation to you."

"It's the percentage move," Cam said. "It doesn't cost anything to believe in God and heaven. If you're right, you win big. If you're wrong, you lose nothing, you're just dead. But what if you *don't* believe and you're wrong? Then you're fucked."

I laughed. "Yeah, that's it, Cam. It's just one big casino game and you've figured how to beat the house. OK, but suppose there's a heaven and we're up there skating around and some of those goons from the Philadelphia Flyers show up. Then what?"

"I find it highly unlikely that any Philadelphia Flyer could enter the kingdom of heaven," Cam said. "But if that happens, we do the same as always. Beat the crap out of them. If you want peace, fight for justice. Gotta have peace and justice in heaven."

"Thank you, Monsignor Carter. And on that enlightened note I'm going to bed," I said.

"Not till you tell me you'll at least think about rejoining the human race this season," he said. "Gotta get back on the horse."

"How do you know I wasn't on her last night? Three more seconds I win the bareback. Took the gold buckle in the calf roping," I said.

"She likes that sort of thing?"

"What?"

"The roping?"

"Nah. I was kidding. I stayed home and watched the Sox."

"You want Tamara and me to set up something in a couple of weeks? What about Elaine Neely?"

"The PR lady at Carter & Peabody?"

"Yeah. Smart. Single. Looker. About our age. Why not?"

"Corpspeak," I said, going into my imitation of a corporate PR executive. "'Strategic initiatives launched from a broad platform of technological innovation will allow C&P to achieve increasing synergistic advantages going forward.' Jeez, I get horny when they talk like that."

Cam ignored that. "What about Alison what's-her-name? The chick who bought the house next to yours?"

"Alison Dufrayne? Had coffee with her when we ran into each other at a bookstore café. Neutral-zone trap. She talked for twenty-five minutes about window treatments and wall coverings. I couldn't get the conversational puck out of my own end. It was like playing New Jersey."

Cam kept pressing. "Hey, you know who's in Boston now?" he said, then answered his own question: "Faith McNeil."

"Faith from Vermont?" Faith and I had been friends in college. Her name got my attention.

"Ran into her at a golf tournament a couple of months ago. Divorced. No kids. Going back to grad school. Faith scored big when she and her husband started an Internet company in the nineties. She cashed out during the divorce and before the dot-com bubble broke."

"She was always a winner," I said. "You're wearing me down, man. Tell you what. Let's get through two-a-days and maybe you and Tam and I can do a foursome with Faith. Dinner maybe?"

Cam reached out and clinked his brandy snifter against my empty glass. "Ladies and gentlemen," he said, putting down the snifter and cupping his hands to his mouth in an effort to sound like a stadium announcer, "back in the saddle and coming out of Chute Three, that calf-ropin' bronco-bustin' barebackin' buckaroo from Boston—Jean Pierre SAVAAAAAARD." Then he imitated a crowd cheering.

I went to bed.

I'd met Faith McNeil in my freshman year at Vermont, where Cam and I were on scholarships for hockey and Faith for basketball. Actually, Faith and I were on the full rides. Cam's family was so well off that he gave back his scholarship so Coach Indinacci could sign Gaston Deveau, a speedy center. "That little frog is faster than a hooker at a truck stop," Indinacci said of Deveau. Coach was never one to get overly technical. Deveau put up numbers that belonged on the Chicago Mercantile Exchange and led us to the NCAAs three years running.

Faith was a well-proportioned six-foot forward with auburn hair she usually wore in a ponytail. She lived on our floor. She was a premed major and kind of a smart-mouth. Early in the year we'd passed each other in a Burlington restaurant on a Saturday night. We were with our dates. I waved. She nodded. The next day she was carrying a laundry basket down the dorm stairs just as I was coming up.

"Get much?" she said.

I really hadn't (it was only September), so I laughed and said, "Close. Hit the post."

"Keep shooting. One hundred percent of the shots you don't take don't go in," she said, and laughed one of the deepest, throatiest laughs I'd ever heard. She was down another level of stairs before I yelled down the stairwell, "How about you?"

"Naw. He had no touch from outside and couldn't drive the lane," she said, laughing again.

I went to some of her games, she came to some of mine, and we had a few meals together, but we never really dated. I was a little afraid of Faith McNeil.

·　·　·

You wouldn't think a WASP like Cam would go to a state school, but Cam's grandfather and father were UVM grads, so it's a family tradition. Also, it tends to make life in the classroom a little easier when three buildings, a library wing, a hockey rink, and two faculty chairs carry your family name.

Cam and I were roommates but that was Indinacci's decision. I didn't become friends with Cam until the third week of practice. Indinacci had recruited two good classes in a row, so a lot of freshmen and sophomores—including Cam and me—were pushing the juniors and seniors for jobs. There was a lot of bad feeling and I thought Indinacci was making it worse when he matched the freshmen and sophomores against the juniors and seniors in an intrasquad scrimmage that turned out to be bloodier than the Crimean War. We—the freshmen and sophs—were beating the upperclassmen pretty bad when Indinacci whistled a penalty against one of our guys, thus giving his vets a five-on-four power play. A power play was the only time senior Monti Andersen got on the ice. Andersen was huge. A Zamboni with legs. His job was to stand in front of the opposing goalie while his teammates blasted away. The first time, it worked. I got beaten by a shot I never saw. But Cam was on the ice for the vets' next power play. That was the end of Monti Andersen's hockey career. Andersen took up his usual stance just outside of my goal crease. I was hopping around trying to see through his legs or around him or anything when *whooomp*, he was gone. Just like that. What happened was that Cam came across the front of the net full bore and cleaned Monti Andersen's clock. Steamrolled him in a move that was about four separate penalties—charging, cross-checking, interference, and intent to injure—and probably a couple of felonies to boot. Andersen fell awkwardly, dislocating his left shoulder. As the senior writhed on the ice Cam stood over him and said—loud enough for everyone to hear—"You can stand on Park Place, Monti, but you've got to pay the rent."

After that I figured Cam might be a pretty good guy to be friends with.

Hockey is big at UVM and the team's rabid following includes a small battalion of women known among students as "puck bunnies." Players call them "puck fucks." Screwing a puck fuck is about as hard as hitting an empty net. I did OK but I think Cam was on his way to setting a New England single-season freshman screwing record until March, when he met Tamara MacDonald, a freshman at St. Michael's College in Winooski, a few miles from campus. Met her at the Slapshot, a downtown bar and restaurant that wasn't too picky about matching your photo ID with the real you. We were at the bar waiting for a table when Cam spotted Tamara standing with a group of her friends. I think it was some kind of WASP attraction. Genetic programming. Tamara—which she pronounces Tam-AH-rah—is from Nantucket, Massachusetts, an island with more money than the United Arab Emirates. There was nothing overtly sexy about Tam. She looked like a page out of a Brooks Brothers catalog—light blue cashmere V-neck sweater and off-white chino pants. Not exactly the tight-jeans, bare-belly, push-up-bra look we'd more or less gotten used to.

"I know her from someplace," Cam said.

"Been to any Republican inaugural balls lately?" I asked, but by then Cam was walking toward Tamara and all of a sudden they were shaking hands and laughing and Cam was writing her phone number on a cocktail napkin.

"Wish you'd jump on loose pucks that fast," I said when he got back.

"Nantucket Yacht Club dance a year ago," Cam said. "My parents dragged me there. Her parents are members."

After that it was the Cam & Tam Show all the way through college. They got married right after graduation and before Cam signed with Boston.

Cam, Tamara, and I did a lot of foursomes for dinner and concerts, but until I met Lisa I was always with someone different—a puck bunny or maybe a woman I met in class. I actually went to class, which is something a lot of hockey players don't do.

I majored in history for no reason other than that I can't do math except for figuring my save percentage.

A couple of times in my first two years I went out with Faith McNeil but it was a kind of friendship thing where we were going to dinner with Cam's parents and I knew from experience that an airhead wasn't going to make the cut. Faith could hold her own even with a guy like Cam's father, a likable, hard-drinking blowhard.

We were at a Burlington restaurant one night when Cam's father—having slammed down three single-malt scotches before we'd even placed our orders—leaned back in his chair and said: "OK, boys, you can pick only one—money, power, or sex— what's it going to be?"

I said sex to try to be funny. Cam said money because it's what he thought his parents expected him to say.

"You guys are *really* dumb," Faith said, staring at us and shaking her head. "Pick *power*, dummies. If you have power you get the other two."

Of course that was the answer, and Cam's dad laughed so loud we were getting stared at by people at the other tables until Cam's mom said, "Shush, Cameron." To tell you the truth I think Cam's dad would've taken a run at Faith if he thought he could get away with it. But Cam's mom, Diana, had grown up with a little money and she wasn't one to sacrifice self-respect just to keep a country club membership. Cam told me that when he was about twelve his father "got caught with lipstick on his dick." That indiscretion cost Cam's dad a small chateau in France and some new Limoges china to replace the pieces Diana broke throwing them at him. "Got me with her goddamn out pitch—soup tureen, sidearm, pecker high," Cam's dad said to us one night a few years ago when Diana wasn't around and he was drunk and recounting the incident and the stupid way he got caught. He'd taken his mistress to a Red Sox game and they sat in the first row behind the plate. Diana saw them on TV. "Wouldn't have caught us if it wasn't for the left-handed DH.

You couldn't see us behind all the right-handed hitters. I've always been against the goddamn DH rule."

That affair ended interconference play for Cameron Carter Jr. Now he gets his kicks watching Cam and me play and betting on hockey, horses, and football.

Diana liked Faith. "That's the kind of girl I like to see you with, JP," she whispered to me one night at dinner after Faith had left the table to go to the ladies' room. "Not these . . . these . . . well, these other women you go out . . ."

"The puck bunnies?" I said.

She laughed.

"Mrs. Carter, life is hard enough without unnecessary challenges." I said.

She said I needed more confidence.

I said confidence was the forty saves I'd dropped on Minnesota in our 2–1 championship win at the Christmas Classic. "Hockey is hard. Women should be easy."

After I left college I never saw or heard from Faith until Cam and Tamara invited her to dinner.

The Carters waited a week into training camp—the end of two-a-days—before they invited Faith and me to their house.

They should've scheduled it earlier because it fell two days after Cam fought Davey Canfield in training camp, so Cam's face was still swollen. Canfield was a rookie left wing for our farm team in Providence. His first-year stats were three goals, seven assists, and 402 penalty minutes. Canfield is an enforcer, a guy whose best chance to make the NHL is as a fighter. You read a lot of stuff these days about the so-called new NHL and the alleged disappearance of fighting. Fighting isn't as important as it used to be when there was at least one brawl per game, and that old line from Toronto Maple Leaf founder Conn Smythe pretty much said it all: "If you can't beat them in the alley you can't beat them on the ice."

But even today the stat sheets show there's at least one fight every three games. That works out to about thirty fights per season per team. You lose too many of those and other teams will begin running you out of the rink. Every contending team in the league carries at least one fighter. We carry two.

One of the unwritten rules of the Hockey Code is that heavyweights fight heavyweights, and another part of the Code says that the incumbent heavyweight has to give the newcomer a chance. This meant that sooner or later Cam or Kevin Quigley, our other tough guy, would have to drop the gloves with Davey.

Canfield was professional about it, I'll give him that. We ran into him in the rink lobby before practice. The kid was only twenty but Cam and I were impressed by his approach. "Think we should go today, Cam?" he said.

"Let's do it early," Cam said. "Maybe Packy will throw us out and we'll get the day off."

We were scrimmaging five-on-five when Cam and Davey began jousting in front of my net. Play stopped when the gloves came off and Canfield began throwing bombs at Cam's head. Landing them, too. Hit him on the left side of the head with three rights, the second of which knocked Cam's helmet off. Cam staggered and almost went down—something that would've brought Davey one step closer to making our team and Cam one step closer to losing his job.

Cam, recovering, used his right hand to pull Davey in close and they waltzed around a little bit. I thought Cam was just hanging on. You could tell these guys were pros because there was no yapping. In hockey good fighters don't talk a lot. "Why rattle before you strike?" as Cam puts it.

"Let 'em go," said Packy, who didn't want any of the players to break up the fight, something veterans are inclined to do when a teammate is losing.

Canfield threw a few harmless rights into Cam's back before Cam reached into his bag of tricks. In a sudden shove with his right hand, Cam pushed Canfield away, thus setting him up for three hammering lefts, two to his face and one to his throat. Then Cam grabbed the bottom of Canfield's hockey pants and tipped him over. When they fell to the ice both were bleeding but Cam was on top, the clear winner.

Canfield was a pro to the end. "Jeez, why didn't somebody tell me he's a lefty," the kid said, picking up his gloves.

"The winnah and still champion," said Kevin Quigley as he skated over to my net. Quigley is a local guy with a strong Boston accent, the kind where most Rs become Hs.

"Close, though," I said. "Kid's tough. Think you can take him?"

"Don't think I'll have to. The Mad Hattah will send him down," said Quigley.

I looked up in the stands to my right, and sure enough, there was general manager Madison Hattigan—the Mad Hatter—sitting alone, cell phone pressed to his right ear, his dark cadaverous eyes on the ice, seeing everything.

Cam and Davey skated to the medical room for stitches. If you didn't play hockey for a living you'd think there'd be some danger that a couple of guys who'd just tried to beat each other's brains out might go at it again. But Cam and Davey are dispassionate professionals. Emotion didn't enter into it. This was ritualized combat, something that goes on in all thirty NHL training camps. Not that the fights aren't real. I laugh when fans say hockey fights are faked. I'm with Wayne Gretzky, who said, "If fights were faked I'd get in a lot more of them."

Cam made it back for the last fifteen minutes of practice. I think he just wanted to send a message to the team and especially to the rookies. As Cam says: 'The first rule of life, love, and hockey is the same rule—you've got to play hurt.' "

Cam came into our dressing room after practice, dumped his gloves and helmet in his locker, then headed back out the door. I saw him take a right toward the rookies' dressing room. He told me later he went there to talk to Canfield. "I told him it was a good scrap. If they send him down all he has to do is take care of business for a season or two and he'll be in the Show. Maybe not here but somewhere. The kid can throw 'em."

Quigley was right. The next morning the Mad Hatter shipped Davey to Providence, and later that season he traded him to Edmonton. Best break the kid ever got. He caught on with Edmonton and has been in the NHL ever since.

"Cameron Cabot Carter the Third, you look like someone hit you with a bag of shovels." It was the deep rich voice of Faith McNeil coming from the foyer of Cam and Tam's house. "JP here?" she asked.

"In the living room," Cam said but by then I was off the couch and headed for the foyer. What awaited me there was Faith McNeil wearing the Montreal Canadiens power play—Saint Laurent, Chanel, Givenchy, Tourneau, and Vuitton. The ponytail was gone and in its place was a hairstyle best described as early Katharine Hepburn. She looked like what she'd become—an alpha female.

"Hey, Faith, all your sweats in the wash?" I said, trying to set the tone and get in a preemptive shot.

"Along with your game, JP. I heard about the intrasquad," she said. Faith won that exchange. We'd had our Black-versus-Gold intrasquad game the night before and I'd given up five goals playing only a period and a half.

I went to shake hands with her—I hate social hugging and kissing, it's insincere—but she grabbed my right hand and pulled me into a hug that included a head-on with the same breasts that used to make the block-lettered "VERMONT" on her game shirt look like a section of track for the Tilt-A-Whirl.

The Carters could afford as much household help as they wanted but they didn't want any. They were getting the meal themselves, so Tamara excused herself and went back to the kitchen and Cam went with her to make a couple of gin and tonics for Faith and me. As soon as they were gone Faith turned serious. "I heard about Lisa. I'm sorry," she said. "You've had a tough time."

I thanked her and said I heard she'd taken a hit herself what with the divorce.

"Not the same," she said. "Pete and I made a choice. You and Lisa didn't. Besides, he was in love with someone else. Anyway, it worked out OK"—she hesitated a half beat—"securitywise." I'd been around Cam's family long enough to know "security" was one of the upper-crust code words for serious wealth. Cam told me Faith cleared twenty mil when she sold her stock in the company she'd helped start.

It was here that I broke the first rule of goaltending—I committed myself too soon. "Maybe we could grab dinner some night and catch up," I said as Cam entered the room with the drinks.

"I thought that's what tonight's for," Faith said. "Grad school starts next week. And to tell you the truth, JP, I'm in a relationship. He's a cardiologist at Mass General. Between my classes and his job we won't get to spend much time together." She took her gin and tonic from Cam and headed to the kitchen to see if she could help Tamara.

As Cam handed me my drink he let loose a long low whistle followed by the equally low rumble of an explosion. I knew what he meant. I'd just gone down like one of those Japanese fighter planes in the movie *Midway,* smoke and flame belching from the fuselage before it crashes into the Pacific.

Tam didn't need help so Faith returned to the living room.

Scrambling to recover, I asked her where she was going to grad school.

"Boston University. First year."

"Business school?" I asked.

"Med school," she said. I almost spewed my drink. Here I was doing the same thing I'd been doing since I was eight years old—putting my body between pucks and their intended destinations—and here was Faith McNeil, who'd built a business, made about ten times as much money as I had, and was now on the road to being a doctor.

I can handle beautiful women. And I'm OK with beautiful and smart. But hit me with an alpha female—beautiful, smart, sophisticated, successful, stylish, and rich—and my self-confidence goes farther south than Enron. I spent most of dinner stickhandling asparagus tips around my plate.

When Tamara and Cam started clearing away dishes Faith turned to me and said, "I hear Cam's been giving you a rough time."

"Cam's worried that I don't date much, but to tell you the truth I don't want to," I said.

"You know what you need, Jean Pierre?"

I said I sure didn't.

"A rehab start," she said.

I laughed. A rehab start in baseball and sometimes in hockey happens when you're coming off an injury and your team sends you to its minor-league affiliate to get in a game or two before you come back to the bigs. The only bad thing about a rehab start is sometimes they don't recall you. They leave you in the minors.

"I know a lot of single women, JP. I can make sure you meet some of them. Dani, my personal shopper, would be perfect for you. She loves sports."

Two weeks later Faith invited me to a private party at the Museum of Fine Arts and introduced me to Danica Purcell, a twenty-two-year-old looker who was lighter than a Macy's Parade balloon and whom I started dating almost immediately. It was nice to go out for a change. And Dani wasn't an alpha so I felt comfortable with her. Dani also liked sex almost as much as she liked her commissions from Saks and Bloomingdale's. I went out with Dani for three months before she dumped me for an Italian designer. No matter. By then I was back in circulation. It's not hard for a pro athlete to find agreeable women. Faith's rehab strategy worked. Except for one thing. I never came back from the minors. It was as if I kept dating the same woman over and over—midtwenties, good-looking, good job, killer clothes. Puck fucks but with taste and style. It wasn't their fault they weren't Lisa.

I was thinking of Lisa as I drove Boss Scags onto the Bourne Bridge, the westernmost of the two suspension bridges over the Cape Cod Canal. Driving over the Bourne Bridge is like taking off in a plane. Your car climbs the steep roadway while the land around you falls away until you're at the highest point of the bridge, the surging water of the canal below and the huge green scrub-pine expanse of Cape Cod stretched out before you. Twenty minutes after crossing the bridge I pulled the Ferrari up to Cam's parents' house. An hour later we were on the water over Horseshoe Shoals, which lies south of the Cape and north of Martha's Vineyard. Cam let the boat drift and we worked tube-and-worm jigs, sending the weighted lures to the bottom and retrieving them fast. We hooked up on our first try. Bluefish don't nibble. They hit hard and fight harder. Mine was ripping line off the reel. When I tightened the drag to slow him the line snapped. I turned to help Cam land his fish. I stuck the butt of my rod in one of the rod holders and put on a pair of gloves so I could grab the wire leader without cutting my hands. Cam worked his fish close to the stern and I reached over the transom, grabbed the leader, and pulled the bluefish into the boat. It was an eight-pounder. We threw him in a chest of ice. We always keep the first fish on the off chance we don't catch another.

"How'd you lose him?" Cam asked me as I rerigged my rod.

"Tightened the drag too much," I said.

About a minute went by before Cam said: "Yeah, it's like that with kids and players; Set the drag too loose and you can't control 'em; set it too tight and you lose 'em. Got to set it just right."

Hang around with Cam long enough and you're going to hear a few things worth writing down.

As usual, we were on the porch shortly after sundown, and—also as usual—Cam had something to say.

"I think we're down to our last shot, JP," he said, pouring a couple of ounces of Cognac into two of his parents' Austrian-made crystal snifters.

"Your dad has a lot more Cognac where this came from," I said.

"I don't mean the Cognac. I mean we're getting old. Our team's getting old. If we don't win a Cup this year I don't think we're going to win one. Getting close to last call, *mon ami*," he said.

"Cam, we're thirty-one. You've got what? Two years left on your contract? I'll probably get one more five-year deal. We're still making it into the All-Star Game. We've got a few more kicks at the can."

"I know, but I'm getting tired, JP. Tired of coaches telling me I have to be in my hotel room by midnight, of fighting guys I don't dislike—and don't think Lindsey isn't starting to notice that—and having no-talent guys like the Mad Hatter telling me what to do all the time. Where to be and what time to be there."

"At least you have a soft spot to land," I said, sounding a little jealous, which I was. Trying to soften that, I told him that no matter what happened he'd had a hell of a run.

"The run's not over, Jean Pierre," he said. I didn't say anything, because when Cam uses my full name instead of calling me JP it means there's more coming. Sort of like when your parents called you by your first, middle, and last name. Nothing good ever happened after my mother or grandmother started a sentence with "Jean Pierre Lucien Savard . . ."

"The only thing left that I really want to do," he said, "is get my name on the Stanley Cup."

"You and six hundred and fifty other guys on thirty teams," I said.

"Yeah, every team wants the Cup, but there are only five or six teams that are legitimate contenders."

"Cup or no Cup, we've had great careers."

"But winning a Cup defines a career. *Not* winning one also

defines a career. The best thing about winning the Cup is that they engrave your name on it. It's forever, JP. Winning the Cup is immortality."

"At least that's an immortality I can believe in," I said. We raised our glasses and moved to clink them together. But I misjudged the distance. I hit Cam's glass too hard, shattering my snifter and sending shards of glass and a dribble of Cognac onto the floor.

Two

It was raining as I drove to Cam's house on Beacon Hill to pick him up for our preseason game against the New York Islanders at Boston Garden. The arena is the second Boston Garden. The original building closed in 1995 but everyone calls the new place the Garden, which in Boston they pronounce "GAH-den." I live less than a mile from Cam in a condo on Marlborough Street, a place I bought after I sold the house Lisa and I owned.

In nice weather Cam and I walk to the rink. We go up the west side of Beacon Hill, then down the north side to the Garden. The north slope was Boston's red-light district in Colonial days. Now when we walk past the statehouse on top of the hill Cam says, "The whores moved uptown."

Lindsey—Cam and Tamara's eight-year-old—answered the door. "Hi, Mr. Savard," she said. "Daddy said he'd be down in a minute. I like your car."

"Thanks, Lindsey. How you doing?"

"Fine. I hope you and Daddy win tonight."

"Thanks."

"And I hope you don't let in any of those really long shots. Like remember against Montreal?" she said.

"Me, too," I said.

"You remember that really, really, REALLY long one?"

"Hard to forget."

"The one that just rolled along the ice?"

"Just rolled along," I said.

"I think I would have stopped that one," Lindsey said, bending over and sweeping aside an imaginary puck with her imaginary stick.

"Probably would have," I said.

"Maybe even Caitlin would have stopped it."

"Caitlin's only five," I said.

"But she's almost six and she's in Learn-to-Skate."

"Where is Caitlin?" I asked but Lindsey ignored the question.

"How did that puck ever get into the net?"

"Bad bounce," I said.

"I hope you won't let it happen again."

I said I'd try not to.

"Hey, Linds, Mom wants to see you," Cam said, bounding down the front stairs. *"Bonjour,* Jean Pierre. *Comment ça va, eh?"* That's Cam's way of needling me about my being the only French-Canadian player he knows who can't speak French. I spoke French as a child but I lost the language when Mom and I moved to Maine. Lewiston is a partly Francophone city but I went to schools where they spoke English.

"So how's it going with Julie the Account Exec?" Cam asked as he got in the car.

"You're one behind. It's Sheri the Equestrienne. She teaches at a riding academy in Weston."

"A horsewoman? How'd you meet her?"

"The Ferrari," I said. "Sheri saw me hand the keys to the valet at Sonsie. It was love at first sight." Sonsie is a swank Newbury Street bar and restaurant where people go to be seen or just to say they've been there.

"So we're into boots and riding crops, are we?" Cam said.

"She takes off the spurs. Too tough on the sheets."

"She go to the whip much?"

"Only in the stretch," I said. "She sure likes to be on top."

"You OK with that?"

"Cam, Sheri the Equestrienne could ride a guy to a win in the Breeders' Cup," I said, nosing Boss Scags through the rain-slicked streets toward the Garden's underground garage.

I could afford to be loose. Reginald "Rinky" Higgins, our backup goalie, was starting against the Islanders. Packy was saving me for our final two exhibition games. In the greatest preseason scheduling I'd seen in nine seasons, we were playing a Thursday-night game against the New York Rangers at their training camp at the University of Vermont in Burlington, and then two nights later we'd play Montreal in Quebec City, one of the greatest restaurant towns in North America. The best part was the itinerary. We'd fly to Burlington on Wednesday—the day before the game—so we'd get a free night on the town. After Thursday's game we'd bus to Quebec, where we'd stay at the Château Frontenac, a castle on the north bank of the St. Lawrence River. We'd have Friday night to enjoy Quebec before we played the Canadiens on Saturday.

That schedule had to be Packy's doing. The Mad Hatter usually arranges our itinerary so we play more back-to-back road games than any other team in the league. On a back-to-backer we charter out right after the first road game, check into our hotel at some ungodly hour of the morning, play the second game that night, and charter home after the game. It saves a few bucks on hotels and cuts down on the chance of a player hitting for the cycle—getting drunk, drugged, laid, and arrested. But it beats the hell out of you over the course of an eighty-two-game season. It also makes us feel like children.

We beat the Isles 3–2 Saturday night and Packy canceled Sunday's practice so he, the assistant coaches, and Madison Hattigan could trim the roster from thirty players to twenty-five. I suppose that's when the Mad Hatter surprised everyone by announcing he was *adding* a player. The player was Cole Danielson, a mouthy twenty-year-old punk who wore his orange-dyed hair in a mullet, stood a well-muscled six-three, 225, had the acne and nasty temper of a steroid user, and carried a reputation as being some kind of fistic hell for the Johnstown Chiefs of the East Coast Hockey League. The ECHL is two steps below the NHL, and the only reason a roided-up moron like Danielson was within a hundred miles of an NHL camp was to audition as a goon. Well, that and to help the Hatter put pressure on Kevin Quigley.

Quigley was in the last year of a three-year deal that paid him $575,000 a season, which is light money in this league. But Danielson—like dozens of other marginally talented hit men—would come even cheaper. And rumor has it that Hattigan gets to pocket 10 percent of the difference between the NHL salary cap and our team's actual payroll, always a few million dollars under the cap. So Quigley is a guy forever on the bubble, only as good as his last fight.

A fighter is like a nuclear weapon—you don't have to use it but you'd better have it. Or as Packy said when we signed Quig five years ago after we'd been pushed around by Philly in the playoffs, "We should've bought the dog before the house got robbed."

Today's tough guys have to be more than brawlers. They have to be able to play. Quig takes a regular shift on our second line.

There was no undercard that Monday at practice. We went right to the main event. I was skating around lazily before the coaches came on the ice when I saw Danielson come up behind Quigley and tap him on the left shoulder. "Hey, Quigley, just so ya know, I don't start nothin' I don't finish," Danielson said.

"You asking me to dance?" Quigley said real loud, so we all turned our attention to him. Quig slowed to a stop behind one of the goals and dropped his stick, helmet, and gloves on the ice, a silent invitation to Danielson to do the same. The rookie dropped his gloves and stick and then slowly—reluctantly, I thought—took off his helmet.

There was no sparring. Quigley, who's at least four inches shorter than Danielson but built like a mailbox, bull-rushed the rookie, pushing him backward across the ice and slamming him into the doors to the Zamboni entrance. The unlocked doors swung open and Quigley and Danielson went rolling down the ramp and onto the concourse, where they toppled a pretzel kiosk, knocked over a stack of empty beer kegs, and flailed at each other—Quigley getting all the better of it—until they slammed against a large blue trash bin labeled "RECYCLABLES—INTERMINGLE." The truck-sized garbage can overflowed with plastic bottles and aluminum cans. By now Quigley had committed an assortment of atrocities on an overmatched Danielson. The fight should've been over except that Kevin doesn't fight like Cam. Cam fights for tactical reasons, to redress legitimate grievances and to right miscarriages of justice. Kevin fights to hurt people.

In an attempt at a grand finale, Quigley tried to throw Danielson into the recyclables bin, but the bin tipped over, spilling hundreds of cans and bottles onto the combatants. So Quigley grabbed Danielson by the shoulder pads and flung him into the now half-empty, sticky-wet, smelly container, emphatically ending pugilistic competition for the morning.

"Sorry about the recyclables," Kevin said to the three janitors surveying the wreckage they'd have to clean up. "He should go out with the regular trash. He's not recyclable."

By now Packy and the coaches were on the ice and everyone was gathered at the Zamboni entrance when Kevin returned.

"The hell was that all about?" Packy asked.

"Punk asked me to dance," Quigley said.

"Good thing he didn't ask you to fight," Packy said.

Kevin Quigley went to get his skates sharpened. Cole Danielson went to Johnstown.

. . .

Wednesday morning we boarded the charter for Burlington at ten o'clock and I took my usual bulkhead window seat at the left front of the coach cabin. Cam sat beside me, which is unusual. He normally sits in the back.

"Saw Faith McNeil at my father's office yesterday. We manage her investments," he said. "She told me to say hi. And to ask if your rehab's ever going to end."

"About the same time she's worked her way through the top half of the Forbes 400," I said. I'd run into Faith at parties and charity events three or four times a year in the three years since our dinner at Cam and Tam's. For the first two years Faith was always with that cardiologist Sherman Wolfe. Of course he'd prefer it if you and I and everyone on earth called him *Doctor* Wolfe, but I liked to call him Sherm because I knew it annoyed him and he couldn't say anything about it without sounding like a jerk. Faith dumped him last year. "There was a quarterback controversy" was how she described it to me, adding, "Either I start or I don't play." Since then, whenever she and I met, she'd be introducing me to a CEO or a Wall Street heavyweight and I'd be introducing her to a Sheri the Equestrienne or a Missy Taylor the New England Patriots Dance Team Coordinator.

"Faith's going to be at the Meet the Bruins deal next Tuesday," Cam said. Meet the Bruins Night is our annual preseason dinner for premium seat holders and corporate sponsors. It's a fund-raiser, with the proceeds—after the Mad Hatter deducts everything but the cost of air-conditioning—going to one of the Bruins' favorite charities, the Greater Boston Boys and Girls Club, of which Faith and Tamara are trustees.

"Who's she going with?" I asked.

"You'll be surprised," Cam said.

"Christ, does high school ever end?" I said. "OK. I'll bite. Who?"

"No one," he said, standing up and heading for the back of the plane.

We were to play the Rangers in the new 10,000-seat SportsPlex on the UVM campus, the one that recently replaced the old 4,035-seat Carter Field House that Cam and I had played in and that Cam's grandfather donated. The Cart was one of the great old barns in college hockey. The university was going to tear it down but it's still standing because of something Cam's father said to the university trustees. Cam's dad—who refused to give any money to the SportsPlex—said that if they pulled down Carter Field House he would personally go to the new library wing he and Diana had donated "and tear it down brick by brick until you have to find a goddamn welfare hotel to store all those volumes of Shakespeare and that mither-ficking Chaucer." I thought the Olde English was a nice touch.

The Cart is shaped like a blimp hangar with this big curved roof. The walls of the concourses are covered with framed photographs of former teams and players. We found a picture of Cam blocking a shot in a game against St. Lawrence and a photo of me robbing Paschal Fleming on that breakaway in the BC game the night I got tickets for Lisa. There I was holding the puck in my glove in front of the goal line with the rest of me sprawled in the net. I'd embellished the save by holding the pose longer than was necessary, something I used to do in college when I got carried away with the crowd and the band and the general mayhem and maybe with an inflated sense of my own importance.

Cam and I walked from the Cart to the SportsPlex, one of those new places with private suites, a souvenir shop, wide concourses, huge concession stands, and restrooms big enough to hold a barn dance. "Great place to eat and take a leak," Cam said. The new arena is used for basketball and hockey. Men's and women's hoops are big at Vermont, bigger than when Cam and I were there. We came across a display case with photos of former UVM women's basketball greats. There was Faith Mc-Neil, number 31, hair in a ponytail, high cheekbones and squinty gunfighter eyes adding a menacing intensity to her even then regal features. The photo showed her launching a jumper from the corner. "She wasn't afraid to jack it up," I said. "Even with the game on the line."

"Especially with the game on the line," Cam said. "Girl had brass ovaries. Still has 'em. You should see her portfolio. Faith's not exactly risk averse."

The caption under the photo read: *"Faith McNeil: America East Rookie of the Year . . . Two-Time America East Second All-Star . . . One-Time First All–Star and All–New England . . . Four-Time Academic All-America."* She was an alpha female even then.

We had a light skate midafternoon on Wednesday just before the Vermont varsity's regular practice. I'd showered and dressed and was sitting on the UVM bench watching the players—the goaltenders mainly—and waiting for Cam, who was doing an interview with the *Burlington Free Press*. As soon as I sat down, the goalie on my right skated out of his net toward me. "Excuse me, you're J. P. Savard, right?"

"What's left of him," I said.

"I'm Rudy Evanston. I met you when I was a kid. I was one of Lisa Quinn's patients. I heard about you and Lisa from Coach Indinacci. I'm sorry about, uh . . . what happened."

I was so shocked all I said was, "Holy Moly. Rudy Evanston. I remember you. Jeez, you've come a long way." I didn't want to say that when I first met him in the cancer ward I thought he was a dead boy walking.

"Been cancer-free for nine years," he said. "Scary waiting for the test results every six months. Beats the alternative though." He told me he was in his senior year but he'd redshirted his freshman year, so he had two seasons of eligibility left and he thought he had a shot to start or at least split the job with a freshman Indinacci had recruited.

"How's Coach Marco treating you?" I asked.

"Coach sure knows some horny women tutors in the Academic Support Group," he said.

"Hey, Rudy, don't talk to this guy. He'll wreck your game." It was Marco Indinacci skating toward us. "Don't set foot on the ice, JP. If the NCAA catches a pro on the ice with these kids they'll launch an investigation. It'll be death by committee meeting. . . . Rudy, get in the net."

I shook hands with Rudy and wished him luck. "Luck doesn't have much to do with it," he said. "Got to work at it."

"Kid's got one of the greatest attitudes I've ever seen," said Indinacci as soon as Rudy was out of earshot. "Sat on the bench most of the last two years. Never complained. Worked his ass off in practice. I think he's my starter."

"How much longer you going to coach?"

"I don't know. This year and next will give me twenty-five. Maybe that's enough. Maybe not. I still like it. Beats working. . . . Hey, JP, I gotta go run this circus. I'll be at your game tomorrow."

I was still watching practice when Cam slipped up behind me. "Remember when we thought this was good hockey?" he said. "Now it looks like they're moving in slow motion."

Speed is the main difference between college hockey and the NHL. Not so much individual player speed but the quickness with which players make decisions and move the puck. Speed kills. And there's nothing it kills faster than false hope of an NHL career.

Cam showed up and we boarded the bus for the hotel. I made a mental note to tell the Bruins' scouts to check out Rudy Evanston. And to bring along the Grit-O-Meter or whatever scouts use to measure the size and depth of a kid's heart.

There was no team dinner Wednesday, so while most of the guys headed for downtown Burlington restaurants—and some tried their luck trolling for college chicks—Cam and I took a cab to the Inn at Essex, where the New England Culinary Institute runs a gourmet restaurant.

A lot of players cheat on their wives and girlfriends on the road. Hell, a few of them cheat when we're home. Cam isn't one of them. And not to sound self-righteous, but I wasn't either in the years I was married. Even now I don't go looking, but I'm not one to pass up an empty net. I had a pretty good night with that lady caddy Serge Balon hooked me up with at his golf tournament. "She'll regrip your irons," as Serge put it. Then last January there was Deirdre the TV sideline reporter in Ottawa. I wasn't starting that game and the team bench was crowded so I sat in a folding chair in the runway where Deirdre did her stand-ups. Stand-ups are live reports from ice level where the reporter gives injury updates and stuff while fans behind her wave like fools at the camera and the people in front stick pens up their nose trying to make the reporter laugh on air. Deirdre did good stand-ups. But not as good as the one we combined on after the game under the five-speed shower at the Château Laurier. I suspected Sheri the Equestrienne and Missy Taylor the Patriots Dance Team Coordinator played by the same rules. But by hanging out with Cam I cut down on what the priests in my parish used to call "occasions of sin."

At dinner we talked about the team and whether or not we had enough talent and grit—grit is a blend of passion and courage; it's what supports talent—to make a serious run at winning Boston's first Cup since 1972 and the days of Bobby Orr and Phil Esposito. We figured we had a good core group and that winning it all would come down to our top guys staying healthy and playing like top guys. That and goaltending.

A team can dress twenty players for a game and we usually carry twenty-five on our roster. But there were only a half dozen guys who—with Cam, Quig, and me—would determine how far we'd go.

Phil "Flipside" Palmer is Cam's partner on defense. Flipside is our music expert, a human discography of rock, rap, jazz, pop, classical, and country. Only guy in the world besides the Kingsmen who knows the words to "Louie Louie." One day last season Takagi "Taki" Yamamura, a Japanese-Canadian and our second-line center, came into the room and said, "Hey, Flipper, betcha don't know the only Japanese song by a Japanese singer to chart in the U.S. Top Forty." Without even looking up from the stick he was taping, Flipside said, " 'Sukiyaki' by the late Kyu Sakamoto, 1963. Covered in the eighties by A Taste of Honey." You don't screw around with Flipside.

Bruno Govoni is our number three defenseman and a great penalty killer, which is a good thing because, otherwise, he's an immature punk. Bruno is a strip club and porn fan. The ring tone on his cell phone isn't a ring at all but the recorded orgasmic moanings of Canadian porn star Loretta "Lash" LaRue. Of course Cam and I know his phone number and dial it at strategic moments. Like last season when his phone went off—so to speak—during our meeting with the Sisters of Charity about a hospital fund-raiser. "Whoa. Get back, Loretta," Bruno said, taking out his phone and shutting off Loretta midmoan. A couple of nuns smiled.

Our first-line center and top scorer is Jean-Baptiste "JB" Desjardin. JB will score forty to fifty goals a year and get close to a hundred points. He'll also irritate most of the English-Canadian guys on the team because he's an outspoken separatist. JB thinks Quebec should separate from the rest of Canada and form a new French-speaking country. "Hard to build a national economy on doughnut shops and chain-saw repair," Cam tells him just to piss him off.

Jean-Baptiste's right winger is Luther Brown, an African-Canadian from Niagara Falls, Ontario. Luther almost always has his headphones on. For his first three seasons on the team I figured he was listening to Dr. Dre or Ludacris or various rappers who sing about hos and bitches and going down to the candy store and other lyrics you can't play at the junior prom or in pregame warmup. One day last season when he was taking off the headphones before practice I asked Luther whom he was listening to.

"Count Basie," he said.

Rex Conway, another of our forwards, is a combination shit disturber and Bible-thumping fundamentalist. Rex could score five goals in a game but he wouldn't get on TV because every producer knows they'd blow the start of the ten o'clock news while Rex talked about how he owed his goals "to my personal relationship with my Lord and Savior Jesus Christ," just as if it were Jesus and not JB and Luther who'd been feeding him the puck all night.

Taki Yamamura, who can play wing as well as center, is the fastest skater in the league but not even the best athlete in his own family because that has to be his wife, Su, a principal dancer with the Boston Ballet. Taki brought some of us to the opening of *The Nutcracker* last November. We had one of those eight-seat private boxes like Abe Lincoln got himself shot in. At intermission—or "halftime" as Kevin Quigley called it—we hit the champagne pretty hard. Had a couple of glasses in the lobby and brought a tray of them back to our box. So when Su, as the Dew Drop Fairy, did a beautiful *grande jete*—a leap in which she hung in the air like Kobe Bryant—we clapped and whistled. Later we booed the army of mice and Quigley threw a plastic champagne glass at the Rat King. Taki told us the next day that Su said if he ever brought us to the ballet again she'd do things to him that would make Iwo Jima look like a Boy Scout jamboree.

We'll have a dozen other guys shuttling up and down from Providence. We call them the Black Aces. Packy calls them spare parts. The Mad Hatter calls them flotsam and jetsam.

At dinner with Cam on the night before our preseason game with the Rangers, I was set to plunge a dessert fork into the Inn at Essex's killer crème brûlée when Cam said, "We really gotta have it between the pipes this season, JP."

"What the hell have you had for the last nine years?" I said, miffed that Cam seemed to have forgotten that I consistently put up good numbers and usually pass up a potential three-day mid-season vacation and sex rodeo with a Sheri the Equestrienne by getting myself picked for the All-Star Game. The only mark on my rap sheet is that three or four times a year I'll let in a long one.

"This can be a special year, JP. Gotta stay dialed. Can't let in one of those rollers like against Montreal."

I looked up from the crème brûlée. "You son of a bitch you heard everything Lindsey said."

Cam was chuckling now.

"Your own daughter is tuning me up and you let her."

"What'd you want me to do? Cross-check her into the living room? Besides"—he was laughing now—"she was right."

"It was one stinkin' goal."

"Cost us the game."

"It was a best-of-seven series for Christ's sake, Cam."

"Cost us home ice."

"Think of all the saves I made."

"That goal was like letting in a sectional sofa."

"I'll get even, Cam. Payback's a bitch, babe."

Cam was joking but he'd made a point. It's harder to be a good good-team goalie than a good bad-team goalie. A good bad-team goalie knows he's going to get a lot of shots—a lot of chances to be a star—and his team isn't expected to win, so there's less pressure. All a good bad-team goalie has to do is keep it close, and because what a goalie does is so obvious to fans, he's a hero. It's different on contending teams like ours. There's more pressure because there's more at stake. The job isn't about making forty saves a game. It's about making the two or three saves that make winning possible. Goaltending for a good team is less about being a star than about overcoming fear, injury, fatigue, sickness, circumstance, and other people's mistakes to do what needs to be done when it needs to be done. Not some of the time. All of the time.

We beat the Rangers 5–1 Thursday night. It was a typical pre-season game. I didn't recognize half of the Rangers players because they were all minor leaguers auditioning for jobs. Most of them would end up back in the AHL. But the game meant more than most exhibitions because part of the proceeds went to the Lake Champlain Medical Center, where private donations were funding one of those hostels where parents can stay while their kids are being treated.

There must've been a lot of Vermont fans in the building, because Cam and I got cheered every time we touched the puck even though the Rangers were supposed to be the home team. Cam scored one of his rare goals—slapshot from the right point that dinged in off of the crossbar—and the fans chanted, "Go, Cats, Go." The college atmosphere made me think of the great times I'd had playing in Burlington. A minute later I blew the shutout by giving up a sixty-footer. It was embarrassing. The first thing you want to do is smash your stick over the crossbar, partly to let out the frustration and partly as a cheap way of publicly apologizing for your gaffe. But I'd learned not to do that. I learned it the same way I learned everything else I knew about goaltending—the hard way. It was mostly Chantal Lewis's fault. Chantal and I were freshmen at St. Dominic's High School. She was a cheerleader. I was the JV goalie. I thought she was prettier than a five-goal lead, which is the main reason I never got up the nerve to talk to her. She used to show up for the third period of some of our games because the varsity played the next game and she was dating a sophomore defenseman. Chantal Lewis was worth a goal a game to the opposition any time I knew she was in the rink. And knowing she was there wasn't hard, because only a dozen or so people came to JV games. Take Chantal Lewis out of my high school and I would've had a better goals-allowed average and more than one college scholarship offer. It was a Saturday in February when I went out for the third period and saw Chantal and her cheerleader friends sitting in the stands behind my goal. We had a one-goal lead at the time but not for long because in the first minute I let in a shot that skidded under the stick blade that I should have had on the ice. Embarrassed and frustrated I smashed my goal stick over the crossbar. Right away our coach pulled me out.

"Grab some pine," he said as I took a seat on the end of the bench and watched our backup goalie play—and play well—in a game we'd go on to win 4–2.

"You know why I pulled you?" Coach asked me after the game.

"Because I let in a bad goal," I said.

"Guess again."

"Because I smashed my stick?"

"You're getting close," Coach said. "I pulled you because you showed how much you were hurt. JP, in the goaltending business you never—ever—show how much you're hurt. Get up, shut up, and stop the next shot."

About a half hour after our exhibition win over the Rangers I was walking across the rink parking lot to our bus when Marco Indinacci caught up with me. "Good game, Ace, except for that last goal," he said. "Hey, you asked me when I was going to retire," Marco said. "What about you? When you going to hang up the tools of ignorance?"

"Four or five seasons," I said. "One more contract."

"Don't stay too long, JP," my old coach said. "There aren't many happy endings in the NHL."

It was after 2 a.m. when the bus pulled up to the Château Frontenac. Packy told us we had practice at Le Colisee from eleven to noon.

I'm an early riser, which is a good thing if you want to get one of the few copies of the *Toronto Globe and Mail* at the Frontenac's front desk. I think breakfast with the sports section is one of life's minor pleasures. I was reading an NHL Notes column while finishing my coffee when I saw the news that, in the aftermath of the Rangers' loss to us, New York had called up my old UVM teammate Gaston Deveau. I knew most NHL GMs thought Deveau was too small—he's about five feet nine, 160 pounds—to play in the the Show. So Gaston went overseas and for six seasons tore up Europe like the plague. The Rangers signed him two years ago but buried him in the minors. I was happy he'd get his first shot at the bigs.

We coasted through practice. Guys were more interested in what restaurants and clubs they'd hit than in Packy's penalty-kill and power-play drills. Bruno Govoni tried to round up a party to hit a suburban strip club. He asked Rex Conway to go but our Christian right winger said he wasn't a big fan of strip clubs because, as Rex put it, "Like Moses ye shall see the Promised Land but ye shall not enter." About once a year Rex gets off a good line. I figured that would about do it for the season.

You'd need three weeks to hit all the great restaurants in Quebec City. Some of the guys went to Le Continental or Aux Anciens Canadiens, both across the street from the Frontenac. But Cam and I had been to those places in our early days when Quebec City had an NHL team, the Nordiques. That team moved to Denver, where it's now the Colorado Avalanche. I wanted to try someplace new, so Cam, Luther Brown, and I went to Le Saint-Amour on rue Ste-Ursule, also an easy walk from the hotel. I had the caribou steak grilled with wild berries and served with poached pears in red wine. Cam ordered a château-bottled Bordeaux—"*Château de Deuxième Hypothèque,*"

Cam said to the waiter while pointing to what must have been the most expensive wine on the list. The waiter laughed. "Château de Second Mortgage," Cam translated for us. He wasn't kidding. Our bill looked like the tote board at Saratoga. Cam paid.

Luther and I like jazz, so I suggested we catch the first set at L'Emprise, a jazz bar in the Hotel Clarendon. Cam was surprised there was no cover charge or minimum. He laughed at the sign on the door: *"Consumption Obligatoire."*

We got the last three seats at the narrow bar that borders three sides of the small stage. The group that night was the Quintette Joelle Clarisse. The woman I assumed was Joelle—a striking young blonde in a black sheath dress—was the vocalist, and four young guys were on piano, drums, bass, and tenor sax.

Joelle said a few words in French—she lost me after *"Bon soir, mesdames et messieurs . . ."*—and began a set sung mostly in French but with one song, "Maybe You'll Be There," in English and another, "Bésame Mucho," in Portuguese. The group was good but by no means memorable. Or not until the end of the set, after a guy at the bar handed Joelle a slip of paper. She read it, smiled, turned to the band, and said, "Summertime."

I nudged Cam. "They're playing your song," I said, hitting him with a quick lyric—"Your daddy's rich and your mama's good-lookin' . . ." Cam flipped me off. Luther laughed.

From the first notes and the woman's full, clear, sultry "Summertime . . ." the song ached with sensuality. On the woman's left the sax player, eyes closed, swayed back and forth losing himself in his instrument, playing with passion and an almost erotic abandon. Most people stopped drinking and the two waiters put down their trays. Halfway through the song the woman turned to the saxophone player—the bass and piano had receded now and the drummer worked softly with the brushes—and it was just the two of them wrapped in the music. Singing and playing to each other. They had to be lovers, I thought. Or to have been lovers once and now the music was all they had left.

When the song ended, the sax player leaned back and looked at the ceiling. The woman dropped her head briefly. Then, turning away from the sax player, she said something and the group segued into a break with "Take the A Train." That's when the applause began and the people stood.

"Passion beats talent if talent isn't passionate," Cam said. I borrowed a pen from Luther and wrote it on a cocktail napkin. I thought it would make a good theme for my season. Or maybe for my life.

We left L'Emprise and walked toward the hotel. As we neared rue des Carrières and the Frontenac I decided it was too early to go to bed, so I walked the fifty yards to Dufferin Terrace, the railed boardwalk on the edge of a cliff, two hundred feet above the river. I stood at the rail and stared at the St. Lawrence. I knew from a history class that I was looking at the stretch of water where, on a moonless night in September 1759, a flotilla of British troops slipped undetected under the French guns guarding the city. The British landed near the only climbable pathway up the cliffs. By dawn more than four thousand English troops had assembled in battle formation on the Plains of Abraham west of the city. In one of the greatest understatements in military history the surprised French commander, the Comte de Montcalm, looking out at the British troops, said, *"C'est sérieux."*

The Battle of Quebec was over in minutes with Wolfe dead, Montcalm mortally wounded, and the English in possession of the city and, with that, in control of Canada.

"Don't jump," Cam said suddenly appearing beside me.

"Just thinking about the battle," I said.

"History majors," Cam said derisively.

"History to you is the Dow Jones Five-Day Moving Average," I said.

"At least I can make money with that. How's your room?"

"Cornered the market on oak and mahogany," I said. "Yours?"

"Great view of the river. Only one problem."

"No one to share it with."

"Bingo."

I told Cam a line Lisa had gotten off on our last vacation at the Frontenac. "The best sex is hotel sex," she'd said. Cam thought it would be a good marketing slogan for Westin or Fairmont.

We lost 5–3 to the Canadiens Saturday night and hardly looked like a team that would challenge Montreal for the division title much less one that could compete for the Cup. And this time we couldn't make the excuse that we were just playing a meaningless exhibition. This was the final preseason game for both teams, and both coaches dressed the guys they planned to play on opening night. But our defense played like a road company rehearsing for a train wreck, our offense got only fifteen shots on goal (to thirty-seven by the Canadiens), and I let in what Lynne Abbott said in her story was "Savard's soft-serve du jour," an unscreened fifty-foot slapper by Montreal captain Tim Harcourt, a defenseman who's lucky if he scores five goals a season.

Kevin Quigley gave us our sole highlight but I was the only one who appreciated it. Early in the first period I got blindsided by the Canadiens' Rheal Duchamp. There was no penalty on the play. Packy went out of his mind. "You're going home in a body bag, Duchamp!" he yelled, jumping up on the bench and tapping Quigley on the shoulder. Quig skated out for the face-off, where he lined up opposite Duchamp. I figured the fight would break out as soon as the linesman dropped the puck. Instead I heard Quig say to a nervous Duchamp, "Excuse me, Rheal, but do you plan on doing that to our goaltender any more?"

"Oh, no, no, Kev, that was an accident," said the chickenshit Duchamp in a reply made up of equal parts fear and common sense. Duchamp didn't come near me for the rest of the game and Quig didn't have to serve a penalty for instigating a fight. It's funny how being known as a good fighter often means not having to fight at all.

Thankfully, that game marked the end of training camp. We'd play for real starting Thursday. *C'est sérieux.*

Most of the players don't bring wives or dates to Meet the Bruins Night, because we have to sit at this long dais and any woman we came with would be left shifting for herself among the season ticket holders and corporate types—the suits—sitting at the round tables set up on the Garden floor. The anal-retentive Mad Hatter makes us sit in the order of our jersey numbers. Because I wear number 1 I sat at the left end of the dais, just above table 1, which was reserved for the trustees of the Boys and Girls Club. Tamara Carter and a half dozen men were already seated when Faith McNeil walked in, moving as she always had with the lupine grace of an athlete, her stride and carriage suggestive of vast reservoirs of strength and speed. Even in low heels and a dark gray wool-and-silk business suit Faith was a head turner. Cam was right. She was alone. Faith took the last open seat at the table, her back to the dais and to me. There was a day I would've tossed a sugar packet on her head but instead I called down: "Hey, Faith, I didn't play *that* bad. You could at least say hello."

She turned, smiled up at me, and walked to the end of the dais. I stepped down to meet her.

She told me she'd come to present the Boys and Girls Club Man of the Year Award to Kevin Quigley for the hundreds of hours he volunteers. Then she asked me whom I was with.

"No one. Too awkward. Sheri's back at the condo."

"Sheri the Equestrienne?" Faith asked, smiling.

"You've been talking to Cam."

"Oh yeah. And good luck in the Breeders' Cup. Ride 'em, cowgirl," she said, pretending to hit a horse on the flank with a cowboy hat. "Whose silks is she wearing? Kentucky Stables or Victoria's Secret?" Then she laughed the same throaty Hepburnian laugh I'd first heard echoing up the stairwell of a college dorm.

I couldn't think of anything to say and I'd started back to the dais when Faith asked me if I could give her a ride home. "I took a taxi because I hate parking in this area. I live close. Chestnut Hill."

"First castle on the left?" I said. Chestnut Hill is a neighborhood of multimillion-dollar Tudor-style homes near the Boston College campus. It's an easy drive from the Garden so I said I'd give her a lift. But I'd have said that if she lived in Iowa.

You might think it's odd that a guy like Quigley, who most fans see as a brawler, would get the Man of the Year Award from the Boys and Girls Club. But look around the league and you'll see that in almost every city it's the enforcers and shit disturbers—Serge Balon in Philly, Davey Canfield in Edmonton, Quig and Cam with us—who do the most community service work. You want someone to give a hockey clinic, open a playground, or visit a hospital, the so-called goon is your guy. Faith, who doesn't waste a lot of words, did the award presentation. "Most of you know what this man can do with his closed fists," she said, "but tonight we honor him for what he does with his open heart." Quig got a standing ovation. Ever since the days of Terry O'Reilly they've loved the bighearted, two-fisted Irish guys in Boston.

Players had to hang around and sign autographs after the dinner, so it was about quarter of ten before Faith and I and Boss Scags headed for Chestnut Hill. It was small talk most of the way until she told me what everyone seems to ask any athlete over thirty. "How much longer are you going to play?"

I said goalies could last a little longer than most players. Some—Johnny Bower and Jacques Plante—played into their forties. "I think I can go another five years."

"Then what?"

"Then I'll retire."

"And . . . ?"

"And what?"

"What will you DO?"

"Take ten strokes off my handicap."

"Seriously, JP?"

"I won't DO anything," I said. "I'll be retired."

"You won't do anything for what? Thirty years? That's a long time to not be doing anything. Let me put it another way. What would you do if you weren't a player?"

"I don't know. Teach and coach maybe," I said, though it was only something I made up on the spot. Then, mainly to change the subject, I asked Faith why she was going to medical school. "Cam says you're set for life. Why put yourself through something as tough as med school?"

"I was a premed major, remember?"

"But that was before you broke the dot-com casino."

"I think the secret of life—of a happy life—is having something to do. Something you're good at. I think I can be a good doctor."

"I think I can be an excellent retiree," I said. Faith didn't laugh. She gave me directions to her house.

"Don't get out," she said when I pulled up under the portico. "I know this is the part where I'm supposed to invite you in but I can't. I've still got about an hour of studying to do . . . and you've got Sheri the Equestrienne waiting to . . . um . . . saddle up?" We both laughed. She started to close the car door, then stopped and said, "We ought to grab lunch sometime."

"Sounds like a plan," I said. But we didn't set a date, which meant we wouldn't do it.

Faith went in the front door and flicked the porch light, signaling me that it was OK to leave. I drove west on Beacon Street toward Kenmore Square and directly into a traffic jam caused by 36,692 people leaving Fenway Park after the Sox' 9–1 win over Oakland in the opening game of the playoffs. The Boss and I sat in traffic through an entire John Coltrane album and it was after eleven when I got home. Sheri the Equestrienne was hotter than a crawfish boil.

It wasn't so much my being late that bothered her. It was my being, as she put it, "the only person in America besides Charlie Fucking Manson who doesn't have a cell phone."

I've always seen phones as unlocked gates through which people can barge, univited and usually unwanted, into my life. Not being inclined to barge into anyone else's life, it irks me when people barge into mine. I have one phone in my condo but it's mainly for ordering takeout. "If I had a cell phone people might call me and talk to me," I said.

"That's the wonderful thing about phones, Jean Pierre," Sheri said as if she were talking to a six-year-old. "Phones connect people. They let us communicate. They bring us closer." Then she said she was going home because she had to give an early-morning lesson. Dressage? Undressage? I forget.

When she left, the rodeo announcer in my mind—the one I'd hoped would be yelling, "Good ride, cowboy, good ride"—was instead announcing J. P. Savard as a healthy scratch.

That's when I decided that maybe Sheri was right about telephones. I grabbed my only phone and called Faith McNeil. We set a date for lunch.

High School

Holly Van Gelder never looked at me. When it came time to pass our geometry homework to the front row, Holly—without turning around—extended her open right hand behind her like a relay runner waiting for the baton. I put my homework paper in her hand; she added her homework and passed the papers up the row. Holly never spoke to me either, probably because she spent most of her class time whispering to Aaron Scanlon, a junior who sat to her left and who was our starting quarterback, point guard, and pitcher, the best athlete in the school and a pretty good guy.

Holly's family lived in Westview Estates, the part of town where the doctors and lawyers had cornered the market on BMWs and Volvos. I lived in the section of town called Little Canada, which in terms of money and social standing was about as far from Westview Estates as it was from Mars or Venus. Except that she looked like a fifteen-year-old Scarlett Johansson, Holly Van Gelder was enough to make me wish St. Dom's had stayed an all-boys school. But my attitude changed on a Friday afternoon in late February.

It was the day of our last regular-season varsity hockey game and we were playing crosstown rival Lewiston, the city's public high school and one of the best teams in the state. I was a sophomore and was on the varsity but only as a backup to Bernie Fortier, a cocaptain and two-year starter. Bernie was being recruited by a lot of NCAA Division I colleges, none of which was Harvard or Princeton. Bernie was so dumb that on the day before the Lewiston game he plagiarized an op-ed column from the Lewiston Sun-Journal, got caught by his English teacher, and was suspended by our assistant principal, Mary "No Charity" Garrity. This meant I was starting.

We usually played Lewiston at night but because of a concert at the old Central Maine Civic Center our game was at 3:30 in the afternoon, which meant that for the first time all season hockey players would get dismissed early. I'd just put my homework paper into Holly Van Gelder's open hand when the announcement came over the PA system: "Would all varsity hockey players please report to Coach Lennon in the team room." I scooped up my books and headed for the door.

"Good luck, JP," Aaron Scanlon said.

"I'll try to keep it in single numbers," I said. Lewiston was loaded as usual.

The Saints (that was us) versus the Blue Devils was about as big as high school hockey gets in Maine. I was used to seeing a few hundred people at our games. It surprised me to see a few thousand in the stands when we took the ice for warm-ups. I was skating behind the net when I heard a rap on the glass and looked up. It was Aaron Scanlon giving me a thumbs-up sign. He was with Holly Van Gelder, who, to my surprise, smiled and waved.

I let in a lot of goals in warm-up but there's an old saying in hockey: Bad warm-up, good game.

Andre LeBlanc scored for us in the first minute and the cheering was the loudest I'd ever heard. But Lewiston came right back to tie it when one of their wingers ran me over and a trailing defenseman shot the puck high into the net. It should've been goalie interference but I think the ref was scared to call it. Lewiston had more fans than we did.

Andre's gave us a 2–1 lead late in the first period when he buried a rebound off his brother Paul's shot. And that's where the score stood right down to the last minute of the third period.

We'd been getting shelled but I was stopping everything. I was also getting tired. I'd seen mop-up duty in a few games but this was my first varsity start. I kept sneaking peeks at the clock wanting the game to be over. With 1:03 to play we got a two-minute penalty and the Blue Devils rolled out their power play, which featured the state's leading scorer, Geoff Cutting, at center and a couple of howitzers on the points.

Cutting won the face-off and drew the puck to the right point man, who slid it left and, whomp, a shot I didn't even see bounced off my left leg pad. Cutting got the rebound but I got my stick glove on his shot. Paul LeBlanc grabbed the rebound and started behind the net with two forecheckers hounding him.

"Two on you, Paul . . . Two on you . . . Up the boards!" I yelled. Paul rimmed the puck up the boards, where it was intercepted by a Lewiston player and shot back in on me. I held on for the face-off. There was still 0:51 to play. Lewiston pulled its goalie for a six-on-four advantage. Adrenaline canceled fatigue and I was playing on instinct. Arms and legs moving in the ingrained patterns learned on driveways, ponds, and rinks over the previous eight years. No time to think. With less than thirty seconds to play I dived across an open net to get a stick onto a shot that was headed in. Geoff Cutting clanged the rebound off of the crossbar, and one of our defensemen flipped the puck into neutral ice. The Blue Devils went back to retrieve it. 0:27 to play. They came back on us with six players moving to the attack. The puck went left to Cutting, who accelerated past our defenseman, skated to the top of the face-off circle, and blew a laser into our net high to my stick side. Goal. The Lewiston stands erupted in cheers. Then they heard the whistle. Offside. Now the St. Dom's fans started cheering. I looked at the clock: 0:21. Face-off outside the zone. But it came back in fast. A shot. A skate save. Another shot. The puck went into my glove. "Hold *it, JP . . . Hold it!" It was an exhausted Paul LeBlanc kneeling in front of me, shielding me with his body and not wanting to get up on exhausted legs. 0:11 to play. Fans on their feet. Both sides screaming. Cutting managed a shot off the face-off. It went over the net into the corner. A Blue Devil player slid it up the boards to the point. Two of my teammates blocked my view. "Gimme a look. . . . Gimme a look!" Our left defenseman spun out of the way just in time for me to get a pad on a low slapshot. The puck skidded into the corner, where they had two guys on it and another headed for the low slot. We were collapsing. . . .*

And then the horn, the only thing that could save me and free me. Paul and Andre got to me first, jumping on me just as they had when we were kids on the Skating Pond. Then our bench emptied and I was on the bottom of a pileup of black-and-white uniforms and sticks and gloves, and somewhere above the pileup people yelled and clapped.

We went through the handshake line, where I got a few "great game" compliments from the Lewiston players, which made me think they were probably pretty decent guys.

I skated off the ice into the arms of Coach Lennon, who gave me a hug. "Looks like you'll be opening the playoffs for us," he said. Coach didn't know that the lawyer Bernie Fortier's father hired would help Bernie weasel out of the plagiarism rap, but that's another story.

A lot of our fans were still milling around the lobby when I left. They included Aaron Scanlon who was with Holly Van Gelder who was with Chantal Lewis and a whole posse of kids who pretty much made up the social A group at our school.

"Way to go, JP," Aaron said, emphasizing the remark with a right-handed fist-pump.

"I didn't know you PLAAAAAAYED," Holly Van Gelder said, and said it just like that—PLAAAAAAYED—as if she'd discovered I could fly or something.

"Gonna be playin' for the next two years," Aaron said. "Gonna be brickin' up that net, baby. Yeah."

"*Tomorrow night I'm having a party at my house. Mostly basketball and hockey guys. And cheerleaders,*" *Holly Van Gelder said, glancing at Chantal Lewis.* "*Why don't you come over, JP.*"

I said I would. That moment in the lobby of the civic center was when I discovered there's a difference between playing hockey and being a hockey player. I liked both.

Three

Every shot is a snowflake. No two are alike. Shots differ in speed, distance, and angle. They come at you out of a kaleidoscope of swirling bodies. Pucks can dip, rise, get tipped by an opponent or deflected by a teammate. A lot of things can happen on a shot. Most of them are bad. That's why I throw up before games.

Fifteen minutes before warm-up for our game against the Ducks at the Garden I grabbed my bottle of mouthwash, headed for the last toilet stall, and vomited the tea and toast I'd had a few hours earlier. I never throw up before preseason games, only regular-season games and playoffs.

I throw up because I'm afraid. Not afraid of getting hurt—today's equipment is so good that goal is the safest position on the ice—but afraid of being responsible for losing a game we might have won. And afraid of being publicly embarrassed.

I don't like throwing up but I know it's a sign I'm ready. I look at anxiety as energy I haven't used yet. It's like when I'm stopped at a traffic light with the clutch in and the Ferrari's engine revving. When the light changes, I pop the clutch and the revs become motion. It's the same with anxiety. Fear fuels performance.

I play better scared. But there are nights when I wish they'd never open the dressing-room door and that I wouldn't have to play. Then I remember something Lisa used to tell her patients— "The only way out is through."

A few seasons ago I wrote that line on the four-by-six file card I have taped to the left side of my dressing stall. I read the card before every home game. It says:

1. Watch the puck not the game.
2. Make aggressive choices.
3. There are no easy saves.
4. The only way out is through.

The reminders and the throwing up didn't do me any good. We lost 4–1 to Anaheim, got outshot 33–21, looked almost as disorganized as we had in Montreal, and—except for Jean-Baptiste, who scored our goal—couldn't have found the net with a satellite positioning system. And I don't think we hit anybody all night, although as Cam said: "Do you even want to hit a guy with a duck on his shirt?"

If you were listening on radio you wouldn't know any of this, because if our radio commentator Spence Evans were any more of a Homer he would've written *The Iliad.* According to Spence, we lost because of "lax officiating" and "bad breaks." Spence is an ex-Bruin from back in the days when players needed summer jobs to support their family. He knows the Mad Hatter gets approval—and disapproval—of the team's radio and TV announcers. He also knows he's lucky to have a job where there's no heavy lifting. He isn't about to screw that up by being objective.

Yesterday after practice Spence tried to get me to say that our standard early-season six-game, thirteen-day road trip while the Ringling Brothers Circus comes to the Garden is "a great opportunity for the guys to come together on the road and jell as a team."

I said it was more like a great opportunity to lose four or five games, for the younger guys to lose confidence, for fans and media to write us off early, and for us to be chasing Montreal until St. Patrick's Day. Which is precisely what it is.

What I didn't tell Spence is that the trip used to be worse because of a hazing ritual that Cam single-handedly put an end to in our rookie year. What used to happen on a team's first long road trip was that on a night off the rookies had to take the veterans to dinner. Of course the vets ordered the most expensive dishes on the menu along with $500 bottles of wine. By the end of dinner guys who couldn't tell a Château Haut-Brion from grape Kool-Aid would be ordering Cognacs that would have maxed out Napoleon. And the team's rooks would be stuck with a bill that looked like the Treasury balance.

Only someone with major family money and a Zamboni full of self-confidence could have done what Cam did. There were four rookies on that team—Cam, Jean-Baptiste, Flipside, and me—nine years ago when Cam stood up in the dressing room in St. Louis after practice and said: "Just want to let you guys know the rooks are doing things differently this year." He said that instead of wasting money on a feedbag extravaganza, the four of us were going to pony up five grand each, and the $20,000 total would be matched three-to-one by the Carter & Peabody Foundation and donated to whatever registered charity the veterans voted on. The gift would be in the name of every member of the team. "But you don't have to go along with this," Cam said, really putting the screws to the vets. "If you've got your heart set on filet mignon and a first-growth Bordeaux, Tamara and I will take you and your wife or girlfriend—together or sequentially—to any restaurant you like when we get back to Boston." A guy would look like a complete hoser if he took Cam up on that offer. There was a lot of grumbling at first because veterans don't like a rookie telling them what to do. But I don't think Cam was ever a rookie at anything, not even life. And nobody seemed to mind when the team got credit in the national media for what amounted to a $60,000 gift to Boston Children's Hospital, a gift that cost the veterans nothing. I never understood the power of money until I met Cam. Money makes you bulletproof.

When the Mad Hatter made Cam team captain in Cam's third

season it seemed less of a surprise than a confirmation of the natural order of things.

At least this season we played three home games before the long trip. We beat Atlanta 4–3 and Washington 4–0. The only bad thing about the Washington game was this guy who proposed to his girlfriend and had it televised on the Garden's JumboTron. I don't understand people who propose at a sports event. What's the point? An engagement should be a personal moment of commitment, not a public spectacle. I set the marriage over-under at eight years for people who get engaged on JumboTrons.

Sheri the Equestrienne wasn't at any of our home games and didn't have time to see me before we flew to Minneapolis on Monday for Tuesday night's game with the Wild. We flew commercial, which is unusual. We normally charter but I suppose the Hatter can save a few bucks by putting us through the traffic jams and unmitigated logistical torture of driving to Boston's always crowded Logan Airport instead of letting us charter from Hanscom Field, an easy-to-get-to airport in suburban Bedford.

Like most NHL teams, the Bruins would sooner allow lepers than journalists on team charters. But even the Mad Hatter can't control who buys seats on a commercial flight; thus Lynne Abbott, the *Boston Post*'s hockey writer, was on our flight, as were the radio guys, Spence Evans and play-by-play announcer Mike Emerson. The rest of the Boston sportswriters and broadcasters were home trying to invent ways to get their editors to assign them to a Red Sox playoff.

Most of the players like and respect Lynne, who's been covering the team since before my time here. One thing we admire about her is that if she rips you in the paper she'll be at practice to face you the next morning. Lynne says she'll come in even if it's her day off. She doesn't hit and run like some of these national writers and local columnists who show up in the dressing room once a year, hammer you in their stories, and then disappear. And

Lynne's not a pecker checker. Most of us wear robes or towels in the dressing room but there are times you'll be butt naked at your dressing stall and Lynne will be on deadline. She just comes over, looks you dead in the eye, asks her questions, and leaves. She's as much a pro as we are. And she's not a woman you want to hassle. A year ago we called up Brendan Fitzmorris, who was playing his first game in the NHL. He scored a goal and the next day at practice the kid was strutting around like he's Wayne Gretzky. He tried to harass Lynne. "Hey, lady, you know what this is?" said Brendan, holding on to his penis as if it were a fishing rod and he was hooked up to the marlin in *The Old Man and the Sea*. Lynne took him out fast. "Jeez, I dunno, kid. It looks like a penis. Only smaller."

Cam made Brendan apologize. Brendan said it wouldn't happen again. Lynne said that was too bad because "I'd like to be the first woman to own the Bruins."

Lynne is in her midthirties. Her shoulder-length blond hair frames a thin face highlighted by huge blue eyes behind wire-rimmed glasses. She's from Boston but she dresses country. She's big on blue jeans and cowboy boots. Monday she wore a $2,000 pair of custom-made boots she bought in Calgary last year. They're monogrammed LBA. I asked her what the B stood for. "Depends on the situation," she said. "My parents say it stands for Bethany."

Packy nicknamed Lynne the Knower of All Things. He did that four years ago when she broke a story on a Mad Hatter trade that even Packy hadn't known about. Lynne is seriously sourced, as writers like to say.

It's different with broadcasters. They're entertainers not journalists. Except for Mike Emerson, our radio play-by-play guy, who does more homework in a week than I did in three years of college. We were flying back from Vancouver on a red-eye last season. It was about 2 a.m. and I had to take a leak, so I was walking down the aisle and the only reading light still on was the one over Mike's seat. He was updating the stat sheets and file cards he keeps on each player. "Sleep is overrated," he said as I walked by.

The only trouble with Mike is that he thinks he knows music. But Mike's in his late forties and probably couldn't name a song recorded in the last fifteen years. That doesn't stop him from taking an occasional run at Flipside.

"Pop quiz. What were Sonny and Cher's real names?" Mike asked Flipside just after we boarded.

"Salvatore Bono and Cherilyn LaPiere," said Flipper, who then undid his seat belt, stood up, and pretended to swat away a basketball while he yelled at Mike: "Get that stuff OUTTA here, Emerson." I think Flipside did that only to embarrass Mike and keep him from asking more questions.

Fans have a romantic view of a road trip. They think it's a group vacation where someone else pays the bills. It isn't. I've gone to Buffalo forty times and still haven't been to Niagara Falls. Baseball players go to a city and stay three or four days. Hockey players are in and out. Here's our schedule for the day after we arrive in Minneapolis: Bus from the hotel to the rink, light skate, bus back to the hotel, have a team lunch and meeting, go to our rooms and try to nap, bus back to the rink and play the Wild. Then we can either bus to the hotel for a postgame meal or go out on our own, which is what Cam and I will do. Wednesday morning we bus to a suburban rink for a midmorning practice, then bus to the airport for our flight to San Jose. But I'm explaining, not complaining. When we fly over a city and I see all those office buildings containing all those cubicles I think of what life would be like working nine to five Monday through Friday. I know I'm lucky to do what I do.

At first it looked as though the middle seat between Kevin Quigley and me might go empty. No such luck. Just before the plane pulled away from the gate a fortyish-looking woman in a black pantsuit and white oxford shirt scrambled down the aisle and settled into 16-B. She began flipping through a folder and pulled out a brochure titled *Understanding the Angry Child*. With her big black-rimmed glasses and blond hair pulled back and fastened with a clip that looked like a leghold trap, she had the classic librarian look, the one giving rise to the fantasy that—fortyish or not—if you took off those glasses and freed her hair from the leghold trap you just might uncork a sexual Vesuvius quaking on the brink of long-supressed eruption. But I have a policy about talking to people on planes. I don't do it. Not unless I know them. There's too much risk that the person will be in sales or academia and will bore me into a tongue-lolling stupor. But Ms. Vesuvius must have overheard some of us talking and figured out who we were. Sort of. About an hour out of Boston she turned to me and said: "Are you people the Red Sox?"

"No, ma'am. We're the Bruins. A hockey team," I said, observing another of my in-flight survival rules, namely that any attractive woman who speaks to me on a plane will be addressed—at least at first—as "ma'am." Pretty women aren't used to being called "ma'am." It handcuffs them. Puts them down 0–1 in the count. They feel vaguely offended but they can't say anything because, on the surface, it looks as though I'm just being polite.

She said she was a social worker with the Archdiocese of Boston's Catholic Charities and was on her way to a national conference in Minneapolis. Her name was Nan O'Brien and she ran what she called "a family-preservation program" that tried to help dysfunctional families and prevent child abuse and neglect.

We were making our descent into Minny when Nan O'Brien gave me her business card:

Nancy C. O'Brien—LICSW

DIRECTOR

Catholic Charities Family Preservation

I asked her what the LICSW stood for. "Licensed independent clinical social worker," she said. Then she asked me if I could donate some equipment to her program's annual fund-raising auction. "Maybe some autographed sticks and balls."

"Pucks," I said. "We're a hockey team. We use pucks."

"Oh, of course. Sticks and pucks then?"

I said I'd give her a couple of game-used goalie sticks and a few pucks.

"I'll get you a stick from everyone on the team," said Quigley in a voice suggesting that any player who didn't give Kevin an autographed stick might be endangering his health and general well-being. Nan gave Kev her business card.

The trip was a nightmare. We lost 2–1 to Minnesota and 3–2 to San Jose. I played both games. Rinky Higgins got his first start of the season in Phoenix and he threw thirty-seven saves at the Coyotes but we lost 1–0. Whenever I watch a game from the bench I'm surprised at the speed and violence. When I see the game from the goal crease I'm focused on the puck, the whole play is in front of me, and the players are just colorful swirling chess pieces whose movements I have to keep track of. But when I sit on the bench the game moves horizontally and speed is more obvious. Once or twice a game a player will get checked into the boards in front of me, the force of the collision shaking the bench and making me wonder how a skater—a nongoalie—can take that kind of pounding for eighty to a hundred games a year. Cam tried to explain it to me once: "There's an anesthesia that goes with playing," he said. "Mostly you only hurt after the game."

I was back in goal in Anaheim, where we lost 4–1.

We had an off night in Nashville and Cam thought it'd be a good idea if we forgot our 0–4 road record and took in some country music. During a break by the band—the all-girl Cotton-Eyed Jo—Cam and I went to play the jukebox. I remember when you could hear a song on a jukebox for twenty-five cents. This machine wanted fives, tens, or twenties. "Someday it'll cost you ten shares of Google just to hear a little Alan Jackson," Cam said as the machine inhaled his ten and he punched up some Gretchen Wilson, Tim McGraw, and the Dixie Chicks. The best part of the night was watching Lynne Abbott, an easterner, out-dance half of the Stetson-hatted, I-was-country-when-country-wasn't-cool, phony cowboys in the joint. Some of them tried to hit on her but she always slipped back to the safety of our table. The team had an 11:30 curfew (is that demeaning or what?) and it sure looked like there were a lot of unhappy counterfeit cow-boys when Lynne decided she'd be safer walking back to the ho-tel with us than staying in the honky tonk. Surrounded by players Lynne looked like a twelve-meter yacht in a convoy of destroyers.

We beat Nashville 2–1 and headed into Toronto an abysmal 1–4 on the trip and 3–5 for the season. We had a late-morning practice at the Air Canada Centre, the new rink the Leafs moved into when they left Maple Leaf Gardens a few years ago. We were in the dressing room about ten minutes before practice when Packy walked in and right away one of our rookies, Billy Shannon, started yapping. "Gotta have this one tonight, guys. . . . Gotta bring it. . . . Little sandpaper in the game . . ." Billy shut up as soon as Packy was out of earshot in the trainer's room.

"Hey, rook, shut the fuck up. You haven't hit anyone or blocked a shot in three games," Flipside said.

Flipper was right. All that chatter was fake hustle. Not even the coaches are fooled by it. But I don't like hearing that tone be-tween teammates. That's what losing does.

We had a free afternoon, so after lunch I joined Cam on a short walk from the hotel to the Hockey Hall of Fame on Yonge Street.

We entered the hall through a food court in an ultramodern office-and-shopping complex. Once inside it was like stepping back in time not only because of the exhibits and old photos of players without helmets but because the Hall of Fame is located in what was a branch of the Bank of Montreal built in 1885. The building's weathered stone exterior and polished oak paneling are a sharp nostalgic contrast to the glass-and-steel architecture of modern Toronto.

We headed straight for the hall's sanctum sanctorum—as my religion teacher at St. Dom's would've called it—the old bank vault on the second floor, home of the Stanley Cup. There was the Cup itself, a gleaming silver bowl atop a column of concentric silver bands, each glittering with the engraved names of former winners. Display cases around the room held the older engraved bands that had to be taken off so the trophy wouldn't stand too high. Some of the greatest names in hockey are on that Cup: Fred "Cyclone" Taylor, Maurice Richard, Jean Beliveau, Bobby Orr, Wayne Gretzky, Mario Lemieux. And Georges Vezina, a Montreal Canadiens goalie from the twenties who had my all-time favorite sports nickname, the Chicoutimi Cucumber. The writers called him that because he was from Chicoutimi and was so cool in net. But it might also be worth noting that Vezina fathered twenty-two children. His wife, Marie-Stella Vezina, should have her name on a trophy. Each year the Vezina Trophy goes to the best goalie in the NHL as voted by the general managers. I've been runner-up three times. I'd like to win it. But I'd rather win the Stanley Cup.

While I walked around reading names Cam stood and stared at the Cup as if it were the Holy Grail or the Hope Diamond. "Money can't buy that," he said. "Which is why it's worth winning."

If you win the Cup you get to keep it for a day. A few years ago when Dallas won the Cup a defenseman, Penrose Holiday, put his five-week-old infant son in the bowl for what he thought would be a cutesy nude photo for the family's Christmas card. Of course the kid did what babies do. Then he did the other thing babies do. You might want to remember that the next time you see a player swigging Dom Pérignon out of that bowl.

"I think it's this season or never," Cam said more to himself than to me.

"It'll be never if we don't get some scoring," I said. The truth was our defense and goaltending had been solid after opening night but only J.-B. Desjardin and Taki Yamamura were scoring with any consistency.

"Pisses you off that the Mad Hatter was too cheap to get into the free-agent market and get us a scorer or two," Cam said.

"It's not just the Hatter," I said. "It's Gabe's money." Gabe Vogel has owned the Bruins for twenty years. We're part of a worldwide media empire based mainly on cable TV.

"In Gabe's eyes we're just programming," Cam said. Vogel is listed annually in *Forbes* magazine as one of the four hundred richest people in the world. Word around the league and among our fans is that his mandate to the Mad Hatter is to build a competitive team but one not quite competitive enough to win the Stanley Cup and cost Gabe a whole lot of money in player contracts. I think Madison Hattigan does what he's told. We're always $3 million or $4 million under the cap. And if the rumors about Hattigan getting a percentage of that money are true, then the Mad Hatter is pocketing $300,000 to $400,000 every season.

I doubt Gabe Vogel would know a puck from a whoopee pie. He hardly ever comes to our games and when he does he sits in his luxury suite. I've seen him in our dressing room only once and that was last season after we were eliminated by Montreal in the playoffs. He looked relieved.

I left Cam staring at the Stanley Cup while I wandered downstairs to an exhibit that shows the evolution of the goalie mask. It's hard to believe but for more than half a century goalies didn't wear masks. There had been a few unsuccessful experiments with goalie masks but it wasn't until November 1, 1959, that Montreal Canadiens goalie Jacques Plante put on a mask in an NHL game and changed hockey forever. In the first period of a game against the Rangers at Madison Square Garden, Plante came out of his net and checked the Rangers' Andy Bathgate behind the Montreal goal. On his next shift Bathgate—who had one of the hardest shots in the league—deliberately put a back-hander into Plante's face, smashing the goalie's left cheekbone and slicing the side of his nose. In those days team's didn't carry backup goalies. If Plante hadn't returned to the game the Canadiens would've been forced to use the Rangers' practice goalie, an amateur who was one of the Garden's electricians. Plante had been practicing with a mask of his own design but his coach, Toe Blake, had refused to let him wear it in a game. Blake said it blocked the goalie's vision at his feet and, worse, was a tacit admission of fear. "If I jump out of an airplane without a parachute does that make me brave?" Plante asked his coach. Realizing the leverage he had, Plante made it a condition of his returning to play that he be allowed to wear the mask. Blake caved. Plante wore the mask and Montreal won the game. And the next game. And the one after that. And the Stanley Cup, their fifth in a row. Plante's invention didn't only prevent injuries. It saved lives. Anyone who ever plays goal owes something to Jacques Plante, the most important goaltender of all time. No him, no me, I thought.

During dinner at Giovanni's in Toronto's Little Italy I asked Cam what he'd do if he had the Cup for a day. "I'd have to take it to the Carter & Peabody offices because it'd net the company a zillion dollars' worth of publicity," he said. "But what I'd *like* to do is take it back to Vermont. Haul it into our old rink and let Indinacci and everybody get their picture taken with it."

I said I'd bring it home to my mother and grandmother. Display it at St. Dom's High School and maybe at my grammar school. "I'd try not to let a politician get within a five-iron of it," I said.

"I don't remember seeing your mom on opening night. She come down?"

"Couldn't. Said she didn't want to leave my grandmother alone. She's seventy-eight and her health's slipping. I invited them for Thanksgiving. Told Mom I'd send a car for them and hire someone to look after Mammam so my mother can get to our Friday-afternoon game."

The next night we lost 2–0 to the Leafs to close out one of the worst road trips since Lee went to Gettysburg. It was the second time in nine games we were shut out. The only good thing was that Flipside apparently got through to Billy Shannon. The rook had three hits and blocked a shot. Unfortunately he tried to block another shot in the third period. That one ended up in our net. It was a dumb rookie play. One of their shooters was about twenty feet away to my left when Shannon slid out at him pads-first. The puck ticked off of Billy's leg and over my shoulder into the net. The first thing I wanted to do was yell at Billy. Or point to him and show him up the way I've seen a lot of quarterbacks show up receivers who run the wrong routes or pitchers show up fielders who make errors. But that's not part of the hockey culture. We don't show up a teammate. Ever. We need each other too much.

After the game I had a talk with Billy. I told him it's OK to try to block a shot from beyond the face-off circle. If he misses, then I still have time and space to see the shot and react. "But when a shooter is in close either check him or drive him off the angle but don't try to block the shot," I said. Billy nodded.

We limped back to Boston 1–5 on the trip, 3–6 for the season, and grateful the Red Sox and Patriots were keeping us buried on page 3 of the sports section. In a quirk of scheduling we had to play Toronto again at our place. Rinky Higgins got the start and we won 2–1. When a coach changes goalies and wins he usually comes right back with the same goalie. Rinky started again versus the Rangers but we lost 4–1. So Packy switched back to me and we closed out October with a 3–2 win in Chicago and a 4–3 loss to New Jersey.

We lost the New Jersey game on a power-play goal in the last minute. Their right point guy faked a slapper, then dished the puck to the left face-off dot, where their winger one-timed it into the net. *Thunk.* Goalies don't see goals. We hear them. We either hear the puck clank in off the pipes, crossbar, or metal center-piece or we hear a muffled thud like someone hitting a bass drum when the puck strikes the padded base plate of the goal. If the puck hits the netting then we hear the roar—or collective groan—of the fans. It used to be worse. In high school the steel base plate wasn't padded and a low shot that beat you would slam into the net with the sharp *clank* that meant instant humiliation. I hate the sound of a goal.

One of the few good things to happen in October was my lunch with Faith McNeil. Because the team had a Sunday-morning practice, Faith and I planned to have a leisurely brunch at Sonsie. But Faith checked out of that. When I pulled Boss Scags into her driveway I found her dressed more for the NCAA Women's Basketball Final Four than for brunch. She wore baggy string-tied gray shorts, a sweat-soaked gray T-shirt, and a pair of beat-up Reeboks. She was shooting a basketball at a hoop suspended over her garage. Her hair was in a ponytail the way she wore it in college.

"Leave it to you to buy the only house in Chestnut Hill with a backboard and basket," I said.

"The house didn't come with those. I bought them," Faith said, launching a twenty-five-foot jumper that was nothing but string music.

"Three-pointer," I said. I passed the ball back to her and made what I hoped looked like a token effort at playing defense (actually I was trying but I didn't want it to look that way). Faith drove by me and laid the ball in left-handed.

"Why don't we have lunch here and watch the Pats game," she said. It wasn't a question.

Faith went upstairs to shower and I flipped through the Sunday papers. Lynne Abbott wrote her Sunday column on how the Bruins weren't going anywhere if we didn't get more scoring.

Faith made Cajun crabcakes—heavy on the crab and cayenne, light on the bread crumbs—and lobster salad sandwiches. We ate sitting on her couch watching the Pats-Jets game. She had a half bottle of Veuve Clicquot champagne on ice. I rarely drink at lunch so I took a pass and had a Coke. Faith poured a few ounces of the champagne into a fluted glass. Strange. I'd never known her to be much of a drinker. It was even stranger when she poured herself a second glass just before halftime.

Halftime was a smile. The TV people did a feature on none other than Patriots Dance Team Coordinator and my ex-girlfriend, Missy Taylor. Missy said the Pats dancers were "an integral part of the total entertainment philosophy of Patriots ownership and a vital channel for the expression of fan enthusiasm and support."

"Silly me," said Faith. "I thought they were a T and A show."

Midway through the third quarter with the Pats up by seven and driving, Faith laid her empty glass on the coffee table on top of a stack of *Robb Report* magazines, tucked her feet onto the couch, and laid her head on my right shoulder. I figured it was the champagne, the lunch, and the basketball workout combining to make her sleepy. I thought that for four more plays when, with the Pats first-and-goal from the five, Faith slid her left arm around my neck and said, "Rehab's over." I was about to say "Mine or yours?" but I couldn't because at that moment I had a mouthful of Faith McNeil's tongue. Out of the corner of my left eye I saw the Pats score on a quick-out to the tight end just before Faith hit the Off switch on the remote and pulled me down on top of her. Why do women get to decide everything?

We missed the fourth quarter. We also missed Oakland versus Seattle at 4:15 and Giants versus Cowboys at 8:30, and we would have missed the 'Skins-versus-Colts Monday-night game if I hadn't had to get out of bed for a morning practice. On the continuum that has sex at one end and lovemaking at the other, Faith and I gave each other both.

At midnight we were at the kitchen table eating scrambled eggs and English muffins. She said it was so late I might as well stay at her house.

"You like living alone?" she asked.

"I don't find myself bad company," I said. "I spend so much time with the guys, it's nice having a little time for myself. You?"

"I don't like Sundays," she said.

"That explain tonight?"

"No," she said. "What explains tonight is that I've known you since we were freshmen in college. You were the only guy I could talk to without thinking you were going to hit on me."

"I didn't try out because I didn't think I could make the team," I said in one of the hundreds of sports metaphors that had passed between us. We used the language of sport not as affectation but as a way of making ourselves clearer. I reminded her of the day when our history professor was almost finished taking attendance and Faith came rushing into the classroom. "You beat the throw," said the prof, a baseball fan.

"Nope. I slid in under the tag," Faith said, a better metaphor.

We cleaned up the kitchen and went back to bed.

I wouldn't have expected Faith McNeil to be a cuddler or a babbler but she was both. She had her left arm around me and for most of an hour walked me through her childhood and adolescence. She grew up in Cambridge, a suburb of Boston, and went to a Catholic grammar school and Cambridge Catholic High School, where she earned twelve varsity letters, four each in soccer, basketball, and softball. She sounded like one of those lost-in-the-glory-days guys we all know as she described almost every game of her high school career. I fell asleep with Cambridge Catholic trailing Wakefield by five in the Eastern Mass quarterfinals with two minutes to play and Faith on the line for the front end of a one and one.

When I woke up it was 8:30, which really pissed me off because it meant I wouldn't have time to go home and change before practice. Faith had asked me if I'd wanted to set an alarm and I'd said no because I'm a light sleeper and I've always had an internal alarm clock I can set for whatever time I want to wake up. On the road I leave a wake-up call if we have an early flight but that's just for backup. I'm always awake when they call. But I must have been so relaxed from my night with Faith that I slept an hour more than I'd planned to. I took a fast shower. Faith was half asleep when I kissed her good-bye. She said something that sounded like "Mmmmaahhbye . . ."

I felt happier, more buoyant, than I had in years as I drove Boss Scags through the back streets of Boston toward the Garden. But if there's one thing I've learned about Happiness it's that when Happiness is up and dancing it's only because Trouble is taking a nap or making a run to the convenience store for cigarettes and lottery tickets. Trouble doesn't stay gone long.

We had a ten o'clock practice and it was 9:30 when I came scrambling into the dressing room, the last guy to arrive. I'm usually the first. It didn't go unnoticed that I was wearing the same chinos and golf shirt I'd worn the day before.

"Even in college you had two sets of clothes," Cam said.

"GQ called. They want you for the cover," Jean-Baptiste said.

"Jean Pierre Savard, one of the eight hundred and twelve best-dressed players in the NHL," Kevin Quigley said.

There were other remarks but I stopped listening when Cam, who has the locker to my left, said, "Gotta talk to you."

I suited up and headed for the ice with Cam behind me. We skated to the visitors' bench, where we always stretch before practice. No one else was within earshot when Cam asked, "You spend the night with Faith?"

"And a fine night it was."

"Good. Should've happened a long time ago. Guys she's been going out with are lighter than the women you've been going out with. But that's not the problem."

Cam and I each put a leg up on the dasher board in front of the bench and began stretching when he said: "Sorry to screw up the afterglow, JP, but I've got bad news. The Mad Hatter's trying to trade me."

Trouble was back from the convenience store.

Four

The vampire bats attacked me the moment I opened the door.

"Trick or treat, Mr. Savard," said the first vampire bat, who was Lindsey Carter decked out in a bat costume the wings of which Tamara had made out of the remnants of an umbrella. "Trick or treat," echoed the smaller bat, Caitlin Carter. Tamara and Cam stepped in behind the bats. I'd almost forgotten it was Halloween until Faith came over to watch *Monday Night Football*, bringing with her a few packages of miniature candy bars and two pumpkins. She'd also brought a scalpel with which to turn the pumpkins into jack-o'-lanterns. Lindsey and Caitlin went to the kitchen to watch Faith perform some tricky maxilofacial surgery on the pumpkins. Meanwhile Cam updated me on our GM's move to trade him.

It was Lynne Abbott, Knower of All Things, who told Cam that the Hatter was offering him around the league, trying to swap Cam, a proven defenseman (and the one guy Hattigan can't control with money) for the forty-goal scorer we needed. Lynne said she'd heard it from her front-office sources in Vancouver and L.A. Lynne told Cam she planned to break the news later in the day on the *Boston Post*'s Web site. Cam said if she waited two days she'd have a better story but that he wouldn't elaborate. Lynne said she'd give Cam only one day because of her fear of being scooped. Cam acted fast.

While Cam could have killed a trade by retiring on the spot, he was troubled and angry about three things: the public embarrassment of being traded as if he were a used Zamboni; the fact that if he refused the trade he'd probably have to retire—or be suspended—immediately, thus forfeiting his last chance at winning the Cup; and his awareness that somewhere in another city a fellow player would be hung out to dry, knowing his team tried to trade him but he was stuck with that team because Cam torpedoed the deal. Cam went for the preemptive strike. He met with Madison Hattigan Monday after practice.

"No matter what the goddamn question is, the answer is always power or money," Cam's father likes to say. Cam learned the lesson. The Mad Hatter has authority but authority isn't power. Security guards have authority. Rich guys have power.

Cam didn't let on that he knew Hattigan was trying to trade him. Cam said he'd been thinking it over and he was going to retire at the end of the season. He wanted to give the club the "courtesy"—how the Hatter must have winced at that patronizing touch—of letting it know a day before he told the media. That bit of news and the certainty it would be made public the next day effectively canceled Hattigan's ability to trade Cam. No one is going to give up a scorer for a guy who's announced he's going to retire in eight months and can well afford to do so.

At first Hattigan, apparently forgetting whom he was dealing with, took the news as Cam's way of renegotiating. "Look, Cameron, if it's your contract . . . we can rework that. Have Denny Moran call me." Moran is a lawyer and senior partner at Carter & Peabody. He's doubled as Cam's and my agent since we came into the league.

"It's got nothing to do with money," Cam said. "I could make more money in the family business." Cam wasn't bragging. "This is about going out on my own terms while I can still play. I'd rather leave two seasons too early than two shifts too late." Then Cam pressed his advantage. "You'll be saving almost five million on my salary over the next two seasons," he reminded Hattigan. "I know how you can spend a fraction of that and solve our scoring problems."

"MIT won't clone Gretzky," Hattigan said, trying to sound dismissive.

"Gabe Vogel wouldn't pay Gretzky," Cam said. "And every GM in the league knows we can't score; they're not going to help us by dishing us a big gun." Then Cam became what he described as "conspiratorially friendly." "Madison," Cam said. "There's a guy with the Rangers you can get for a torn puck bag. They've buried him on the fourth line. Paying him $475,000. The minimum. He gets maybe four shifts a game and when he's on the ice they use him as a checker. I'm sure you know Gaston Deveau, but no one in this league has any idea how good he is. Or could be if someone gave him a chance."

"He's too small for the NHL," Hattigan said.

"Henri Richard was small and he's got his name on the Stanley Cup eleven times. A record. I'd like my name on the Cup *once*," Cam said. "JP and I played with Deveau in college. He should have won the Hobey Baker his last two seasons." The Hobey Baker is the trophy that's supposed to go to the best player in college hockey but usually goes to a good player whose college has the best sports information director. "Gaston's thirty but he can still fly. You see what he did in Europe?"

"Look what Hitler did in Europe until the Allies sent in the varsity. Europe isn't the Show," the Mad Hatter said, showing the typical NHL old-timer's prejudice against the European leagues. And against small players. But Hattigan—probably to end the conversation—said he'd think it over. He also said he thought the club should set up a formal press conference to announce Cam's retirement. "Let's you, Packy, and me take all the questions at once," Hattigan said.

Cam said no. He told the Hatter that Lynne Abbott had the story and would break it in the next morning's paper. Cam wasn't going to give up control of the message. He didn't want anyone thinking the decision to retire was anyone's but his. "I don't want any of that 'by mutual agreement' bullshit" is the way he put it.

"By the way," Cam said as he left Hattigan's office. "You've been in this game a long time, Madison. You ever get your name on the Cup?" Cam closed the door before the Mad Hatter could answer. Cam doesn't ask many questions he doesn't know the answer to.

Cam repaid Lynne by giving her news of his retirement a day ahead of everyone else. He also told her he'd hold an informal press conference in the dressing room after our Tuesday-night game with Edmonton.

"Look at this, Daddy," said Lindsey, who came into the living room carrying a pumpkin in which Faith had carved earholes she'd filled with disks of summer squash and a circular nose hole from which extended a droopy carrot.

"It's a Jean Pierre-o'-lantern," Faith yelled from the kitchen.

Caitlin carried the other pumpkin, an elaborately carved gargoyle the product of Faith's artistry and scalpel. If I ever get a face transplant, Faith's got the gig. She gave the Carter girls the gargoyle and put the Jean Pierre-o'-lantern on my coffee table.

"Is she your girlfriend?" Lindsey asked me.

"Lindsey, that's not a polite question," said Tamara as she and Cam shooed the bats out the door.

"Well, are you?" I asked Faith when the door closed.

"I hope so," she said.

"Me, too," I said.

Faith was staying overnight for what she'd called "the second game of the home-and-home." We watched the Colts beat the 'Skins 28–21, a nice midseason win for Indianapolis fans but not enough of a margin to cover the seven-and-a-half-point spread, which is the only thing a gambler like Cam's father cares about. The Colts would have covered if their Lithuanian placekicker hadn't blown a late-game field goal by banging the ball off of the left upright. I'd just turned off the TV when Cam phoned. He was laughing so hard he could hardly talk. "My father had ten grand on the Colts" (hysterical laughter). "It'd be worth the ride home just to watch him tear up the den." Whenever Cam's dad loses his bets on the NFL Sunday games—which is most of the time—he tries to get even on the Monday-night game.

"I just called my father and he didn't even say hello. Just picks up the phone and says, 'Goddamn Lithuanian gypsy choke artist . . . You didn't see disregard for the Vegas line in Johnny U's day.' So I tell him John Unitas was Lithuanian and he says, 'Well he goddamn well must've been human on his mother's side.' "

Mr. Carter's football disappointments can lead to major den wreckage when his team wins but doesn't cover or when they lose by more than the spread. From the tantrums I'd seen watching games with Cam's dad I could imagine what was happening in Cam's parents' house.

I reminded Cam of the time we were watching with his dad when a wide-open Dallas receiver dropped a pass in the end zone on the game's final play, that moment of carelessness costing Cameron C. Carter Jr. twenty thou. The eruption began quietly with Cam's father mumbling about "the integrity of this god-damn league . . . druggies snorting up the thirty-yard line . . . Take away the betting man and the NFL couldn't out-Nielsen Dora the goddamned Explorer. . . ." Then Cam's dad kicked the coffee table and threw the remote at the plasma TV (missed, wide right) before storming off to bed. I had to hold a couch pillow over my face to keep from laughing out loud.

The memory of it had Cam and me laughing so hard we were gasping for breath when Faith, who had heard only my side of the conversation, stood up and said, "It must be great to be seventeen forever." She didn't seem angry. Just curious, I thought. Maybe even wistful. She knows my teammates and I live in a world that gives us more cheap laughs than a Three Stooges film fest. Faith and I talked about it later. I told her about the baby powder Quig sprinkled in JB's hair dryer, the live lobster from a hotel kitchen Cam once placed on a napping Taki Yamamura's chest. Almost scared Taki back to Vancouver. And about the time three of us snuck out of lunch early, went to Rex Conway's hotel room, and put all of the furniture into the bathroom and left the Gideon Bible where the bed used to be. It took Rex more than an hour to get his room back together. I rationalized that the stunts are childish but the laughter is real. It cuts across cliques and team status. I claimed that laughter helps connect us and hold us together through the long season. "We need it," I said.

"Oh," she said. "I thought you were just immature."

That's how I learned Faith McNeil doesn't chase pitches outside the strike zone.

We beat Edmonton 2–1 thanks mainly to Cam, who played his best game in two seasons, assisting on both goals, blocking four shots, and playing thirty-one minutes, more than half the game. But the big news came after the game when Cam met with the media.

The dressing room was more crowded than usual because of all the reporters who wanted to talk to Cam about his retirement. I got dressed fast just to be out of the way of the media crowding around Cam's dressing stall. It was the usual feeding frenzy where Lynne and other writers get whacked in the back of the head by TV lenses wielded by guys who think a dressing-room press conference is a reenactment of the bayonet charge at Little Round Top.

Cam is slick with the media and he didn't have any problems until toward the end. That was right after Bruno Govoni bolted to the shower and Jean-Baptiste quietly switched on Govoni's cell phone, then placed a call to it. When a writer asked Cam if his retirement plans included "bringing Carter & Peabody into the area of sports franchise ownership," what we heard before Cam answered was the breathless voice of Loretta "Lash" LaRue moaning "Yes . . . Yes . . . FUCK . . . OHHHH . . . YESSS . . ."

"That goes for me, too," said Cam as the press conference ended.

Two nights later we stole a 1–0 win at New Jersey, then returned to Boston for a five-game home stand. I got shelled 5–3 by Minnesota in the first game, so Packy switched to Rinky Higgins, who lost 5–1 to Columbus. We were 7–10 and in fourth place, eight points behind Montreal, when we faced the Canadiens at the Garden on a Saturday. Packy reminded us this was a four-pointer. If Montreal won they'd be ten points ahead of us— that's a lot of ground to have to make up—but if we won we'd be six points out of first, close enough to have the Canadiens peeking in their rearview mirror. The game was a laugher. I can't explain it but we beat them 9–3 and it was as if all the shots we'd been missing were suddenly jumping into the net. JB, Quigley, and Taki had two goals each and I got an assist when I shoved a puck to Cam, who passed it to JB, who roofed a laser that knocked Montreal goalie Claude Rancourt's water bottle off of the string holding it to the top of the net. Quigley then flipped the bottle into the crowd, which goes a long way toward explaining why the teams had a combined 217 minutes in penalties. The fight was so bad that even Claude Rancourt and I paired off, not because we wanted to fight but because part of the game's code is that when a melee breaks out the goalies fight each other. But Claude and I just waltzed around pulling on each other's jerseys and talking.

"I need Sox-Yanks tickets next season, Jean Pierre. You can do this, *mon ami?*"

"Get you into the Carters' private box," I said. "Can you get me anything for the Canadian Grand Prix?"

"Pit pass. No problem," Claude said, twisting the neck of my shirt.

Goalies like and understand one another in a way other players don't. We're united in a brotherhood of apartness and fear.

After the game, Alvin "Captain Baritone" Crouch asked Quigley why he'd flipped Rancourt's water bottle into the stands.

"Retaliation," Quig said.

"Retaliation for what?" Captain Baritone asked.

"For nothing. I retaliate first," Quig said.

We closed out the home stand with two more wins—5–4 over the Devils and 3–1 over the Sabres. One of my teammates—I still don't know who it was—got me pretty good before the Buffalo game. The day before every game our video guy leaves a DVD in my locker. It shows my saves, the goals I let in, and all of my passing and puck handling in the previous game against the opponent we're about to play. I use the DVD to review my own game and to remind myself of what the other team's shooters are likely to do. I usually look at it on the TV in the players' lounge but the day before the Buffalo game I was in a hurry to get home, so I brought the disc—labeled "JP vs. Buff"—home with me. I put it on just after dinner. Porn movie. Girl on girl. Faith howled. I wouldn't have minded so much if I'd had the real scouting tape along with the porn movie. But I played well against the Sabres, so maybe this whole scouting thing is overrated. Or maybe I should watch more porn movies.

Faith and I became an item. One indicator was that Tamara asked Faith to take part in the Bruins Wives Benefit Carnival in February. "Wives" is a misnomer. It should be called the Bruins Girlfriends Benefit Carnival because most guys on our team are single. The other indicator was that Faith asked me if she could "keep a few things" at my condo. I asked her if I could do the same at her house. I wanted to be with her, and for reasons that go beyond sex. I didn't like only the way I felt about her. I liked the way I felt about myself when I was with her. I think that's the difference between a Faith McNeil and a Sheri the Equestrienne. And between love and infatuation.

Thursday night after the game we thought we'd skip sex. "Tonight's an optional skate," is the way Faith put it. We lay in the dark talking. She asked me what I like about what I do.

"I like being good at something. I like the recognition. And the money," I said; then after a few seconds I tacked on the rest of the truth. "A rink is the only place I feel important."

"Great while it lasts," said Faith. Then she told me that the program for our game with Montreal last Saturday carried an interview with Canadiens retired veteran Phillippe Dorais. "You know what he said about retiring?" Faith asked, not stopping for me to answer. "He said that on the day he went to the press conference to announce his retirement he felt like he was going to jail. Like he was stepping into a life so bleak he'd never even imagined it."

"I'm a long way from retiring, hon, and I'm going to have plenty of money when I do. But hockey is the only thing I know."

"Money's important, Jean Pierre. And so is doing something you're good at. But pretty soon you're going to have to live that life you've never imagined." Then she giggled and pinched my left nipple. "Always wanted to cop a feel," she said. So much for the optional skate.

We chartered into Montreal on Friday after practice. It's a short flight, so we were in our hotel, the Queen Elizabeth, by early afternoon. The Queen E is home to one of Canada's oldest restaurants—the Beaver Club, a name dating back to the day when Montreal's chief industry was the fur trade. "I made dinner reservations for us at the Beaver Club," Cam told me as we got off the bus. Bruno Govoni overheard him. "Why would anyone want to eat at a strip joint?" Bruno asked.

After the team lunch I took a walk by myself south on rue University, then east on rue Notre-Dame until I came to the Notre-Dame Basilica. The only time I go to church is when I'm in Montreal or Quebec City. I don't go for religious reasons but to be alone for a few minutes in a beautiful and familiar place. I like the smell in a Catholic church—burning candles mixed with the faint fragrance of incense lingering from a now forgotten service.

My first thought on seeing Notre-Dame's carved wood altar, gilded woodwork, and vaulted ceiling covered with thousands of twenty-four-karat gold stars is that this would be a great place to play Wiffle ball. I've already made up the rules. Anything into the pews is an out. Down the aisles is a single, beyond the pews is a double, the first balcony is a triple, and the second balcony or organ loft is a home run. Anything off of the balcony facade is a double. Hitting a Station of the Cross or statue of a saint is a double play. Fouling one back into the crucified Christ is automatic side retired.

I sat in a pew near a small side altar next to a metal stand flickering with votive candles. I think lighting a candle for an intention is almost as illogical as Madison Hattigan switching hotels to win a hockey game. I had a religion teacher at St. Dom's who said that to pray *for* something is not to pray at all. I tried to imagine Cam's dad trying to straddle that semantic blue line: "Heavenly Father, we beseech Thee not that the Packers win but that their loss be by less than the six-point spread. And thus may Your scourge fall on the Wizard of Odds and all bookmakers, for they are the vile money changers in the temple of sport. Amen."

Illogical or not, I stuffed a Canadian $20 bill into the metal offerings box, pulled a wooden stick from the small sandbox filled with sticks, and lit candles for my mother's happiness, for my grandmother's health, and for Faith not optioning me to Muskegon. Then I lit one in memory of Lisa. I was going to leave it at that until I figured that twenty bucks should buy me the Total Conflagration Package, and I lit a candle for Boston winning the Stanley Cup. Maybe my high school religion teacher was wrong. He had to be at least partly wrong; he taught religion.

The only time I ever went to Mass at Notre-Dame was for Rocket Richard's funeral. We'd just been eliminated from the playoffs in late May of 2000 when Richard died. Five of us—Cam, Kevin Quigley, Jean-Baptiste Desjardin, Phil "Flipside" Palmer, and me—represented the team at the wake and state funeral.

It's hard to grasp the importance of Richard to the French. "He was our flag," said my grandmother, who was born in Montreal and who, even after the family resettled in Maine, continued to follow the Canadiens. Richard was the only one she ever spoke of as if he were the fleur-de-lis made flesh.

The Rocket restored French-Canadian pride during the 1940s and 1950s, a time the old French still call "La Grande Noirceur," the Great Darkness. Back then to be French-Canadian was to be consigned to an underclass of factory and mill workers forever under the thumb of English bosses. French-Canadians saw Richard, Montreal's biggest star, as a man who stood up to the English. Who did what millions of working poor wished they could do. And who did it with a menacing ferocity not since seen in the NHL. Novelist William Faulkner, when he first saw Richard in a game at Madison Square Garden, wrote in *Sports Illustrated* that in Richard's face there lurked "something of the passionate, glittering, fatal, alien quality of snakes." For decades hockey was to French-Canadians what basketball is to many African-Americans—the road up and out.

The only smile in the otherwise solemn Richard funeral came just before the start of Mass, when the organist began playing *Ave Maria* and NHL deputy commissioner Scott Josten's wife, Tatum, sitting a row in front of us, said in a stage whisper intended to make obvious her vast knowledge of classical music, "Oh, I just love Bach's *Ave.*"

In an equally loud voice Flipside said, "Actually this one's Schubert's." Flipside was right, of course. But Flipper is toast if he has to go before the deputy commish in a disciplinary hearing.

On the walk back to the hotel I began thinking about my father, something I do only when we play in Montreal. Well, then and on Father's Day. I wonder if he's alive? Is he in Montreal? Will he be in the crowd at our game tomorrow? Watching on TV? I even wonder if he knows who I am, seeing as how my mom changed our name from his—Lachine—back to her family name, Savard.

"How could a guy walk out on a young wife and a five-year-old?" I asked Cam at dinner. "Must've been a major scumbag."

"Either he thought he'd be better off without you or you'd be better off without him," Cam said. That's the trouble with Cam. He's too logical.

"He had the better-off-without-him part right," I said. Growing up, I was sometimes glad not to have a father. Especially where hockey was concerned. I saw the way some of my teammates' fathers drove their kids to be the player the father never was. The only thing my mother drove me to was games and practices. She waited around to watch me play, then bought me a hot chocolate and said something nice even if I hadn't played well. I never had the feeling that how I played had anything to do with how she felt about me. If I ever get my hands on that Cup she's the first person I'm passing it to.

There was a bus to take us to the Saturday-morning skate. But the rink—the 21,273-seat Bell Centre—is only a few blocks from the hotel, so Cam and I walked. Instead of going in through the players' entrance we detoured into the box-office lobby to see a reproduction of the Canadiens' dressing room the way it was in the old Montreal Forum. The display includes the famous sign painted on the dressing-room wall under pictures of the Canadiens players elected to the Hall of Fame. The sign reads: "*Nos bras meutris vous tendent le flambeau, a vous toujours de le porter bien haut!*" and under that the English translation: "To you from failing hands we throw the torch, be yours to hold it high."

Hockey is serious business in Montreal.

. . .

The Canadiens hammered us 6–2. It was old-fashioned fire wagon hockey. They skated us into the ground. One play—their fourth goal, late in the second period—pretty much captures the way Montreal used to play and, sometimes, still does. Tim Harcourt beat Quigley to the puck in the corner, and just before Quig drilled him, Harcourt passed to a breaking right winger, who head-manned it to the center, and all of a sudden I'm looking at a three-on-two. The center dropped it for the trailing left winger, who one-timed a shot that beat me top shelf. Tic. Tac. Toe. And everything at full speed. Say this for the Canadiens: they play the game the way it should be played. Except for that pest Reggie Harper. The guy dives like a soccer player. Late in the second period Harper was rushing the puck with Quigley back-checking on him and closing. Quig reached ahead with his stick to play the puck but Quig's stick brushed Harper's leg and Harper fell to the ice like he was shot with an assault rifle. The ref whistled Quig for a tripping penalty and Harper got to his feet smirking. "You know what you guys are doing?" Quig yelled at the ref. "You're rewarding dishonor." At least it took the smirk off of Harper's face. But Montreal scored on the power play. Sometimes dishonor wins.

After the game, Cam said something to me about none of my pregame rituals bringing me any luck. But that doesn't stop me from doing them. At the start of every game I use the tip of my right skate blade to make a small Sign of the Cross on the ice. I know that sounds hypocritical. And neurotic. But it's something I've done since high school. I also put on my equipment the same way I did in high school—left side first—and I tap both posts and the crossbar with my stick before warm-ups. I find safety in ritual. It's calming because what you do next is predetermined, whereas in a game you're forced to react to others or make them react to you. Or maybe I just don't like surprises. Or anything I can't control.

. . .

In the two games before Thanksgiving we beat Vancouver 3–2 at home then got shut out 2–0 in Toronto. "Lack of oh-fense is killing the Bruins, eh?" as one Toronto sports talk radio guy put it.

Packy disappointed me in Toronto. In his pregame talk—which I think should be about Xs and Os and who's matched up against whom—he said we wanted to head into the Thanksgiving break with a win and then rambled on about Thanksgiving being a great family day and then—the oldest coach's cliché in the book—about how our team is like a family and we have to support each other and watch each other's backs. That family stuff is a crock. In the first place, most of our guys are Canadian, and Canada's Thanksgiving is in October. And it's not as if we didn't know why we'd gotten on a plane and flown to Toronto. The family metaphor in pro sports is ridiculous. Family members don't get cut, traded, waived, benched, or sent to the minors. A team isn't remotely like a family, but coaches in all sports and at all levels keep saying it is. Hockey at our level is a business. While Packy was talking most of us stared at the floor, embarrassed for him.

My mother and grandmother arrived Wednesday afternoon shortly after I got home from practice. Faith was there, too. She planned to have dinner with my family and me on Wednesday, then join her family in Cambridge on Thanksgiving. Faith had met my mother a couple of times at the University of Vermont. "It's been a long time, Mrs. Savard," Faith said.

"Jacqueline, please," my mother said, pronouncing her name Jacque-LYN, with a soft J and the accent on the last syllable in the Quebec way and not JAC-kwi-lyn, with a hard J, the way most Americans pronounce it.

My grandmother's name is Huguette but I've always called

her Mammam. My grandmother went immediately to the kitchen and began searching the cupboards and the fridge to see what she'd cook for dinner. I told her that Faith and I could make dinner but my grandmother wouldn't hear of it. I think she feels as important in the kitchen as I do in goal. But it wasn't too long before Mammam came into the living room and sat on the couch, wheezing. "I get tired," she said.

"The doctor says her heart's weakening," my mother said after Mammam went back to the kitchen. "He gave her blood thinners and a bunch of other pills but they don't seem to do much good."

Faith told me later that my grandmother probably suffered from congestive heart failure. "The pump breaks down after seventy or eighty years," she said.

Mammam was born in Laval, just outside of Montreal. She was six years old when her parents moved to New England. They were among the nearly one million French Quebeckers who moved to the United States between 1830 and 1930. Most came to escape hardscrabble farming or the slums and poverty of life in the working-class sections of Montreal. The arriving French found year-round jobs in New England's mills, factories, and forests. And when they came they brought hockey with them.

Heart trouble or not, Mammam could still wheel in the kitchen. My mother brought in a cooler containing one of my grandmother's *tourtières*—the traditional Quebec meat pie made of ground pork and beef with potatoes and spices—and a bean pot half full of Mammam's baked beans made with molasses, dark brown sugar, pieces of onion, and salt pork. It's poor people's food but it's what I grew up eating and I still love it.

Fortunately, my grandmother, tired from the trip, went to bed early. That's when Faith gave us some much-needed comic relief. Digging deep into her handbag, she came up with, "Ta-da . . . *A Charlie Brown Thanksgiving*," she said, holding up the DVD. Then, reaching into the bag again, she pulled out a jar of popcorn.

We made a large communal bowl of popcorn and watched the movie. I laughed at the scene where Snoopy gets tangled in a folding beach chair. I think that scene is a metaphor for life— you can't always make it unfold the way you know it's supposed to.

Faith left early to drive to her parents' house and I wanted to turn in early because we had practice in the morning. I asked my mother what her plans were for taking care of Mammam when her heart got worse. I told her I'd cover the costs.

"I'll keep her home as long as I can," my mother said. "I don't want to put her in a nursing home. But I'm too tired to talk about it tonight."

My mother's got a right to be tired. She worked full-time in the grocery store until I signed with the Bruins. She scheduled all of the cashiers and baggers. She hired me for a couple of summers. That probably looked like nepotism until, in my first week on the job, she suspended me for a day. That happened when Mrs. Chevalier asked me, "Where can I find cereal, young man?" And I said, "In the cereal aisle."

My mother is fifty-one and still attractive. She's what people of her generation call "a handsome woman"—tall and thin with long legs and highlighted blond hair that refuses to turn gray. She usually wears it in a chignon, a carryover from her working days. It gives her an all-business look.

After we moved back to Maine she went on dates but she always came home. I'd wake up for a few seconds when she opened the front door. I suppose she got her sexual needs taken care of but I never thought of that then and don't like to think of it now. She never went on a trip with a guy and never did anything to make me feel I was going to be relegated to second place.

I missed my tenth consecutive Macy's Thanksgiving Day Parade telecast because of our usual Thanksgiving morning practice.

We'd been skating for three months by then, so I didn't really think we needed the ice time. But Packy knew that if we got a day off, then lost on Friday, he'd leave himself open to criticism by fans and media. Coaches in all sports deny it but I think they make a lot of their decisions defensively based on what fans and the media might say.

We nonchalanted it through practice. Or the so-called players did. The NHL rule book distinguishes between players and goalies as if goalies are, somehow, less than players or different from players. One difference is that goalies can't coast through practice as easily as players. You're forced to react to the shots taken at you, and when you have twenty-two players and a couple of dozen pucks you're going to face a few hundred shots. Rinky Higgins and I worked hard in practice but we were the only two who did.

The most emotion the other guys showed was when we came back into the room and saw the big trunk containing what's called our third alternate jersey. Instead of wearing our usual game shirts with the spoked B on the chest—one of the game's oldest and most respected logos—for Friday afternoon's game we were going to have to wear a gold jersey with the head of a bear who looks like Winnie the Pooh's stoner grandfather. Cam held up one of the shirts at arm's length and said, "What it lacks in ferocious panache it more than makes up for in cuddly insouciance."

We hate the goddamn shirts but Gabe Vogel loves them because it means hard-core fans who already own our home and away shirts will shell out another $200 for the third alternate shirt. Every team does this. And most of the older teams also have retro shirts based on designs of fifty years ago. I wouldn't fall for that if I were a parent or a fan.

Cam's father invited my mother to watch the game from the Carter & Peabody luxury suite. I'd arranged for a nurse to stay home with Mammam so my mother could relax and enjoy her afternoon. Sort of. "I'm proud of what you do but I don't like watching you do it. I worry. Goalies get too much blame," she's told me dozens of times. We also get too much credit.

My mother watches all of our games on cable TV but it makes a difference to me when I know she's in the building. I mentioned this to Cam in the dressing room before the game and he said, "For Christ's sake, JP, how many NHL players still care about what Mommy and Daddy think?"

"All of us," said Kevin Quigley, who'd overheard the question.

I didn't play great but I was adequate and we beat Tampa Bay 6–3. Rex Conway scored the fourth goal—the game winner—when his shot from a bad angle bounced in off Tampa defenseman Igor Brashinsky. Lynne Abbott asked Rex about the goal and of course Rex launched into his sermon about "I have to give a big assist to the Man Upstairs," which is when Lynne snapped off her tape recorder and said, "The assist went to Quigley and the goddamn shot went in off Igor Brashinsky's butt, for Christ's sake, Rex."

"The Lord works in mysterious ways, Lynne," Rex said.

Cam's dad took a bunch of us to a pricey steak house for an early dinner after the game. "Detroit and Dallas won and covered yesterday. The Deuce is feeling flush," said Cam. Technically, Cam's dad is Cameron Cabot Carter Jr. but he hates the word "Junior" so we sometimes call him the Deuce. He likes that. Besides Cam and his parents, our party included Tamara, my mother, Faith, Lindsey Carter (who seemed almost as happy to be with us as she was that Caitlin was home with a babysitter), me, and a surprise starter—Cam's and my agent, Denny Moran. Denny's a good guy. Midfifties, divorced for as long as I've known him. His ex-wife loved Denny's ex–best friend more than she loved Denny. It made him distrustful of wives and friends and helped turn him into a workaholic. Denny's a good-looking guy in an aging Robert Redford sort of way. And he's honest and ethical. But that's not to say I wanted him hitting on my mother. I think he hip checked Lindsey and almost broke a couple of chairs trying to sit next to my mom. First Denny tried a few conversational gambits about the game and how proud she must be of me and so forth. Then he blew himself up. "So, Jackie," he started a sentence.

"Jacqueline, please," my mother said in a voice colder than Nome.

When Cam heard that he pulled in his chest like a batter avoiding a high fastball. I thought I was the only one who saw the gesture but Faith leaned over as if to pick up a napkin and whispered to me, "So much for Denny crowding the plate."

When Cam's father got the check he reached into his jacket pocket and pulled out a small leather-bound book embossed with the words "Business Journal." He uses it to keep track of his expenses for tax deductions.

"What's that, Grandpa Carter?" Lindsey asked.

"This," said Cam's father, holding up the book, "is the greatest work of fiction in the English language." I like the Deuce.

As we left the restaurant, Faith and I found ourselves walking together and out of earshot of everyone else. She asked me why I seemed so happy that my mother had brushed back Denny Moran. I said I didn't know but maybe it was a habitual reaction left over from childhood.

"Well I think your mom knows you feel that way. So don't."

"Don't what?"

"Don't feel that way."

"Can't help it."

"Can too."

"Can not. And why should I?"

"Because your mother deserves it," she said. "And because you're not eleven years old anymore."

My mother and Mammam left on Saturday morning before I went to practice. "We'll see you at Christmas, Jean Pierre," my mother said. Then the verdict came down. "I like Faith very much" was all she said. But she'd never said anything—good or bad—about Sheri the Equestrienne or Missy Taylor the New England Patriots Dance Team Coordinator or any of the women I'd introduced her to since Lisa.

We had noon ice at the Garden and then a charter flight to Philly for a Sunday-night game with the Flyers. I hate playing in Philly. Toughest fans in the league, maybe in the world, not counting German soccer hooligans. Cam and I were walking from the Philly airport terminal to our bus when a kid maybe fifteen years old and standing about fifty feet away recognized me and yelled, "Hey, you JP Savard?"

"Guilty," I said.

"You suck!" the kid yelled. "Flyers gonna kick your fuckin' ass!"

"Welcome to Philly, the town that booed Santa Claus," Cam said, and told me the story of Santa Claus being booed and pelted with snowballs during halftime of a Philadelphia Eagles football game years ago.

We beat the Flyers 3–2 in a meat grinder of a game marred for me only by Serge "the Weasel" Balon scoring a garbage goal. I was juggling a shot that bounced off of my chest when Balon bunted the puck to the ice with his stick, then backhanded it into the net. The way he chopped at me I thought the ref could've whistled him for slashing. I also think I should have handled the first shot cleanly. But that wasn't the bad part. On his next shift, with the face-off to my right, Balon looked over and winked at me. A TV camera caught it, so it was all over the sports news and highlight shows. Pisses me off just thinking about it.

We chartered back to Boston after the game. Cold rain driven by a northeast wind lashed the tarmac as we touched down at one in the morning. I'd heard weather reports about a cold front sweeping in behind the rain. It's after Thanksgiving that we enter the heart of the season. Training camp and the first two months of the schedule seem like so much overture. Spring and the playoffs—if we make them—lie unreachably far away. It's the dark cold time when, as Lisa used to say, "you have to carry your sunshine around with you." I'm not good at that.

Five

If there's reincarnation the Mad Hatter is coming back as a weasel.

Lynne Abbott, Knower of All Things, broke the story. In a box on page 1 of the *Boston Post* Monday sports section, Lynne wrote that she'd "learned from multiple sources with direct knowledge of the trade that the Bruins and Rangers will today announce a deal bringing New York's seldom-used fourth-line center Gaston Deveau, 30, and two third-round draft picks to Boston in exchange for Bruins forward Brendan Fitzmorris, 21." Lynne also pointed out that in trading Brendan, Madison Hattigan was unloading about $1 million in annual salary while assuming only the league-minimum $475,000 on Gaston's contract.

"Un-fucking-believable," Cam said when I picked him up for the drive to practice. "The Mad Hatter saves Gabe Vogel $525,000 in payroll, probably pockets a $52,500 rake-off for himself, and we lose a good young prospect. We could've had Gaston for two minor leaguers. Tops."

We arrived at the Garden to find Lynne leaning against the wall in the corridor outside our dressing room. "You don't want to go in there yet," she said, nodding toward the dressing room, from which we heard muffled shouts coming through the cinderblock wall. I couldn't make out every word but "salary-dumping parsimonious motherfucker" came through pretty clear.

"Brendan hasn't been this mad since his girlfriend used the parental controls to block the Spice Channel on his cable," Lynne said.

Just then the Mad Hatter came storming out of the room, pausing to stab a bony finger at Cam's chest and shout, "You're captain. You wanted Deveau. You talk to Brendan. And you goddamn well better be right about Deveau!"

"Probably rushing off to look up 'parsimonious,' " I said as Hattigan scurried away.

Cam went into the dressing room and I stayed outside for a few minutes, ostensibly to talk to Lynne but really because I never know what to say to a guy who's been traded. There are maybe a dozen guys in the league who have no-trade clauses in their contracts. The rest of us have to sweat it out every season. Being traded isn't just disruptive, it's humiliating. I've seen more than a few guys cry when they're told they've been traded.

When I finally went into the dressing room Cam and Brendan were sitting together. I heard Cam say, "You're right. There are twenty great guys here. But you know what? There are twenty great guys on the Rangers, too."

Brendan nodded and buried his face in a towel, his anger giving way to sorrow and resignation. Then he wiped his face, threw the towel in the laundry cart, and started packing his equipment bag. By the time he finished, most of the guys were in the room and Brendan went around shaking everyone's hand and saying good-bye. It was a classy way to go out. When he came to me he said, "Watch out for Broadway Brendan, JP." Then he asked me if Lynne Abbott was around. I said she was still outside in the corridor. I shook his hand and wished him luck in New York. But not against us.

"What'd Brendan want?" I asked Lynne a few minutes later as I clomped out to practice.

"Remember that stunt he pulled with his penis in the dressing room last season?" she said. "He wanted to apologize again. He said the first time he apologized only because Cam made him. But this time he really meant it."

"You believe him?"

"Yeah. Guys change, JP. People grow up."

"Not hockey players."

"Even hockey players," she said. "It just takes you longer."

I was stretching before practice when Kevin Quigley asked me if I'd help him deliver the sticks we'd promised Nan O'Brien, the social worker from Catholic Charities. Except Quigley never actually *asks* for anything. What he said was, "Hey, peckah-head, we got to get those sticks ovah to Nan O'Brien today because we go to Ottawa tomorrow and she needs them for her fundraisah." *OLD NEIGhBoRhooD EXPRESSioN SomERVILLE 1940-50*

I asked him why he needed me, seeing as how he was the one with the SUV. "Her office is in Government Centah and you cahn't pahk there," Quig said. "I figure we can carry them over in two stick bags. It's only a few blocks."

Kev got everyone to give him an autographed stick, then borrowed two stick bags from Les Sullivan, our equipment manager. Kevin and I each carried a bag through a cold rain to the Catholic Charities offices.

"You think she's a free agent, JP?" Quig asked.

"She wasn't wearing a ring when we met her on the plane," I said.

"Maybe she's just not married on the road. Like most of the guys in the league. How old you think she is?"

"Late thirties. Maybe forty. Too old for you, Kev," I said. Quig is twenty-seven. "Besides, she didn't sound like she's from Charlestown." I'd never seen Quig with a woman over twenty-five and who wasn't a member of his hometown parish, Holy Family. I think Kev holds the NHL record for dating women named Colleen or Bridget. Most of his girlfriends talk in that

Greater Boston Irish-Catholic patois that even the best actors can't imitate. The woman Quig was with at last year's team Christmas party tried to tell me I'd played well against Ottawa the previous night. How that came out was: "You played wickud pissah against the Senatahs, JP."

The name plate on the wall beside an open office door read: "Nancy O'Brien—Family Preservation Program." Nancy was behind her desk when Quig and I walked in, dripping wet and carrying stick bags.

"Oh, thank you. This means so much to us," she said, stepping out from behind her desk as Quig and I took the sticks out of the bags and propped them in a corner of her office. I have to say that Nancy O'Brien, LICSW, was looking good in a classic Mrs. Robinson sort of way. She still had the leghold trap holding back her hair but gone was the pantsuit she'd worn on the plane and in its place was a black chalk-stripe business suit, the skirt of which stopped about four inches above her knees. "If I had legs like hers I'd wear skirts, too," I told Quig later. She still wasn't wearing a diamond or a wedding ring.

Nancy told us the signed sticks would bring in thousands of dollars, most of which would go directly to her program. "If we don't clear at least fifty thousand dollars on this dinner dance and auction I'm going to have to lay off a caseworker," she said, adding a wry, "Merry Christmas."

"So where do you want to have lunch?" Nan asked. Kevin hadn't told me lunch was included in the deal, probably because, for me, it wasn't.

"Union Oystah House is good with me," Quig said. "JP cahn't stay, though. We promised Sully we'd get the stick bags right back to him. He's packing us up for Ottawa and Atlanta."

I picked up the audible. "Yeah, I've got to take the bags back," I said to Nan. "Besides, I told Cam I'd go to the airport with him to meet Gaston Deveau." That wasn't true. I was just trying to help Quig. Maybe pick up the assist if he nailed Nan O'Brien.

"I heard the guys in the office talking about that trade," Nan said. "It must be awful to be owned by someone who can trade you away."

"It's not like we don't get paid," I said. But Nan was right.

I grabbed the empty stick bags and walked back to the Garden, stopping briefly in Quincy Market, where a store specializing in old photos had an eight-by-ten black-and-white studio publicity shot of the late actress Anne Bancroft as the aging seductress Mrs. Robinson in *The Graduate*. I bought the photo and, a few minutes later, taped it to Kevin Quigley's locker. The dressing room was quiet so I spent a couple of hours answering mail. I try to answer every letter except the ones from the wackos who never sign their name or give a return address. And who, I suspect, never in their wussy life set foot on a rink, field, court, or anyplace they wouldn't enjoy safety and anonymity. "You can't hide on the foul line," Faith once said. You can't hide in a goal crease or a batter's box or a tennis court either, which is why I respect anyone who has the guts to play anything more than a video game.

It was about 4:30 and getting dark when I pulled Boss Scags into Faith's driveway, surprised to see her Lexus parked outside and the lights on in the garage. I entered the garage through the side door and found Faith placing strings of Christmas lights on the floor. "Testing them before I string them on the house," she said.

"When you doing that?"

"This weekend."

"I'll help you do them now if you want. Rain's letting up."

"Nope."

"Why not?"

"Premature illumination," she said.

. . .

Over dinner I told Faith about Quigley apparently taking a run at Nan O'Brien, who must be ten or twelve years older than he is.

"What's Kevin like? He's the only guy on the team I can't figure out," she said.

Next to Cam, I consider Quig my closest friend on the team, so it surprised me that I couldn't tell Faith more than I did. Just that Kevin's a local guy who played college hockey at Boston University and still lives in the parish he grew up in. The only time he ever goes anywhere is when we play a road game. Quig had a tough childhood. His father is a Boston cop, a gruff guy I'd met a few times. "Get too close to him and you could catch a bad cold," Cam says of Quig's dad. Once when Quig was drunk he told me his father used to slap him around a lot and that his mother was too mousy to do anything about it. The abuse ended when Kev was seventeen and hit back. Dropped his father with two punches—"a body shot and a head shot. We got along better after that," Quig told me. Quigley was a linebacker in high school and still wears number 63, his old football number. But he knew he had a better future in hockey. Kevin's a great guy to go to a ball game with and everyone on the team knows he'll cover your back. And he might lead the NHL in charity work. But, aside from that, no one really understands him.

"He's a strange man," was all Faith said.

We practiced Tuesday at the Garden before we flew to Ottawa. Our won-lost record was 13–12 entering December, still eight points behind first-place Montreal in the Northeast Division but only two behind second-place Ottawa. It was important that I play wickud pissah against the Senators because a win would tie us for second place.

I stopped at my condo to pick up a few things for the trip. By the time I got to the dressing room Kevin Quigley had already torn up the photo of Mrs. Robinson. But not before most of the guys saw it and figured out what was going on.

"Hey, Flipper, the answer is the Starland Vocal Band. What's the question?" Taki asked Flipside Palmer.

"Who recorded 'Afternoon Delight,'" said Flipside, adding, "Hey, Quig, 'Afternoon Delight' was a one-hit wonder, just so's you know."

"Kev, is it true women hit their sexual peak just before menopause?" Cam asked.

Quig did the smart thing, which was to turtle—take the hits and say nothing.

"So what's the story on Nan O'Brien?" I asked Kevin after most of the guys had gone out on the ice and I was replacing a broken toe strap on my right leg pad while Kev taped a couple of extra sticks.

"Widow. One daughter. Kid's in her second year at Holy Cross. Husband died about seven years ago. Stroke. She lives out in Framingham."

"So is she a free agent?"

"Free and unrestricted, near as I can tell."

"You find out her age?"

"Thirty-nine. Be forty in January."

I didn't ask Kev anything else, partly because he wasn't in a particularly expansive mood but mainly because I had to go out and face a whole bunch of shots I didn't feel like facing. So it surprised me that just as I was putting on my mask, Quig said, "She's a nice person, JP. A kind person."

He said it with un-Quigley-like sincerity and with a finality that told me our conversation was over. A *kind* person? That didn't sound like the Kevin Quigley I'd known for five seasons.

Just as I was walking out to the ice who do I see running through the building—suitcase and equipmet bag in hand—but Gaston Deveau. I flipped up my mask so he could see it was me. "Bonjour, Gaston!" I yelled, genuinely happy to see my old college teammate.

"What is so *bon* about the *jour*, Jean Pierre? Boston traffic is worse than New York. I thought the cab would never get here from the airport." We shook hands and I told him to hustle up. That Packy had already listed him in Brendan's old slot at right wing.

"*Tabernac . . . mon Dieu . . .* I'm a center," Gaston said, angry and disappointed he'd be playing out of position. I knew that *tabernac* and *mon Dieu* were strong French-Canadian profanities even though *tabernac* means "tabernacle" and *mon Dieu* means "my God." While American profanity is usually sex-based—seems I hear "motherfucker" and "cocksucker" in our dressing room from time to time—French-Canadian profanities are religion-based. My grandmother—who wasn't above the occassional "*calice*" when something went wrong in the kitchen—told me that for centuries the Church had such an iron hold on everyone's life that to use a religious word in a profane way was more shocking than to use a sex word. *Calice* means Chalice.

The defense and I played well in Ottawa but it wasn't enough. We lost 2–1 and Gaston on right wing wasn't reminding anyone of Gordie Howe. On his first shift he carried down the right side—jersey flapping, full head of steam—but as he cut left at the top of the circle the defenseman put a hip into him and sent Gaston cartwheeling through the air, stick and gloves flying. The hit made it onto ESPN's *SportsCenter*.

Gaston still has great wheels, and the twenty pounds he's gained since college are all muscle. But he's been a center since youth hockey, and working along the wall doesn't allow him to create and exploit space. I can't blame Packy for playing him there. We've got two great centers in Jean-Baptiste and Taki. So the only way Gaston plays center is if he drops to the third line—a checking line for us—or the fourth line. A martini gets more ice time than our fourth line.

We won 3–2 in Atlanta but Gaston didn't figure in the scoring and had only one shot on goal. He told me on the flight back he was nervous: "I'm squeezing maple syrup out of the stick," he said. I reminded him his sticks are made of compressed graphite.

Because Cam, Gaston, and I make Boston the only NHL team with three alumni from the same college, *Sports Illustrated* decided it wanted a photo of us wearing Vermont game shirts and standing in front of the gold dome on the statehouse, on which the magazine planned to paint the Vermont logo. You can't believe the clout *SI* has. I'd like to say the *SI* shoot is why we lost 4–1 to the Penguins that night, but why we lost is mainly because I sucked and let in two of the first five shots. Gaston had only one shot on goal and, worse, more turnovers than Sara Lee.

Sunday was also Rex Conway's birthday. If we play a home game on a guy's birthday we let that player pick out the music for pregame warm-up. But that doesn't apply to Rex, because two years ago on his birthday he led off our warm-up set with a Christian-country song: "Backhand Me, Jesus, to the Top Shelf of Life." You think skating around to that wasn't embarrassing?

Packy started Rinky Higgins in goal on Tuesday when we beat Buffalo 4–2. Late in the game with the score 3–2 Rinky made a spectacular blocker save on a shot that looked like it had the top corner. He lost the rebound but he made a left pad stop on the second shot, then caught the puck as it popped in the air and held on for the face-off. I get mixed feelings watching something like that. On the one hand I want us to win. But I know if Rinky keeps playing like that my job will be in jeopardy.

Packy came back with me Thursday in Pittsburgh, where I got some revenge on the Penguins in a 4–3 win.

The Fitzmorris-for-Deveau trade continued to look like the most lopsided deal since the Louisiana Purchase. We lost 5–2 to the Flyers Wednesday night at the Garden and not only was Gaston pointless again but he was on the ice for three of the Flyers' even-strength goals. He looked lost out there. Back when he played center his job in the defensive zone was to provide coverage in the high slot. But as a right wing he's supposed to cover the left point man. The score was 2–2 midway through the Flyers game when Gaston got confused and picked up Philly's high forward in the slot. "My man. I got him," JB yelled at Gaston, but it was too late. The winger on the half-wall slid the puck back to the open point man, who blasted a laser into our net, low stick side. That was the game winner.

It was no surprise that Gaston and I were seated next to each other on the bench Thursday when Rinky played in goal and we lost again, 3–2 to Atlanta. We also lost Taki for a few games because Atlanta defenseman Ulf Bjorke—a notorious cheap-shot artist—leg checked him. Kevin Quigley beat the snot out of Bjorke but the only thing we got from that was satisfaction and a five-minute penalty to Quig. Well, maybe I shouldn't say "all," because when I walked into the dressing room on Friday, Packy had changed the lines around and Gaston was centering our second line.

He also told us I'd start in goal against the Canadiens—"Got to have this one, JP," he said. Later, Faith doubled the pressure by telling me I had to meet her parents at their house on Sunday, the day after the Montreal game. I'd met Faith's parents ages ago when they'd visited her at college. But that was no biggie because back then Faith and I weren't dating and now . . . well, you just never know how parents are going to feel about the guy who's screwing their daughter.

The media went crazy with Saturday's game. TV-8's Alvin "Captain Baritone" Crouch called it "a statement win" and Lynne Abbott called it "the defining win of the season thus far." What happened is that we hammered the Canadiens 5–0 in one of the fastest, most wide-open games we've played in years. I had twenty-nine saves for my fourth shutout; and finally—at last— Gaston scored. Then he scored again. And added an assist for second star of the night, as voted by the media. Away from the boards and free to create, Gaston was everything he'd been in college and in Europe—elusive, imaginative, free. He scored his first goal on a breakaway after he'd slipped the puck between Tim Harcourt's skates and the second on a quick wrister from a face-off to the right of the Montreal net. Gaston could have had a third goal, I thought, but after drawing goalie Claude Rancourt to his knees Gaston slid the puck to Quig for an easy tap-in. The crowd went crazy. But Gaston's best move came late in the game when a defenseman—who must have seen the TV highlight of the hit Gaston took against Philly—tried an open-ice hip check and caught nothing but air as Gaston danced around him, leaving him with his butt sticking out and looking ridiculous. It was an important move. Word gets around in this league and if guys think they can hit you they're going to do it until you show them they can't.

I had one of those nights where I feel like a big Velcro basket and everything coming my way sticks to me. I felt like I was wearing the game. Goaltending is a lot like sex or golf—the more you think about what you're doing, the more likely you are to do it badly.

Of course the Mad Hatter, who rarely visits our dressing room until the media leave, came into the room right after the game, no doubt to make sure he got his props for our acquiring Gaston and sticking with him through six unproductive games. It was actually Packy who'd stuck with Gaston.

The only bad thing about the win came in our dressing room after the game. The Canadiens bring a huge contingent of media everywhere they go. JB answered their questions, switching smoothly from French to English and back. Apparently one of the writers had asked JB about his views on Quebec separatism and JB said, in English: "The French are a separate people. We should have a separate country." That's when Jimmy Porter, the left wing on Jean-Baptiste's line, threw a towel into the laundry cart and said, loud enough for the players near him to hear, "Fucking frog."

"Hey, Jimmy. Lighten up. I'm a frog too," Gaston said.

"Yeah, Gaston, but you don't want to jump out of the fucking pond."

Gaston didn't say anything and Jimmy stalked off to the shower. That stuff bothers me because I never know if it's a benign tumor or a cancer in our room. But I felt so good about the win that it was an hour before I started getting nervous about meeting Faith's parents. By Sunday morning I was sitting on the edge of the bed, a towel in my hands and teetering on the edge of full throw-up mode just as if it were forty-five minutes to game time.

"Why are you so anxiety stricken about going to my parents' house?" Faith asked. It's the same kind of question people have asked me since my first day of grammar school. It's hard to explain except to say that I wasn't completely joking when I said my first rule for a happy life is not to meet anyone I don't already know. I never know what to say after I've met someone. It's why I say no whenever Denny Moran approaches me about making some extra money by playing in a corporate golf outing or making an appearance at a sales meeting. You'd think that being a high-profile player makes socializing easy, that people come to you with their autograph requests and questions like "What's Jean-Baptiste Desjardin really like?" But being a player only gets you to conversational first base. The truth is I don't know much about business, politics, or world affairs, and I find that your average adult isn't all that interested in the nuances of the Bruins' right-side overload power play. My idea of socializing is what Lisa used to call "bump-and-run"—a quick hello and handshake, maybe a remark about the team, then an "I'll catch you later" and I'm off to stand in line at the bar or pull a bump-and-run on someone else. But I couldn't bump-and-run Faith's family. To my relief and surprise I didn't have to.

Faith had used a chunk of her dot-com money to buy her parents a house in suburban Winchester. The house is about a hundred feet from a pond that on that mid-December Sunday was covered with black ice, that early-season ice that's so clear you can see through it to the dead leaves and muck on the bottom of the pond. Even though Faith's money meant that her parents could retire, her father, Jim, kept his job as a history teacher and boys varsity basketball coach at Cambridge Catholic, and her mother, Susan, did a lot of volunteer work for the Winchester Hospital. Faith's younger brother Jim Jr., twenty-five, in his last year at Tufts University Dental, was at his parents' house for the weekend. While no one in Faith's family had played organized hockey they're all pretty good natural athletes, and they'd skated enough to be comfortable in the nearly two-hour pickup game we played with various neighbors and kids. It was just like when I was growing up. We marked the goals with boots and had a rule about no lifting the puck because no one was wearing pads. I played defense so I got to skate a lot and carry the puck for a change. There must've been ten players per side and it took me fifteen minutes and about a dozen giveaways before I figured out who was on my team. This was hockey the way it was first played, with creativity demanded and rewarded by open ice. There were no subs; everybody played. And there was no ref, because we didn't need one. When I held Faith's mom to keep her from getting to a rebound in front of my team's goal she tripped me with her stick just as I was skating away with the puck. If I got hurt out there it would have taken Denny Moran and a platoon of Carter & Peabody lawyers to keep me from being found in violation of my Bruins contract. But I didn't care. I was having too much fun, the kind of spontaneous good time that's become a foreign concept to most NHL players, including me. If there's a better game than pond hockey on black ice I've never played it.

While we played, Faith's dad had racks of ribs cooking over hickory chips in a couple of smokers. If you think pond hockey followed by smoked ribs, cold beer, and the Patriots beating the Dolphins 49–7 in the 4:15 game isn't a great way to spend a Sunday afternoon, name me a better one. Sex? The line on sex versus pond hockey is 6–5 pick 'em.

Just before we left, Faith's dad embarrassed her by taking me into his den, the walls of which fairly drip with photos of Faith as a basketball player. Even as a sixth-grade CYO Leaguer, Faith, all knees and elbows, had the gunfighter eyes.

Her father told me he was thinking of dropping down to assistant hoops coach at the high school. "We lost two games all of last season, won our league, went to the playoff semifinals, and the parents are still unbearable," he said. He told me that the first three rules of high school coaching are: "Never trust a parent. Never trust a parent. Never trust a parent."

I believe him. And I'm glad no coach ever had reason to say that about my mother.

"I had a great time," I said, tossing my skates in the backseat and handing my car keys to Faith, who'd had two beers to my four. "I'd love to have grown up in a family like that," I said, instantly wishing I'd kept quiet because I felt as though I were being disloyal to my mother and grandmother, who did a good job under tough circumstances.

"Maybe you'll create a family like that," Faith said as she headed toward Boston a lot faster than Boss Scags usually gets driven.

"Maybe we could make a family like that," I said. Or maybe the fourth beer said it.

"You proposing?"

"Nah. I was going to do that live on the JumboTron at the Garden."

"Maybe that's something we should talk about."

"Proposing on the JumboTron?"

"I'm oh-for-one in marriage," she said. "But love's a funny thing. You can lose a hundred times, win once, and you win the whole tournament."

"I'm one-for-one but it was an abbreviated schedule," I said.

"Serious question," she said. "You grew up without a father. Ever think of what kind of father you'd want to be?"

"Cam Carter," I said. "I watch him closer than he knows. He gives Lindsey and Caitlin a lot of his time and he doesn't push. I think he's got it dialed. What about you?"

"My dad says being a parent is like being a good ref: 'Call it tight early and you can let 'em play late. Let the players decide the game.' I want my kids to trust themselves."

"Christ, we've been going together for less than three months and we're talking about kids?"

"Clock's ticking, Jean Pierre. We're in our early thirties. But let's get through Christmas. We can talk about it later."

"We're not going to live till Christmas," I said as Faith gunned Boss Scags past the Museum of Science, downshifted through the right-hand turn at Leverett Circle, then accelerated onto Storrow Drive as if she were coming out of the pits at the Monaco Grand Prix. The Arthur Fiedler Footbridge and the Hatch Shell were blurs as Faith, shifting like Michael Schumacher, took the Ferrari above ninety miles per hour for the first time since I'd owned it. "Why'd you buy this car?" she asked.

"To help me meet chicks," I said.

A mile went by before Faith said: "You know, JP, you should stop thinking this Ferrari is a better car than you are a person."

We had a great Christmas schedule. A quick trip to Long Island on December 22, then no games until the day after Christmas when we played Ottawa at home. We beat the Isles 4–2 with Gaston getting a goal and an assist. Packy told us we'd practice on the twenty-third and twenty-fourth, take Christmas off (loud cheer), and have a mandatory pregame skate on the morning of the twenty-sixth. He also told us that the team's annual Christmas skating party would be on the twenty-third at the Garden. Some of us think this so-called Christmas party is really more of a PR photo op. That's why Flipside said he'd have an unofficial team party later that night at his house in Medford. "Wives, girlfriends, or paid escorts. No kids," Flipside said.

The biggest surprise at the team's official Christmas party was Kevin Quigley showing up with Nan O'Brien. That ended all the older-woman and Mrs. Robinson jokes. As soon as we know a teammate is serious about a woman—and Kev wouldn't have brought her if he wasn't—all joking stops. Team rule.

The biggest nonsurprise was the Mad Hatter skating around trying to get himself into photos and on TV. Madison Hattigan was at the top of his PR game, kissing more kids than a guy running for reelection. Lynne Abbott had warned her paper's photographer about our self-promoting GM, so the next day's *Post* carried pictures of players and children only. The *Post* had a nice shot of me in the net with Lindsey Carter, who was imitating my goaltender's crouch and holding one of my sticks. Cam told me that in the early years of youth hockey kids get to volunteer to play goal on a game-to-game basis instead of committing to that position for the whole season. He said Lindsey volunteered more than anyone. "Linds loves playing goal," Tamara said. "I don't know where Cam and I failed."

I skated over to Nan O'Brien. "You have to lay off a caseworker?" I asked.

"Are you kidding? I'm hiring a caseworker. We cleared seventy thou at the auction and dinner dance partly because of the way people bid up those signed sticks. You guys really helped us."

"Kevin's the guy who made the play," I said.

Faith arrived at the party just as Paul Bertrand, the Bruins' anthem singer, showed up dressed as Santa Claus and singing Christmas carols while he handed out gifts to the kids. If you don't think a guy singing Christmas songs can precipitate an argument, you don't know our team. Cam and Flipside got into it when Cam said Nat King Cole's "The Christmas Song (Chestnuts Roasting on an Open Fire)" is "the greatest pop Christmas song of all time."

"Wrong," Flipper said. "The greatest Christmas song of all time—in the Pop Division—is Bing Crosby's 'White Christmas.' And while we're on the subject, the greatest song in the Ecclesiastical Division is 'Silent Night.'"

"And in the best-of-seven final?" Cam said with a touch of sarcasm.

"'Silent Night' in a sweep," Flipside said. Most of us agreed although Quig said Bing Crosby should be disqualified because he was an abusive father.

"True but artistically irrelevant," Flipside said.

"Can we get out of here?" asked Faith, who failed to grasp the importance of the Great Christmas Carol Debate and Playoff. Faith and I almost made it to the Zamboni door when Rex Conway skated over, Rinky Higgins in tow. "Jean Pierre, I need you and Reginald to sign something for my church," he said. Rex was the only guy who wasn't going to Flipside's party, because Rex's total commitment to spiritual salvation (and to picking up naive, dewy-eyed, incredibly good-looking Christian fundamentalist chicks) required that he speak at a church service that evening. Like Nan, he wanted Rinky and me to autograph a stick to be raffled off. Unlike Nan, he wanted more than our names. "I need you to put my church's name on it," Rex said.

"Sure. What's that?"

"Sign it 'To the Foursquare Bible-Believing Church—Merry Christmas, Jean Pierre Savard," Rex said. Now I know why he wanted Rinky and me. Our goalie sticks were the only ones big enough to hold all that.

Faith and I went back to my place to kill the two hours between the end of the Bruins' party and the time we had to leave for Flipside's. I spent most of that time wrapping Christmas presents, with particular attention to the big one I'd bought for Lindsey Carter. I got her a complete set of junior-size goaltending gear—leg pads, catch glove, blocker, goalie pants, body and arm protector, mask, the works. I got everything into a huge box, then wrapped the box, tied it with a red ribbon, and put one of those stick-on bows on top. Then I taped two notes to the box—a simple gift card to Lindsey and a sealed note to Cam and Tamara. The sealed note read:

> Cam and Tam,
> No one suffers like the parents of a goalie.
>   Jean Pierre

That was the payback for Cam letting Lindsey beat up on me back in September.

I'd waited too long before trying to hire a town car to bring my mother and grandmother to Boston on the morning of the twenty-fourth. Denny Moran solved the problem by sending one of Carter & Peabody's corporate jets. "Give my regards to your mom . . . I mean to Jacque-LYN," he said, pronouncing her name correctly. "She's pretty particular about the name, eh?" Denny added, then laughed.

"Just moving you off the plate," I said.

Mammam probably wouldn't know the difference between a Gulfstream IV and a one-horse open sleigh, but I wondered what my mother would think climbing aboard. "She'll be embarrassed by the ostentation," Faith said.

The party was in full swing when we arrived at Flipside's house. Some of the married guys brought their wives. You might have recognized Jean-Baptiste and Renee Desjardin from that photo of them in the *Sports Illustrated* swimsuit issue. JB was the one wearing a top. I was surprised Taki's wife, Su, got the night off, because the Boston Ballet was in the middle of its annual *Nut-cracker* run. To be honest I wondered if she'd really want to be with us, since the world she works in is a lot more sophisticated and cultured than ours.

One of the coolest things about Flipside's house is that he has two jukeboxes. He's filled one with singles and albums from the

1990s to the present. He calls it the one-name jukebox because most of the artists in it seem to have one name—Eminem, Coldplay, Incubus, Ciara, Shakira, Deerhoof, Ludacris, and so on. The other jukebox—the one that got Flipside his nickname—is filled with vinyl records released mainly in the 1950s, '60s, '70s, and '80s, when the music industry produced 45-rpm discs with one song on each side, a "hit side," also called the A side, and a flip side or so-called B side. Flipper had the jukeboxes fixed so you didn't have to put in any money or Treasury notes. We started out playing mostly the one-name jukebox, but as the party heated up, there was a big demand for the older stuff and Flipper plugged in the second jukebox. The later it got and the more we drank the older the music we wanted to hear.

Nan O'Brien was looking at some of the older stuff when she saw "96 Tears" by a group listed on the label as "? and the Mysterians."

"Ooohh. I know this. I know Question Mark's real name," she said. She should've simply told us and left it at that. But she pressed her luck. "Philip," she said to Flipside—Nan has trouble calling people by their nicknames—"what was Question Mark's legal name? Nobody ever knows this."

"Rudy Martinez," Flipside said, then rolled up the score: "The Mysterians were named after characters in a Japanese sci-fi movie and the song's original title was '69 Tears.' The flip side is 'Midnight Hour.' Anything else you need, Nan? Something from the bar maybe?"

Nan got a round of boos and hisses. "Welcome to the NHL," Quig said to her. She laughed. That was about all Quig said all night. I noticed he was drinking more than he usually did. And that's a lot.

I suppose I shouldn't have been surprised that Su Yamamura was the best dancer in the room. Put on a tune and Su turns into some kind of Janet Jackson. It's like Cam's father says: "Banking, baseball, or barbecue, a goddamn pro beats a goddamn amateur every time."

"We have practice in the morning, hon," I said to Faith around midnight as I launched into what I knew would be at least a twenty-minute campaign to get her out of the party.

I asked Flipside where our coats were. "Upstairs, first bedroom on the right," he said. "You got the claim check, right? . . . Just kidding, JP, just kidding."

At the top of the stairs I opened the first door on my right. It wasn't a bedroom. It was a dimly lighted den. I was stunned by what I saw. There was Kevin Quigley, his back to the door, crying uncontrollably, his head resting on Nan O'Brien's right shoulder, his huge back heaving with sobs.

I stopped, shocked, my right hand on the doorknob. Nan had both arms around Quig and was whispering to him. When she saw me she flicked the fingers on her right hand as if she were brushing me out of the den with a whisk broom. I closed the door softly, certain that Quig hadn't seen or heard me and wishing I'd never opened it.

I found the coats piled on a bed in the next room. I'd retrieved my Burberry and Faith's butter-soft black cashmere and was headed toward the stairs just as Loretta "Lash" LaRue began moaning from somewhere in the bottom of the coat pile. I retrieved the phone from the plaid horse blanket of an overcoat that I knew was Bruno's and rushed downstairs shouting, "Telephone for Mr. Govoni . . . telephone call for Mr. Govoni," while holding up the phone, the better for guests to hear Ms. LaRue's breathless gasps of pleasure. Everyone except Bruno and the girl he was with seemed to think it was amusing.

We were headed back to my place, Faith driving Boss Scags again, when I told her what I'd seen upstairs.

"Are you going to tell anyone?"

"No."

"Not even Cam?"

"No one except you. I figure it's between Kevin and Nan unless one of them wants to talk about it . . . whatever *it* is."

"Whatever it is, if it's causing him that much pain it's going to come out," Faith said. "Emotions leak."

"They can leak after the season," I said.

Christmas Eve morning I was at practice (if you want to call it that; half the guys were hungover), so Denny Moran sent a limo to Hanscom Field to meet the C&P jet carrying my mother and Mammam. They were at my condo when I got home.

"Really, Jean Pierre, was all that private-jet and limo business really necessary?" my mother asked.

"That's what agents are for. They're problem solvers," I said.

"They're enablers," my mother said.

Our Christmas plans were dictated by Mammam's weakening condition.

Cam's parents and Faith's parents invited my mother, Mammam, and me to Christmas dinner but I said no because I didn't think my grandmother was up to it. The earliest I could hire a nurse to stay with her on Christmas Day was 5 p.m. and that cost me triple the usual rate. So our plans called for Faith to come over for dinner on Christmas Eve. Then on Christmas Day we'd play what Faith called "a split-squad game." She'd have Christmas dinner with her parents, I'd eat with my mother and grandmother, and then we'd meet at Cam's parents' house at about six o'clock.

Faith and I exchanged presents on Christmas Eve. She gave me an Italian-made black leather jacket with the prancing-stallion Ferrari logo on the left sleeve and my jersey number—number 1, "the loneliest number," Faith said—on the right sleeve. I gave her small custom-made diamond-and-gold earrings that from a distance look identical but up close you can see that one is the numeral 3 and the other the numeral 1—31, her basketball number.

Faith and I each took one for the team on Christmas Eve. Faith brought my mother to early-evening Mass at St. Ignatius

Church while I stayed home in man coverage against my now constantly wheezing grandmother. "Give her the short routes but don't let her beat you deep," Faith whispered to me as she left the house.

My mother and I cooked Christmas dinner. My grandmother couldn't even work in the kitchen anymore, the place that had always been the center of her life. As soon as the nurse arrived, my mother and I headed for Weston and Cam's parents' open house.

Cam's mom and dad live in a porticoed mansion that looks like the White House. The butler had barely opened the door for my mother and me when we were greeted by the Deuce himself, hospitable and engagingly drunk: "Merry Christmas, JP. Jacqueline. Come on in. If you're lucky you won't have to put up with Diana modeling the fur coat I gave her. And don't give me any of that goddamn political correctness PETA crap, because Lindsey already gave it to me. My own grandaughter for Christ's sake. What Linds doesn't understand is that a warm wife is a happy wife and a happy wife is one less goddamn problem."

Faith had arrived before us. And I was surprised to see Denny Moran there. He was sipping what looked like a Cognac and standing by himself next to the bar when my mother went over to him.

"JP says I have you to thank for the plane and limo, Denny," my mother said.

"Dennis, please," said Denny Moran.

My mother looked taken aback for a second. Then she smiled. "Got me," she said.

"Thanks for the goalie stuff, Mr. Savard," said Lindsey, coming up on my blind side.

"You're a sick and demented person, Jean Pierre," said Tamara, kissing me on the cheek. "But Lindsey loved your present. We had to make her take off the mask so she could eat dinner."

I told Lindsey I could get Harry Flask of Masks by Flask Inc.

to design whatever she wanted on her mask and helmet. Harry did up my outfit with a drawing of Montreal great Jacques Plante's first goalie mask on the front and with three crossed flags—the American flag, the Canadian maple leaf, and the Quebecois fleur-de-lis—on the back.

Lindsey said she wanted her mask painted "pink with a picture of Belle from *Beauty and the Beast*."

"Harry can do it but people might laugh," I said.

"Not if I stop the puck," she said.

We left Cam's parents' party early because our schedule called for a morning skate and a game against Ottawa on the twenty-sixth. When we got home the nurse handed me a slip of paper with a phone number and a message to call Nan O'Brien.

"It's about what you walked in on at Philip Palmer's party," Nan said when I reached her at home. "Have you mentioned that to anyone."

"Only to Faith," I said.

"Please don't talk about it to anyone else," she said. I promised I wouldn't and asked if she could tell me what was going on.

"All I can tell you, without betraying a confidence, is that Kevin is dealing with some serious problems from his past."

"No one has problems anymore, Nan. They're 'issues' these days. Didn't you get the memo?"

"I call things what they are, Jean Pierre, and this one's a problem," she said. I told Nan she should get a national award for being the first social worker in a decade to use the word "problem" instead of the wimpy euphemistic "issue."

"How can I help?" I said.

"Kevin might want to talk. Not now but eventually. Listen to him. Otherwise just watch him. I think you might see changes in him, and in the short term, they might not be good. Either for him or for your team."

I said I'd keep an eye on Quig. "But it's tricky when you don't know what you're watching for."

"Sorry, Jean Pierre," she said.

If our Christmas schedule was good our New Year's schedule was terrible. Right after our game on the twenty-sixth—a 6–2 win over an Ottawa team that played as if the guys wished they were home with their families—we hit the road for a four-game southern swing including a New Year's Eve game at Dallas. That's where I faced my first penalty shot. Dallas's speedy center Greg Adamson got around Flipside, who turned and tripped Adamson even though I beg our guys not to do that. I'd rather face the breakaway in the heat of the game than have to stand around and wait for a penalty shot. Most fans don't know it but the stats on penalty shots favor goalies. We stop about 60 percent of them. I didn't actually stop Greg Adamson. He hit the post. I watched a rebroadcast of the game and heard the dumbass announcer say, "Adamson beat J. P. Savard but his shot hit the post." That's bullshit. His shot hit the post because I played the angle like goddamn Pythagoras. Adamson should've deked. I think a shooter's best chance on a penalty shot is a deke and a backhand to the top shelf. But I'm not about to tell them, and most of them are too dumb to figure it out for themselves.

My mother and grandmother got another complimentary flight to Lewiston courtesy of Denny Moran. Carter & Peabody handles the State of Maine Employees Association pension fund and Denny had a meeting in Bangor on the twenty-seventh. He said it would be easy to make a quick stop in Lewiston. When my mother told me this she tried to imitate Denny Moran, who'd been imitating Cam's father: "When you're a private company you can do what you goddamn want without answering to any goddamn whiny shareholders."

My mother does terrible imitations.

We had back-to-backers at Florida and Tampa Bay on the twenty-eighth and twenty-ninth. I won my start 7–1 (Gaston Deveau scored two more goals) and Rinky Higgins held us in the game against Tampa Bay until we scored five in the third period for a 5–3 win, our fifth in a row. I picked up thirty-eight saves in a strong showing against Carolina but it wasn't strong enough. The Hurricanes beat us 2–1, a tough loss to one of the league's legitimate Cup contenders. I was in the shower when Cam stuck his head in and said, "JP, Sully's got a phone call for you."

I wrapped a towel around my waist and found Les Sullivan pitching our equipment bags into a van for the trip to the airport. Les handed me his cell phone. It was Faith relaying a message from my mother. Mammam was dead.

Six

Mammam died of an aortic aneurysm, which Faith said "is like a volcano of blood erupting in your chest." She died at home, collapsing at the kitchen sink while drawing a glass of water. "It was fast, Jean Pierre. She didn't suffer," Faith said.

Shock, sadness, and relief jumped me at the same time. I felt guilty about the relief but I knew Mammam's death freed my mother from caretaker prison.

Time was when an NHL player could miss games only for the death of a wife, child, or parent. Today it's common in all major pro sports for a player to miss a game or two for a grandparent's death. Packy was good about it. He asked me to fly with the team to New Jersey in case Kent Wilson, the goalie the team called up from Providence, didn't make it to the rink by game time. But as soon as Kent arrived I could grab a flight to Boston and Packy would start Rinky Higgins against the Devils on Thursday and against Toronto in Boston on Saturday. My grandmother's wake was Friday and the funeral Saturday.

Kent, thrilled at the call-up, was in New Jersey before we were. By late Thursday I was in Faith's Lexus heading north on I-95, which route number she apparently mistook for the speed limit.

After checking into the Holiday Inn we went to my mother's house, which by this time—about 8 p.m.—was crowded with neighbors and relatives, many of whom I hadn't seen since I'd left Lewiston to go to college. Most of my grandmother's older friends spoke to each other in French. They'd brought enough food to fill an NHL training table.

It was there in the parlor that my mother told me that my grandmother had long ago arranged with Monsignor Faucette that her funeral Mass would be the traditional High Requiem. Mammam had also said she wanted the altar boy at her funeral to be none other than her grandson, namely me. "A thirty-one-year-old altar boy?" I almost shouted at my mother. "I should be with you."

"You should be with your grandmother," my mother said.

"What's a High Requiem?" Faith asked.

"About an hour. Fifty minutes if you're lucky," I said. "Good music, though." I took Faith's hand and led her toward the stairs.

"Where are we going?"

"My bedroom."

"For God's sake, Jean Pierre, not now."

"You're going to run some lines with me," I said.

My old room was almost the same as I'd left it thirteen years ago. Yellowed newspaper clippings covered the walls, ceiling, and closet door. There were posters of the University of Maine hockey team; Go Black Bears! (I've forgiven them for not recruiting me); photos of ex-Bruins Ray Bourque and Cam Neely and of the Celtics' Larry Bird; and a framed black-and-white glossy of Bobby Orr joyfully belly whomping through the air after he scored the overtime goal giving Boston the 1970 Stanley Cup back before I was born. "The greatest player in his greatest moment," I said when I saw Faith staring at the photo.

I knelt to rummage through the bottom drawer of my old desk. "Got it," I said, pulling out a six-panel folding card entitled "Mass Server's Responses." On it the priest's lines appeared in red type and the altar boy's lines in black.

"Read me the red lines," I said to Faith.

"I go unto the altar of God," Faith read.

"To God who gives joy to my youth," I said.

"Yesssss. Nailed it," said Faith. She kept reading the priest's lines and I kept giving the right responses. I was on a roll until we hit the Apostles' Creed. "I believe in God, the Father Almighty, Creator of heaven and earth; and in Jesus Christ His only Son, Our Lord; who . . . who . . . aw, shit, I could never remember this."

"Who was conceived by the Holy Spirit, born of the Virgin Mary . . . ," Faith said.

"No wonder I can't remember it. I don't believe any of that," I said.

"I don't either," Faith said, "but you're going to have to know the words by Saturday morning."

"Give me that," I said, reaching for the altar boy card, then tearing out the Apostles' Creed and putting it in my shirt pocket.

"Great. You don't like a tenet of your religion you tear it out. What do you call that, JP? Religion à la carte? Wish I could tear out sections of the capital-gains tax laws," Faith said.

"I'm going to tape it to my left wrist like a quarterback's play sheet. The altar boy's back is to the congregation when he recites the Apostles' Creed so no one will know I'm reading it."

Faith smiled. For the next few minutes in my old bedroom we talked about the religion we'd been brought up in and had turned away from. Faith and I went to Catholic grammar schools and high schools. We'd each had deeply religious parents and grandparents. Catholicism was as much a part of her Irish culture as it was of my French culture. Yet neither of us believed anymore. "When did you lose your religion?" I asked her.

"Sophomore year at Cambridge Catholic when Burlington High came back from seventeen points down and that bitch Hazel Anne Worthington beat us with a three-pointer at the buzzer in the state finals. She didn't have both feet behind the line but the zebra gave it to her anyway," Faith said.

"No. Seriously," I said.

"When I got to college. Got away from my parents."

"My grandmother used to tell me stories her mother had told her about how the priests controlled the French in Canada. French Canadians believed in what they called *revanche à berceau,* the revenge of the cradle. Since they'd lost Quebec to English Protestants on the battlefield they thought they'd get it back in the bedroom by producing enormous numbers of little French Catholics. Families with ten, twelve, fifteen children were common. All that did was guarantee a life of poverty."

"But your grandmother never let go of her religion."

"Religion offers hope, cheap at any price. Keep the rules, go to Heaven. I think religions begin with our fear of death."

"What do you think comes after death?" ✳

"Eternal nothingness," I said. "Our work is our immortality."

We left my old room and headed for the stairs.

"Wait a minute," I said, and led Faith to my mother's room, where I snapped on the TV. "I just want the score."

The Bruins were up 6–3 over New Jersey with a few minutes to play. I was about to click off the TV when I noticed Kent Wilson was in the Boston net. Then I heard the TV announcer say Rinky Higgins had given up all three New Jersey goals, all in the first period, and Packy had benched him for the start of the second period. The shelf life on loyalty to a goaltender is about twenty minutes or three goals, whichever comes first.

I spent most of the wake standing between my mother and Faith in the receiving line and trying not to look at my grandmother's body lying in an open casket a few feet away. Faith told me later that viewing the body "helps people accept the reality of death." I know she's right but I'd rather watch curling than look at a dead body.

My mother was a rock through it all except for the final closing of the casket on Saturday morning before the funeral-home guys loaded it into the hearse for the trip to the church. She cried then but not for long.

✳ SEE PAGE 257

Faith sat with my mother in church while I served the Mass. I'd worn a black Hugo Boss suit, white shirt, and black silk tie for the occasion. But Monsignor Faucette found a size XL altar boy's black cassock and white surplice that fit over my suit so I had to parade around dressed like a ten-year-old. At least the long sleeves of the cassock hid the cheat sheet I'd taped to my wrist. But as with goaltending, all the responses and actions came back to me once the Mass started. It was as if I were a kid again and serving morning Mass in front of pews filled with murmuring kerchieved women, their rosary beads clacking against the backs of oaken pews.

Toward the end of Mass the soprano soloist sang a song in French. I think beauty transcends language; this was one of the most moving songs I'd ever heard, yet I didn't understand a word of it. Later my mother told me the song was "Ceux qui sen vont." It means "To Those Who Leave," she said.

"I wish I remembered my French," I told her.

"Your heart remembers," she said.

Take this to the bank; in relationships between the sexes, one family crisis, successfully negotiated, equals one hundred good dates. "Thanks for coming here with me," I said to Faith when, long after dark, we left my mother's house for the drive back to Boston.

"You'd do it for me," she said.

"I would. But not as gracefully."

"Do you ever miss it? Catholicism?" she asked.

"Sometimes. I miss the comfort of it. Most of those people in church, especially the old frogs . . . I envy them their certainty. And you?"

"Same thing. God's gone but I miss Him."

"What would it take to make you believe again?" I asked.

Faith hesitated a minute. "I think if the world went dark and the dead rose from their graves and God stepped out of the sky and told everyone that bitch Hazel Anne Worthington didn't have both feet behind the three-point arc and that CC really won the Massachusetts girls hoops title and then God handed me the trophy in front of the billions of risen souls and Hazel Anne Fucking Worthington."

Had to laugh at that. We rode a few miles in silence. We'd just gone through the Hampton, New Hampshire, toll booths when I said, "We ought to make some time to talk about us. Where we're going. Weren't we going to talk about that after the holidays?"

"We'll talk, JP. But not in a car. Not tonight."

That was the second time I'd brought up our long-term prospects only to have Faith ice the conversational puck.

I snapped on the radio and punched up the Bruins game just in time to hear announcer Mike Emerson say that Gaston Deveau had given Boston a 1–0 lead over the Maple Leafs on a power-play goal at 2:58 of the first period. "Jeez. Packy put Gaston on the first power-play unit. That's a shocker," I said. But it wasn't as much of a shock as what Emerson said a few seconds later, which was "A great glove save by Kent Wilson to rob Toronto's Ken Brewer."

"What's with Kent Wilson starting again? Do we have a quarterback controversy here?" Faith asked.

"I'll find out tomorrow," I said. But I was pretty sure I knew why Wilson was starting. I explained it to Faith: "If the Mad Hatter brings up a new kid and the kid plays well, then it lowers my value and Rinky Higgins's value and gives Hattigan leverage in contract talks."

"By the way, your mother asked me why Hattigan hasn't met with Denny Moran to start working out your new deal."

"How the hell does she know that?"

"Denny—excuse me, Dennis—told her."

"Jesus Christ, I'm thirty-one years old and my agent is tattletaling to my mother."

"You sure that's all he's doing?" Faith said, and laughed another of her rich throaty laughs.

"Look. If the Bruins don't sign me, then I'm an unrestricted free agent. There'll be plenty of offers."

"Great. You want to go to Vancouver? Dallas maybe? How 'bout them Stars?" Faith asked, and began singing Alabama's "If You're Going to Play in Texas (You've Got to Have a Fiddle in the Band)."

"No. I'll give Boston a hometown discount. I'll play here for less than I'd make somewhere else. I told Denny that. It's just that the Mad Hatter wants every edge he can get before they start talking. And the longer he delays, the greater the chance my stock will fall. Or Kent Wilson's might rise, which amounts to the same thing."

"If the team loses you to unrestricted free agency, then they don't get anything in return, right?"

"Right," I said.

"Then it'd be best for them to trade you now and get something for you than to just let you walk away. So why wouldn't Hattigan deal you?"

"Could happen," I said. "A lot of teams would like an experienced goaltender for the playoffs." I told Faith that if I was traded it would have to be by March 18, the NHL's trade deadline, about eight weeks away.

"If they deal you will you go?" she asked.

"Have to. I'm not exactly in Cam Carter's financial position," I said.

"And where will a trade leave us?"

"First, I don't think I'll get traded. We're going to the playoffs and my playoff record is better than my regular-season record. Rinky has never even played two consecutive playoff games. Second, you're in your last year of med school. You'll be a doctor. You can work wherever you want," I said.

"Jean Pierre, we have to talk," Faith said.

"But not tonight," I said in high-pitched chiding mimicry.

"How about tomorrow night? Dinner? My place. I'll cook."

"Done deal," I said just as Mike Emerson's voice on the radio told me that Toronto had tied the game on a fifty-footer. I felt bad for the team. But I have to confess there was a part of me that was glad Kent Wilson had let in a softy. I don't feel that way when Rinky plays. OK, maybe I don't want him to play his way to immortality, but I want him to win because I want the team to win. And while I have nothing against Kent Wilson—we barely said hello in training camp—I knew a great game by Kent would put more pressure on me. As if I didn't have enough of that already.

Toronto beat us—and Kent Wilson—2–1.

The first thing to catch my eye when I walked into the dressing room Sunday morning was the makeshift nameplate—black felt-tip pen on white adhesive tape—over one of the spare lockers. "KENT WILSON" it read. Two goalies on a team is a necessity. Three is a problem. It means there's always going to be someone who's unhappy because he's not playing and not even dressing. More mind games by the Mad Hatter, I thought, but I made it a point to introduce myself to Wilson as soon as he walked into the room. The kid's only doing what I did ten years ago and what any rookie would do—trying to play as well as he can and maybe make it to the Show.

The only good thing about having Kent Wilson around is that I face fewer shots in practice.

At the end of practice Packy called us over to a corner of the rink well out of earshot of the beat writers. All coaches do this as if newspaper reports will compromise national security on what they say. All Packy said was that I'd start Tuesday at home against Washington and Thursday at Pittsburgh and that Rinky would be the backup. Three minutes later Packy was telling Lynne Abbott: "I haven't made up my mind yet" about which goalie would start on Tuesday and that Thursday was "too far away to even think about." Coaches don't lie because they're bad people. They lie because the flow of information is one of the few things they can control. Coaches like control.

I was nervous driving to Faith's house late Sunday afternoon. The only time I'd ever talked about marriage was with Lisa years ago. And we didn't really plan it as much as we drifted into it. I hoped Faith and I were on that same easy, natural path and that our conversation would end in an unofficial engagement with a wedding date to be named later. I figured if we wrapped it up fast we'd have time to watch the NFL Wild Card playoff between Green Bay and San Francisco. A pretty good match, I thought. But that was before I knew about the Match.

"Part of the problem I have—I mean *we* have, Jean Pierre—is the Match," Faith said almost before I had my coat off. She told me that the Match is the national program that assigns graduating medical school students to internships at hospitals across the country. Students can research and apply for various internships listed on the Internet. But it's the hospital that has the final say. Students get assigned to an internship. And those students who don't get a match, or don't want to accept the one they get, have to scramble for whatever leftover openings they can find. "We find out on March 17," she said. "It's sort of like a trade deadline for med students. We report to our hospitals July 1."

"So you could get sent to Utah or some godforsaken place?" I asked.

"Theoretically but not really," she said. "I'm applying to Mass General here in Boston—"

"Great. Walking distance from the Garden," I said, interrupting her.

"—and to Lake Champlain Medical Center in Vermont. It'll be one of those two," she said, putting a handful of shrimp into a sauté pan.

"Lake Champlain is a goddamn par-five from here," I said. "So which one do you think it'll be?"

"Whichever one I want."

"Getting a little cocky, aren't we?"

"Put it this way, Jean Pierre, they both want the quarter mil I'll pledge to their capital campaigns."

"That's crass and arrogant," I said.

"That's reality," she said. "Life's a power sweep, JP. Saint Vincent Lombardi said that, according to my father." I looked at her. Looking back at me were the same Clint Eastwood eyes I'd seen in the basketball pictures in her father's den. Faith McNeil was about to take the medical establishment to the hoop. I was afraid she might take me too.

"So how's the decision shaping up?" I asked.

"Mass General is one of the biggest and best hospitals in the country. But if I go there I'm a spare part. Just another body on the JVs. Lake Champlain is opening a new oncology center. If I go there I'm on the varsity. I'm a player. And I want to be a player, JP. Always have."

"So where would that leave us? Besides two hundred and fifty miles apart."

"We can't know that until we know where you're going to be playing."

"I think I'm going to be right here in Boston for four or five more seasons. But you never know. Sometimes a contending team will rent a player for the playoffs."

"*Rent* a player?"

"They'll find a guy like me who's got only a few months to go on his contract, then trade for him, knowing they have to pay him only through the playoffs. Sometimes that's all they want him for."

"Then what?" Faith asked.

"Then the player is a free agent and can sign with anyone. It could be a nice deal financially but I dread being traded. I have the job I want. Let's assume I keep it."

"Well, we'll always have summers together. Even if I'm in Vermont I'll get to Boston as often as I can. But they tell me the first year of a medical internship is rough. You work about a million hours. We wouldn't see each other much for the first year."

I sat in a kitchen chair feeling—and maybe looking—like a losing boxer slumped in his corner between rounds. "It's one thing to put your career above me but I think you're putting it above *us*," I said.

"And what are you doing by playing into athletic old age? It's not like we need the money."

"Playing hockey is what I do, Faith. It's all I know how to do. All I've ever done. Or all I've ever done well."

"I want to be good at what I do, too," she said. "And I think I can be. And for a long time . . ."

She didn't want to say what I knew came next, so I finished the thought for her: ". . . and what you'll be doing is a lot more valuable than what I do," I said. "So should I tell the Boston Garden JumboTron guy to forget showing the scene where I propose on bended goalie pad?"

"Not forget it. Maybe postpone it for a year."

"Faith, if you're not the best-looking single woman in northern Vermont you'll be in the top five. You're going to get hit on by every doctor in that hospital. And the married ones first."

"I've been known to hit back," she said, placing two dishes of shrimp pasta on the table, then pulling the cork from a chilled bottle of Pinot Blanc and looking at me again. Clint Eastwood was gone this time. "There's no one else, Jean Pierre. And I don't plan for there to be anyone else . . . not until you and I know for sure. I lost on my first marriage. I don't like losing. I'll pay the price to win."

"But not if it means taking one excellent internship that would keep us together over another excellent internship that will keep us apart but advance your career?"

"Let's not fight. It reminds me of my first marriage. It's why I kept putting off this conversation."

"There's no one else in my life either. And I don't want there to be. But I need time to think about this. Give me a few days, OK?"

"Sure. I think there are ways to do this. But there'll have to be a lot of compromise."

"Yeah. Mostly by me," I said, instantly feeling whiny.

"Let's give it a week or so, Jean Pierre."

"OK, but the series moves back to my place next time. I need the home-ice advantage. I'm already down 0–1," I said, trying to lighten the mood.

"What is this? Best of seven?"

"Best of whatever it takes," I said.

We did the dishes, at the end of which I used a hook shot to launch an SOS pad at the wastebasket. My shot was going long but Faith reached out with her right hand and slammed it into the basket with an authoritative alley-oop flourish. "You get the assist," she said, pointing at me as if we were on a basketball court.

"I think I should go home tonight," I said.

Faith said she understood.

We kissed good night in a perfunctory way. I drove home unhappy and confused and wishing my Ferrari had an automatic transmission so I could spend less time shifting and more time feeling sorry for myself.

It was strange that I didn't throw up before our Tuesday-night game with Washington. That happens two or three times a season but never before home games, where the pressure is greater than it is on the road. I also didn't play very well but we won 7–4, which is all that counts. Quig and Cam had a busy night. That's because the more Gaston Deveau scores—and that's a lot since he moved to center—the more he gets hammered by opposing checkers and goons. The tactic is as old and as primitive as the game, but a lot of time you see another team's fourth-liners, fringe players, sent out to rough up a scorer. Washington's Drew Campbell, a spare part who's lucky to be in the lineup, started hacking at Gaston early in the game. The theory here is that if

Gaston retaliates and both players get sent to the penalty box, then our team loses its number two scorer and all the Caps lose is a no-talent stiff. Worse, if the refs catch only Gaston retaliating and don't see the original infraction—and that happens a lot—then Washington gets a power play. Someone had to stop it and that someone was Quigley. It was worth the instigator penalty to watch Quig drop Campbell with a two-punch combo—*Splat! Splat!*—you could probably hear in row 15. The guys on our bench were standing up pounding their sticks on the boards—the age-old hockey players' applause—when Quig effectively won us the game by challenging the Washington bench. He skated over to within ten feet of the bench and used both hands in a gesture that said, "Come on. Who's next?" There were no takers. And there was no one hassling Gaston for the rest of the game. Set the price high enough and no one will pay it. I don't know where our team would be without Kevin Quigley. Out of the playoff run probably. That's why I was shocked by what happened a few weeks later in Detroit.

We played in a sold-out and screaming Joe Louis Arena and won 3–2. I had thirty saves, twelve of them in the last period, when we were just hanging on and the Detroit crowd—one of the greatest in hockey—was in full roar. Packy liked Gaston at center so much that he moved Taki to right wing. Quig's line was on the ice late in the game when I smothered a puck with my catching hand and the Red Wings' Bobby LaForrest whacked me with his stick on the back of my glove trying to get me to cough up the puck. The ref didn't whistle a penalty, probably because we were in the late stages of a close game. Refs say they don't officiate the clock or the score. Refs lie. Hockey's Code requires that an opposing player taking liberties with a goaltender has to answer for his crime, so I wasn't surprised to see Quigley skate over to LaForrest. I was surprised when all Quig did was point to the scoreboard and tell LaForrest, "You're not worth taking a penalty on." I've seen Quig beat the shit out of guys for less—close score or no close score. It was a very un-Quigley-like thing to do. I filed it in my memory.

I didn't see Faith when we got back to Boston, partly because she was getting ready for her last semester of med school and partly because we had back-to-back games. We beat L.A. 5–0 at the Garden on Saturday afternoon. That was my fifth shutout of the season and I was starting to think I might have a shot at playing in the All-Star Game in early February. In another surprise move, no doubt dictated by the Mad Hatter, Kent Wilson started Sunday at the Garden against the Islanders, and the boy wonder got blown out 5–4. I thought Wilson might get sent down but he was still around at Monday's practice. And now he had an official nameplate above his locker.

Rinky started at Washington, where he lost a 1–0 heartache, and I had a comparatively easy seventeen-save game in our 5–2 home win over Ottawa. Then it started to unravel.

I lost three in a row, 2–1 at St. Louis in the opener of a home-and-home, 4–3 to St. Louis in Boston, and an embarrassing 8–4 loss to the Rangers in Madison Square Garden where Packy had to take me out in the first period. Packy usually makes his goalie changes between periods, which Rinky and I like because it's a lot less embarrassing than making that long skate to the bench in front of seventeen thousand people during a stoppage in play. But we were down 4–0 in the first twelve minutes of the game. After the fourth goal, Packy sent Rinky over the boards and called me to the bench. I got a loud mock cheer from the Ranger's fans, who rank with Philly's as the toughest in the league. After the game we were filing off the ice when a fan chinned himself up on the glass and called Luther Brown a nigger. Luther and Bruno Govoni climbed the glass and went into the stands after the guy but he'd run away by the time they dropped into the seats like paratroopers from the 82nd Airborne. Kevin Quigley, always our last guy off the ice—just in case he has to engage in a rearguard action—made a move to go into the stands but changed his mind.

"That scumbag's gone. They'll never catch him," Quig said. That surprised me too. Common sense never stopped Kevin before.

We chartered out of New York right after the game, arrived in Ottawa at 2 a.m., and that night suffered our fourth loss in a row, 4–3 to the Senators, with Rinky Higgins in net. We were still in second place but ten points behind the Canadiens and only two in front of Ottawa when we came limping back to Boston.

We had midweek home games against Florida and Chicago, then a rare open weekend, the Sunday of which was reserved for the Bruins Wives Carnival to benefit the Boston Boys and Girls Club. We beat Florida 4–2 thanks to Jean-Baptiste's hat trick, then knocked off Chicago (hands down the best uniforms in pro sports) 2–1. I started both games but Kent Wilson was the designated backup against Chicago, which meant Rinky watched the game from the press box.

"Hard to be happy about that," he told me.

Faith phoned me a few times after our unhappy talk at her house but we didn't see each other until the Wives Carnival. Tamara Carter, the carnival's organizer, had Rinky, Kent, and me in our goalie gear, and we took turns standing in front of a net facing shots from kids whose parents paid $10 for four pucks. A few hours of that is damn tiring if you want to know the truth. Faith wandered over a couple of times mainly because located to the left of the shoot-on-a-pro-goalie area, Kevin Quigley was conducting a shooting clinic. "I just come over to hear Kevin talk," Faith said right after Quigley had explained to a bunch of kids the difference between the slapshot and wrist shot: "You don't always have to use the slappah, the wristah is bettah because you get it off quickah."

"Stick around. Pretty soon he'll talk about the backhandah," I said to Faith.

"Cam and Tamara invited us for dinner," she said. "You OK with that?"

"Sure. The series moves to a neutral site," I said.

"Let's not argue tonight, Jean Pierre. Promise?"

I promised but I didn't really have to. Faith and I had decided months earlier that any couple who argue in front of other people are major losers and automatically out of our social rotation.

Topic A at Cam's house was Kevin James Quigley. "He's playing like he has tenure," said Faith, who'd seen all of our recent games either at the Garden or on TV and to whom it was obvious, as it was to Cam and me, not only that Quigley was becoming a reluctant enforcer but that he wasn't even banging in the corners and getting the puck to Taki and Gaston.

"It's like he thinks he's in the NHL for his hands," Cam said.

"He is. Sort of," said Tamara, curling her hands into fists and striking a laughably bad pose as a boxer.

"You can't crank it up for all eighty-two," I said, reiterating a fundamental tenet of an NHL season: that no matter how much we deny it, even to ourselves, there are games where we simply take a night off. It's not premeditated. It's not that we consciously want to do it. It's just that the season is so freaking long and the only part that really counts is at the end. So I think it's our mind's way of preserving our body. The writers like to use the phrase "so-and-so thinks he can turn it on and off like a faucet." That isn't true. The damn faucet sometimes turns itself on and off. The main thing is that it's on in April, May, and June for the playoffs.

"Kevin was great with the kids. As usual," Tam said.

"Hell be great with the kids in Providence freaking Rhode Island if he doesn't go back to being his ornery old self," Cam said.

"You want to invoke the No-Hockey Rule?" Faith asked.

"Moved and seconded," said Tamara. "All in favor?" The four

of us raised our hands. The No-Hockey Rule is when we don't allow shoptalk at the dinner table. It can be a great idea in the middle of a long season. So for the rest of dinner and far into that cold January night we were just four old friends talking about movies, music, books, and our parents. Faith never mentioned her internship choices and I never brought up the trade deadline. "Is it a violation of the rule if I ask what's up with our agent and your mother?" Cam asked.

"Major violation," I said, but we all laughed because we all knew something was up.

"Just have to let 'em play it out. So to speak," Faith said.

Afterward, Faith and I went back to my condo and made love like sex-starved teenagers. Sex doesn't solve problems but it restores an emotional balance—"mental homeostasis," Faith calls it—that makes problems less scary.

We were scheduled to close out January with a Wednesday-night game in Montreal. On Monday morning Cecilia Lopes, the team's PR director, asked Cam, Gaston, and me to come to her office after practice because a feature writer for the English-language *Montreal Gazette* wanted a phone interview with us—the three Vermont alumni—for what Cecilia called "a big takeout in Wednesday's paper."

It was dark with temperatures in the low teens and a north wind whipping icy snow against the bus windows as we rode from Trudean Airport to downtown Montreal late Tuesday afternoon. It was the part of the season when, as Cam says, "You're sick and tired of being sick and tired." We were also banged up. Cam was playing with a sprained left shoulder, Flipside had been hacking and coughing since Monday's practice, Luther Brown was back in Boston with the flu, and Bruno had a bruised ankle from a shot he blocked in the Chicago game. Bruno finished the game only because he refused to let trainer Richie Boyle take off the skate boot. "If you take it off my ankle will swell and I won't be able to get my foot back into the boot," Bruno said in a re-mark that tells you all you have to know about how hockey play-ers see injuries.

I was happy to see that—bruised ankle notwithstanding—Bruno's sense of humor remained intact. We were stuck in down-town rush-hour traffic when Bruno borrowed the bus driver's microphone to read us a selection from *Letters to Penthouse*. But instead of reading it as it was written, Bruno kept substituting Rex Conway's name for the name of the guy in the letter, who I think was having sex with three sorority sisters in a cornfield. "*Oh, Rex, do me next, moaned the writhing brunette . . .*" We were all laughing except Rex, who said, "And the men of Sodom were very wicked, and sinners before the face of the Lord, beyond measure. Genesis thirteen, thirteen." Rex has a way of making the Bible sound funnier than *Letters to Penthouse*. Or maybe you had to be on our bus.

Cecilia Lopes wasn't kidding about the *Montreal Gazette* do-ing a huge takeout on Cam, Gaston, and me. The story started on page 1—right up there with the wars, murders, and political scandals—then jumped to the sports section. There were all sorts of photos of the three of us going all the way back to our years at Vermont. The writer made a lot out of the friendship between Cam and me—"the Beacon Hill Brahmin and heir to the Carter fortune and the blue-collar kid abandoned by his father and raised by his mother in gritty working-class Lewiston, Maine"—as if it were surprising that a couple of guys from different social worlds could be good friends and teammates. But that's the great thing about sport. It's a meritocracy, especially a blood sport like hockey. In this business we give up our bodies for each other and judge each other only by what we do and how well we do it. I don't think it's that way in most business offices. It's one of the reasons I want to play as long as I can and never go into the world of cubicles, annual reviews, and staff meetings.

. . .

It was snowing too hard for me to take my usual walk into old Montreal, which is why I was hanging around my room after dinner when Gaston called. "Hey, JP, heads up, our old alma mater is on TV tonight. Playing UMass-Amherst. Go, Cats, go."

"Thanks. Tell Cam," I said.

"Already did. We're watching it in your room."

Burlington, Vermont, is so close to Montreal that we could pick up the telecast of a rare midweek college game. Vermont ranked seventh in the nation and was second, behind Boston University, in Hockey East. Goalie Rudy Evanston was playing like an all-American. At least that's what I'd read in the papers. What I saw on TV was appalling. Two of Rudy's first three stops were spectacular glove saves but only because Rudy was farther off of his angles than I was in high school trig.

"*Tabernac.* Get me a stick. I score ten goals on this guy," Gaston said.

Rudy had a great catching hand, so on any shot from center to the left wing he positioned himself by cheating to the stick side and tempting the shooter with the seemingly open glove side. You might slide by with that in college but it isn't going to work in the NHL, where shots are harder and more accurate. And it wasn't working all that well against UMass, which won 5–4, with two of those goals scored low to Rudy's glove side. Too low to catch.

"Who've they got for a goalie coach? Derek Jeter?" Cam asked.

"An unpaid volunteer assistant. I forget his name," I said.

"Well, they're getting their money's worth," Cam said.

The next morning I called Marco Indinacci at Vermont to tell him what I'd seen, which was that "when it comes to playing angles no one's going to confuse Rudy Evanston with Minnesota Fats."

"We got a goalie coach. Guy played minor pro. But he works full-time for the city and he's missing half of our practices because a new supervisor changed his hours," Marco said. "Any chance you could sneak up here for a couple of practices? Rudy would love it. So would I."

"Not a prayer," I said. "We go from Montreal to Columbus, then home for a game with Buffalo, and then we get the All-Star break." I explained to Marco that I wouldn't be at the All-Star Game. Fans didn't vote me to the team. The team's third goalie would be named by the Eastern Conference All-Stars head coach and that was Montreal's Jean Picard because his team won the conference championship last season. Picard would pick his own goalie, Claude Rancourt.

"OK. But give Rudy a call. Tell him what you saw," said Marco, giving me the number for Rudy's off-campus apartment.

I phoned Rudy. A woman answered. "Just a minute, I'll get him," she said.

I'll bet you will, I said to myself.

"Rudy? It's J. P. Savard. To whom did I just have the pleasure of speaking?"

"Oh my God, Mr. Savard . . . ah, that was Claire."

"Consoling you after last night's loss, was she?"

"Don't tell me you saw that. I sucked."

"Right on both counts. I saw it on TV—we're in Montreal—and you sucked. Hey, you're going to have to stop cheating to your stick side."

"It was working well until last night. I've had a pretty good season."

"Rudy, I watched the game with Gaston Deveau and he was drooling on himself thinking about how many goals he'll score on you if you get to this league, which, the way you played last night, you won't. You've got quick hands, but it's all about positioning in the NHL. You give NHL forwards a lot of glove side to shoot at and they're going to hit it. These guys score goals for money."

"I guess it wouldn't hurt if our goalie coach showed up more than once a week," Rudy said.

"No one's more alone than a goalie, Rudy. You're going to have to work it out on your own. NHL scouts look for good fundamentals. Don't make the position look harder than it is. The only people you'll fool will be fans and writers."

We talked for a few minutes. Rudy said he'd "checked out OK on the last cancer screening" and that the biggest decision he faced was whether or not to turn pro after this season or stay for a final year of college. I wanted to tell him to stay in school because he wasn't ready for the pros. But that would've sounded hypocritical coming from me, a third-year college dropout. All I told him was that whenever he was ready I'd hook him up with Denny Moran. "Meanwhile, keep square to the puck."

He thanked me for calling.

I told Rudy I'd take him and Claire to dinner the next time I was in Burlington "if Claire's still on the traveling team."

"She'll be on it. She's the one," he said.

"Not a puck bunny, then?"

"Definitely not. Hey, you'll love this. She's a nursing major."

"Make sure she doesn't put your game in intensive care."

"Did a good job of that myself last night."

We wished each other luck and said good-bye. I went down to the bus thinking of my own college days and how simple and good that time was.

We should have bottled the game with Montreal. It was that great. The Canadiens were flying. We were flying. The crowd was into it as only a Montreal crowd can be, roaring start to finish. It was wide-open up-and-down hockey with shots off the rush and quick counterattacks. There were so few stoppages that we made more changes on the fly than we did on face-offs. At one point in the second period I looked up and saw Canadiens defenseman Justin Pelletier wheeling at top speed through center ice looking like a fourth forward, his eyes darting left and right as he looked for someone to pass to. He dished to an open teammate who one-timed a shot I stopped with my blocker. Pelletier, trailing the play, tried to sweep the puck past me but I dived and stopped it with the wide paddle of my goal stick. Cam grabbed the rebound and sent a home run pass up the middle to Gaston, who broke in alone only to be stopped by Rancourt, with the puck instantly coming back our way again. It was like that all night. The score was 3–3 with three seconds to play and a face-off in Montreal's zone to Rancourt's left when Packy waved me to the Boston bench. He figured Montreal couldn't score in three seconds, so he put out a sixth attacker. Gaston took the face-off with Jean-Baptiste and Taki behind him at the top of the circle and Quig and two other forwards stacked in front of the Montreal net. Everyone in the building knew Gaston was going to try to win the draw back to JB or Taki for a quick shot. Everyone was wrong. When the linesman dropped the puck, Gaston pushed away the Canadien center's stick, corralled the puck, and wristed a quick shot that beat Rancourt high to his glove side a fraction of a second before the horn sounded. We went crazy on the bench, piling over the boards as if we'd won the Stanley Cup.

It was in this giddy collective mood that we went whooping and hollering our way through the short corridor leading from the ice to the visitors' dressing room. Usually the only people you see on that walk are cops, arena security guys, and photographers or writers. I guess that's why the man wearing a black suit and well-tailored camel's hair overcoat and holding a newspaper caught my eye. The man reached out and grabbed Cam's elbow as Cam walked by. Cam stopped and talked to the guy, who I figured must be a Montreal writer I didn't recognize.

In the dressing room, we gathered around the TV to watch replays of the goal, cheering like high school kids every time the puck went into the net.

I was taking off my leg pads when Cam came into the room, tapped me on the right shoulder with his gloved hand, and motioned me toward the trainer's room. I was still in my sweaty long underwear and game pants when I followed Cam into the small room. "Give us a second, will you, Richie?" Cam said to Richie Boyle. Richie left and Cam closed the door.

"You see that guy who stopped me after the game?" Cam asked.

"Yeah. Writer, TV producer, or con man?" I said.

"His name is Rogatien Lachine. Says he's your father. He wants to talk to you."

Seven

I couldn't say anything as I struggled to comprehend the fact that a man claiming to be my father was standing outside our dressing room wanting to talk to me. The struggle didn't last long. "I have two answers for him, Cam, a short one and a long one. The short one is no. The long one is no fucking way."

"That's what I figured," Cam said. "Can't blame you."

"Un-goddamn-believable. A guy walks out on his wife and child and a quarter century later decides to come back for a little how-dee-do? Tell him to take a hike."

"Why me? This is your chance to tell him yourself."

"Fuck him. I'm not talking to him. I should high-stick him. And how do I know he's really my father?"

"You see the nose?" Cam asked. I had to smile at that. "I think you should talk to him, JP. Or at least listen."

"No. And why is he coming at me through you?"

"He read the story in the paper. Knows we're friends. Look, it'd only take a minute. You can always walk away."

Richie Boyle stuck his head in the door: "Hey, guys, I need the room. Got walking wounded out here."

I left the training room and went to my dressing stall with Cam behind me, still pressing. "It's your life, JP. Like it or not, parents are a part of it."

"That fucker stopped being a part of my life a long time ago. What'd he say to you?"

"I'll tell you on the flight. Go talk to him."

I reached into my equipment bag and pulled out my catch glove and blocker.

"What the hell you doing? He wants to talk, not shoot at you," Cam said.

"These are in case he tries to shake hands," I said, pulling on my gloves and walking out of the dressing room.

"I'm Jean Pierre Savard," I said, walking fast and, I hoped, menacingly toward the man in the overcoat. My voice came down hard on my last name, my mother's maiden name. I didn't extend my hand and neither did he.

"I'm Rogatien Lachine. I came here to tell you I'm sorry for what I did to you and your mother." The man spoke with a French accent. His black eyes looked straight into mine.

"Yeah, well, you and your sorry are twenty-five years too late. And why bother me now?" I said, not wanting to make this easy on him.

"I was a drunk for twenty years. The people who help me recover tell me I should apologize to everyone I hurt. It takes me years to get up the courage to do this. I know it doesn't change anything. I know I can't make it up."

"What do you really want?" I asked, figuring that he wanted to cash in on my success somehow, although from the way he was dressed he didn't look like a guy who was missing any meals. But it's a fact of any player's life that once you come into the big money you find relatives and alleged friends coming out of the woodwork. Everyone wants a piece of you.

"I only want you to know I'm sorry. I'm ashamed of myself. And always will be. That's my punishment."

"Good. You ought to be ashamed of yourself," I said. "And how'd you get in here anyway? You got tickets?"

"A suite. It's for the business."

"What's your business? Impersonating a father?" I said, landing what I thought was a pretty good shot. But the man never changed expression or tone of voice.

"Excavation and construction. We do OK. There's a lot of building in Montreal."

"Hey, JP, bus rolls in five minutes. Let's go." It was Packy yelling down the corridor.

"I've got to go," I said. "Not that I want to stay."

"You should be proud of what you've made of yourself."

"Wish I could say the same for you," I said.

"Au revoir. I have to leave too," he said.

"At least that's something you're good at," I said, ripping in one last shot as Rogatien Lachine turned and walked toward a door leading out to the cold Montreal night.

I took my usual bulkhead seat on the charter and, in an effort to be alone, threw my coat on the empty seat. Didn't work. Cam tossed the coat into an overhead bin and sat beside me. "Have a nice father-son chat?" he asked.

"Can you believe that guy?" I said.

"I can believe he's remorseful and you're pissed."

"So what'd he say to you?" I asked Cam for the second time.

"He gave me this," Cam said, reaching into his pocket and pulling out a business card that read *Rogatien Lachine— Construction & Excavation* and carried a Montreal street address, fax, and phone number. "And he said he wanted you to know he made your mother the beneficiary on a million-dollar life-insurance policy. He didn't want to tell you himself."

"I hope she collects soon," I said, handing the business card back to Cam, who slipped it into his shirt pocket.

"My work is done here," Cam said, hoisting himself out of his seat and walking back a few rows to kibitz on one of the ongoing card games played during team flights.

· · ·

Rinky got the start in Columbus, where we won an 8–0 laugher. Taki had two goals and could've had a hat trick if Kevin Quigley had passed him the puck on a two-on-one late in the game. Instead Quig shot and missed the net. "Make the goalie make the save!" Packy yelled at Kevin when the line returned to the bench. Packy doesn't yell much and I think it's been about three seasons since anyone yelled at Quig, who just sat and hung his head.

Back-to-back games are bad enough but in a ridiculous bit of scheduling we had Buffalo at the Garden the night after we'd played Columbus on the road. I started against the Sabres and lost 3–2 in overtime. I got beaten five hole on the game winner. It always looks bad when a goalie gives up a goal between his pads. But if a goalie in today's game stood with his pads tight together—the way goalies played a half century ago—we'd give up a lot more goals to the four corners of the net. I usually close the five hole by dropping to the ice and bringing my knees together and keeping my stick blade on the ice and directly in front of me. This time I was a tenth of a second late. It wasn't a bad goal, it was a great shot. Guys in this league can drive nails with the puck. But it must've looked like a bad goal, because I heard a few boos from the crowd. Players say they shrug off boos and that being booed doesn't hurt. But it does.

Quigley was benched for the game. I hoped Kevin got the message. Cam and I wanted to take him to lunch after the next day's practice but he said he was having lunch with Nan O'Brien. "Union Oystah House?" Cam said, mimicking Kev's accent.

"Kev, are oysters really an aphrodisiac?" I asked. But Quigley was walking to the shower and didn't answer either of us.

It was after five o'clock when I headed to Faith's house, driving west on Commonwealth Avenue toward a sun that was setting almost an hour later than it had in December. The last rays of an early-February sunset are the first noticeable glimmers of light in the long dark tunnel of a New England winter. The days start getting longer in late December but it's only in February that I notice and begin to think about the playoffs—and the trade deadline.

"Can you believe the nerve of the guy?" I said to Faith after I'd told her about my father showing up at the Montreal game.

"I can believe a lot of things where money is concerned, Jean Pierre. You sure he isn't going to hit you up?"

"If he does he'll be my sixth shutout of the season. He told me he only wanted to say he was sorry."

"He didn't ask you to forgive him?"

"Nope. Good thing. I wouldn't have. I haven't."

"It's a basic technique in alcohol and drug recovery to have the alcoholic or addict go back and apologize to everyone he ever hurt, and to make restitution if he can. So what's the problem?"

"I don't want him back in my life."

"He doesn't seem to be coming back into your life. I doubt you'll hear from him again."

"I hope not."

"You can forgive him in your heart without letting him into your life."

"Bullshit. He gets nothing."

"You don't do it for him, JP. You do it for yourself. You've been carrying this anger around for a long time. What good does it do you? What did I hear you tell Lindsey Carter about goal-tending? Once the puck is in the net, forget it; the only shot you can stop is the next one. Forgiveness is the next stop."

"I can't do it. It's not just me. The lowlife walked out on my mother, too."

"From what I've seen of your mother, she's put a lot of it behind her."

I told Faith about the life-insurance policy naming my mother as beneficiary. "She'll be a million dollars richer when the son of a bitch dies. Which I hope is tonight," I said.

We beat Florida 4–1 on a Wednesday night before the All-Star break. The score was 2–1 midway through the third period when Cam teed one up from the point and blasted the puck right into a Florida forward's shin pads. The puck bounced back into neutral ice, where Ricky Lange, the Panthers' top scorer, picked it up and skated in alone on me, Cam in furious and futile pursuit. Lange skated straight down Broadway, faked a shot, pulled the puck back with a toe dribble, and cut around to my left just as I hit the ice. He then lofted a backhand over me and into the top of the net. Well, almost into the net. In a desperate move I shot out my left leg. I got the toe of my skate on the puck, sending it over the goal and into the netting that protects the spectators and makes them think they're looking at a game through a fog bank. "You're lucky, Savard!" yelled a fan in a Panthers jersey. That, of course, is utter bullshit. I don't admit to any lucky saves. After the game a writer asked me if I didn't feel lucky to have stopped Lange from scoring a goal that might have changed the game. I said I felt stupid falling for the fake but after that I made the only move I could make and it was good enough. What I didn't say is that if fans and writers are going to blame me for the rain, then I'm going to take credit for the sunshine.

Jean-Baptiste, Taki, and Cam were Boston's representatives in the NHL All-Star Game. That gave me a four-day break before a three-game road trip. Faith was busy at school so I drove up to Maine to see how my mother was doing. Before I left I asked Cam and Faith if they thought I should tell my mother about my father's appearance. Cam bailed out: "Do what feels right," he said.

"I'll bet he talked to her before he talked to you," Faith said.

. . .

Piles of muddy snow narrowed the salt-stained streets of Lewiston. I slalomed Boss Scags around the potholes and puddles en route to my mother's house. Most Ferrari owners put their car in storage for the winter. But most Ferrari owners have more than one car.

My mother was on the phone and laughing—something she hasn't done a whole lot in her life—when I walked through the unlocked front door.

"Here he is now. . . . Here, hon, Dennis wants to talk to you," she said, handing me the phone.

Denny told me the Mad Hatter had finally scheduled a meeting to talk about my contract. "He says he'll see me a week from next Monday," Denny said, adding, "You don't make the All-Star team and all of a sudden Hattigan has time to talk to me. What a coincidence."

I told Denny I wasn't looking to bring down the casino. "Just get me another four or five years and for Christ's sake keep me in Boston."

"Shouldn't be that hard," Denny said. "Put Jac—put your mother back on for a second."

I handed the phone to my mother, who laughed at whatever it was Denny said. Two laughs in three minutes. A personal best.

We ate boudin blanc for dinner; it was from the last batch of sausages my grandmother had made, and which my mother had kept frozen. My grandmother made her version of boudin with pork, chicken, cream, butter, plain bread crumbs, and a combination of spices known only to her. Thank God she never made boudin noir, which contains pig's blood and which my grandmother called "blood pudding." We ate in the kitchen, which smelled as it had when my grandmother was alive. "I hate to screw up a good meal, but a guy claiming to be my father showed up after the Montreal game," I told my mother.

She didn't act surprised, because she wasn't. "I thought he might."

"Thanks for the heads-up."

"I didn't know for sure and I didn't want to distract you."

"So you've seen him?"

"No. He wrote to me about a month ago. He wanted to say he was sorry."

"What did you say? Have you answered him?"

"Not yet."

"You going to?"

"I'll let him know I got his letter and that it's good—good for him—that he feels remorse. It's good he's in recovery. I wish him well with that. But that's all. I don't want to see him."

"Did he want to see you?"

"He didn't say that."

"Can I see the letter?"

My mother went to her room and came back with a small hand-addressed envelope from which she handed me a folded one-page handwritten letter.

Jacqueline,

Il y des péché qui sont impardonnables . . . "You know I can't read this," I said, handing the letter back to her. She smiled and read it to me:

"Jacqueline,

"Some sins are unforgivable. Mine is one of them. But I want you to know the sorrow I feel, and will always feel, for what I did as an alcoholic. And for what I did not do as a husband, a father, and a man.

"I have been sober more than five years. The people at the alcohol program at Hotel Dieu—that's the French Hospital in Montreal," my mother explained—"say I should apologize to all the people I hurt when I was drinking. But I had to wait until the sorrow grew so heavy that I wanted to express it and was not doing so only because someone told me to.

"I am working up the courage to apologize to our son. I am sure he is angry and will remain so. I see in the papers what he has done and am proud of him and of you and ashamed of myself. No apology is adequate.

"Then he told me about the insurance policy," my mother said, folding the letter and putting it back in the envelope.

"That's the only part of this that doesn't suck," I said.

"You're not in the locker room, Jean Pierre."

"Sorry. But the hell with him. We should talk about something else."

"First tell me about your meeting with him."

I told her what happened outside the dressing room in Montreal. "I have no intention of forgiving him. I told him that," I said.

My mother ignored that. "Denny says there's some progress on your contract," she said.

"Denny and the Mad Hatter are meeting a week from Monday. The deal will get done, but God knows when."

"And what's Faith doing next year?"

"Same thing she always does—whatever she wants," I said with more bitterness than I'd intended. I told my mother about Faith's internship choices and how she was leaning toward the Lake Champlain Medical Center in Vermont.

"Then you two have some talking to do," my mother said. "Faith's a good woman, Jean Pierre. And very strong."

"We'll work it out," I said, even though I wasn't sure we would. Or could.

I stayed overnight at the house I'd grown up in and slept in my old room curled up under a patchwork quilt my grandmother made. I slept eight hours—something I hadn't done since the season started—and awoke to the smell of bacon and coffee. My mother and I ate breakfast together. We didn't talk about my father. After breakfast I read the *Lewiston Sun-Journal* and saw that the Mainiacs, the local Junior A team, beat Quebec City 1–0 with Lewiston goalie Demetre Fontaine picking up a thirty-five-save shutout. I knew that Fontaine—a nineteen-year-old from Trois-Rivières—was the Montreal Canadiens' number one draft pick the previous year. Another kid who—in a few seasons— would take a veteran's job the same way Rinky Higgins or Kent Wilson could take mine.

I waited until the morning traffic cleared before I headed back to Boston, a ziplock bag of boudin blanc on Boss Scag's floor. "When are you going to get a sensible car?" my mother asked as I was leaving.

"When I grow up," I said.

There were two calls on my phone when I got home. Faith wanted me to go to her house on Sunday to watch the telecast of the NHL All-Star Game. Denny Moran wanted me to call him at his office.

"Get a life and stop working Saturdays," I said to Denny when he answered his own phone at the Carter & Peabody offices.

"That's what I want to talk to you about, JP."

I said that would be more fun than talking about the $50,000 bonus I'd blown by not making it to the All-Star Game.

"Maybe not," Denny said. "This is awkward, JP, but since we picked up that Maine State Employees account I'm spending more time in Maine than a moose. Look . . . Christ, I can't believe I'm saying this. . . . I've got to be in Portland next Friday and I'd like to take your mother to dinner. But I won't if it bothers you."

"If it's OK with her it's OK with me, Denny. And I think it'll be OK with her. She's been stuck in that house a long time. It'll do her good to go out. Might even do you some good."

"I appreciate it, JP. That almost makes me forget my cut of the fifty thou All-Star bonus you blew."

"Have her home by eleven," I said.

"I've been hit on harder at the Ritz bar," Faith said of the predictably nonviolent NHL All-Star Game, where no one hit anyone or blocked a shot and the final score was something like Eastern Conference 172, Western Conference 138. Or maybe it was 14–9 the way the paper said. Our guys did well. JB and Taki each scored and Cam picked up two assists. The only downer was seeing my fellow goalies get lit up like tiki torches. That and watching Montreal goalie Claude Rancourt being helped to the bench in the third period after a Western Conference forward lost an edge and fell on Claude's right knee. I suppose most fans think I should be glad that our archrival's goalie got hurt. Maybe I'd feel that way if it happened to another player. But goalies are a strange breed and we mostly wish each other well. We all belong to the Goaltenders Union, which isn't a real organization in that we don't collect dues or hold meetings. I tried to explain this to Lynne Abbott a couple of years ago. The best I could do was to say that the Goaltenders Union is a freemasonry of spirit and empathy, an unofficial brotherhood of guys held together by our apartness. And it doesn't matter what level you played at. If you were a goalie in peewee hockey, then you're in the union. It doesn't even matter if you don't play anymore. Being a goalie is like being a Marine—you're never an ex-Marine or an ex-goalie. Lynne said she understood but I don't think she does. I think only goalies understand.

We had a tough trip after the All-Star break; a Tuesday-night game in Denver followed by an all-night charter and a Wednesday-night game in Vancouver before we had to fly back across the country to play the New York Islanders on a Saturday. We lost 5–2 to the Colorado Avalanche, a team we could meet if we get to the Stanley Cup finals. Packy started Rinky Higgins in that game. That's a little game coaches play. The unspoken message to the Avalanche was: OK, you beat us, but you didn't beat our top goalie, which you'll have to do when the money's on the line.

I got the start the next night in Vancouver. The team was tired from a 2 a.m. arrival and from having played the night before. We were hanging on to a 2–1 lead late in the third period when there was a scrum in front of the net. All I remember is that I was trying find the puck amid all the skates, sticks, and legs when someone banged into me from my right side, twisting my mask around so I couldn't see. I threw off the mask like a baseball catcher going after a pop-up and just as I did someone hit Flipside Palmer, who came crashing into me, knocking my unhelmeted head against the left post. All I saw was an explosion of yellow in a field of black. When I regained consciousness, Richie Boyle was shining a flashlight in my eyes. "Probably a mild concussion," Richie said. "You're done for tonight, JP."

Flipside and Cam helped me to the bench and Rinky came in for the last five minutes. That was a tough spot for him but he made a couple of stops and we escaped with the W.

I had a headache so I popped three ibuprofen and spent a long time in the shower letting a hard spray of hot water play on the back of my neck. "Got my bell rung. No biggie," I said to anyone who asked. I fell asleep in my room at the Westin Bayshore at about midnight. An hour later I woke up and vomited. I didn't want to wake Richie—trainers keep worse hours than players—so I took an over-the-counter sleeping pill and an antacid tablet and sat hunched over on the edge of my bed for the next hour until the sleeping pill kicked in.

When I woke up at about 6 a.m. I still had a headache. I called Richie, who came to my room and told me he wanted me to go back to Boston to see our team doctor, Jack "Send 'Em In" Wynn. A team doctor is about the last person you want to see when you're hurt. Team doctors are hired and paid by the club, which most of us see as meaning that the Hippocratic oath gets twisted around so that the phrase "but first do no harm" becomes "but first don't lose your gig with the club." I think if my head got knocked off of my body and was spinning around in the face-off circle the team doctor would retrieve it, sew it back on, and tell management I'd be good to go in two or three games. It's only rookies who don't seek out independent doctors and get second opinions. But my contract says I have to see old "Send 'Em In," so I flew back to Boston via Toronto, arriving too late to see anyone. Thursday morning I took a cab to Massachusetts General

Hospital, where Doc Wynn shined more lights in my eyes, did some other tests, and surprised me when he said: "You've got a slight concussion; you're out until the headaches are gone for at least five days. You could be out a week. Maybe more. That said, it's only ten a.m., so you've got plenty of time to go get your second opinion." No matter what they say, no doctor likes it when a patient gets a second opinion. But I think the fact that Doc Wynn knew I *always* got a second opinion is what kept him honest in the first place. It's a crazy game but you have to play it. I ignored his remark about a second opinion and asked him, "What's the story on internships here? Good program?"

"Mass General is one of the best hospitals in the world, JP; getting an internship here is like being signed by the Yankees or playing Carnegie Hall. Why? You making contingency plans in case Hattigan doesn't sign you?"

"My girlfriend graduates from med school this year," I said. "She might intern here."

"If she's lucky," Wynn said. "We're highly selective."

"So's Faith McNeil," I said, heading for the elevator.

I didn't want to drive because of the headache and blurred vision, so I called Faith and invited her to my place. "Bring your little black doctor's bag," I said. "I need a second opinion on this alleged concussion."

"I could've made that diagnosis off of TV and this phone call," she said. "You've got blurred vision, you were throwing up, and you still have a headache. Textbook concussion."

"I'm sure it'll feel better if you come over and rub my head."

"Ha! Which one?" she said.

I tried for a quick nap after I'd talked to Faith but the phone rang. It was Denny calling to tell me that the Mad Hatter had rescheduled the meeting to discuss my contract. Hattigan wouldn't meet with Denny for another two weeks. "You get hurt. The meeting gets delayed. All part of the negotiations game, JP."

"I think we might be losing the game," I said.

"Haven't lost one yet," Denny said. That was true. Denny had always negotiated good deals for Cam and me. But I was getting a bad feeling about this one. Denny also told me he was taking my mother to dinner in Portland. I suggested Pat's Café on Stevens Avenue, a restaurant I'd come to know on trips to Portland during my days in the AHL. "Great food and a lot of tables set in little nooks and corners. Good place to talk, which is all you're going to be doing," I said.

I watched on TV as we beat the Islanders 4–3 in one of those new tie-breaking shootouts where three players from each team take turns skating in alone on the goaltender just as they would on a penalty shot. Rinky stopped one of the Isles' three shooters, and Jean-Baptiste, Gaston, and Taki scored for us. I began to wonder if Rinky was at the point where he could be a number one goalie. My thinking went like this: He's good, he's younger than I am, and he'd come cheaper. And at this point in his career he's either going to have to win my job outright, resign himself to being a career backup, ask for a trade, or wait until his contract expires next season and become a free agent. I think his first choice would be to win my job. My getting hurt gave him a good chance to do that.

A lot of injured players like to watch the game on the dressing-room TV or to see it live by standing in the runway near our bench. They think that if they go up to the press box they'll be fair game for writers and broadcasters. But I don't mind talking to the media. I know whom to avoid (most of the writers in New York, a few in Toronto, and any gossip columnist) and whom I can trust. I see writers as a link to the fans and not as people looking for dirt to dish. Most of them are as professional about their jobs as I am about mine.

Before I went to the press box I stopped by our dressing room.

I told Rinky to keep track of the 'Canes big center Ned Croutty, who likes to one-time the puck from the slot and who's strong and determined enough to take the beating routinely handed out to guys who like to hang in front of the goal.

It's true in all professional sports that when you're hurt, you don't feel as though you're part of the team. So as soon as the guys went out for warm-ups I took the elevator to the press box and started walking to the players' seats. I didn't get far. A Channel 3 TV producer asked me if I would do an interview between the first and second period, and our radio analyst, Spence Evans, asked me to go on air with him between the second and third periods. I said yes to both. I don't worry about broadcast interviews. The questions are usually softballs. But if Spence Evans is a belt-high marshmallow over the heart of the plate—"I'll bet you're eager to get back out there, JP," is a typical Evans nonquestion—the print journalists, especially Lynne Abbott, are tougher. As soon as she saw me, Lynne said: "Excuse me, JP, but why is Kevin Quigley playing like a wuss?"

"I haven't noticed he is," I said, lying to protect Quig.

"I don't know what it looks like from down there but from up here he looks like Disney's Princesses on Ice."

"Quig will be there when we need him," I said.

Lynne said that was what she'd thought at first "but he's been playing soft for more than a month." I didn't know what to say so it was lucky that Lynn changed the subject and asked about my concussion. I said the headaches were gone and that I'd probably miss only one or two more games.

I sat at the end of the press box with a couple of guys up from Providence, both of whom were healthy scratches. The main thing I noticed watching from a press box was that you have a fraction of a second more than you think you have when you're on the ice. I think that's the difference between good players and great players; great players have a higher panic point; they use that extra millisecond. And the immortal players—Bobby Orr, Wayne Gretzky, Mario Lemieux, Gordie Howe—seemed to have no panic point. If an opponent did X they did Y. Sort of like the talking cobra in Kipling's *The Jungle Book:* "If you move I strike. And if you don't move I strike."

The other thing I noticed was that Kevin Quigley was in fact playing like a wuss.

"Jesus, Quig, you've got to drill him on that play," I said to myself as Quigley took a curving route into the Hurricanes' left corner and tried to stick-check the puck from a Carolina defenseman. The play there is to staple the defenseman to the boards and either take the puck or leave it loose for a teammate to swoop in and pick up. Instead the defenseman kept possession and skated a few strides before sending a home run pass up the middle to Ned Croutty, who skated in alone and slid the puck under Rinky for a 1–0 Carolina lead in a game they'd win 6–2. Packy benched Quig for two shifts but that didn't do any good. Even when Kev came back he still played softer than cashmere.

"See what I mean," Lynne said as I walked past her on my way to the broadcast booth for my TV interview.

For the rest of the game Quigley played so poorly I was embarrassed for him. I wanted to talk with him but it would've been easier scheduling talks with the North Korean government. He'd been a different guy ever since he hooked up with Nan O'Brien.

"Cam's the captain. Can't you get him to talk to Kevin?" Faith asked me as we drove back to my place after the game.

"We've tried setting up a lunch, we even invited him to a couple of Celtics games, but he's always got some reason he can't go. And that reason is usually Nan O'Brien. Was she at the game?"

"Saw her in the Family Room," Faith said, using the new, politically sanitized title for what used to be the Wives' Room. "She's at all the home games."

A light snow fell as I pulled Boss Scags into the tiny garage behind my condo. I was looking forward to catching the NHL highlights on TV while enjoying some postgame pasta and a glass or two of wine, a nice overture to what I hoped would be some relaxing late-night sex. That hope lasted until we took off our coats and Faith hit me with the buzz kill: "I've decided on my internship," she said. "I'm going to Vermont."

Hurt

I knew what it was as soon as I felt it. It happened in December of my first season with Vermont. It was early in the first period of a game at Northeastern. I was on my knees and off balance at the left post with a Northeastern forward about twenty feet in front of me looking at a mostly empty net. He shot and I stuck out my right leg in a desperate move. The pain was as if someone had strung a hot wire high on the back of my leg from below the butt to above the knee. Hamstring. I made the save but that was it for the night. Our trainer, Bobby Breyer, helped me to the dressing room.

I was on the trainer's table when the guys came into the room after the first period.

Coach Indinacci glanced at me but talked only to Bobby. "How long's he out for?"

"Hard to say. I'll have a better idea tomorrow," Bobby said. Coach walked away.

On the trip back to Vermont I sat on the left side of the bus with my right leg stretched across the aisle and resting on a right-side seat. About ninety minutes into the trip one of the assistant coaches had to use the bathroom at the back of the bus.

"Excuse me, JP," was all he said as he stepped high over my outstretched leg. On his way back to his seat he didn't say anything.

You spend more time at the rink when you're hurt than when you're healthy. I cut a few classes to get some early-morning treatment. I was on the trainer's table one morning when Coach Indinacci came in.

"Morning, Coach," I said.

"Bobby around?" Indinacci asked.

"Right here," said Bobby Breyer emerging from a supply closet.

Indinacci and Bobby stood about five feet from me as they reviewed the injury report.

"Knowles?" Indinacci asked.

"Good to go," Bobby said.

"Schaeffer?"

"No contact for another week."

"Savard?"

"Another week at least. Maybe two."

Indinacci didn't say anything. He turned and walked to his office.

"Was it something I said?" I asked Bobby, confused by Indinacci's coolness.

Bobby didn't answer.

Even when you're hurt you have to show up during practice hours. Players would come in, see me on the trainer's table, and ask me how I was doing. I had a bunch of them laughing one afternoon as I explained how my hamstring started killing me during sex with a puck fuck. "Had to abort the mission. Freaking embarrassing," *I was saying just as Indinacci walked up to our group.*

"All right, guys, that's it. On the ice in ten minutes," *he said, clapping his hands. The group around me dispersed and I was again alone on the table.*

The cold front lasted for about a week. None of the coaches was rude to me. No one tried to rush me back. No one implied I was faking it. But they spoke to me only if I spoke to them first.

One day after practice I went into Indinacci's office.

"Talk to you, Coach?" I asked.

"Talk," Indinacci said.

"I didn't get hurt on purpose. I got hurt making a save," I said, getting to what I thought was the bottom line.

"I know. Hell of a save, too," Indinacci said.

"Then why am I all of a sudden a nonperson?" I asked.

Indinacci leaned forward over his desk. "You're not a nonperson, JP. You're a nonplayer."

"So that means I'm chopped liver?"

"No," Indinacci said. "That means you're irrelevant."

I didn't make the weekend trip to Orono for two games against Maine. I started practicing on the Monday after that series. That week we had a rare Thursday-night home game against New Hampshire. "You think I can play?" I asked Bobby.

"Probably. But if I were you I'd give it another few days. Play on Saturday," he said. On Wednesday Coach Indinacci came up to me at the end of practice.

"What do you think about tomorrow?" he asked.

"I can play," I said.

Eight

I spooned puttanesca sauce over two bowls of linguine. "Isn't puttanesca supposed to be an aphrodisiac?" Faith asked.

"When Bruno gave it to me he said it gets its name from *puttana,* the Italian word for 'whore,' " I said. "Bruno's grandfather told him that some Italian ladies in the whore industry made puttanesca sauce because they thought men were aroused by the smell. Maybe it's the anchovies."

"Gross."

"Of course it doesn't work when your girlfriend tells you she's taking an internship two hundred and fifty miles away."

"Do we have to go through this again?"

"Yes."

We spent the next half hour running the same familiar laps around the same well-worn track; arguing about her decision to pass up an internship in Boston, which I said would be perfect for us, to take one in Vermont, which she said would be perfect for her, or at least perfect for her career. "We'll have all of July and August and most of June together," she said.

"Great. What do we do for the other two hundred and eighty days?"

We weren't getting anywhere until Faith asked the only question that counted. "Do you think we should break this off?"

"No. Do you?"

"No." Then she smiled and said. "This puttanesca stuff making you horny?"

"No."

"Me neither."

We skipped sex and went to sleep, each clinging to opposite edges of the king-sized bed, our bodies silhouetted like two mountain ranges, a cold desert of sheets and blankets stretching between us—the demilitarized zone.

Meanwhile, a rising northeast wind brought in moisture from the Atlantic and turned a flurry into a near blizzard.

Sidewalk plows were pushing aside a foot of heavy wet snow when I left for practice the next morning. I couldn't find an empty cab and the streets were too snowy to drive on so I walked to the Garden.

When I got to the dressing room Luther and Flipside were in the process of ranking the months of the year. They disagreed on all of them except March. They ranked March last and not only because of the weather. For a hockey player one of the worst things about March is the NHL trade deadline. A lot of guys are on edge until that day comes and goes. The delays in my contract talks made me wonder if I should be worried. Faith going to Vermont would be a home-baked cherry pie compared to my being dealt to L.A. or Vancouver.

"You're not going anywhere. Hattigan's just dicking you around so he can stay way under the salary cap," Cam said. "Starting goalies don't get traded. If the Hatter deals anyone it'll be Quig."

"You talked to Kev?" I asked.

"Tried to but you know Kev. He's always got somewhere to go, something to do. He won't even admit his game's fading faster than AM radio."

"So what do we do?"

"Go with Plan B," Cam said.

Before I could ask what Plan B was, Packy stopped by to tell me the team wouldn't be taking me to Buffalo but that he planned to start me three days later at home against Philly assuming I was free of all concussion symptoms.

"Philly," Cam said and laughed. "Nice way to ease back into things. At least you know where Serge Balon's first shot is going."

"Right at my melon," I said. "At least he won't score if he hits me on the head."

"Goalies have strange priorities," Cam said.

We lost 4–3 to Buffalo with Rinky in net. Watching the game on TV, I noticed how quickly Rinky recovers. He'll drop down into his butterfly and in a fraction of a second be back up on his skates. Lately I've noticed that it takes me longer to recover, especially late in a game when my legs are tired. I hope no one else has noticed it. Maybe I can lose some weight, work on my leg strength in the off-season and be as quick as I used to be. Or maybe I'm kidding myself and it's little things like this that begin that final slide. In most businesses people get better as they age. But not in pro sports. The life cycle of a player is from hopeful rookie to dependable starter to aging-but-wily veteran to a beaten-up guy just trying to hold on for one more payday. It's always ugly at the end.

The loss to Buffalo dropped us into a third-place tie with Ottawa in our division. The way the playoffs work is that the three divisional champions in our conference—the Eastern Conference—are automatically seeded first, second, and third for the playoffs. The next five teams with the best won-lost records—no matter which division they come from—are seeded four through eight. The top four seeds get home-ice advantage for the first round. By early March we were nine points behind Montreal. Possibly too much ground to make up in the last month of the season. But if we finished a strong second in our division we might get the number-four seed and home ice.

I had two good days of practice before our Saturday-night game against Philly. Sure enough Serge "the Weasel" Balon launched a missile at my head on his first shift. I caught it. "Makin' sure you haven't lost your nerve, JP," Serge said as he skated past the cage before the face-off.

"Hey, Serge, the idea is to *miss* the goalie," I said.

Serge is always a pain in the ass but that night had me wishing the NHL called penalties for criminal mischief. In the course of the first two periods, Balon slashed Taki, tripped Gaston, and ran Rex Conway into the Philly bench, where three Flyers punched him before he extricated himself.

The game was 1–1 after two periods. Packy gave us a few minutes to settle down before he came into the dressing room. "Enough's enough, Quig. You got to send a message to Balon, you know what I'm saying? The refs aren't doing it," Packy said.

Quig nodded and took a swig of Gatorade, probably so he wouldn't have to say anything.

The Flyers scored on their second shift to make it 2–1. When Philly put Balon's line on the ice right after the goal, Packy countered by sending Quigley's line over the boards. I figured the fight would start right after the face-off. But Kevin went up and down his wing like a toy player in a tabletop hockey game. To make it worse, Quig coughed up the puck to Balon, who came flying into our zone and was lining up a shot when Cam hit him and—as Cam's father later described it—"put the goddamn Weasel on Queer Street." Cam's hit brought the crowd to its feet but didn't save the game. We lost 4–1 to drop into fourth place in the division. We'd be lucky to make the playoffs.

Packy called Quig to a closed-door meeting in the coach's office after the game. When Kev came out he changed into his street clothes, went straight to the Family Room, picked up Nan O'Brien, and took off. He left without talking to any of us.

"That's it. I've had it," Cam said.

We had two days of practice before we headed for Montreal. Sunday was just a light skate. Cam had the day off because he'd been playing about thirty-two minutes per game. Monday was a different story. That was the day Cam unveiled Plan B.

We skated through a few passing drills and worked on the power play before Packy decided he wanted to finish practice with a twenty-minute scrimmage—first and third lines and defense pairings against second and fourth lines and defense pairings. That matched Cam, a right defenseman, against Quigley, the left wing on our second line. Normally our late-season scrimmages feature less contact than the Ladies Auxiliary Square Dance and Strawberry Festival, so I thought it was odd that when Quigley carried the puck into the corner to my right Cam unloaded on him. Splattered him into the boards. Play moved up ice before Quigley regained his feet and skated out of the zone.

"Can't leave it there, Kev!" I yelled just in case he needed a reminder that a hit like Cam's—even in practice, even from a friend—has to be repaid. The hockey checkbook has to balance. I was also thinking that it wouldn't be the worst thing in the world if we had what the writers call "a spirited scrimmage." Sometimes that can jump-start a team or, in Kevin's case, a player. But when Cam had the puck in the corner with Kevin coming in on the forecheck, Kev just tried to play the puck. He never bodychecked Cam. As Cam and Quig fought for the puck along the boards—working their sticks like a couple of kayakers—two other players moved in, creating a rugbylike scrum. Packy blew the whistle to restart play. As the scrum broke up Cam gave Kevin a face wash. That's where a guy rubs the sweaty palm of his glove in your face. It's not exactly a punch so refs rarely call it, but it's annoying, and demeaning to the recipient. A face wash has been the preface to some memorable scraps. But Quig ducked away and started skating into position for the face-off. Cam skated after him and cross-checked him across the back of the shoulder pads. "What the fuck's the mattah with you?" Quigley said, turning to face Cam.

Cam didn't answer. Instead, holding his stick in both hands, he kept cross-checking Kevin. Once. Twice. Three times. Kev tried to spin away and head back toward the face-off circle but Cam kept after him.

"Let it go," Packy said as Flipside reached out to grab Cam.

With that, Cam dropped his stick and gloves in hockey's most inescapable challenge. For a moment Quigley stood there. "There's no way out, Kev," I heard Cam say. That's when Quigley dropped his stick and gloves and two of the best heavyweights in the league began circling like a couple of boxers. Even the janitors in the stadium stopped sweeping and leaned on their brooms to watch. Cam, a left-handed puncher, used a right jab to keep Quig away, then landed two looping lefts to the right side of Quigley's head, cutting his hand on Quig's helmet with the second punch. I don't know if it was the hits to his head or the sight of blood but Quigley went postal. He rushed Cam, grabbing him by the shoulder pads and hammering him against the glass, where Quig unleashed a flurry of punches to Cam's midsection. When Cam doubled over, Quig threw a right uppercut that caught Cam in the face, sending him slumping to the ice, blood gushing from his nose and trickling from his mouth. If it had been a professional boxing match the ref or doctor would have stopped it. I guess all of us thought Kevin, the clear winner, would stop, which is why no one moved in the split second it took Quig to rip off Cam's helmet. Cam's bare head was propped up only by the boards. I couldn't believe it when I saw Quig draw back his right arm for a kill shot. As Quig brought his fist down toward Cam's unprotected temple I reacted the only way I could. I caught the punch. Stuck out my catch glove and grabbed Quig's fist inches before it crashed into Cam's head. It was the biggest save of my life.

Quig glared at me. For a second or two I thought he might come after me. Then Quig looked at Cam. Kev started to say something but whatever it was got choked off by the same kind of heaving sobs I'd heard when I walked into the wrong room at our Christmas party and found Quig crying on Nan O'Brien's shoulder. It wasn't even ordinary crying as much as an anguished twisted cry rising from the bottom of a personal hell. "Fucking liahs . . . fucking liahs . . . all of them," Quig cried.

"That's it, guys. Off the ice. Let's go," Packy said, breaking up the huddle around Quig. A few of the Black Aces went to the opposite end of the ice for some so-called extra practice (I think they mainly do that to try to impress the coaches) but Packy ordered them off the ice too. There was just Cam sitting against the boards and bleeding a river, Quigley doubled over on the ice, and me standing there not knowing what to do.

"Who's a liar, Kev?" I asked.

"All of them . . . my phony fucking parents . . . couldn't tell me the truth . . . and my give-up mothah; loved me so much she gives me away . . . cop stepfathah beats me up about once a week till I coldcock him," Quigley said, blowing his nose into his hand, then wiping it on his practice shirt. He looked over at Cam: "Jesus, Cam, I'm sorry—"

Cam cut him off. "Never mind the scrap. I started it. Tell me who lied about what."

What came out in the next few minutes, as Quigley regained emotional control, was a story of rejection and deceit. Kevin Quigley was adopted and never told about it. He'd been given up at birth by his unmarried mother and adopted into a family that told him he was theirs.

"It's typical old-time Irish," Quig said. "Never talk about anything. Pretend everything's OK. My own mothah puts me on waivahs and I have to find out twenty-three years latah from a social workah."

"Now you have the chance to deal with it," Cam said.

"Yeah. The truth will set you free. But it'll beat the shit out of you before it does," Quig said.

Quig started apologizing again for the fight when Leadfoot Larry Jankowski yelled at us: "Let's go, guys, got to resurface. We got *Sesame Street on Ice* tonight." Leadfoot Larry drives the Zamboni as though he thinks it's a tank and he's George Patton. Hockey players and Zamboni drivers are natural enemies.

It was a Zamboni driver, not a psychiatrist, who invented the fifty-minute hour. When we were kids our team would pay for an hour of ice rental but at ten minutes before the hour the corner doors swung open and out would roar the Zamboni with the driver screaming, "You little bastids get off the ice. We got the high school on next." That doesn't happen in the NHL but we players still harbor simmering residual dislike for Zamboni drivers.

Leadfoot came straight up the boards, blipping the throttle as he drove right at the three of us. Quig and I could have skated out of the way but Cam, still bleeding, was using the dasher board to hoist himself to his feet as Leadfoot gunned the Zamboni toward him. Quigley went crazy again. Only this time he was the Kevin Quigley we'd known and trusted. Kev charged the Zamboni and hauled Leadfoot off of his perch. The machine stopped and stalled. But Quig was just getting started. He grabbed the flailing Leadfoot by the collar of his nylon jacket and the belt on his denim work pants. "Curling's a great sport, Larry, you fucking arrogant moron. You like curling, Larry? Curling's where you take this big dumbass stone and throw it down the ice. . . . Like this . . . ," said Quig, using two hands to send the skateless Jankowski skimming across the Garden ice and into the middle of the spoked B, our center-ice logo. "Stay there till we're off the ice, Janko. Don't go near this fuckin' machine!" Quig shouted as he pulled the ignition key from the Zamboni and threw it into a corner of the rink from which a slip-sliding Jankowski would have to retrieve it.

Behind me, Cam was stifling a laugh. "Quig's back," he said.

"What was that all about?" Lynne Abbott said as I walked past her toward the dressing room.

"Plan B," I said.

"Cam almost got killed out there. Nice save on that last punch," Lynne said.

"Please don't write that."

"I won't."

. . .

Few subjects are off limits in a team's locker room. Wives and kids maybe but that's about it. Religion, politics, physical quirks are all fair game for teammates' gibes. So it was no surprise that when Cam, Quig, and I pushed through the locker room door the first thing we heard was Flipside humming the theme song from *Rocky* and Taki making like a ring announcer. "And in this corner the Brawling Brahmin from Beacon Hill . . . Cameron CAAAAR-terrr."

"About time you hit someone, Kev, but it's supposed to be the guys on the other team," Jean-Baptiste said.

Cam shadowboxed his way into the trainer's room to get stitched up. Quigley slumped in front of his locker exhausted but smiling.

I love Faith McNeil but you wouldn't have known it in the weeks after her decision to take an internship in Burlington, Vermont. We'd stopped talking about it but our disagreement put a chilly distance between us. So did the team's schedule. We ran our losing streak to four games in a 5–3 loss at Montreal, a game in which I played poorly at least partly because I was distracted by thoughts of whether or not my father was up in one of those luxury suites staring down at me. It was like that creepy feeling you get at a movie where a guy walks through the jungle and can't see anyone but wonders how many unseen eyes are watching him.

At least the trip to Montreal let me catch my old college team on TV. They lost 3–2 to Maine but Rudy Evanston played well in goal. He had thirty saves and had stopped cheating to his stick side.

Rinky Higgins started in goal in Atlanta and picked up a shutout in a 3–0 win. Rinky also started at the Garden against Calgary, where he again played well and we won 3–2. The crowd was taking a liking to Rinky and cheering him the way they once cheered me when I was wresting the job away from a veteran. Rinky gave us our third win in a row with a thirty-eight-saver against the Rangers in New York. He played even better—forty-one saves, three on breakaways—in Toronto but we lost 2–1. That loss was probably the only reason Packy started me at home against Detroit. We won 2–1 but I heard a few boos on the one goal I gave up, a long slapper from center ice. It's hard for me to understand booing. I don't think I've booed anyone since I was a ten-year-old on a school field trip to Fenway Park. I booed a second baseman who'd booted a ground ball. But I did it only because the grown-ups around me were doing it. I think people who boo are mostly the same losers who yell at their kids at Little League and peewee games, mostly people who never played and have no idea what it's like to be in the arena, to put themselves out there. I wonder how they'd like it if every time they made a mistake at work a red light went on and people booed.

Our home crowd's biggest cheers were for Quigley. Kevin was hitting hard, clean, and often; nailing people to the boards, cartwheeling a couple of guys in open ice, and generally putting the sandpaper back in his game and ours. The result was that his line mates, Taki and Gaston, came out of scoring slumps that had coincided with Quigley's temporary experiment with pacifism.

The win over the Red Wings was our third in four games and we were all feeling pretty good at practice the next day. The guys had more bounce and jump in their legs, and passes hit sticks with a clicking sharpness you don't hear when we're dragging ourselves through the motions. Shots came at me harder and arrived quicker than they had in several weeks and I felt good stopping them, almost as if I'd put my body on goaltending autopilot. I even stayed out a few extra minutes and took some shots from the Black Aces. When I arrived back in the dressing room, Jean-Baptiste told me, "Packy wants to see you." I still had my pads on when I flopped into a folding metal chair in front of Packy Dodd's desk.

"You're not going to like this, JP, but I'm going to alternate you and Rinky. He starts tomorrow against Phoenix; you get the first game of the road trip at Buffalo."

I was surprised and disappointed. But you don't show that. Not to a coach. Not to anyone in management. Never let them know you're hurt. "What's the matter with the play-till-you-lose thing we've been doing lately?" I asked.

"Front office wants to see more of Reginald. See if he's ready to help us in the postseason."

I knew when Packy said "Reginald" and "front office" he was telling me that the Mad Hatter had ordered the change. Hattigan rarely calls anyone by his nickname.

"I guess the Hatter wants to see if Rinky's ready to take the starter's job for less money," I said.

"It's a business, JP," Packy said, leaning back in his chair and pushing at his temples with the heels of his hands. "I know you have a contract coming up. We both know what's going on here. But I've got to do this."

What was going on was that the Mad Hatter was gaining more negotiating leverage on Denny Moran. How could a goalie who plays only every other game be worth north of $3 million? Besides devaluing me, Hattigan was also playing to a vocal and growing group of fans who were falling in love with Rinky. And out of love with me.

I went back into the dressing room and told Cam I had to talk to him.

"Stop by the house for lunch on your way home."

I banged the polished brass knocker on Cam's front door half expecting I'd summoned the ghost of Jacob Marley. But it was Tamara who answered. "Cam just called. He'll be late. He forgot he had to pick up Caitlin at kindergarten," she said. "You OK with a chicken salad sandwich?"

"Don't let me cut into your day, Tamara. I'll call Cam tonight."

"You're not cutting into anything. Besides, I want to talk to you."

"The last person who wanted to talk to me told me I was losing half my job. And the person who talked to me before that told me she was going to Vermont." I told Tamara about the new system of alternating Rinky and me.

"Well, you can end that by outplaying him," she said. Say this for Tamara MacDonald Carter. She may not know much about hockey but she has an instinct for the bottom line. "Come out to the kitchen. I want to know more about you and Faith. She told me she was taking the Vermont job."

For someone who supposedly wanted to talk, Tamara did a lot of listening. I spent the next twenty minutes ranting about Faith moving to Burlington when she could have taken an internship in Boston "that's only three freaking public transit stops from my condo."

"I see your point, JP," she said.

"Great. Call Faith and tell her. Not that anyone can change her mind."

"I don't want to change her mind. She's doing what she believes is best for her . . ." Here Tam hesitated a fraction of a second searching for a word I thought would be "career." But it came out "vocation."

"What about my vocation?" I said.

"The question is what's best for both of you. Faith could work as a doctor for thirty years. She should be where she believes she's needed. And you two can be together most of that time. Cam says you'll sign one more contract, then retire."

"Probably."

"And then what will you do?"

"I guess I won't have to do anything."

Tamara ignored that. "A wise old man—my grandpa MacDonald—told me the secret of happiness is work that you love to do and that's good when it's done. Faith can have that. And should have it."

"And I should have less of her?"

"Yes. Temporarily."

"Why?"

"Because less for you means more for her and more for her will mean more for both of you—eventually."

"I was with you right up to 'eventually.' "

We were interrupted by Caitlin Carter running into the kitchen. "Hi, Mr. Savard. Did you see Lindsey's trophy?" Caitlin said as she brandished a small trophy, a metal statue of a goalie screwed onto a wooden stand. A brass plate on the stand read: "First-Team All-Star—Greater Boston Girls Hockey League."

"No. I didn't. And I haven't seen you in a long time," I said, picking up Caitlin under the arms. "Are you going to be a goalie too?"

"No. That's no fun. I scored a goal on Lindsey."

"You did. When?"

"Saturday. I shot a tennis ball into the fireplace."

"Smelled great when it burned," Tamara said.

"It wouldn't have burned up if Lindsey saved it," Caitlin said. "Put me down. I'm hungry. I want lunch."

"Caitlin, that's no way to ask," Tamara said.

"I want lunch PLEEEEEESE," Caitlin said with mocking insincerity. "Mr. Savard, did you know Daddy had a fight with Mr. Quigley? . . . POW . . . BAM," Caitlin said, thowing a left and a right into the air.

"That's enough, Cait," Cam said, lumbering into the kitchen and sitting down at the table.

"So what was the big confab with Packy about, JP?"

I told Cam that from now on Rinky and I would be alternating in goal and that I thought the move was ordered by the Mad Hatter.

"That's his MO," Cam said. "He risks screwing up team

chemistry and losing a number one goalie to free agency for the sake of saving a few more dollars under the salary cap and then getting his kickback on what he saves. Makes me glad I'm getting out of the business."

I said that with the playoffs a month away there probably wasn't enough time for me to win back the job. Not unless Rinky had a total collapse, and that wasn't going to happen the way we'd been playing lately. And I didn't really want it to happen. Montreal goalie Claude Rancourt's knee injury in the All-Star Game had put him out for the season. Without him the Canadiens had lost six of their last seven games. We were only four points behind them with nine games to play, and two of those games were with Montreal. We could still win the division and have home-ice advantage in the playoffs.

"So screw it. Don't sign. Go free agency. You'll have so many offers, Denny won't be able to answer the phone fast enough," Cam said.

"With Faith in Vermont I don't want to play in any other city. A trade or free agency will put us farther apart."

"The only way out is to play your butt off, JP. Make it impossible for Packy not to play you. Or for the Hatter to let you walk."

"Yeah. The only way out is through. Been that way since I was seven years old." I thanked Tamara for letting me rant about Faith's decision. "What you said makes more sense than what anyone else has said," I told Tam. "I'm beginning to think you're right. I should look beyond the next game for once in my life." I told Cam and Tamara that I had to get going. "Faith's coming over for dinner and discussion number five thousand nine hundred and twenty-seven about what we're going to do. Or not do."

Cam grabbed a tablespoon, held it in front of me as if it were a microphone, and asked, "And what's your position on that question, Senator?"

"I plan to march under the Arc de Capitulation," I said. "I don't like her decision but I love her."

"That's the spirit, JP. Unconditional surrender. The greatest aphrodisiac in the world."

"I need all my fighting spirit for the rink," I said.

"Mr. Savard, you get in front of the fireplace and I'll try to score on you," Caitlin said.

"No thanks, Cait. It's been a bad enough day."

"You can use the shovel for a stick."

"OK. You get one shot."

I grabbed the small brass coal shovel from a rack of fireplace tools and crouched in front of the open iron grate while Caitlin grabbed her sawed-off hockey stick and a lemon yellow tennis ball. Caitlin pushed the ball to within ten feet of me, pulled her stick back to shoulder height, and brought it down on the ball. The shot came in about a foot off the carpet. I kicked it out with my right leg. Easy save, I was about to say until the ball hit the leg of an armchair and bounced back at me, past my flailing shovel and into the cold ashes of the fireplace.

"Goal! That counts!" yelled Caitlin, putting her stick in the air and high-stepping around the living room like the actor who played Mike Eruzione in *Miracle*.

Tamara buried her face in her hands to hide her laughter.

"You got scored on by a chair, JP," Cam said.

"Been that kind of day," I said to Cam, handing him the shovel and heading for the door.

There were two messages for me when I got home. One from Faith saying she'd be over at six. The other from Nan O'Brien asking me to call her at the Catholic Charities office before 5:30. It was only 3:30 so I phoned Nan.

"It's about Kevin, Jean Pierre," she said. "He finally got around to telling me the whole story about the fight at practice. I'm glad someone besides me knows what Kevin's been going through."

"He almost went through the side of Cam Carter's face," I said. "Cam's the hero in this one, Nancy."

"I've already thanked Cam," Nan said. "I don't think that sort of treatment is listed in the therapeutic manuals but I have to say it worked. Kevin's talking openly and with less pain than he has since Christmas."

"Kev's better at handing out pain," I said. "What happened anyway?"

"Catholic Charities used to handle more adoptions than any agency in New England," Nan said. "The woman who's now my supervisor was the case worker on the Quigley adoption. When she heard Kevin and I were . . . um . . . dating she told me she was pretty sure Kevin didn't know he was adopted."

"Why'd you tell him? Isn't that a violation of some sort of rules you people have?"

"Truth trumps rules, JP. Kevin was in a bad situation. His adoptive father turned abusive and that abuse went on for a long time."

"Until Kevin laid him out," I said.

"There were a lot of bad years before that," Nan said. "But what really hurt Kevin is that I also found out his birth mother is dead so he has no chance of ever seeing her or talking to her. He felt rejected. Unwanted both by her and by the family who took him in. I met Kevin's so-called parents and I can see why he'd feel that way. But he's better now."

"Had to be a bitch for Kev to be lugging that around for the last couple of months."

"When these things come out they tend to come out in tidal waves. It won't last long. He's on his way to being rid of it. Well, mostly rid of it."

"Cam and I have him covered," I said. "God knows he's watched our backs long enough."

"Thanks, JP. Oh, the other reason I called—nice save."

I laughed and hung up.

I stretched out on the couch and thought about where I was in life. Rinky Higgins was pushing me. I'd push back. Maybe I'd win back my job. I probably would. This time. But what about the next time? Maybe Rinky would ask for a trade to a team where he could be the main goalie. But then our team would bring up Kent Wilson or wheel in some other guy to push me. I've seen too many guys stay too long. It's ugly. First you alternate starts. Then the other guy gets the big games. Then one day they send you down but they don't call it that. They say, "We just want you to get more playing time in Providence" . . . or Wilkes-Barre or Binghamton or wherever. And then they might call you back, but more likely they forget you. The next thing you know you're thirty-eight years old and alternating with a teenager. Then some AHL GM is telling you they're sending you down to the ECHL but "just so you can get more playing time." I remember Gumper Dreesen, the other goalie in Providence during my season in the AHL. Dreesen was thirty-seven and barely hanging on. They sent him down to the ECHL a few days before Christmas. I lost track of him until five years later when *Sports Illustrated* did a big feature on hockey among the Cajuns of southern Louisiana. A photo captioned "Win One for the Gumper" showed forty-two-year-old Gumper Dreesen playing for the Bossier-Shreveport Mudbugs of the Western Pro League, which is about as far from the NHL as Neptune. By then Gumper was divorced and living in a trailer park with his dog, Five Hole.

I called Denny Moran to tell him that if it helped his bargaining position I didn't need a four- or five-year deal. I figured I'd get what I could for three years, then call it a career. Go out on my own terms, or something reasonably close to my own terms. Of course, Denny wasn't in his office, because he was in Maine servicing Carter & Peabody's account with the Maine State Employees Association. I wondered what else he was servicing. I could've reached him on his cell phone but instead I asked his secretary to flip me over to Denny's voice mail. I left a message, then stretched out on the couch again for what I thought would be a short nap, but I didn't wake up until six o'clock when I heard Faith coming up the stairs. "Can I tell you about our specials, sir?" she said, bursting through the door with a bag of groceries.

"Pasta carbonara," she said, putting the bag on the kitchen table and hanging up her coat. "We got your pancetta, your olive oil, your parmigiana, a little Romano, a few eggs, a little cream . . . a heart attack in a bowl except for . . . THIS," she said, lifting a bottle of pricey Barolo wine out of a paper bag. "It's the wine that'll keep you heart-healthy, Jean Pierre. Trust me. I'm a doctor. Bar's open. Get you something? A little eye-opener? You look like you need one."

"Earl Grey tea with honey," I said, sitting up on the couch and rubbing my eyes.

Faith nuked a cup of tea and set it down on the coffee table.

"Sit down for a sec before you start the great experiment in arteriosclerosis," I said, patting the couch beside me.

"What up?" she said sitting down.

I took a sip of tea, put down the cup, took Faith's hand, and said, "We'll have a nicer evening if you know right now I'm with you on this Vermont move. It's the best thing for you. Someday it'll be the best thing for us. I still like what I do. But I know I can't do it much longer. It's time to think about something besides the next practice, the next trip, the next game. I love you, Faith."

Then Faith McNeil did something I'd never seen her do. She took her hand out of mine, put both hands to her face. And cried.

"Jeez. First Quig, now you. What happened to all the hard guys?" I said.

She choked out a "Thank you, Jean Pierre," followed by a sentence that sounded like it was caught in a run-down between laughter and tears; "I haven't cried since we lost to that bitch Hazel Anne Worthington in the states." She slid the napkin out from between my teacup and saucer and dried her eyes with it. "What made you change your mind?"

"A lot of things. Age maybe. It's not so simple. But I talked it over with Tamara today. I think she told me what I already knew. It's time to start thinking beyond the next shot. Sometimes I wonder if anyone can teach us anything we don't already know. That's enough. We can talk about the rest later. And, ah, maybe the rest should include picking out a diamond."

"You're supposed to surprise me, not tell me."

"I was afraid I might pick out something you wouldn't like."

"You know, JP, I've always wondered how you can play hockey with so much confidence and not have the same confidence about . . . well, about almost anything."

"Maybe because I haven't done anything besides play. It's the only thing anyone ever told me I'm good at."

"I know one other thing you're good at," she said, walking over to the living-room window and closing the drapes on the gold-and-gray remains of a late-winter sunset.

"What happened to the pasta carbonara?"

"The chef is substituting a new special," Faith said, stepping out of her skirt and laying it across the back of a chair.

"Let's not wreck the couch," I said, taking her hand and leading her to my bedroom. Our lovemaking lately had been mechanical. It was just sex really. Basic maintenance. But that night began better, as much communion as sex. My years of conscientious field work have established that the simultaneous orgasm is about as rare as a truthful NHL general manager. So I've always been a ladies-first guy. But after one of the best starts in the history of foreplay, Faith became strangely detached.

"What's the matter?" I said.

"You go ahead, Jean Pierre. It's OK."

"No. What's wrong?"

"I think I'm too happy," she said.

"We can stop for a while. . . ."

"No. You go ahead. I want you to."

And so I lost myself in Faith McNeil while she kept saying "thank you" and I kept saying her name, neither of us seeing beyond the moment, or around the corner.

Nine

It was grisly. We were playing the Rangers in a matinee—our last home game before a four-game trip. Late in the game Taki tore into the New York zone at full tilt. He cut around a defenseman and pushed hard to the net, then he lost an edge and crashed skates-first into the boards. You could hear the bone break.

Taki lay on the ice a long time before the EMTs took him off on a stretcher. The trainers told me that when they got Taki in the ambulance, cut away his game sock, and took off his shin pad, they saw a piece of bone sticking through the skin below his knee. He was done for the season and maybe for all seasons.

Our first concern was for Taki, but buried under that was the unsettling knowledge that he was our team's second-leading scorer and 20 percent of our offense. Without him and with Gaston playing with bruised ribs we were a one-line team. And one-line teams are toast in the playoffs. With three days before the NHL trade deadline we knew Madison Hattigan would have to swing a deal for a scorer. Either that or we could all call our country clubs and book tee times.

"There's no goddamn distinction in potential," Cam's father says. He means that as pros Cam and I are judged only on what we do—not what we want to do, could do, ought to do, or used to do. That's what makes pro sports such a cold business, and it's one of the reasons players get nervous as the trade deadline approaches. That deadline was only two days away when Cam picked me up for the ride to the airport and the start of a week-long trip with games against Buffalo, Florida, Tampa Bay, and Carolina.

"Who do you think the Hatter will deal?" he asked as the Buick idled in traffic.

I said Rex Conway, who hadn't been scoring lately.

"We'll have to give up more than Rex to replace Taki," Cam said. "It's gotta be a big deal, JP. Either that or our season's over."

I knew Cam was safe because he'd already announced he'd retire at the end of the season. The more I thought about it the more I worried about myself. A lot of teams like to rent players for the postseason. That is, find a guy like me who's at the end of his contract, trade for him, and have to pay him for only three or four months. After that they can re-sign him or let him become a free agent. The risk to the team is minimal. And a lot of teams would like an experienced goalie in the postseason. "Maybe I'm not so safe," I said.

"Naw. You're OK. The only team that needs a goalie is Montreal and teams in the same division almost never trade with each other. But we're going to lose someone," Cam said.

Every player hates the thought of losing a teammate and friend because of a trade. Every trade is an ugly reminder of how little control we have over our life.

Most of the guys were milling around in a private lounge near the boarding gate when Cam and I arrived. As we walked in I saw the woman behind the desk reach for the handheld microphone, and I thought we were about to get the first early boarding call in the history of U.S. domestic aviation. But what came over the public address in that phony-polite Stepford Wives dis-embodied techno voice you hear at airports and on recorded messages was:

"Your attention please. Will passenger Jean Pierre Savard go to the nearest airline courtesy desk. . . . Passenger Jean Pierre Savard, please go to the nearest courtesy desk."

"Excuse me," I said to Cam as I started toward the woman behind the counter in the back of the lounge.

"Maybe it's Denny. Maybe you've got your deal," Cam said. "Hope so."

I hoped so too. But some instinct made me fear the call.

The lady behind the counter handed me the phone.

It was Madison Hattigan. "You really oughtta buy a cell phone, JP."

"We're getting ready to board here," I said in a tone I hoped told the Mad Hatter I didn't want to chitchat.

"Look, Jean Pierre. I wanted you to hear it from me first. We've traded you. We had to. . . . It's to Montreal. We needed a scorer. They needed a goalie."

I felt sick. Helpless. I looked for a chair but there wasn't one nearby so I leaned on the counter, my head down and my stom-ach turning. The rest of Hattigan's message was just bits and pieces of information coming through my ear into a mind so stunned it could barely comprehend. Hattigan was telling me that the Canadiens had sent Henri Brisette, a proven forty-goal scorer, plus a future first-round draft choice to Boston for me. ". . . and, frankly, we feel Reginald is ready to step up and if we don't give him a chance we're going to lose him. I'm the one who's going to take the heat on this thing, JP. You were a popu-lar guy here, and a great player. Listen, the best thing you can do is call Jean Picard as soon as you can." Hattigan gave me the Montreal coach's phone number. I scribbled the number on my boarding pass. I was too shocked to say anything.

"Jean Pierre? You still there?"

"Not for long," I said, and put down the phone.

Cam was standing behind me. I think he'd figured out what happened from my reaction.

"I've been traded," I said. "Montreal."

"Jesus Christ Almighty, JP, I'm sorry." Somewhere in the background the Stepford Wife was making the boarding call. Across the lounge a line of players and coaches shuffled toward the boarding concourse. "I guess you're the only guy I get to say good-bye to," I told Cam as Flipside Palmer, the last guy in line, disappeared into the walkway leading to the plane.

"Gentlemen, we're boarding your flight," the lady behind the counter said to Cam and me.

"I gotta go, JP. I'll call you tonight. Bitch of a business. I remember when it used to be a game. Hey, you want to take the car?" Cam said, fishing in his pocket for his keys.

I said I'd take a cab. Cam boarded the flight. I stood in the lounge holding my garment bag.

"Sir, you're not boarding?" the Stepford Wife asked me. I said no and walked away adrift in a miasma of humiliation, isolation, rejection, abandonment, anger, confusion, helplessness, self-pity, and fear of the unknown.

On the cab ride home I couldn't even think about Montreal. All I could think about was my being ripped away from teammates and friends, some I'd known for ten years. I wasn't even going to get a chance to go around the dressing room and say good-bye, to go out the classy way I'd seen other guys go out. Ten years, nine hundred and some-odd games, thousands of flights, bus rides, parties, and dinners with guys I felt closer to than to anyone except Faith and my mother. All ripped away in a two-minute phone call. I figured Cam would tell the team on the plane. I wondered what they'd think. What they'd say. I knew how Rinky would feel. The same way I felt when I was a rookie and the team dumped Harry "Head Case" Harrington and I knew I was in the Show. I didn't blame Rinky nor was I resentful of him. Four, five, maybe six seasons from now the same thing would happen to him and, later, to whoever replaced him.

We're all in the game's food chain, all part of an endless cycle of consumption. And in the end we all wear the spoked D—Dump City.

I heard the trunk lid pop as the cabbie pulled up to my condo. I put the fare and a $10 tip through the tiny door in that annoying protective plastic barrier separating the cab's front and back seats. The bulletproof shield reminded me there are lots of jobs more dangerous and demanding, and less lucrative, than playing hockey.

I figured Faith had already left for her meeting at school so I planned on leaving a message on her phone. I wanted her to hear the news from me before it broke on TV or radio. Then I'd call Denny Moran, my mother, and maybe Jean Picard in Montreal.

But Faith was just coming out the front door as I walked up the stairs with my suitcase. "What are you doing home? You look awful. Are you sick?" she said.

"Worse. I got traded."

"Oh my God. Where?"

"Montreal."

Faith held the door for me, then went to the phone and canceled her meeting. "Tell me about it," she said. She didn't seem as upset as I'd expected her to be. Or maybe as I'd hoped she'd be.

I told her how Hattigan called me at the airport just as the flight was boarding. "What it comes down to is that Montreal was desperate for a goaltender and Boston was desperate for a scorer. No other teams would trade with them so they traded with each other. The Canadiens are only obligated to pay me the rest of the contract I had with Boston. After that I can re-sign with them—if they make an offer—or I can become an unrestricted free agent."

"Do you think they'll make an offer?"

"Yes, if Claude is finished."

"Good."

"Why good?"

"Because you don't have to be Henry the Navigator to see that

Montreal is about a ninety-minute drive from Burlington, Vermont. We'll be closer with you in Montreal than if you were in Boston. This must be what my grandfather meant when he said, 'You never know when you might be getting a break.' "

"Your grandfather ever get traded?"

"There wasn't a big market for Cambridge city workers who booked baseball and boxing bets on the side," she said. "Look, all I'm saying is that this deal might not be as bad as it feels now. And you don't have to go. You can quit today if you want to."

"And then what?"

"Well . . . I don't mean to kick you when you're down, Jean Pierre, but that's a question I've asked you before. What next?"

"I'll call my mother, Denny Moran, and the Canadiens," I said.

"That's not what I mean."

"I know."

I phoned my mother, who, like Faith, didn't seem as upset as I'd thought she'd be. "It will all work out for the best, Jean Pierre. It always has. I think God has a plan for you," she said, tumbling back into the net of Catholicism that had broken so many of life's falls for her.

"If God's plan is to make me sick, lonely, pissed off, publicly humiliated, and unhappy He's doing a helluva job," I said.

"Stop feeling sorry for yourself."

"I'll call Denny and he can feel sorry for both of us," I said.

"He's not in his office. He's at the Portland Marriott," she said.

I almost asked her how she knew what hotel my agent was in but then I thought better of it. There was a new lilt in my mother's voice since she'd started seeing Denny. I was happy for her.

"Montreal will want to keep you, JP," Denny said. "I hear Rancourt's all done so they'll have his slot under the salary cap. And their GM, Lou St. Martin, will be a lot easier to deal with than Hattigan. The money will be about the same as in Boston.

It's only a question of how many years you want to play. I think we could get four. Maybe five."

"No. I don't want to play more than three, Denny. Make it two if that'll push up the salary and make-able bonuses."

"How about we make it two years and a hundred hours of community service. Christ, JP, you're the only guy I know who can make earning three million for nine months' work sound like a prison sentence."

"Talk to Sweet Lou and keep me up to speed. I have to call Picard."

"One more thing, JP."

"What?"

"Does your mother like sushi?"

I hung up on Denny and phoned Jean Picard, who said his club needed me "as soon as that Ferrari you drive can get you here. Tomorrow?"

"Tomorrow afternoon," I said. "I can practice Friday and play Saturday if you need me."

Picard said they needed me and that they'd reserved a suite for me at the Queen Elizabeth.

I hung up, turned to Faith, and said: "A free suite, minibar, cable TV, and twenty-four-hour room service. This would be a great job if it wasn't for the puck."

By now the city's two all-sports radio stations had broken news of the trade and my phone was ringing incessantly. I took a call from Lynne Abbott and gave her the usual vanilla quotes about a trade: "I'll miss Boston . . . thank the fans for me . . . a door closes, a door opens . . . blah, blah, blah." None of it said how I really felt, which was awful.

"Either we shut off the phone or we get out of here," Faith said.

We walked the length of Newbury Street to Sonsie, where the diners Faith referred to as "louche Euro-trash" wouldn't recognize a hockey player from a pile of eggs Benedict.

"I have to leave in the morning," I said.

"I want to come with you. We can split the driving. I'll fly back Monday."

"Thanks. It'll help if you're there."

We got back to my place to find my old-fashioned answering machine maxed out on messages, the best of which was from Cam's father:

"I just heard the news, JP. I'm so goddamn mad I might call Gabe Vogel and buy his goddamn team just so I can send that goddamn Hattigan scouting in the Ukraine. If you don't feel like putting up with this bullshit you can have a job with me. And next home game I'm having a lease-breaking party in our corporate suite. Fill that thing with so many drunks and hookers it'll look like Forty-second Street."

"You know it's really an option, JP," Faith said. "Why not take a job with Cam's dad and end this right now?"

"Because I could never figure out how to play the angles in a business meeting. I'm a professional player. A professional is an amateur who didn't quit."

We took Boss Scags and left early. Faith did most of the driving, which meant we were in Montreal in time for lunch, after which Faith went back to the hotel and I walked to the Bell Centre to meet Jean Picard.

"Jean Pierre. Bonjour. Hello. Welcome to Montreal," the coach said, rising from behind a desk the size and shape of Manitoba. Picard looked like one of those older male models you see in upscale men's magazines: salt-and-pepper hair perfectly parted, navy blue pin-striped suit and a white shirt with French cuffs held together with small gold monogrammed links, an almost dainty counterpoint to his massive gold Breguet watch. It struck me that Picard had traveled a long and prosperous road from the scrappy hatchet-faced left wing he'd been in his twelve seasons playing for the Canadiens to his current position as coach of one of the most distinguished sports franchises in the world.

Picard asked me if I liked to know ahead of time if I was starting. It was the first time a coach ever asked me that. Knowing days ahead that I'm going to start makes me nervous, I told him. "But I'd rather be nervous than surprised. I can program anxiety."

"Well, you're playing Saturday against Toronto. And probably most of the games we have left. Including the first one against Boston. And the second one if we haven't clinched the division."

He told me he was sure Claude Rancourt's career was over and said I was their guy for the rest of the season "and I hope many seasons to come. We have a good chance at the Cup, Jean Pierre. And, believe me, in Montreal winning the division or the conference means nothing. This team is measured by how many Cups we win. I think it's like playing for the New York Yankees. But it has been a long time for us. Much too long."

The Canadiens last won the Cup in 1993 when they had the great Patrick Roy in goal. The club's twenty-four championships is an NHL record, but, as Picard said, "We won most of those in a six-team or twelve-team league. Now there are thirty teams. Much harder. And I'll warn you, the media coverage of us is like nothing you've ever seen. We've scheduled a press conference for you tomorrow morning at ten. Before practice. Get it over with, eh?"

I told Picard I didn't mind talking to the media.

We talked for a few more minutes, then Picard got up to walk me to the elevator. As I turned toward the door I saw what I think is the most revealing hockey photograph ever taken, even more dramatic than the Bobby Orr picture. The old black-and-white photo hanging on Jean Picard's office wall was taken April 8, 1952, in the Montreal Forum after the Canadiens eliminated Boston in the seventh game of a Stanley Cup semifinal. The picture shows Boston goalie Sugar Jim Henry, his right eye blackened and nose broken, bowing slightly as he shakes hands with the Canadiens Rocket Richard, who has blood streaming down his cheek onto his game shirt from the sloppily bandaged cut above his left eye. Richard suffered a concussion in the first period of that game. The team doctor stitched the cut but could do nothing about the concussion that kept Richard lying on the trainer's table until the game was almost over. Late in the third period with the score tied 1–1 Richard returned to the Montreal bench, where he asked teammate Elmer Lach the score because Richard couldn't focus his eyes on the scoreboard. With three and a half minutes to play, Richard jumped onto the ice on a line change, took a pass from defenseman Butch Bouchard, outskated two Boston back-checkers, beat both defensemen, and sent an ankle-high shot past Jim Henry. That goal won the game and clinched the series. Minutes after the photographer caught the battered Richard and Henry shaking hands, Richard went to the Canadiens dressing room, and—just as Richard's father entered the room to congratulate his son—the Rocket began sobbing uncontrollably, went into convulsions, and had to be sedated.

"He was on fire all the time, the Rocket," Picard said when he saw me staring at the photo that captures the dignity, chivalry, violence, and bravura of our game as does no other.

"Makes me proud to be a hockey player," I said.

Picard ushered me through the door and past two secretaries who could have been podium finishers in a Charlize Theron look-alike contest.

"Oh, one more thing. You can't have jersey number one. It was Jacques Plante's number. We retired it."

I asked Picard for number 31. Faith McNeil's number.

I got back to the hotel to receive a blizzard of phone calls, most from my ex-teammates.

Taki Yamamura relayed a message from Su. "She says skip the Montreal Ballet. They bump into each other."

Bruno Govoni said: "Christ, JP. Some guys have all the luck.

Montreal. Strip Club City. There's clubs there that have more stages than Wells Fargo and more poles than Warsaw."

Flipside called to say he was burning me a "Jean Pierre Savard Trade-to-Montreal" theme album. He was pretty sure Ray Charles's "Hit the Road, Jack," Tom Petty and the Heartbreakers' "Don't Come Around Here No More," Steam's "Nah Nah Hey Hey Goodbye," the Beatles' "Ticket to Ride," and the Alkaline Trio's "Fuck You Aurora" will be on it. "It'll be sort of a sentimental thing, probably make you cry," Flipper said.

"Let's go out to dinner and I'll tell you about hockey in Montreal," I said to Faith.

"I hear it's like soccer in Brazil."

"Bigger than that."

The phone rang again just as we were leaving. Faith answered it and I'm sure was ready to tell the caller I wasn't in. But the caller was Marco Indinacci and Faith knew I'd want to talk to my old college coach.

"Jeez, JP, I'm sorry about the trade. Hattigan's got to be crazy. No one trades a goaltender to a division rival."

"Hockey is still most goals wins, Marco. Boston was desperate to replace Taki. Montreal was desperate for a goalie. It's business."

"Well if you ever get tired of being in a business where you get jerked around, I've got an option for you. I'm retiring after next season. Twenty-five years. It's enough. I'm looking to hire an associate coach who'll step up to head coach when I leave. You've got first refusal."

"Thanks, Marco. I appreciate your thinking of me, but I couldn't step down to that kind of money. I mean—"

A suddenly angry Marco Indinacci cut me off. "Step DOWN? Did you say DOWN? Hey, ace, I didn't know big-shot NHLers were spending their time working with kids. I guess you must be busy curing cancer and straightening out the Middle East on your off days, eh?"

"I'm sorry, Marco," I said, embarrassed at the insulting

implication of what I'd said. "I didn't mean it that way. I apologize. I know what you did for me, and for a lot of other guys. All I meant was that a couple or three more years in the Show and I can do anything I want."

"And what's that, ace?"

"I don't know, Marco. I'll figure it out when I get there."

"Well, I just thought if you came here I'd get an assistant, a successor, and a goalie coach all in one package. And let me tell ya, Rudy Evanston needs a goalie coach. His last six games were brutal. He's staying with us as a fifth-year senior next season, and frankly, it's because no pro team wants him."

"I appreciate your thinking of me, Coach. Really. Maybe if it were three years from now I'd jump at it. My girlfriend's a doctor. She'll be doing her internship at Lake Champlain Med Center."

"I know. Cam told me. That's why I thought I'd have a chance. Guess I didn't factor in the step-down angle. Wouldn't want an NHLer slumming it, ace."

I apologized again. I'd really stung the guy. And I'd violated one of my mother's rules of good manners: "A lady or gentleman never hurts anyone by accident."

"Well, good luck up there, JP. Hope it works out for you."

"Thanks again, Marco. Nice of you to call. I've been a little mixed up for the last couple of days," I said, but by then Indinacci had hung up.

We took a cab to Les Remparts in the predominantly French east side of the city. At dinner Faith asked me if I'd be distracted knowing my father was going to be at the games.

"I can block out anything once they drop the puck. I'll shut down my heart if I have to."

"You really hate him, don't you?"

"With good reason."

"No doubt about that. Do you think you'll ever let it go? I mean what he did. Or in your case didn't do?"

"No. I can't."

"You can. But you choose not to," Faith said.

I didn't have an answer for that. For the rest of the meal we talked about the logistics of my move to Montreal, of Faith's move to Burlington, of cars, insurance, the sale of our homes, and all the little things that can suck the life out of a love affair.

The press conference was easier than I'd expected. I had a little fun with a young reporter from *La Presse Canadienne*. The kid asked if my goaltending style was butterfly or stand-up. "It's a combination. I call it the butter-up," I said. There were a few snickers throughout the room. But, sure enough, my so-called butter-up style appeared in several of the next day's papers.

Practice was short and up-tempo with a lot of skating and puck movement and a few hundred shots for me. I felt good playing goal again, feeling the dull thud of pucks off of my leg pads, the *thwack* as they hit the broad blade of my stick, and the sharp tug as it disappeared into the webbing of my glove. Being in goal gave me a sense of control. Even the sweat and fatigue felt good. And there were no headhunters on the Canadiens. Nobody blasting close-in shots up high the way Rex Conway would sometimes do in Boston. Or at least the way he did until a few years ago when he hit me on the side of the helmet when I wasn't even looking. I threw my goal stick at his head and chased him around the rink. I've heard of goalies getting in fights with headhunters. When a reporter for the *Hockey News* asked me what I'd do if I were NHL commissioner for a day I said that any idiot who goes head hunting in practice should have to play goal for fifteen minutes.

Tim Harcourt told me that Picard gradually reduced the length of practice as the season wore on. "We come here, skate hard for maybe forty-five minutes, and we're done. This is a good place to play. As long as we win," he said. Tim also told me that the buzz among Montreal players and front-office people was that Madison Hattigan's job with the Bruins was on the line. Few GMs ever make a major trade within their own division, because that GM is toast if the guy he traded comes back to beat him. "If we beat Boston in the playoffs Hattigan is archives," Tim said.

Tim and a couple of other players invited me to lunch after practice but I told them I had to do some shopping for Faith.

"Your wife?" Tim said.

"Girlfriend," I said.

"Plenty of those in Montreal," he said. "No need to import."

Arriving at the hotel, I ducked into one of those expensive boutiques on the first floor, made a purchase, then took the elevator to my room.

I gave Faith the diamond ring a few hours later during dinner at Les Halles on Crescent Street. "This is for you, whether we get married or not," I said. "But I hope we do."

"Jean Pierre Lucien Savard, that's an odd way of asking me to marry you."

"Will you marry me?"

"Yes. Of course. Thank you." Faith was never one for gushy scenes but when she slipped the ring on her finger she spontaneously held it up to the view of the young couple dining at the table next to ours. I guess they'd had a few drinks, because they immediately raised their wineglasses to us, and the woman, laughing, took Faith's hand and held it up for the entire restaurant to see. This set off a sudden joyful commotion as other diners broke into applause and toasts. A smiling Faith was the center of attention until a man at a nearby table recognized me. "Hey, J. P. Savard. *Bienvenue au* Montreal," he said, pointing to me and setting off another round of cheering. The maître d' sent a split of champagne to our table. "To love and hockey," I said, clinking my glass against Faith's.

"Love I understand," Faith said, setting her glass on the table. "But hockey?"

"The game brings people together," I said. "Very important."

"Why?"

"Because everyone is lonely."

Back at the hotel we slipped into those white Turkish towel robes with the Fairmont Hotels logo. I don't know what it is about those robes—maybe the easy access they offer—but it wasn't long before we were making love as we had on that autumn Sunday at Faith's house so many months ago.

The digital clock read 2:11 a.m. when I woke up. Faith was asleep on her stomach. I starting rubbing the small of her back as I felt my need for her rising again.

"Ernie Banks," Faith murmurred out of a half sleep.

"Huh?"

"Let's play two," she said, repeating the mantra of the old Chicago Cubs infielder as she turned over and slipped her arms around me. Faith is a gamer.

I don't think my trade to Montreal truly hit home until our Saturday-morning game-day skate. There, hanging in my locker, was the *bleu, blanc, rouge* Montreal Canadiens game shirt with the number 31 on the back and sleeves and "SAVARD" sewn onto the back above the number. It's the most storied uniform in the history of hockey and one of the most respected in the world of sport. My grandmother would have liked to see me in this jersey, I thought as I pulled it on over my chest and arm protector.

I don't usually think a lot at practice. I find it best to let my body react instinctively with the moves so long embedded in muscle memory. But as I skated to the Montreal goal for the first time I couldn't help but think that I was the latest link in a chain of Canadiens goalies stretching from me to Patrick Roy, Ken Dryden, Jacques Plante, Gerry McNeil . . . all the way back to George Hainsworth and Georges Vezina. It's an honor to play goal for Club de Hockey Canadien. Which is all the more reason I shouldn't have tossed my shirt toward the laundry cart after practice. I missed. The sweaty shirt hit the side of the cart and fell to the floor, where a tall silver-haired gentleman in a dark impeccably tailored suit picked it up and walked over to where I was sitting. "We don't do that here, Jean Pierre. Our colors don't hit the floor," the man said, taking my shirt and placing it on a hanger in my locker, then brushing the CH logo with his hand as if to knock off any dirt it may have picked up. The man introduced himself but he didn't have to. He was Jean Provost, a team vice president but, a generation ago, the first-line center and captain of the Canadiens. He helped Montreal win ten Stanley Cups and, since Rocket Richard's death, had become the public persona of the Canadiens—Gallicly elegant in his dress and deportment, seethingly passionate in his love for the game and the team.

"You got off easy," Tim Harcourt told me after Provost left. "The old-timers tell me that when Big Jean was in his first year as captain a rookie took off his game shirt and dropped it on the floor. Jean grabbed the kid around the throat. Took four or five guys to pull him off."

When I came out of the shower Louis St. Martin, the team's GM, was waiting by my locker. "Welcome to Montreal, Jean Pierre. Come upstairs for a minute when you're through," he said. "But before you get out of here I am sure a lot of reporters will want to know the intricacies of, what did you call it? The butter-up style of goaltending."

Twenty minutes and a dozen media questions later, St. Martin and I sat in overstuffed chairs pulled up to a glass coffee table in an office big enough to have its own area code. "Your father is one of our luxury suite owners. You know this?" St. Martin said.

"You know my father?"

"I know all our corporate partners," he said. "And I should tell you I'm the one who let him pass through security when he talked to you a few weeks ago."

I didn't know what St. Martin was probing for so I went for the conversational delay of game. "OK. It's your building."

"He told me the whole story. Said he wanted to tell you he was sorry. Which, by the way, I know he is."

"Sorry finished out of the money," I said.

"I understand. I only want you to know that I don't think he will try to see you again. And if he does it will not be with my help."

"He won't be a distraction to me, if that's what you're asking," I said.

"I suppose it is. Or was. We need you, Jean Pierre. We could win the whole thing. Again. For the twenty-fifth time."

"You won't even win tonight if I don't get lunch and a nap," I said, getting up to leave.

I ate toast and soup for lunch and tried to nap, something I'm usually good at. But I was troubled by Lou St. Martin's bringing me one degree of separation from my father. Too close. I tossed and turned for an hour before finally falling asleep at about 3:30, a half hour before I'd told Faith to wake me up, which she did by putting her cold hand down my Tommy Hilfiger boxers.

"Hey, I have a game tonight . . . and not THAT kind of game," I said, removing her hand.

"Have a good sleep?" she asked.

"Not enough. Doesn't matter. I like to be a little logy when I get to the rink. The nerves kick in fast enough."

We were playing the Toronto Maple Leafs and the game would be televised on *Hockey Night in Canada,* the most popular television program in Canadian history. In homes across the country the Saturday-night national telecast of a hockey game turns a TV set into a kind of a family hearth with sometimes two and three generations gathering to watch. And when the matchup is Montreal-Toronto the game takes on undertones people don't like to talk about. "To be blunt," I told Faith, "Montreal versus Toronto is French versus English; Catholic versus Protestant; working class versus ruling class. That's oversimplified and is less true now than it was a generation ago. But it's still more true than false."

"You make it sound like the Crusades," she said.

"Nah. Way more important."

I got to the rink at five o'clock, three hours before game time. Besides Tim Harcourt I also knew Tim's defensive partner Reggie Harper, first-line center Joe Latendresse, and a couple of other guys I'd met at Serge Balon's golf tournament. Latendresse was with Boston five seasons ago. The Mad Hatter traded him on the day Joe and his wife, Renee, closed on a house. I'd introduced myself to the rest of the guys at practice. It's easy for a traded player to go into a city and have twenty ready-made friends. The burden of a trade falls on wives, girlfriends, and children, who enter their new neighborhoods and schools as strangers. There are huge rewards that come with making it to the NHL. But there's a big price, too. It starts with our parents driving us to frigid rinks on frigid mornings. And, for a pro player with a family, the price can include a scared child in a new school and a wife wondering how long it will be before her husband gets traded, sent down, or released and the family has to move again.

"Take 'em out, JP," Picard said as the clock in the dressing room ticked down to game time. I stood up and walked down the curtained runway toward the bright lights beyond. I heard the PA guy begin his announcement *"Bonsoir mesdames et messieurs . . ."* but that was all I heard before I skated into a wall of noise made by twenty-one thousand fans. The TV lights were so bright I could see the marks of skate blades under the newly resurfaced ice and could almost feel the collective stare of the crowd. I kept my head down and skated directly to my net, where I roughed up the crease, using my skates to shave the too-slippery new surface so there would be no sudden slippage of my blades.

The game was a joy. Toronto's Ian Manchester got a break-away in the first minute. He went high to my glove side. My left hand shot up and grabbed the puck. I was peripherally aware of the fans cheering. I'm told they were also standing but I wouldn't know that because I didn't look up. More important than the ovation was that my new team seemed to calm down. Joe Latendresse gave us a 1–0 lead at the end of the first period and we were up 5–0 late in the third when the only question was whether or not I'd hang on for the shutout. I have a theory that a goalie working on a shutout needs one lucky break late in the game. Mine came when a shot broke off of my left pad and spun half over the goal line before a diving Reggie Harper swept it away with his stick.

We won 5–0 and the media voted me first star of the game. The three stars of the game have to stay in the tunnel briefly until being introduced to the crowd, beginning with the number three star. While waiting I glanced up for the first time and saw the out-of-town scoreboard showing that Boston had lost to Florida 6–1. Maybe I should have felt sorry for my old team. But I didn't. In this game friendship lasts, allegiance doesn't. I was a Montreal Canadien now.

I woke up Sunday morning when Faith pulled back the drapes and light flooded our room. She was staring out of the west-facing window. "What's that huge church?"

"Mary Queen of the World Basilica," I said. "Why?"

"I was thinking maybe we could go to Mass. You know, like we did when we were kids."

"You're not throwing your repentent self back into the arms of Mother Church are you?"

"No. It's more of a nostalgia thing. I can't explain it. I'd just like to go to church with you."

I didn't have any excuse not to go because Picard had given the team Sunday off. But I said that if we were going to church we should go to Notre-Dame. "It's a nice day. We can walk there and stop for breakfast on the way back."

We got to Notre-Dame about fifteen minutes before Mass. I told Faith about my fantasy of playing Wiffle ball in the cathedral. I explained all of my rules. This sent her into a giggle fit that lasted most of the way through the Gospel, which was in French so neither of us knew what the priest was saying anyway.

After Mass we walked west along Notre-Dame, then north toward Mont Royal, away from the downtown office buildings and into neighborhoods of elegant old homes. On a shaded side street I saw six kids playing road hockey with a dirty tennis ball. "Got to see this," I said to Faith, and led her down the street.

The boys, all about ten or eleven years old, were talking in French, but every so often I caught a familiar name. "*Le but* Joe Latendresse," a boy in a Canadiens jersey yelled after he'd fired the muddy tennis ball into the netting of one of the small aluminum-framed goals. He held his stick aloft with his left hand and bumped his gloved right fist against the fists of his two teammates as they'd seen NHL players do on TV.

"In the States we called it street hockey. In Canada it's road hockey," I explained to Faith just as a car turned down the small street, forcing the boys to carry both goals out of the way to let the car pass. As soon as the car was gone the boys put the goals back in the middle of the street. The game continued. It was the same game that has been played for a century on streets in Toronto, Winnipeg, Minneapolis, Boston, or anywhere kids love hockey and don't have—or can't afford—the ice to play on. Faith laughed when one of the kids stood in goal, grasping his hockey stick as if it were a goal stick and declaring himself "*le gardien de but—Jean Pierre SAVAARD . . .*"

"In league games we were always ourselves but in street hockey we were our heroes," I said to Faith.

"Who were you?" she asked.

"Patrick Roy," I said.

"Why him?"

"He was a cocky guy. Played with a lot of confidence. I think we pick our heroes because they have something we wish we had." We continued down the street, leaving the hockey game behind us.

As we walked, Faith put her left hand under my right arm and pulled me closer to her. "How many kids are we having?"

"Well, you're Irish and I'm French so . . . let's see, that would mean ten or twelve kids."

She laughed. "I think two would be a good number," she said.

"Yeah. You have three and life is an odd-man rush," I said.

The rest of the day was like one of those soft-focus movie montages where the lovers roam around old Montreal, walking among the columns of Marché Bonsecours, the city's original town hall, now a public market, then climbing to the top of Mont Royal, the hill overlooking the city.

"I was born over there," I said, pointing east in the general direction of the Plateau section of Montreal.

"You want to take a walk there? Find your old home?" Faith said.

"No. I probably couldn't find it. And wouldn't want to even if I could. I just remember it was a dark place."

"I know, Jean Pierre. I know and I'm sorry. But it's over. It was over a long time ago. You won."

I didn't say anything, because I felt a sudden surge of almost primal sadness and was afraid my voice would break. We walked back toward the hotel, stopping for lunch at a restaurant near the Musée de Beaux-Arts. Faith said she'd take a morning flight back to Boston. "I wish you didn't have to leave," I said. I suggested she drive my car to Boston. "I don't need a car in Montreal. And if you don't have to go to the airport then maybe you can stay another half day?"

"Deal," she said, reaching for the lunch check. "You get a free lunch, I get a Ferrari."

"You should be an agent."

"You've got Boston twice this week," she said.

"Thursday there, Saturday here. Even if we split, it should be enough to clinch the division."

The Bruins went 1–3 on their road trip. They were ten points behind us in the standings and thoroughly banged up. Gaston was still playing with bruised ribs, Kevin Quigley was hobbling around on a gimpy ankle, and Rinky Higgins had a bruised catching hand. Picard told us about Rinky's sore hand and told us to blast away with high shots, glove side. Maybe that sounds cruel to some people but it sounded practical to us.

Cam and I snuck out for lunch Wednesday in Boston. We went to a private club his father got us into because neither of us wanted to be seen fraternizing with the so-called enemy the day before a big game.

"Lindsey's grounded," he said.

"For how long?"

"Probably until she goes to college," Cam said. "Tamara's really pissed."

"What happened?"

"The day you got traded Lindsey took her goalie stick and beat the stuffing out of that huge teddy bear my parents gave her for Christmas. Said the bear was Madison Hattigan and she was going to kill him. Beat the shit out of the thing, teddy bear stuffing all over the room. Fucking massacre. Then she called my father and told him to fire Hattigan. Dad had to explain that he couldn't fire Hattigan because he didn't own the team. So Lindsey told him to buy the team. And, you know my father and Linds; he told her he'd think about it."

"I'll call Lindsey. Tell her I'm OK up here. And that Faith and I are engaged and scouting around for flower girls.

"How's Rinky playing?" I said.

"Just well enough to lose. Trading you was stupid. And trading you within our division was beyond stupid. The Boston columnists are all over Hattigan. Lynne Abbott ripped him in her Sunday column. Even called him the Mad Hatter."

"I wish we weren't looking at each other down the gun barrels tomorrow night," I said.

"Me, too. No way we each get our name on the Cup."

"Maybe neither of us will."

"Good luck anyway," Cam said.

"You, too."

We destroyed Boston. Beat them 8–1. Rinky Higgins was on the bench and Kent Wilson was in the Boston goal after the first two periods, which had us leading 6–0. Our first two goals beat Rinky on his glove side.

I lost the shutout to Rex Conway of all goddamn people. I think he one-timed a pass from his Lord and Savior Jesus Christ. Or maybe it was from Flipside Palmer like the PA announcer said.

The win wrapped up the Northeast Division title for us.

Alvin "Captain Baritone" Crouch of TV-8 caught me in the runway after the game. "Tonight's win sets up a big game in Montreal Saturday, J. P. Savard. The Bruins will be desperate."

I had to explain to Captain Baritone and his misinformed viewers that our win put us twelve points up on Boston with only five games to play and that the race was over. Not that he heard or understood a word I said.

"OK, you heard it live on TV-8 from ex-Bruins goalie J. P.

Savard. Our next telecast Saturday night, seven thirty, live from Moan-RAY-ALL," he said.

"EIGHT o'clock," I yelled, hoping Captain Baritone's microphone was still live. I was trying to save a few hundred thousand TV viewers from suffering through an insipid half-hour pregame show.

We chartered back to Montreal after the game, so I got to see Faith only briefly outside the dressing room. She said she'd got the Modern Automotive Grand Slam with the Ferrari—speeding tickets in Quebec, Vermont, New Hampshire, and Massachusetts.

I also saw Denny Moran, who just happened to be with my mother, who just happened to be wearing a couple of gold-and-diamond earrings only slightly less dazzling than the chandeliers in the Copley Plaza. She must have seen me looking at them.

"A birthday gift from Dennis," she said.

"Oh my God, Mom, I'm sorry," I said. In the midst of the trade, the move to Montreal, and my engagement to Faith I'd forgotten my mother's birthday. "I owe you big-time on this one."

"You do not," she said, and laughed in a way that told me she meant it. "Win that Cup and bring it home. That would be the best present." Then she leaned over and whispered, "Your agent's a pretty nice present. So far."

Time was when that statement might have bothered me but that time belonged to a fast-fading past.

We beat Boston 3–2 Saturday in Montreal in a lackluster game I'll remember only because Cam scored on me. He whistled a shot from the right point that kissed in off of the left post. It was his one hundredth NHL goal—not a lot for a guy who's been in the league ten years—but he skated to my net to claim the puck as a keepsake.

"I hope Caitlin shoots it into the fireplace," I said as Cam picked up the puck.

"Just warming up for the second season, JP. The money games," Cam said.

I knew how much Cam wanted to win his first Cup in his last year. And I knew how much I wanted to win it, which was more than I did when the season started. But only three things could happen. He'd win. I'd win. Or we'd both lose.

It was April and we were about to find out.

Ten

The noise shook the building and me.

We'd come into our dressing room after warm-ups. I was sitting in front of my locker running down my mental checklist of where Boston players like to shoot when I first noticed the noise. You can always hear the dull murmur of a crowd from inside a dressing room but this sound rose above normal fan enthusiasm to become a visceral roar pouring from twenty-one thousand throats. We didn't only hear it, we felt it.

"Lost in the past," Tim Harcourt said. He told me that before a home playoff game the arena darkens and old photographs of Canadiens immortals—Aurel Joliat . . . Georges Vezina . . . Boom Boom Geoffrion—are projected onto the ice ten or twelve at a time. The sight of these Montreal Hall of Famers whips the crowd into a nostalgic frenzy. But that's only prelude. The frenzy rises when, one by one, photos of the Canadiens Holy Trinity are projected the full length of the ice. First, Guy Lafleur in full stride, the puck on his stick, his hair flying, the consummate Flying Frenchman. Then Jean Beliveau, Le Gros Bill, the big handsome graceful center with the C on his shoulder, captain for life and forever in the hearts of Montrealers.

The cheers accompanying those two photos are like storm waves breaking ever higher against a seawall. But with the projection of the last photo, the wave goes over the top and unbridled emotion floods the arena. The final picture—taken on the night the team closed the old Montreal Forum—is of Rocket Richard holding a flaming torch. Even in his seventies the Rocket's face was dominated by those piercing angry brown eyes. Angry at what? Opponents who routinely hacked and slashed him? Affronts to the French people? Both? I suppose fans could see whatever they were looking for. Whatever it was, the roar told me that playing hockey in Montreal was different from playing any sport anywhere else in North America.

"*Tabernac.* Got to have this one, boys," Joe Latendresse yelled, standing up and banging his stick on the dressing-room table, thus toppling two pyramids of tape and twenty half-filled paper cups of Gatorade, this to the annoyance of assistant trainer Marc Wilson. "*Tabernac* your fucking self, Joe," said Wilson, who had to clean up the mess. When you're an NHL player there's always someone to clean up after you.

With only two minutes to go before the clock in the dressing room ticked down to 0:00 and we headed for the ice, I knew my nerves were OK. I felt more resolve than anxiety. Maybe it had to do with what Faith told me before I left the hotel. I'd been my usual anxious pregame self, worrying out loud about everything from bad bounces to shaky officiating, when Faith cut me off midlitany: "Take it from an old gym rat, JP—you can only play the next shot, not the whole tournament."

After beating Boston 3–2 in the final regular-season game between us, we'd gone on to win our last four games and wrap up first place in the Northeast Division and in the Eastern Conference. Philly won the Atlantic Division and Carolina took the Southeast Division, so those were the top three seeds for the playoffs. Boston also won its last four games—with Rinky playing well in goal—to take second place in our division and get fourth seed for the first round of the playoffs. The way the playoffs work is that the number one seed plays the number eight seed, number two plays number seven, and so on. So the matchups were: Montreal versus Tampa; Philly versus the New York Rangers; Carolina versus New Jersey; and Boston versus Ottawa. The Bruins had by far the toughest opponent so I and a lot of other people were shocked when Boston won in a four-game sweep. And I was equally surprised when it took us six games to eliminate Tampa, partly because playing hockey in Florida in April is like skating on Italian slush in Naples. "I've seen better ice in my driveway," Justin Pelletier told the media after we'd lost Games 3 and 4 in Tampa. Justin, one of our defensemen, is from Trois-Rivières.

Philadelphia bounced the Rangers in five games with Serge "the Weasel" Balon scoring five goals, picking up three assists, and instigating a near riot. It happened in Game 4 in New York when a Ranger fan threw a dead fish at Flyers goalie Jeff Fishbane after the Rangers scored. Serge put the butt end of his stick in the fish's mouth, then used his stick to sling the fish eighteen rows into the stands, where it hit an ice-cream vendor, knocking him down in an aisle. Some Rangers fans started toward the Flyers bench but—this being New York—they stopped long enough to steal the vendor's ice cream, thus giving the cops extra time to move into the area.

We lucked out in the second round. Because the New Jersey Devils had upset Carolina we played the Devils, while the Bruins had to face the much tougher Flyers.

We broomed New Jersey in four, which gave us a few days to rest and to watch the Bruins struggle with Philly. It was predictable during the off days that the question reporters asked most was whom we'd rather face in the division finals, Boston or Philadelphia. It was equally predictable that we lied. We said it didn't matter, that they were both tough. But the truth, at least for me, was that I'd rather play Philly than have to face Boston and all my former teammates. The second-to-last thing I wanted was to stand in the way of Cam Carter winning the Cup. The *last* thing I wanted was to lose my own chance.

The Boston-Philly series was tied at two games each when I

tuned in for the telecast of Game 5 and saw a pregame graphic telling viewers that Rex Conway would miss his fourth consecutive game. Pulled groin, the TV announcer said. But everyone knows you can't believe injury reports, especially during the playoffs. Lynne Abbott told me that she has a formula for figuring out management's lies: "If they say it's the left ankle it's the right shoulder . . . if they say right knee it's left elbow. . . ."

The next day I phoned Cam to see what the truth was about Rex. Cam's story was moderately amusing. Rex had recently taken to wearing a gold cross about the size of one of my goalie sticks. This to better advertise the fact that Rex has God on speed dial, just in case any of us had missed the news over the previous seasons. It was after the Bruins eliminated Ottawa that Flipside had another of his team parties and Rex showed up with a girl named Christina, a soprano in the choir of the Foursquare Bible-Believing Church. "One of those eye-batting faux-naive-southern types who pretends not to know she's a home-wrecker-in-embryo," Cam said. "So Rex gets her into one of the upstairs bedrooms at Flipper's house and in about two minutes we hear Rex scream and the door opens and out comes Christina the Choir Singer yelling, 'Jesus may love you, Rexall Conway. But ah don't.'" So Rex's alleged groin pull was really some major testicular bruising where Christina speared him with his own cross. "Christina didn't seem to understand why we laughed as she came down the stairs," Cam said. "I don't think Christina spends much time hanging around people who laugh."

"Sorry I missed it," I said.

"Me too. It's been one of the few smiles this month." Cam paused for a second before he said what both of us were thinking. "Could be you and me in the conference finals, JP. There's no part of that that won't suck."

"You have to beat Philly first," I said.

"We can beat Philly. The league finally got around to suspending Serge for the rest of the playoffs for the fish-throwing incident. Flyers aren't the same without him."

Cam was right. After losing Game 5 to fall behind three games to two, Boston bounced back to win Games 6 and 7 and earn a date with Montreal.

Meanwhile, the Western Conference was a bigger upset than the Revolutionary War. Anaheim stunned top-seeded Detroit in the opening round and followed that with an upset of the L.A. Kings. The San Jose Sharks pulled off shockers by eliminating Colorado and Dallas. So the Western Conference Finals came down to Anaheim and San Jose, teams that Boston or Montreal should beat. The winner of the Boston-Montreal series would be a lock to win the Stanley Cup.

The Canadiens had the better regular-season record so Games 1 and 2 were in Montreal. Faith planned to be at Game 1 but then she'd have to go home for graduation from med school. "Graduation doesn't mean much to me but it's a big deal to my parents," she said.

Faith was finished with classes and wasn't scheduled to start her internship until July, so she'd been spending about half of her time with me and the rest either in Boston trying to sell her house or in Vermont looking to buy a place for us. She drove Boss Scags on all of her trips. "Hit seven thousand rpm and it's like sitting in a six-speed cordless vibrator," she said. I told her to call Modena, Italy, and pass that on to Ferrari's ad agency.

Faith also made good on the quarter-million-dollar pledge to the Lake Champlain Medical Center, the gift that was contingent on her getting the internship she wanted. She insisted on the gift being listed as "anonymous," so she never took any public credit for it. "It was just business," she said. I think Faith McNeil has a stronger power play than the Bruins and Canadiens combined.

"How do you feel?" Faith asked me as I was leaving the hotel for the opening game of our series with Boston.

"Like a guy who's eight wins from the Cup he's dreamed about but has to fight his way through his friends to get it," I said.

"Conflicted?"

"No. I want to win."

"You thinking about your dad?"

"He's my father, not my dad."

"Semantics, JP. Is he lurking in your mind?"

"No. The fucker's lurking in his luxury suite."

Boston set the tone early. The Bruins started Gaston's line with Kevin Quigley on left wing. It took twenty seconds for Quigley to come crashing through my crease like the Polar Express, knocking me to the ice mask-first, the jolt bringing back the headache I'd had after my concussion a few weeks earlier. Headache or not I wasn't going to give Quig the satisfaction of knowing he'd rocked me. I jumped up fast. So did Quig.

"Congrats on the engagement, JP," Kevin said as though his running me over were just another day at the office, which, for him, it was.

"Nice of you to drop by, Kev," I said just as our conversation was interrupted by referee Jimmy Simpson.

"That's goalie interference, Quigley. You're gone for two," Simpson said, raising his arm to signal the penalty.

"Bullshit, Jimmy," Quig said, skating toward the ref and apparently preparing to launch a harangue about a miscarriage of justice. But Quig fooled me. "That wasn't intah-ference. It was chah-ging," Quig yelled.

"What difference, Kev? They're both two minutes," Simpson said, sensibly, I thought.

"My image, Jimmy. Intah-ference is wussy. Chah-ging is more my style."

Simpson was already skating backward toward the penalty box and I wasn't sure he'd heard Quig until the public address guy announced the call: "Boston penalty. Number sixty-three. Two minutes. Charging," Simpson said. Quig skated toward the penalty box tapping his stick on the ice a couple of times in what I took to be grateful acknowledgment of the ref's highly evolved sense of semantics and public perception.

The hit from Quigley and the banter we'd exchanged sent a clear message: that even between friends there would be no quarter asked, given, or expected.

We scored a power play goal while Quig sat out his penalty and we went on from there to take a fairly easy 6–2 win and a 1–0 series lead. We outshot Boston 41–19, so you couldn't blame Rinky Higgins for the loss. But the fact is he didn't play all that well. I had a headache throughout the game, a throbbing in my left temple, the same place I'd had a concussion weeks earlier. But it was the playoffs, when everyone plays hurt, so I didn't say anything.

I returned from practice the next day to find a note Faith left before she took off for Boston: "Call Rudy E. Needs 4 tix for tomorrow. 2 for him, 2 for parents."

Tickets are the bane of every pro player's existence and never more than when you're in the playoffs. With every round you win the calls get more frequent and bizarre; a second cousin twice removed whom you haven't seen in seventeen years will try to get a couple of good seats for a playoff game. "Hey, I'll *pay* for them," he'll say as though he's doing you a favor. Or like we get tickets for free, which we don't except for wives and immediate family. In my second year in the league I had a former high school classmate from St. Dom's—a guy I hadn't heard from in six years—call me for Bruins playoff tickets. When I called back to tell him I had his tickets he wanted to know the seat location before he agreed to pay for them. I was young then. Today, I usually don't return calls that might have anything to do with tickets. But I like Rudy Evanston. So I called Jean Picard's secretary, a woman the guys on the team tell me could find four on the aisle for the Second Coming, the Gettysburg Address, or a Beatles reunion. She got me four good seats for Game 2. I called Rudy.

"I hope your parents and Claire enjoy the game," I said.

"Claire can't go. She's cramming for her last two finals. The fourth ticket's for Coach Indinacci," Rudy said. "I hear he talked to you about coaching."

"He invited me to take a two-point-seven-million-dollar pay cut, if that's what you mean," I said. "I like you, Rudy, but not two-point-seven mil worth."

Rudy laughed.

"I'll work with you at Marco's summer hockey camp. You'll be there, right?"

"I'll be there. But I have to work as a volunteer. The freakin' NCAA won't let him pay me."

"Check your shoes," I said.

"What?"

"This summer. After camp. Check your shoes. I worked Marco's camp when I was a student. And the NCAA had the same rule. But while I was on the ice, hundred-dollar bills had a way of growing in my shoes."

"There's a few technical things I want to work on this summer. But I think my problems in the second half of the season were mostly mental. Indinacci is a good coach but he never played goal," Rudy said.

"Goalies don't need coaches, we need gurus," I said. "We'll talk about it this summer."

"Thanks for the tickets. Good luck in the game."

"Aren't you the one who told me luck doesn't have anything to do with it?"

Game 2 was on a Saturday night in Montreal. The first thing I did at the morning skate was introduce myself to Montreal team doctor Wingate Desaulniers. The second thing I did was lie to him. Told him I was getting migraine headaches. I said it always happened in the playoffs because of the pressure. He frowned, wrote me a prescription, and didn't ask any questions.

I took it easy in practice and let my backups—Ryan McDonough and Demetre Fontaine—take most of the shots. Fontaine was the teenager who had played most of the season with the Lewiston Mainiacs in my old hometown. Demetre would likely become Montreal's goalie of the future, but management only brought him up for the playoffs to take a lot of practice shots and to get his first wide-eyed look at the Show. You wouldn't want to start either of those guys in a playoff.

I filled my prescription at the hotel pharmacy. There were still eight hours before I had to play so I took one of the pills, figuring the drugs would be out of my system by game time. While waiting for the pill to kick in, I ordered a salad from room service and called Denny Moran at his office.

"Caught me just as I was leaving," he said.

"What? You don't work all day Saturdays anymore?"

"Taking Jacqueline to the Sox game. Two o'clock start. A little hors d'oeuvre before we watch you beat Boston tonight. What's up?"

"Paperwork," I said. "Can you transfer ownership of Boss Scags from me to Faith?"

"Yeah. Sure. Why?"

"Graduation present."

Fatigue, the headache drug, and a disconnected phone combined to help me get a two-hour nap. I felt good when I woke up at 3:30, but an hour later, as I arrived at the rink, my headache was back. And it was so close to game time that I didn't dare take another pill.

I hadn't heard from Cam or he from me. What could either of

us have said? The playoffs had become a zero-sum game. Like tennis. The point one of us wins is the point the other loses. But we did connect, sort of, during pregame warm-ups. Both teams were skating around in huge counterclockwise circles when Cam and I happened to arrive at the center-ice logo at the same time. It's part of hockey's code that you don't skate into the other team's territory during pregame. Not unless you want to start a donnybrook. But as Cam and I skated close to the center-ice face-off dot I reached out and tapped his shin pads and he tapped my right goalie pad.

We won again but it wasn't easy this time. We fell behind 1–0 when I fanned on a sixty-footer. I think my eyes were slow to pick up the puck. I never played baseball but I know what batters mean when they say that when they're hitting well they can see the stitches on the ball. When I'm at the top of my game I can see the long shots clearly almost as if the puck were approaching in slow motion. But that first goal was a blur. I settled down after that and stopped J.-B. Desjardin on a breakaway and Rex Conway on a rebound, and made that rookie Billy Shannon look like the ex-Yalie he is by poke-checking the puck while he was trying a curl and drag. In a case like that I don't get credit for a save because Billy never got off a shot. Back in high school my coach didn't like to see me attacking a puck carrier like that. "Don't bother a puck that's not bothering you," he used to say. But that's wrong. A lot of goaltending has to do with stopping trouble before it happens.

I also started holding on to pucks. It slowed down the game and kept Boston from building any flow or momentum. Some fans, players, refs, and coaches don't like it when a goaltender stops the game a lot. But I figure the puck is safer in my glove than on anyone's stick, even a teammate's. Besides, I like to jam up the game and to frustrate and annoy attackers. Refs rarely call me for delay of game. There's a part of me that would rather destroy than create. Or maybe destruction and creation are the same thing in goaltending.

We scratched out goals in the second and third periods to take a 2–1 lead into the final minute, when Boston pulled their goalie for a sixth attacker and we scored into the empty net for a 3–1 win and a 2–0 series lead. When the game ended, Cam smashed his stick over the crossbar, something I hadn't seen him do since college.

As soon as we got back in the dressing room I ducked into the trainer's room, closed the door, and popped another headache pill. "What's that?" Marc Wilson asked.

"Headache pill. Desaulniers gave them to me," I said.

"You get a lot of headaches?"

"Not usually. Got my bell rung by Quigley in Game One."

"You got it rung earlier in the season too. Missed a couple of games with a concussion, didn't you?"

"Yeah, but it was only my brain. I'm a goalie, what do I need a brain for?" I said, leaving the room before he could say anything else. I came back into the main dressing room just in time to see Tim Harcourt rip a final stat sheet out of the hands of one of our rookies, Michel Joliet. Tim crumpled the sheet and tossed it in a trash barrel. "The only stat that counts is on the scoreboard," Tim told the rookie. We all check our stats. But for a rookie to be caught studying a stat sheet in front of his teammates is a violation of the game's code. Rookies have to learn. "Adventures in babysitting," Tim muttered as he walked past me to the showers.

I met Marco Indinacci, Rudy Evanston, and Rudy's parents at a crowded Crescent Street restaurant where I had reservations for five but where the maître d' could only come up with a long narrow table for four to which he added a fifth chair at the head. I took that chair. I didn't know it at the time but it proved helpful to have the whole table in front of me when I launched into an extemporaneous lecture. It started with a question from Rudy, who was sitting on my right. "I looked at the video from our last five games. I was playing the angles OK.

But I let in nineteen goals in that stretch. Something's got to be wrong."

I'd seen one of those games on TV and I thought I saw the problem. I explained it the way people in sports usually explain things at the dinner table—with silverware and condiments. "Here's the goal," I said to Rudy, laying my knife sideways on the table in front of me. I used the pepper shaker for a defenseman, the salt shaker for an attacker. "This bottle of Worcestershire is you," I said, plunking down the bottle a few inches in front of the goal-knife. "The game's changing," I said. "Ever since the NHL came back after that lockout and decided to emphasize offense, the refs have been calling everything. And that's seeped down to the college level, too. If a defenseman sneezes on the puck carrier it's a two-minute penalty. Look at this," I said, picking up the salt shaker. "This salt is the puck carrier and he's coming at you down his left wing. The pepper shaker is your defenseman, who has inside position on the puck carrier. What do you do?"

"I go to the top of the crease. Maybe a little farther," he said, placing the Worcestershire sauce eight inches from the knife. "Keep square to the puck, know where the posts are, and take away as much of the net as I can."

"That was years ago, Rudy. Back then if the puck carrier tried to go to the net the defenseman could stop him by hooking, holding, or pulling a Glock from a shoulder holster. The way refs call it today the puck carrier can go hard to the net and there isn't much the defenseman can do without risking a penalty." I moved the salt shaker around the pepper shaker and toward the bottle of Worcestershire. "And God help you if they have an opponent camped in front of your net," I said, putting a water glass to the left of the Worcestershire, "because that guy *doesn't* have the puck so your defenseman trying to protect the front of the cage can't even cast a shadow on him without drawing an interference call."

"So what do you do?" asked Rudy's father.

"The hardest thing to do. Be patient," I said. "We can't go charging way out the way we used to. Stay on your feet a fraction of a second longer. Discipline your impulses. And, in practice, work on your lateral mobility. It's about side-to-side quickness now. We're not like cavalry anymore, out there on the front stabbing away. We're more like infantry moving defensively along interior lines. I was a history major, by the way."

"Only left it thirty-two credits short," Indinacci said. "The university offers tuition remission for staffers, JP. A mid-five-figure salary, tuition, and job security—win or tie. That's my final offer." Everyone at the table smiled because they all knew Marco had offered me the job as associate coach.

"Monsieur Savard, we are pulling the goalie," said the waiter, returning the bottle of Worcestershire to the middle of the table and putting down a basket of freshly baked baguettes and a carafe of red wine. I asked the waiter for a tonic and lime. I knew red wine, or any alcohol, would bring back the headache that Desaulniers's drug was beginning to push out.

The five of us quickly fell into the casual conversation and easy laughter that can make a meal a communion. Marco got the biggest laugh when he provided us with a highlight list of my worst gaffes in college. "My favorite one, JP, was against Dartmouth where the puck flips in the air and you bat it with your stick—right into the freaking net. I remember a guy in the stands yelling, top of his lungs, 'You should kill yourself, Savard.' "

"That was my girlfriend's father," I said.

I enjoyed reminiscing about college days when the game was so enjoyable because the stakes were so small.

Marco offered to drive me back to the hotel in his rental car but I wanted to walk. Maybe relax a little and get rid of my headache. As we said our good-byes on the crowded sidewalk outside of the restaurant, Mary Evanston, Rudy's mother, pulled me aside. "I've watched Rudy play his whole life. I don't see him having fun anymore. Something's lost. Or missing," she said.

"What I think is missing is Rudy," I said. "A goalie can have great physical ability but the personality behind the mask has to be part of his game. That's what turns technique to style. Fun? I don't know about that. The position isn't a lot of smiles. The joy is less in playing than in having played well."

"Right now he's not playing with much happiness or confidence. Do you think he can make it to the pros?"

"What's the essence of your son?" I asked.

"Rudy beat cancer. He's a survivor. A quiet tough kid."

"Then he'll be all right," I said. "Toughness supports talent."

"I wish you could work with him."

"We'll work this summer."

"I mean next season. That's really Rudy's last shot at a hockey career."

"Next game might be mine," I said.

"Oh, we understand. Just wishing out loud. Good luck in Boston."

We shook hands and I started walking south on Crescent Street. I didn't get far before my head started throbbing and thudding with every step. I popped another pill.

We practiced at the Bell Centre in the morning. I went through the motions, stopping the shots that hit me or were within easy reach, letting the rest sail by. About halfway through practice one of the assistant coaches growled at me: "You could at least pretend you're trying."

"I can try this morning or I can try tomorrow night. Which do you want?" I said. Jean Picard heard me but didn't say anything. He knows. This is the time of year when a goalie is like a bank from which there are a lot of withdrawals and few deposits. I can ignore the fatigue and pain in the adrenaline rush of a game. Practice was just something I had to get through.

We chartered into Boston after practice. Picard was great about it when I asked if I could spend the off night with my fiancée and try to take care of some details of my move to Montreal. "Check into the hotel with us, then do what you have to do. Just be at the morning skate. And give us a good game tomorrow. *Tabernac,* did you see that guy today?"

He meant our backup goalie Ryan McDonough, who got lit up like the Rockefeller Center Christmas tree. Fontaine, the nineteen-year old, stopped a lot of shots mainly by flopping around making most saves with his body or the wide paddle of his stick in a style I'd seen played years ago by two-time league MVP Dominik Hasek.

"Tell me again why you called up Fontaine?" I said.

"He keeps the puck out of the net," Picard said. "The only people who care how are other goalies."

I took the team bus from the airport to the Westin, where I checked into my room and called Faith, who picked me up in Boss Scags. "Want to drive my graduation present?" she asked. I didn't. Faith drove the Ferrari better than I did. And enjoyed it more.

We were in bed by ten o'clock, which is when Faith launched Operation Foreplay.

"Sorry, hon. Not tonight. I have a headache."

"Jean Pierre, that is the oldest, most lame-ass excuse in the history of old lame-ass excuses."

"I don't mean I don't want to have sex. I mean I really have a headache. Been having it since Quig ran me over in Game One. Team doc gave me some pills. They help a little."

"Left side of your head? Same place as before?" she asked.

"Yeah."

"How's your vision?"

"I'm seeing three pucks."

"Stop the one in the middle. Old joke," she said, turning to snap on the lamp on my bedside table. She took off the lampshade and shined the light in my eyes. "Pupils are unequal but reacting," she said. "You've got another concusssion. More likely, you aggravated the first concussion. You shouldn't be playing."

"Only a few games left," I said. If we beat Boston we'll beat the Sharks or the Ducks in four, five games. Got all summer to take care of my head."

"It's your brain you're dealing with, JP."

"Gotta play hurt."

"This isn't playing hurt. It's playing injured. You could make it worse. I don't want my husband shuffling around like Muhammad Ali."

"How about if I shuffle like Mr. Bojangles," I said, getting out of bed to take another pill. "Seems I saw you play three rounds of the NCAA Women's Tournament with a bad back junior year. How much Vicodin were you on?"

"Too much. I almost got hooked on the stuff. I know what you're saying, JP. I just wish this season were over."

I told her about Marco Indinacci still trying to get me to coach at Vermont and about my dinner with Rudy, his parents, and Marco.

"College coaching would be a saner life," she said.

"I can't leave three mil a year on the table, Faith. An NHL career is too short. And I want my name on that Cup." She didn't say anything. Not even when I told her the rest of the truth: "And I want to keep being important."

I returned to the hotel with the team after the morning skate. Justin Pelletier gave Joe Latendresse a shoeshine at lunch. A shoeshine is when someone distracts a guy long enough so that someone else at the table can pour about a cup of mayo or Thousand Island dressing on the distracted guy's shoes. The guy getting the shoeshine usually doesn't notice until he gets up from the table and by then the mayo or dressing is all over his socks and the cuffs of his pants. When he stands up we all yell "Shoeshine," then laugh like it wasn't the hundred and fourteenth time we'd seen it. It's stupid but it breaks the tension.

I phoned Faith before I turned in for my nap.

"Cam called," she said. "Said to call him at home before two thirty if you can."

"OK. What's he want?"

"A half million dollars," Faith said.

"You have *got* to be kidding."

"No. Really. Five hundred large," she said, just as though Cam had asked to borrow a cup of sugar.

"What does he want it for?"

"Call him," Faith said.

"Damn right I'll call him."

It was about two o'clock so I phoned Cam's house. Lindsey answered.

"Hello, Mr. Savard. I'll get Daddy in a minute. I heard you'll be coaching at the Vermont hockey camp."

"I'll be helping Coach Indinacci," I said.

"Good. I'm going to the goalie-camp part. The first week."

"You sure, Linds? I don't think Coach Indinacci has a girls' goalie camp."

"It's the boys' camp. Girls are too easy. Caitlin shoots harder than the girls on my team. Caitlin's telling everyone she scored a goal on you."

"It bounced in off a chair," I said.

"No excuses, Mr. Savard. I'll get Daddy."

Cam came on the line: "JP, I need to take five hundred thou out of your account," he said, never one to mince words.

"This is to pay for the heart transplant I'll need when I see my next statement?" I said.

"It's for an investment. Sort of."

"What am I investing in?"

"It's better if I don't tell you now."

"Let me guess. You're betting heavy on Montreal, then throwing the next two games. Shoeless Cam Carter."

"Nah. This is completely legal."

"Cam, this is serious money we're talking about. I can't just—"

"Whoa . . . whoa . . . whoa . . . ," Cam said, cutting me off and doing what he does best, which is closing the deal. "You'll know within three months what we used the money for, and if you don't like it I'll guarantee the half mil. It'll go back in your account. No questions asked. No way you can lose."

"Does Faith know what it's for?"

"Faith knows."

"OK. Do it."

"You played well in Montreal, JP," Cam said, changing the subject before I changed my mind. "You're going to need your big-money game tonight. You'll see a lot of rubber, bro. We lose tonight, we're screwed. Still sucks you and I being on opposites ends of this thing."

"Keep your head up through the neutral zone," I said, using an old hockey cliché just to have something to say.

"Got news for you, JP. This is the playoffs. No zone is neutral."

We said good-bye. I popped another pill and fell asleep wondering why Cam needed a half million dollars of my money.

The Boston fans gave me a nice ovation when I was introduced before the game. But the rest of the night was downhill. Boston took nineteen shots—to our five—in a scoreless first period in which I was as outgunned as the guys at the Alamo.

Luther Brown scored on me in the second period and two minutes later Jean-Baptiste gave Boston a 2–0 lead when he roofed a bottle knocker. Picard pulled me for a sixth attacker with a minute to play and we made it 2–1 when Joe Latendresse wrong-footed Rinky. But that was all we could do. The series stood at two games to one in Montreal's favor. Because we had an early practice I figured it would be best if my headache and I stayed at the team's hotel.

I met Faith outside the dressing room after the game.

"Good game," she said.

"Not good enough."

"How's your head?"

"Still hurts. And I'm not seeing the puck clearly."

"Promise me when this is over you'll get your head checked out by someone who's not a team doctor."

"My fiancée's a doctor."

"Your fiancée would nail your butt to the bench if it was up to her," she said, pulling me toward her for a kiss.

"Hey, none of those goddamn public displays of affection in here." It was Cam's father. He and Diana were on their way to the Boston dressing room to meet Cam. We shook hands.

"Goddamn shame you guys having to play each other like this," Cam's dad said.

"Terrible," Diana said. "I don't see how anyone could let that Hattigan person run a team."

That's when Cam's father told us he'd tried setting up a meeting with Gabe Vogel to make an offer to buy the Bruins. First Gabe turned him over to a couple of corporate vice presidents. "Let me tell you something about Gabe Vogel and his goddamn vice presidents," Cam's father said. "Top-shelf people hire top-shelf people; second-shelf people hire bottom-shelf people."

"So what'd you do?" Faith asked.

"Told them I needed a meeting with Gabe. They asked me for how long. I said ten minutes but I didn't think I'd use all of it."

"What's the strategy?' I said.

"Throw down a cashier's check for twenty percent more than his team is worth and give him ten minutes to take it or leave it. He'll be on it like a goddamn nose whore on a line of coke."

"Why overpay?" Faith asked.

"I don't buy things for what they're worth, I buy them for what I can make them worth. First thing I do when I buy this team is fire Hattigan. Second thing I do is bring JP here back to Boston where he belongs," the Deuce said, tapping me on the chest.

"Come on, Cameron, we'll be late," Diana said, grabbing her husband's arm and pulling him toward the Bruins dressing room.

"If that man ever teaches a course at the Harvard Business School, I'm taking it," Faith said. "Can he do that?"

"Do what?"

"Bring you back to Boston?"

"Sure. Montreal is only renting me for the final months on my contract. I can sign with anyone come July 1. But until then I'm a Canadien."

We were walking toward the team bus when I said: "Don't suppose you'd want to tell me what Cameron C. Carter the Third wants with a half million dollars of my hard-earned if socially undeserved money."

"I promised Cam I wouldn't. I can tell you you'll be happy with the investment."

"Well, if I'm not, Cam guaranteed the half mil."

"Actually, I guaranteed the half mil, JP."

"I'm surrounded by conspirators," I said as I approached the bus. Faith squeezed my hand before she headed toward the elevator to the parking garage.

A casual fan might think it's hard to play against old teammates and friends, especially if you know you might go back to the team you're playing against. But no player thinks or feels that way. No one ever said it better than the late Herb Brooks, who coached the 1980 USA Olympic team to a gold medal. "You play for the name on the front of the shirt not the one on the back." The Bruins weren't enemies but they were opponents. I wanted to beat them.

Game 4 started well. Montreal controlled the play and we

had four power plays to Boston's one, scoring on two of them to take a 2–0 first period lead into the dressing room. I still wasn't seeing the puck well but I was stopping it, which in this business is all that counts.

"Careful next period, guys, the refs'll be looking to even it up," Picard said between periods. He was right. Refs tell you they call what they see. But count the penalties to each team at the end of a game. They're usually close to even.

Sure enough, Justin Pelletier got whistled for interference in the first minute and Boston scored on the power play. Three minutes later we were down a man again and Boston tied the game at 2–2. I figured the refs would let us play in the final period. I figured right.

The third period of that game was the best of the series, a clinic of quick breakouts and tic-tac-toe passing. Rinky made a few unlikely saves. So did I. The Boston fans were going crazy. I got caught up in the excitement, which is probably why I thought I could win a race with Gaston Deveau. We were pressing the Bruins when Cam got the puck and spotted Gaston breaking through center ice behind our defense. Cam hit him with a pass that bounced off Gaston's stick and rolled toward the face-off circle to my right. You don't really think at times like this. You react. I felt I could beat Gaston to the puck so I darted from my net. I hadn't gone ten feet when I knew the race was closer than I'd figured so I dived—headfirst. The game tape showed that I won the race and knocked the puck to a Montreal back-checker. But I don't remember any of that because just as I hit the puck, Gaston's knee hit my head. I felt a thud on the left side of my helmet and then it was lights-out. When I regained consciousness my leg pads, skates, helmet, and gloves had been removed and I was strapped to a stretcher that Marc Wilson and two EMTs were loading into an ambulance. Faith arrived just as the EMTs were about to close the doors. "I'm his doctor," Faith told the EMTs, who let her jump into the back of the ambulance.

"And I should be sued for malpractice," she said to me. As the ambulance doors closed, one of the clubhouse boys handed Faith my street clothes.

What happened back at the Garden was that my backup goalie, Ryan McDonough, went into the game and let in three of the first six shots he faced for a 5–2 Boston win that tied the series at two games each.

What happened in the ambulance was a seminar on concussions conducted by the charming, soft-spoken, and ever compassionate Dr. Faith McNeil. "Jesus Christ All-freaking-mighty, Jean Pierre, can I ask you a personal question? What do you plan on using for brains for the rest of your life?"

"Is there a radio in this thing? Can we listen to the game?" I said.

"No. There's no radio. There's no wet bar. There's no CD changer. There's no cable TV. We're in a goddamn ambulance on our way to Massachusetts General Hospital because you have a concussion. Do you know what happens in a concussion, JP?" I figured that was a rhetorical question so I didn't say anything. "What happens is that a few million brain cells—this would be your alleged brain we're talking about here—slam against the inside of your skull. Basically, a concussion is a bruise on your brain. You'll recover from the symptoms but some of the damage can remain. It can be cumulative. It's very serious, JP."

"So are the playoffs," I said.

Faith looked up, drew a deep breath, exhaled slowly, and took my catching hand, which was all clammy and taped up; she kissed it anyway. "I know it's important, hon. I know it's your life and your work. But head injuries have ended a lot of careers." She mentioned former NHLers Pat LaFontaine and Brett Lindros. "I think you're done for this season. After that . . ." The words hung in the air for a few seconds before she said, ". . . I don't know. It's up to you."

. . .

I said I could walk into the hospital but the EMTs insisted on wheeling me in. One of our trainers had phoned ahead so the hospital was expecting me. "We can do a brain scan right now, Mr. Savard," said a young woman whose name tag identified her as Ella Rae, M.D.—Neurology. "I think you'll be spending the night with us." I asked her if she had a final on the game. "Five-two Boston," she said. "What's the schedule now?" I told her Game 5 was set for Friday in Montreal and Game 6 back in Boston on Sunday afternoon. "If we need a Game Seven it'll be Tuesday in Montreal," I said. "You think I can make any of those?"

"I'm not supposed to guess, but no. I reviewed Dr. Wynn's records before you came in tonight. I know he saw you for a concussion a few weeks ago."

"And I'm pretty sure he got another one in Game One," Faith said.

"Squealer," I said.

"We're going to do some computed axial tomography. A CAT scan," she said. "Should take about twenty minutes. It helps us determine the extent of any damage to the brain tissue. Let me know if you have any questions."

"Do you have a Sharks-Ducks score?"

"Scoreless. Just started," she said.

"Celtics?"

"Lost to Denver 101–98. Iverson had 42. He's on my NBA fantasy team."

"Red Sox?"

"It's 2–0 Boston top of the third in Seattle. Two-run homer by Ortiz in the first. Sweet for me. He's on my baseball fantasy team."

"Am I on your NHL fantasy team?"

"Jesus Christ," Faith said before Dr. Rae answered.

"Truthfully, I drafted Claude Rancourt of Montreal," Dr. Rae said. "But I took you when Rancourt got hurt."

"So did the Canadiens," Faith said.

"Who else is on your fantasy team?" I asked.

"Brad Pitt," she said.

I had the CAT scan and a few other tests. It was almost midnight when I got the official diagnosis of a concussion. "I'm afraid you're out for the rest of the playoffs," Dr. Rae told me after she'd looked at the tests. "We'd like to keep you overnight. We'll probably release you in the morning. We can give you a private room."

"I can take him off your hands," Faith said.

"And your relationship to Mr. Savard is . . . ?"

"Parole officer," Faith said before she explained she was a doctor.

Dr. Rae handed me some pills—"These are milder than what you've been taking," she said, then called for a wheelchair. I stood up to show her I could walk and didn't need a wheelchair, hospital policy or not. I changed into my street clothes and threw my game uniform and chest-and-arm protector into a huge plastic trash bag that I thought was a pretty good metaphor for where my career might be heading. We took a cab back to the Garden to get the Ferrari.

I wasn't nauseated so Faith made us a late-night dinner of a mushroom omelet with a spinach salad and crostini with melted Gorgonzola. I thought about watching the last period of the Ducks-Sharks West Coast game but I didn't really want to. What I wanted to do was sleep.

"I'm sorry I got mad at you in the ambulance," Faith said as we got into bed. "It's just that I hate to see what you've been do-ing to yourself these last few weeks."

"I've just been trying to win the thing, you know. Get my name on the Cup."

"Well, you're off the hook now. You've got a legitimate injury that should keep you out of the playoffs."

"We can argue about that later," I said, turning onto my right side and slipping my left arm around Faith, who was wearing one of my V-necked T-shirts and doing more for it than I ever did.

The sun had been up for a couple of hours when Faith woke up for the very good reason that my left hand had found its way under her T-shirt.

"Mmmm. Feeling better, are we?" she said. "How's your headache."

"Still there but not bad. Like it moved into a back room of my brain."

"Well, we don't want to aggravate it, soooo," Faith said, turning toward me and half rising from the bed. "I'm going to do something that will make this very easy for both of us." And she did. She surely did.

It seemed strange to have a whole day to ourselves. No practice, game, or travel for me. No classes or meetings for Faith. "Let's take a walk," she said.

It was a warm day in mid-May and the morning air smelled of wet earth and new-mown grass. A sprinkle of pink apple blossoms fell from the dwarf crab apple tree on Faith's front lawn. We held hands as we wandered east toward Boston College, past the football stadium—"the House that Doug Flutie built," Faith called it—past St. Ignatius Church, halfway around the Chestnut Hill Reservoir, across several acres of baseball fields, and into the village of Cleveland Circle.

"Got to have a slice of Pino's Pizza. Best in the city," Faith said, leading me toward an unpretentious restaurant with booths and benches and a lot of posters of Italy on the walls. We ordered from a counter at the back of the restaurant. "Have the plain tomato and cheese. No fancy add-ons. That's the only way to tell how good a pizza really is," Faith said.

"People, too," I said.

We each got two slices and what was billed as a medium root

beer but which, in keeping with modern drink sizes, was about the size of a trash barrel. Faith paid. We sat in a booth and talked about what a normal life in Vermont might be like.

"I want a hoop over the garage," Faith said.

"And a driveway three or four cars wide. Great for street hockey," I said. "And no windows in the garage doors. If the basketballs don't break them the pucks and tennis balls will."

"And a flat backyard for a skating rink," Faith said.

"No swimming pool?"

"Everybody has a pool, JP. A rink is way funkier."

"What do we do with it in the summer?"

"Arena football," she said.

I was daydreaming out loud when I said it might be nice to take classes in the morning, then go to the rink and coach in the afternoon and be home for dinner. "And no more trips to Edmonton, Calgary, and Anaheim. A big road trip in college is to Boston for Northeastern on Friday night and BU on Saturday. And even if you go to the Frozen Four the season is still two months shorter than the NHL's. It'll be a good life in a few years," I said.

Faith held up the forefinger on her right hand signaling that she'd have something important to say as soon as she swallowed a mouthful of pizza. "But Marco needs to name an assistant now," is what she said. "And if you want to work with Rudy Evanston . . . well, Rudy's got only one season left."

"Can't do it, Faith. I'm a player first. I think that old sportswriter Jim Murray had it right about pro players—we are what we do."

She thought about that for a minute. "And if you don't you're nothing?" she said. It was a question but I couldn't answer it.

We walked the two miles or so back to Faith's house. "I'm tired," I said.

"You're a professional athlete, JP. How can you be tired from a walk?"

"Maybe it's mental. This is the most relaxed I've been since training camp. No game to worry about."

I slept through most of the late afternoon while Faith went grocery shopping. I awoke to the smell of grilled swordfish wafting up the stairs.

With no hockey game until the next day, we watched the Red Sox on TV after dinner. Just as I clicked on the game the announcer was reminding viewers that a week from Saturday would be a makeup game for the Sox versus Detroit and that the game would be "a day-night separate-admission doubleheader." Faith giggled when she heard that.

"What so funny?" I said.

"We should do one of those," she said.

"One of what?"

"A day-night separate-admission doubleheader."

So we did. And this time I made it easy for her. I surely did.

I fell asleep thinking that I'd just had the best day of my life and I hadn't played hockey or spent money.

Friday wasn't the best day of anybody's life if you played for Boston or Montreal although it was slightly better for Montreal because we won 8–7 in a game in which both starting goaltenders—Rinky Higgins in the Boston net and Ryan McDonough for us—played poorly. Montreal was down 7–6 going into the third period. Joe Latendresse tied it on the power play, then won it for us at 17:18 of overtime when he swept in from the right side, got Rinky going left to right, then shot back across the grain, putting the puck into the place Rinky had just left. It was—as the TV guys like to say—a goal scorer's goal. Montreal held a 3–2 series lead going into Game 6 in Boston.

Cam's father invited me to watch that game from his luxury

suite. I thanked him but explained I was a Montreal Canadien, at least for the time being, and it was best if I stayed down by my team's bench. Faith joined Cam's parents, six or seven Carter & Peabody clients, Denny Moran, and my mother in the C&P box. I stood in the runway beside the Montreal bench. You can't see the game very well from there. But you can feel it, sense its intensity, and glimpse its beauty. Skating is as close to elegance as a man can get.

Gaston was skating to space, his arrival magically timed to coincide with the puck's arrival. Cam was hammering guys. Flipside—his shirt billowing, back-checkers scrambling helplessly in his wake—was a one-man breakout play, sometimes carrying the puck the length of the ice like a fourth forward. Kevin Quigley was banging along the walls. And if that wasn't enough, Boston had three power plays to our one and scored on all of them for a 3–0 first-period lead. We were back on our heels.

I went into the dressing room between periods. The first thing I saw as I entered was Ryan McDonough taking off his goalie equipment. "Going somewhere, Ry? Doctor's appointment?" I asked.

"I always do this when I suck. Change everything. Underwear. Jock. Everything. Fresh start, eh?" he said, snapping off his words like a man badly shaken.

I felt I had to do some freelance coaching. "Don't attribute your ability to outside things," I told him. "You played well enough to make it to the NHL. You're going to have to slam the door now. Resilience is part of ability. Nothing to do with a dry jock. Hey, if we get the next goal . . ." I didn't think I had to explain what everyone in the NHL knows—3–1 is the most dangerous lead in hockey. But my advice didn't do any good. McDonough gave up a softy in the first minute of the second period. That was it. With the game all but officially lost, Packy pulled McDonough and put in Demetre Fontaine. The kid played half the game on his knees or stomach diving around like a circus seal but stopping everything Boston shot at him. "What the hell's he doing?" said Marc Wilson, who was standing in the runway with me. "Stopping the puck," I said. "It's the job description."

Fontaine was named third star of the game even though we lost. Alvin "Captain Baritone" Crouch caught the kid in the runway as he came off the ice. "Demetre . . . Demetre Fontaine . . . Nineteen years old and you're third star in your first NHL game. How do you feel?"

In his French accent the kid said, "I radder win dan be turd star."

"Turd star. Got to love live TV," I said to Marc, who was bent over laughing.

Faith and I met my mother and Denny Moran at the Copley Plaza bar after the game. Denny told me Montreal was hot to sign me for two years "and I think I can push it to three or four if you want."

"No. Two is good. No more," I said.

"Well, this Fontaine kid will be ready by then," Denny said. "His style, if that's what you want to call it, reminds me of the Dominator's." "The Dominator" was the nickname of the great Dominik Hasek. We didn't know it then but in her story the next morning Lynne Abbott would give Demetre Fontaine his own nickname—the Demonator.

We speculated on which goalie Montreal would start in Game 7; the psychologically fragile Ryan McDonough or a teenager with thirty-nine minutes of NHL experience.

"Nasty choice," Faith said.

"They won't dare start a teenage rookie in a Game Seven," Denny said. I said I wasn't so sure. "The kid's cocky and cold-blooded—good things for a goalie in a money game."

"Relieved you're not playing?" Faith asked on the ride back to her place.

"No. I don't miss the nervousness. But I feel . . ." I was going to say "useless" but changed it to "unimportant."

"Someday you're going to have to learn you're more than a goalie," she said.

"I'll take that course in two years."

She gunned the Ferrari past the IHOP on Soldiers Field Road.

Eleven

I thought Faith would give me an argument about driving to Montreal on Monday so I could be at Tuesday's Game 7. She didn't. She understood. And came with me.

"My father had a team rule that a player had to travel both ways on the team bus. No driving home with parents after an away game," she said.

"*Had* a rule? Doesn't he still?"

"Naw. Parents beat him down."

We talked briefly about my taking a pass on the Vermont coaching job.

"If you don't when you can, then maybe you can't when you want to," she said. "Whoever takes the job next could be there a long time."

"It's worth the risk to play another two seasons. I'd give my left one to get my name on that Cup."

"Hey. Careful what you wish for."

I said that if I coached I'd rather be a goalie coach than a head coach.

"Hah. A goalie coach *is* a head coach," she said.

"How you feeling?" she asked as we drove off I-93 onto I-89 in New Hampshire.

"Great," I said. "No headaches. No nausea. I could go."

"Stay like that for a week and if Montreal makes it to the finals maybe you'll be ready to play in Game Four or Five. I wouldn't recommend it but I know how you feel. You wouldn't even have to play. All you have to do is be on the roster to get your name on the Cup, right?"

"Technically. But I don't want to back into it that way. I want to matter."

"If you can dress you'll play. Who else have they got? The Demonator? Stay symptom-free and if the Canadiens win tomorrow you might get your chance."

I decided to tell her what I'd been telling myself since I woke up. "I don't mean I want to play in a couple of weeks. I want to play tomorrow," I said, bracing myself for what I thought would be a tsunami of bewildered anger.

But Faith said nothing. The silence stretched for miles. Finally, without glancing at me, she said in a cold even voice: "What we have here, class, is a case of denial about a concussion that could lead to brain damage. Or, judging from your last statement, has *already* led to brain damage." Long pause: "You've got to be out of whatever mind you've got left, JP."

"I want to play tomorrow. And if we win tomorrow I want to play in the Stanley Cup final against San Jose. Players play. And there's no guarantee I'll ever get this close again."

"A few days ago you were in Mass General. You've had three concussions this season. No doctor in North America would sign off on your playing."

"A team doctor would," I said.

"JP, after a first concussion the chances of a second concussion are four times greater. Even if you take a hard hit on your body the force could get transferred to your brain and that's it. Four concussions. Grand slam. Don't be foolish. You're hurt. There's no dishonor in not playing. This is about your brain."

"It's about my heart, too. In the old no-helmet days guys got their bell rung all the time. And they played. I don't want my heart questioned. Ever. By anyone."

"No one IS questioning it, unless maybe you are. What's this really about, Jean Pierre?"

"It's about paying the price to be the best at what you do. It's about our children taking their children's children to the Hall of Fame and pointing to a name on the Cup and telling them: 'That's your great-grandfather,' or 'your great-great-grandfather.' It's forever, Faith, for all eternity. After you get the money, this is what you play for. No one's forcing me, I *want* to play."

We pulled into the truck stop and restaurant at exit 16 in New Hampshire a few miles east of White River Junction, Vermont. We fueled up the car and bought coffee and snacks for the rest of the trip. Faith got a box of cookies with a drawing of elves on the package. I bought a prewrapped sandwich. "Elves made mine; who made yours?" she said. It was a throwaway line but a casual smile, and there's nothing better than a smile to draw the poison out of an argument.

We didn't talk much as Faith drove us through Vermont and over the Canadian border. We'd crossed the Champlain Bridge into Montreal when she said, "You know, JP, if I hadn't been a player I don't think I'd even try to understand any of this."

"Do you think you will understand it?"

"I want to. It seems to me all players are like this. Especially goalies."

"It's part of the culture. Georges Vezina almost died in net." As Faith pushed the Ferrari north into the heart of the city I told her the story of Vezina's death. On November 28, 1925, in the season opener against Pittsburgh in Montreal the thirty-nine-year-old Vezina began coughing up blood in the first period. By the end of the period he was so weak teammates had to help him off the ice. In the dressing room he kept coughing and spitting blood. Vezina had never missed a game in fifteen seasons with the Canadiens. Over protests of his teammates he insisted on starting the second period. But a few minutes into that period Vezina collapsed in a pool of his own blood. He was rushed to the hospital, where doctors diagnosed him with tuberculosis, a death sentence in those days. After being released from the hospital a few days later, Vezina went back to the rink to get his jersey, the one he'd worn the previous season when Montreal won the Stanley Cup. When Vezina saw his old goalie pads propped up in a corner he sat down and wept. Then he went home to Chicoutimi and died.

Faith let out a long sigh. I didn't know what that meant. We drove into the city in silence.

"You going to see Dr. Desaulniers?" Faith asked me as she drove north on University Street.

"First I'll call Picard. Tell him not to rule me out for tomorrow. Then I'll try to get a decent night's sleep. If the headaches come back then that's the answer. I'm done. If they don't I'll talk to De-saulniers. Shouldn't be a problem. The team needs a goaltender."

The Canadiens were still providing me with a suite at the Queen Elizabeth Hotel. I called Marco Indinacci before I un-packed. I thanked him for his offer but told him I wasn't a can-didate. "Going to play two more seasons," I said. Then I told him I was thinking of playing in Game 7.

"Don't do it, JP," he said. "Too risky. You're with a good team. You could win a Cup next season. You could win two in a row. Sit this one out."

I couldn't tell Indinacci that I'd probably be back in Boston the next season if Cam's father bought the Bruins. "Aren't you the guy who used to tell us you looked for players who wanted to pull the cart, not ride in it?"

"That was just coach's talk," he said. "Can't that doctor you're engaged to talk you out of this?"

"That doctor I'm engaged to isn't happy about it. But I think she'll understand. Hey, you saw her play. She didn't leave much on the floor."

"Didn't leave many loose balls, that's for sure. Faith McNeil was a goddamn human dust mop."

"She's still a gamer."

"So are you, JP. But take care of yourself, OK? I'll be watch-ing on TV. I hope I see you in a suit and tie."

"No ties. We play sudden death," I said.

"Sudden fuckin' death is what I'm worried about," Indinacci said.

"There'd be something nice about you coaching one of Lisa's patients this summer," Faith said at dinner. It was the kind of thing a Sheri the Equestrienne would not have said. She never seemed comfortable when I'd mention Lisa. And I don't think Sheri was a big fan of the few photos of Lisa that I kept around the house. But Faith never minded, I think because Faith McNeil, M.D., was born with more self-confidence than you could stuff in a goalie bag.

Sirens, horns, street drills, and other sounds of the city woke us up Tuesday morning. "How's your head?" Faith asked.

"Just what I was going to ask you," I said, smiling.

"Seriously, JP?"

"I'm good to go," I said. "No pain."

"Not to throw the rule book at you, but you should be symptom-free for a week before you even think about playing. What's it been for you?"

"Two days," I said. "That should be more than enough for any team doctor in any sport in the known universe to clear me to play. Especially if the doc's team needs a goalie in the deciding game of a playoff."

"How did you become so cynical?"

"Life," I said.

I showered. You don't shave before a playoff game. I was set to leave when Faith glanced up from her third coffee. "Hope that's decaf," I said.

"Coffee without caffeine is like sex without orgasm," she said. Then she asked if she could go to the morning skate.

"Sure. Why?" I said.

"I've been through a few thousand basketball practices but I've never seen a hockey practice."

"Hockey practices are colder and less squeaky," I told her. "Go around to the back entrance. I'll leave your name with the security guy." I kissed her and set off for the arena and a meeting with Dr. Wingate Desaulniers. I figured he'd be like the Boston team doc, Send 'Em In Wynne. I'd already nicknamed Desaulniers "Send 'Em In Winnie" by the time I arrived at a small secondary office he maintained at the arena.

"So they weren't migraines you needed the pills for," Desaulniers said, jamming me with his first pitch.

"It was like a migraine," I said. "Hurt like hell."

"You've had two diagnosed concussions within a month and a probable third one that wasn't diagnosed," he said, sounding increasingly unfriendly. I read this as the charade he had to go through to assuage his conscience before he sucked it up and did what he knew the team paid him to do—OK me to play. "Let's run down the list of symptoms," he said.

"Amnesia?"

"And you are?" I said.

"Please, Jean Pierre, I need your cooperation."

I was going to say "and my 1.91 career playoff goals-allowed average" but all I said was "OK."

"Amnesia?"

"No."

"Blurred vision?"

"Not anymore." It was only a small lie. And for a good cause, I thought.

"Nausea?"

"Nope."

"Ringing in the ears?"

I scrapped the Nine-Inch Nails joke and said, "No."

"Sleeplessness?"

"You sleep with Faith McNeil, you're going to lose a few winks," I felt like saying, but again, all I said was "No."

"Headaches?"

"Not in two days," I said, throwing my changeup pitch—the truth.

"Two days? That's all?" Desaulniers said in a tone that made me wish I'd lied. The doctor did the usual flashlight-in-the-eyes trick. Then he sat shaking his head slowly over a sheaf of papers that I figured were test results faxed up from Boston.

"I can't do it, Jean Pierre," he said. "I can't clear you to play."

"Can't or won't?" I said, figuring I'd cut to the chase and raise the specter of what we both knew would be a disappointed team management.

"Both," Desaulniers said. "Three head injuries. Three strikes you're out," he said.

"With baseball fans like you it's a wonder the Expos moved to Washington." I was getting hot now. "I'll sign a release. I want to play. And the GM and coach want me to play," I said, trying to raise the fear factor again.

"It doesn't matter what you sign. If I let you play—or even let you sign a release knowing what I know—I could lose my license. At the very least my reputation would be damaged. The team is important to me. My profession is more important."

"My profession is important to me, too. And right now it's important to a lot of other people."

"I'm sorry, JP. I admire your courage. But my answer is no. I won't. And you shouldn't."

I left the office and headed downstairs for the rink to tell Picard that I was willing to play but that Desaulniers wouldn't sign off on it. There was a crowd of media in the corridor outside the dressing room where Demetre Fontaine, third-string goalie extraordinaire, was holding court. He'd apparently heard about Lynne Abbott's nickname for him and was now referring to himself in the third person as "the Demonator." As in "When his team need him de Demonator is ready." When Lynne asked him if he wasn't being a bit brash for a teenager, the kid said, "De puck does not know how old is de Demonator."

I caught the kid's eye and nodded toward the dressing room, which was closed to the media. The kid followed me in. "Bonjour, Monsieur Savard," he said.

"Demetre, you'll be surprised and disappointed to know I don't speak French," I said. "But I speak fluent hockey, and that was a hell of a—what was it, thirty-nine minutes?—you played two days ago." He nodded. "But let me tell you something that'll help you last a long time in this league. Don't look for the spotlight. Let it find you." I patted him on the shoulder and walked into Picard's office.

"I tried to get Desaulniers to clear me for tonight. He wouldn't do it," I said.

"*Tabernac.* What do I do, Jean Pierre? McDonough's confidence is shot and my other goalie is nineteen years old."

It was an ugly choice and I wasn't going to make it for him. "I just wanted you to know I'm willing to go."

"*Taber-fucking-nac,*" the coach said, burying his face in his hands. "I'm not taking you off our lineup card. Not yet. Maybe our owner knows a doctor who will . . . ah . . . cooperate."

I left Picard's office and walked toward the rink, where a few of the fourth-liners were already skating around, their blades ripping the new ice—*swick . . . swick . . . swick*—their slapshots booming off the boards and pinging off the glass. Why do they all do that? I wondered. Goalies love slapshots because most players have a backswing like Tiger Woods's, so it takes them forever to get off the shot and that gives the goalie time to get ready. Wristers and backhanders are the goal scorers' shots.

I was looking at the ice when Faith, wearing the leather Ferrari jacket she'd given me for Christmas, came up behind me. "Thought you'd be out there," she said, pointing toward the ice. "What's the deal?"

"No deal," I said. "You'll be pleased to know that Desaulniers won't let me play. Leave it to me to get traded to the only club in the world with Hippocrates as its team doctor."

"I guess Desaulniers never heard of Georges Vezina."

"Guess not," I said.

"Well screw him," she said with a vehemence that surpised me.

Faith stared at the few players on the ice for a couple of seconds and said, "Is this all you guys do: skate around and shoot?"

"It's a game-day skate," I said. "It's just for guys to get loose."

"What do you do at a real practice?"

"Skate around and shoot," I said.

Faith said that five minutes of watching hockey practice would do her for the rest of her life and she was going shopping.

I was still hanging around the home bench watching practice when Cam's father and Denny Moran strolled in. I told them I wasn't going to play. "If you don't mind consorting with the enemy I got half a luxury box through a guy on the board at the Bank of Montreal. You and Faith are welcome to join us," Cam's dad said.

"Thanks. I think I'll take you up on it."

"Better not, JP," Denny said. "You're still Montreal property. We don't want photos of you sitting with a bunch of Boston fans."

I hate that word *property*. But I knew Denny was right.

I was still talking to Denny and Cam's dad when the Bruins filed in. They had 11:30 ice.

"I always knew you were a head case, JP. Now it's official," Kevin Quigley said, walking over to us and putting his arm around my neck. "How's the head? Can you go?"

"I want to go but the doc won't let me."

"Who'll you guys start in net?"

"I honestly don't know but if it were me I'd start the Fontaine kid."

"The Demonatah," said Quig, laughing. "We watched him on tape yesterday. We shoot high on that kid we'll put up a numbah that belongs on a cash register."

"Hey, JP, let's talk about our injuries and bore these people to death." It was Taki Yamamura on crutches, his right leg enclosed in a brace that stood out under a pair of sweatpants. I asked him if he thought he could play next season.

"Naw, I think I'm done," he said. "Besides the broken bone, I tore up the ACL. Docs say it's spaghetti in there. Insurance will cover most of the money left on my deal."

Cam's father laughed when he heard that. "Let me tell you guys something about insurance," he said. "Insurance covers every goddamn thing except what happened."

I hung around a few more minutes to watch practice. Ryan McDonough was fighting the puck, dropping to his knees before the puck carrier shot, mishandling shots, and leaving deep rebounds. In the other net Demetre Fontaine was looking large and stopping everything, until Joe Latendresse taught the kid a lesson. Joe, cradling the puck with one hand, knocking away a defenseman's stick with the other, and cutting to the net with speed, looked up to see the Demonator looming in front of him, seemingly blocking the whole net. Joe, now with both hands on the stick and using his butt to fend off the defenseman, snapped a low shot five-hole—right through the tiny triangle between Fontaine's pads. "Welcome to the NHL," Joe said as he skated in front of the beaten goalie. You didn't have to watch practice for too long to know that the Canadiens didn't have a major-league goalie.

As I left the rink to go back to the hotel, Cam's dad invited Faith and me to join him for a pregame meal in the private club for suite holders. I figured there wouldn't be any media there so I thanked him and said we'd see him for dinner.

Paris, New York, Milan, and Montreal are your Final Four in the world of fashion. And if Vegas line setters saw the women in the Canadiens' private club they'd make Montreal a ten-and-a-half-point favorite. They might even do that if all they saw was Faith

McNeil. She'd gone out that afternoon and bought herself a black leather suit, which she was wearing with black leather ankle-strap stiletto heels and a tailored white shirt unbuttoned to the point where the longitude of taste intersects the latitude of titillation. We also had a couple of age-group medalists in the always formidable Diana Carter and that striking newcomer Jacqueline Monique Savard of Lewiston, Maine. My mother had finally released her blond hair from the confines of the businesslike chignon and had it styled so that she looked more like a network anchor than the grocery store cashier she'd once been. The three women plus Cam's father, Denny Moran, and me sat at a table under an old photograph of Rocket Richard.

Our table looked like something from a junior high school dance—boys on one side, girls on the other. Faith, Diana Carter, and my mother sat against the wall looking out into the room. Mr. Carter, Denny, and I sat across from them. Cam's dad told us that if his coming meeting with Gabe Vogel went well he'd buy the Bruins subject only to the approval of the other NHL owners. "You can take Madison Hattigan and color him gone," Cam's dad said.

Faith had told Denny who'd then told my mother that I'd tried to get myself cleared to play.

"I thought this doctor had talked some sense into you, Jean Pierre," my mother said, putting her arm around Faith's shoulders. That move was unlike my mother, who usually gestured little and said less. Throughout dinner my mother had been more talkative than usual. Sparkling. "Vivacious," as they say in the high school yearbooks. It wasn't until we were ready to leave that I saw why. It was warm in the club and I'd draped my jacket over the back of my chair. As I stood to pick up the jacket I looked across the room. That's when I saw my father.

I'd forgotten he was a luxury suite holder and likely to be in the club. My father was sitting with three men. Our eyes locked for an instant but neither of us gave a sign of recognition. I turned away and was slipping on my jacket when Faith came around the table to join me. The others were already headed toward the door. "Don't stare," I said, "but that guy in the blue blazer at the corner table is my father." Faith, pretending to adjust the shoulder strap on her bag, snuck a look across the room. She said nothing but was giggling as we walked toward the door.

"What?" I said.

"Nice nose," Faith said.

"You think my mother saw him?"

"Had to," said Faith. "Even better, he saw her."

"Yeah. Let the scumbag see what he walked out on. Miserable fucker."

"He apparently was a miserable fucker as you so colloquially put it, JP, but for Christ's sake when are you going to let it go? How much control over your feelings do you want to give this guy?"

"Guy like that deserves to be hated," I said.

"Hate destroys the cup that holds it faster than the object it's poured on."

"Plato, Aristotle, or Pliny the Elder?" I said.

"The sisters at Cambridge Catholic," Faith said. "They weren't wrong about everything."

"I can't let it go, Faith. But I don't blame you for not wanting to hear about it for the rest of your life. I'll pick my spots."

"This isn't about me, JP. Look at it this way. For the rest of his life your father's going to have the greatest pain a person can suffer. Remorse. What do you think he felt tonight when he saw you and your mother? What do you think he feels every time he sees you play? His crime comes with its own punishment. Package deal. Doesn't need you."

I nodded as if to say I understood the theory, which I did. But I think Faith knew that even though I could squeeze the theory into my brain, there wasn't room for it in my heart.

We stood against a wall in the corridor outside the club. "You watching the game from the suite?" she asked.

"No. I'll be down by the bench," I said. I asked Faith to meet me outside the dressing room after the game. "Oh. Almost forgot. Here's a pass that'll get you down to the dressing-room level," I said, handing her a plastic-coated card.

I learned the news from the Montreal cop stationed outside our dressing room. "You heard, Jean Pierre?" the cop said as I walked toward the dressing room. "Picard's starting the kid. Fontaine. What'd they call him? The Demonator," the cop said, chuckling, then shaking his head. "A teenager in a Game Seven. *Tabernac.*"

I was talking to the cop when the dressing-room door flew open and Demetre Fontaine led a file of players onto the ice for what was going to be either the last game of the season or a ticket to the Cup finals. Jean Picard was the last one out of the room. "Why Fontaine?" I asked him.

"Because he's too young to be scared," Picard said.

Starting Fontaine in net looked like an inspired choice. Boston launched a cannonade at the Montreal end, getting off the first seven shots of the period and outshooting the Canadiens by an embarrassing 15–5 through the first seventeen minutes. But the flopping, diving Demonator stopped everything until a Gaston Deveau redirection of a Cam Carter shot beat him at 17:28 for a 1–0 Boston lead. Less than a minute later Joe Latendresse scored for us on a breakaway to tie the game and send the Montreal crowd into delirium.

I like watching the game from near the bench. You not only feel it, you smell it—the sweat, the astringent smell of liniment, the faint ammonia smell of the ice, and all of it mixing with the smells of hot dogs and popcorn wafting down from the seats. Like a salmon, I could detect one part of rink in a million parts of fresh air and follow that smell to the nearest game.

I'd been watching Fontaine closely. He wasn't as undisciplined as he'd first looked. When he was on his knees he kept his hands high protecting the top corners. And his dives were so well timed that the surprised puck carrier couldn't do much but shoot into the kid's body. "You got your goalie for the next fifteen years," I said to Marc Wilson, who was standing near the stick rack with me. But I was wrong. Montreal didn't even have Fontaine for another fifteen seconds. I'd no sooner spoken when the puck squirted out of a scrum in front of the Montreal net toward the Boston right point, where Flipside Palmer fired a laser. Fontaine's catching glove shot out and grabbed the puck. But as the crowd began cheering the save, a Boston player got shoved onto Fontaine's fully extended left arm, pushing the arm against the post. I heard the kid scream and figured—rightly as it turned out—that he'd dislocated his elbow and was done for the game and the playoffs.

Marc Wilson jumped onto the ice and headed for Fontaine. At the end of the bench an ashen-faced Ryan McDonough, his confidence as fragile as a Fabergé egg, hauled himself over the boards and began stretching in preparation for tending the Canadiens' goal. Or trying to. No one would say anything disparaging to a teammate during a playoff—especially to a goaltender about to go into a Game 7—but I felt the confidence going out of our team as McDonough skated to the Montreal net.

The Bruins got one shot in the final two minutes. It went in. Cam Carter sent a pass to Flipside, who misfired so badly that the puck skipped in front of McDonough and hopped over the goalie's stick, between his pads, and into the net for a 2–1 Boston lead. I looked at our bench, where half the guys stared at their skates and the other half raised their eyes to the upper reaches of the arena, from whence a few beer cups and many boos rained down.

There was an even louder chorus of boos as the horn sounded ending the first period. I stood at the stick rack waiting for the players to file past me toward the dressing room. Ryan McDonough practically sprinted to the safety of the room. I fell in behind Tim Harcourt, the last guy in line. I was a few feet from the dressing room when I heard the rapid clack of heels on cement and out of the corner of my right eye saw Faith, waving her pass at any security person who cared to see it and bearing down on me like a blitzing safety. She caught me just outside the dressing-room door.

"Hey, JP. Season's over if you don't play in this rodeo," she said.

"Ever think of being a TV analyst?" I said.

"A TV analyst can't clear you to play. I'm a doctor. I can. And will. You up for it?"

"Like I'm up for heaven when I die," I said. "Why the change?"

Faith hesitated a long time. "Your father, mainly," she said. "I don't want you to go through life feeling what he feels, that you weren't there when it mattered. Heads heal faster than hearts."

Faith grabbed the dressing-room door and barged into the room ahead of me. The sudden appearance of a spectacularly attractive woman in a black leather suit in the middle of the dressing room came as an unsettling surprise to Ryan McDonough, who had stripped off all of his gear—as was his wont after a bad goal—and was standing naked beside a pile of goalie equipment. Ryan, who is hung like a race horse, stared at Faith in wide-eyed amazement.

"Nice equipment, kid," Faith said, glancing at Ryan and his pile of gear as she hurried for Picard's office with me two strides behind.

"I'm Dr. McNeil, Mr. Savard's physician," she said, reaching across Picard's desk to shake his hand. "I'll clear Mr. Savard to play. He's yours if you want him."

"Want him? We need him. But I have to run this by Dr. Desaulniers," Picard said, reaching for the phone that would connect him with the Canadiens owner's private lounge. A brief conversation followed, the result of which was that Wingate Desaulniers said he'd be right down with a hand drafted statement that I'd hold him and the Canadiens harmless in the event of further injury and that I had the permission of Faith McNeil, M.D., to play.

"Get dressed, JP," Picard said, smiling. "Winnie's just feeling paranoid."

I went to my locker and started putting on my equipment. I was half dressed when Desaulniers arrived waving his release form. I didn't even stop to read it, just scribbled my name. Faith gave the paper a cursory and contemptuous glance and signed it. Faith can do contemptuous about as well as you've ever seen it done. "This is a big responsibility you're taking on, Dr. Mc-Neil," Desaulniers sniffed.

"JP's my fiancé. What's he going to do? Sue me?" Faith said.

Desaulniers looked at the signatures, folded the letter, stuffed it in his pocket, and left.

One of the assistant coaches almost torpedoed the deal when he reminded Picard that he could only play one of the two goalies listed on the official lineup card. "Not if they both get hurt. New rule," Picard said, then shouted across the room to Ryan McDonough: "Hey, Ryan, I can see that torn Achilles tendon from here. Looks bad." The players laughed, all except Ryan McDonough, who headed for the shower, done for the game.

"Do that number proud, hon," Faith said, giving me a whack on the butt and heading for the door to a round of appreciative stick tapping by my teammates. Faith pushed open the door just as Justin Pelletier said, "Hate to see you go."

"Yeah, but you love watching me leave, Justin," she said, winking and putting an intentionally sexy hip check on the door. *"Bonne chance, gars,"* Faith said as the door closed.

"Waive the five-year rule, son. That lady is Hall of Fame. First ballot," Picard said as we stood up to head out for the second period.

I got a great ovation from the Montreal fans and even a wink from Packy Dodd on the Boston bench as I skated to the net, where Tim Harcourt flipped a few pucks at me in a hurried warm-up before the ref threatened us with a delay-of-game penalty.

I'd like to tell you my appearance in net inspired Montreal and befuddled Boston but it did neither. The Bruins kept pouring on the shots, outshooting us 14–8 in the period but failing to score. Late in the period I went to my knees, hard, to stop a close-in shot. Faith was right. The jolt to my body went right to my head. My headache was back although the pain was momentarily mitigated by an exchange between Rex Conway and Kevin Quigley. I guess Rex was trying to intimidate me when, before the face-off, he said: "JP . . . Woe to that man to whom our offence cometh.' Matthew 18:8."

"It's 'BY whom THE offence cometh,' and it's Matthew 18:7," Quig yelled at Rex. "I went to Catholic school, Rex. Don't fuck with me on the New Testament."

"When you theologians are through I'd like to drop the puck," the linesman said.

The Bruins kept their 2–1 lead into the third period, when Joe Latendresse tied it for us on a shot from the low slot. Rinky Higgins went down a nanosecond too early and Joe snapped the puck over him.

The rest was a blur to me. My head pounded every time I moved. I kept making saves on instinct like a stunned boxer trying to hold on until the bell. For a moment it looked as though that bell would toll prematurely. With two minutes left in regulation, play was at the Boston end when Cam Carter blocked a Montreal shot and took off on a breakaway—nothing between him and the Stanley Cup finals except me. Joe Latendresse turned and sprinted after Cam. Joe couldn't catch Cam but he got close enough to trip him just before Cam shot. The trip called for a penalty shot and that's the way the ref called it, pointing to the center-ice dot, from which Cam would skate in on me alone with the game, the series, a trip to the Cup finals, and hockey immortality his reward if he scored.

The ref signaled to me to see if I was ready. I nodded and got into my crouch. Then the ref looked at Cam. When Cam nodded the zebra blew his whistle and Cam took the puck and began skating toward the goal. If this were a movie you'd see the scene in super slow motion. Cam, sweat dripping off his face, skating in at a deliberate speed cradling the puck on his stick. Me giving ground slowly waiting for Cam to commit to a shot or a deke.

The movie camera would show you Cam fading to his left forcing me to move to my right. Then you'd see Cam shooting the other way. To my glove side. On the movie screen you'd see the puck saucering slowly toward the top corner, drops of water spinning off it and nothing but empty net in front. Then you'd see a glove come onto the screen and suddenly the puck would slap into the glove's webbing inches before it would have sailed into the net. Here the movie would switch from slow mo to real time and you'd see and hear people cheering and our bench emptying as if we'd won the game. But just before the first of the Montreal players arrived at the net to mob me, Cam, skating around behind the net and with his head down so no one could read his lips, yelled, "Nice stop." It was a classy thing to do and I wondered what I might have said if Cam had scored and ended my season and maybe my last shot at the Cup.

All my save did was push the game into sudden-death overtime—twenty-minute periods, first goal wins.

I suppose this would be the part of the movie where the coach comes into the locker room and says something inspirational and his team goes out and wins the game. But all that happened in our room was that Joe Latendresse went into the bathroom and smoked a cigarette, Tim Harcourt leaned into his dressing stall and momentarily fell asleep, a bunch of guys threw their sweat-soaked gloves in the clothes dryer, and Jean Picard told us what we already knew: "In sudden death any shot is a good shot."

The barrage continued into the OT with the Bruins putting eleven shots on me to our seven on Rinky Higgins. The first overtime ended with the game still tied. I was as tired as I've ever been. So were a lot of other guys—on both teams. The coaches had reduced shifts from fifty seconds to thirty-five or forty seconds to try to get players more rest. But goalies don't get rest. I know it looks like we don't have much to do out there besides making our twenty to forty saves. It's not the saves that wear you down. It's the constant moving: Up. Down. Left. Right. Squat. Stretch. Dive. Recover. Most of the movement isn't to make a save, it's to preserve our view of the puck and to maintain position. And of course we do this while wearing about thirty pounds of equipment.

I've never been as tired in a game as I was in that second overtime. But, somehow, when the puck came into our zone, there was always a surge of adrenaline—a fear of losing, of having my season end—to keep me going.

Goaltending is different from most jobs in that a goalie's contribution—saves—comes at the end of one or a series of mistakes by his teammates. Take the face-off to my right late in the second overtime. Joe Latendresse, our center, was cleanly beaten on the drop by Boston's Gaston Deveau, who slid the puck back to Kevin Quigley at the top of the circle. Our right wing was supposed to dart out and cover Quigley. But the winger blew his assignment. Tim Harcourt tried to block Quig's shot but all that did was screen me. As soon as Tim stepped in front of me I butterflied to protect the bottom of the cage and to try to see under the screen. I saw the puck as it flew by Tim's left leg, headed toward the top glove-side corner. Quig's shot was much like Cam's, and Hollywood would have showed it in the same slow motion with the Canadiens logo visible on the flat face of the puck, the top corner of the net seemingly open and the goalie's glove shooting up at the last moment. The only difference this time is that I didn't catch the puck. Quig's shot clanked into the junction of the crossbar and the post. That slow-mo camera would have shown it . . . toppling . . . spinning . . . wobbling . . . toward the ice, where it landed on the goal line and spun—IN.

"THAT'S GOOD!" the ref yelled, pointing at the puck repeatedly with his right hand as though he were killing a snake with a six-shooter. The ref was in perfect position to see the puck roll across the goal line an instant before I scooped it out with my glove. The red light blinked on and a loud collective groan filled the arena except at the far end, where a thousand or so Boston fans screamed and hugged each other.

For a second or two I felt nothing. It was just another goal among the thousands I'd let in since I was a kid. But reality hit quickly. There was nothing I could do. Nothing I could say. I watched the Boston players vaulting over the boards and swarming Quigley. The hardest part of losing isn't your own unhappiness; it's having to watch the other team's joy.

I wouldn't have seen any of this in a regular-season game, because I would've bolted straight to the dressing room. But in a Stanley Cup elimination game you have to hang around to go through the handshake line. It felt strange to be shaking hands with guys who had been my teammates for almost all of my time in the NHL.

Flipside Palmer was first in line and was already singing, "We are the champions. My friend."

Gaston didn't say anything—he just grabbed my right hand and with his left hand pointed to the shot stats on the scoreboard. I'd made forty-one saves in two regulation and two OT periods.

Quigley leaned over and said: "Glad I got it. Wish it wasn't on you, JP." I didn't have the presence of mind to say it, but in retrospect, if someone had to beat me I'm glad it was Quig, a good guy coming off a tough year. Not to mention a tough life.

Just as I came to Cam the PA guy announced the game's three stars: Kevin Quigley was first, I was second, and Cam—who had about fifty minutes of ice time and dealt out more hits than the Mob—was third. "I hope you bet my half million dollars on Boston," I said.

"Much better investment than that. I'll tell you after we beat San Jose," Cam said, giving me a punch on the shoulder the jolt from which went straight to my still-throbbing head.

I lingered in the shower longer than usual, partly to take the edge off of my headache but also because I wasn't all that eager to talk to the media. I've never been one to duck reporters after a loss, but this was an especially painful loss and I didn't want to talk about it. Eventually I put on a robe and went out and told the few remaining writers that Boston is a great team and I wished them well in the finals. Lynne Abbott asked if Tim Harcourt had screened me on the last goal. "Quigley made a perfect shot," I lied.

Faith was waiting for me outside the dressing room. "How's the head?"

"Hurts like hell. But I'm glad I played. Thank you."

We walked toward the Boston dressing room because I wanted to wish the guys well. When I came out of the Boston room I saw Cam's wife, Tamara, and daughters, Lindsey and Caitlin, standing in the corridor waiting for Cam. A tired Caitlin hung on her mother's arm while Lindsey studied the game stat sheet a PR aide had given her. "You were screened on that goal, weren't you, Mr. Savard," Lindsey said, looking up from the stat sheet.

"I saw the puck," I said. But then I thought I should answer the larger question: "Hey, Linds. We're goalies. We make saves, not excuses."

I asked Tamara if she happened to know what her husband had done with the half million dollars I'd given him.

"Sure. I know," she said.

"Well?"

"He made a great investment with it," Tamara said, drawing an imaginary zipper across her lips.

Boston won the Cup, beating San Jose in five games. The Bruins took the first two games in Boston 5–4 and 6–5, lost Game 3, 6–2, in San Jose partly because the Sharks were desperate to save face in front of their fans and partly because Rinky Higgins had another in a series of off nights. Boston won Game 4, 6–4, and the series moved back to Boston.

Faith and I were at the Garden for Game 5. A Boston win would give them the Cup; a loss would send the series back to San Jose. "No way we're doing the Dionne Warwick," Flipside told a TV reporter, then whistled a few bars from "Do You Know the Way to San Jose?"

"You OK with this if Boston wins?" Faith asked as we took our seats seven rows off the ice to the left of the Boston goal.

"Sort of," I said. "I want the guys to win, but it'll be hard not being part of it."

The game was tied 2–2 after the first period and 4–4 after the second. The third period opened with a Sharks goal that Rinky should have stopped. You could feel the air go out of the building. That's when Cam and Quig stepped up and for the next five minutes carried the Bruins on their broad backs. Cam blocked three shots—"What? You think I was going to let Rinky do it?" he told me later—and Quig bulled through two defenders to jam a shot into the San Jose net and tie the game 5–5. The game and the series turned on a play that came two minutes later. Boston was on a power play when Cam took the puck at the right point and did what I'd seen him do about nine thousand times: faked a slapper to freeze the D, then looked to dish the puck to JB at the top of the left face-off circle. The trouble was that Clint Dwyer, the defender on Cam, didn't buy the fake and skated right at Cam. I thought Dwyer was going to steal the puck off of Cam's stick and have himself a breakaway and maybe a shorthanded goal. Instead Cam pulled a spin-o-rama, whirling counterclockwise and dumping the puck off the boards into the right corner, where Luther Brown collected it and threaded a pass to JB, who one-timed it as he curled off the top of the circle.

"Goal," I said to Faith, grabbing her arm just as the puck went into the net and the Garden crowd exploded.

Boston held on for the final five minutes—Cam was on the ice for four of them—while everyone in the building stood and cheered continuously. The crowd counted down the final ten seconds . . . "*Three . . . Two*" . . . I couldn't even hear them yell "*One.*" Pandemonium swept the building and I think it was only the netting, the high glass, and the appearance of a few dozen

Boston cops that kept the crowd from spilling onto the ice. The guys mobbed J.-B. Desjardin and then gave the obligatory hugs to Rinky Higgins. It hurt to watch it and not be part of it.

After the teams went through the handshake ritual—is that a great tradition or what?—ushers wheeled a table onto the ice, and the NHL commissioner handed the big silver Cup to Cam Carter, who hoisted it high and spun around once before he started a slow, stately parade around the rink. Cam passed the Cup to Jean-Baptiste Desjardin, who passed it to Flipside Palmer, who handed it to Kevin Quigley, who got by far the biggest ovation. Eventually everyone on the team got to carry the Cup.

"How you doing with this?" Faith asked me about halfway through the celebration.

"Better than I thought I'd be," I said. Truth is I was jealous. I wanted to be part of it and wasn't sure I ever would be.

I skipped the dressing-room portion of the festivities—champagne spray really stings your eyes—and drove to Faith's house, stopping briefly in Cleveland Circle to pick up a pizza at Pino's.

"What now?" Faith asked after she'd set the pizza on the kitchen table and poured two beers.

"Wait for offers, I guess," I said. "What about you?"

"I have to close on that house I found in Essex Junction. And I still have to sell this place. And, oh yeah," she said with mock surprise. "Don't we have a wedding to plan?"

"Whatever you and your family want is OK with me," I said.

"You're not into weddings?"

"Marriages count. Weddings don't," I said. "A wedding is the last exhibition game before the regular season. It's mainly for the fans. All you want to do in a wedding is get out without getting your starters hurt."

She shrugged and laughed. "Let's get married in September. Next year I'll pull the goalie," she said.

"Pull the goalie?"

"Yeah. No more birth control."

In the next three weeks Faith sold her house but not her basketball hoop. We bought the house in Vermont, then celebrated by slipping away to the Château Frontenac in Quebec City for a few days. On our second day we were in the early stages of what promised to be a memorable afternoon delight when Cam called.

"Nice timing," I said.

Cam told me that he and Gaston Deveau had prevailed on the NHL to let them have the Stanley Cup for an extra day so they could bring it to our alma mater, the University of Vermont. "We've got it until noon on Friday, when some guy from the Hockey Hall of Fame has to fly it to Vancouver so Taki can have his day with it.

"We're having an open house for the Cup at the old Carter rink," Cam said. "We want you there." I told Cam that I'd checked the papers and that he and Gaston—not I—had won the Cup. It wasn't so much that I still felt jealous as that I thought Cam and Gaston might be inviting me because they felt sorry for me.

"Yeah, but we're alumni and old teammates. You belong there. And save time for lunch. My dad's coming up. Wants to talk to you."

I said I'd be there. Faith said she wanted to go too, which I thought was unusual. "Hey, I'm an alumna. I can go," she said.

"You're a what?"

"An alumna. It's the Latin feminine singular. Alumnus, alumni, alumna, alumnae."

Nothing kills sex deader than a Latin lesson.

We extended our stay at the Frontenac and on Thursday drove directly to Burlington, Vermont. We were at the Carter rink at ten o'clock Thursday morning when Cam, Gaston, and Paul Fentross from the Hockey Hall of Fame pulled in with the Stanley Cup. Fentross has a cool job. He's one of two guys who accompany the Cup everywhere it goes. He put on a special pair of jeweler's gloves to lift the Cup from its case onto a draped display table. There's a tradition among players that if you haven't won the Cup you can't touch it. So Gaston and Cam were the only ones who could touch the trophy with their bare hands. That I couldn't touch it didn't make me feel any better. Mostly I felt like a fifth wheel all morning, and I was glad when Fentross repacked the Cup and took off for the airport. "Where we having lunch?" I asked Cam.

"Champlain Medical Center," he said. "They're breaking ground for that new hostel where parents of sick kids—mostly cancer patients—can stay overnight. My parents and the company kicked in a lot of dough for it."

Great, I thought. I'd just had a two-hour reminder that I'd played ten years in the NHL and never won the Stanley Cup. Now I had to go eat finger food, sip soda, and listen to speeches at a ceremonial groundbreaking. "This sucks," I said to Faith as we drove the few minutes to the medical center.

When we arrived at the site of the new building we saw three dozen folding chairs arranged on a flat lawn in front of a podium. Two easels shrouded in white linen stood to the right of the podium. "I admire Cam's parents for funding the thing but I hope they wrap this up fast," I whispered to Faith as we took our seats in one of the back rows beside Rudy Evanston and his parents. "Wish they had one of these when I was a patient here," Rudy said. "My parents lived close but other kids' parents were traveling long distances. Like you don't have enough to do when your kid is sick."

I knew Cam's parents would be there but I was surprised when they arrived in the company of my mother and Denny Moran. I was about to get up and talk to them but the ceremony started on time, which I thought was a bigger upset than the USA beating the Soviet Union in the 1980 Olympics.

Chadwick Thayer III, chairman of the board of the hospital, talked for a few minutes about the importance of "keeping parents close to their children during arduous medical treatments, especially chemotherapy." Then he said he was pleased to announce the naming of the new building. He lifted the shroud off of the first easel to reveal an engraved marble nameplate—"The Carter-Quinn Family Hostel" it read. Below it were oil paintings of Cam's parents and, to my surprise, of Lisa in her nurse's uniform.

"That's where your half mil went, hon," Faith said just as Cam turned around in his seat a few rows in front of us and mouthed the words: "You want your money back?"

I smiled and shook my head. No. I was as over Lisa's death as I'd ever be but I was glad to see her work remembered.

After a phony ceremonial groundbreaking, Chadwick Thayer III went back to the podium to talk about the hospital's tight budget and how projects like the Carter-Quinn Hostel were possible only through private donations. He then pulled another little rope, releasing the shroud covering the second easel and revealing a large oak panel carved with the names of the major donors to the building. There were six names beside the heading that read: "*Founders:* Cameron and Diana Carter Jr., Cam and Tamara Carter, Faith McNeil, M.D., Jean Pierre Lucien Savard." Cam told me later that founding donors had given gifts of a half million dollars and up and that his parents kicked in five million. "I think my father hit the Derby, the Preakness, and the Belmont," he said.

Beneath the founders' names was a lengthy list of other individual and corporate donors. I scanned it for names I knew. There was Serge "the Weasel" Balon—"said he wouldn't make the pledge if we didn't include his nickname," Cam said—Kevin James Quigley, Nancy O'Brien, LICSW, and all of the Bruins players and coaches. There were contributions from Le Club de Hockey Canadien; Dennis Moran; Jacqueline Savard; Dolph and Mary Evanston; and Harry Flask of Masks by Flask. The names were carved on separate sections of oak to allow for the listing of future donors. Near the top of the listing was a blank space where one of the glued-on panels had apparently fallen away. "Should use screws to attach those names," I said to Cam. "It looks tacky when a panel falls out."

"Remind me there's something I have to talk to you about before you leave," Cam said.

"Can't even get a goddamn bourbon in this place," said Cam's father, who looked like he'd had it with the white wine. "Let's hit the Slapshot. Got to talk to you guys," he said, tossing a half-full glass of alleged Chablis into a plastic-lined trash barrel.

"You go ahead. We'll see you there," Cam said. "I've got to talk to JP for a minute." Cam led Faith and me to a table behind the plaque listing the names of the donors.

"I need you to make a decision," Cam said. With that he lifted a small white towel that covered a strip of oak paneling, the strip that I'd thought had come unglued and fallen from the main plaque. "I took this down because I didn't know if you'd want it up there," Cam said, showing me the small wood panel carved with the name *Rogatien J. Lachine.* My father. "He pledged fifty thou," Cam said. "You want him on or off the plaque?"

"If he's off do we still get the dough?" I asked.

"Already got it. No strings attached."

"Then he's gone. Archives," I said.

"OK. Just needed a decision," Cam said.

"Wait a minute, Cam." The voice came from behind me. It was my mother. She put an arm around me and rested her hand on my left shoulder. "It's time to let it go, Jean Pierre. Past time. Let it go for your own sake," she said.

Cam stared at my mother and me. Faith stood by silently. Denny stayed in the background. "Put it up, Cam. It's all right," my mother said in little more than a whisper.

"JP?" Cam said.

I nodded. "It's all right," I said, and reached for Faith's hand. The anger receded and all I felt was tired.

. . .

It was like old times at the Slapshot, where Cam and Tamara, Cam's parents, my mother, Denny, and Faith and I crowded around a wooden table in a back corner of the old college sports bar. "Open a tab and keep an eye on us," Cam's father told the waiter, slipping him two twenties and ordering a round of drinks.

Before the drinks arrived, Cam's dad leaned forward in his chair and said, "It's a done deal. I bought the goddamn team."

"There go another forty-two nights a year," Diana said.

"More than that because we're going deep in the playoffs," Cam's father said. "Whole deal didn't take but ten minutes." We laughed as Cam's father told us how when he walked into Gabe Vogel's office and Gabe said any discussion would be "preliminary to give you time to set up your financing."

"Already got the goddamn financing," Cam's father said, reaching into his suit jacket pocket and throwing a cashier's check for 225 million onto Gabe's desk. "I told Gabe he could have the check and the cable TV rights. Take it or leave it. He took it so fast I was back on the Lear before they had it refueled. Landed in Boston in time for the Sox game. Ahhh, that's all life is anyway. Get up in the morning and do what you have to do, then come home and do what you goddamn want to do."

The drinks arrived.

"You boys are going to have to get yourselves a new agent," Cam's dad explained. "Denny will be running the team, and I don't want any conflicts of goddamn interest."

"Mom's representing me," Cam said. I think he was joking. Then he told us that he was going to play another two seasons. "Harvard B School will still be there," he said.

"You're a free agent July first," Cam's dad said, looking at me. "We're spending to the cap and we're signing you. We'll top whatever Montreal offers. I can't watch any more of that Higgins kid jumping all around in there. Goosing goddamn ghosts is what he looks like he's doing. We're going to sign that Evanston kid as a free agent. Probably start him as the number two in Providence. But he'll be in camp with us next year. I want you to work with him."

"My pleasure," I said, relieved to know for certain I'd be going back to Boston.

"Hey, now who's taking a job that will keep us apart?" Faith asked.

"Only for two seasons," I said. "We can work it out."

"Seems like we just had this conversation," she said, laughing.

"Life's a busted play, hon," I said.

"But that doesn't mean you can't win," she said, squeezing my arm with one hand and with the other making a circular motion signaling the waiter for another round of drinks.

When the second round arrived, Cam's dad raised his glass of Jack Daniel's in Faith's direction. "Lady, you're a goddamn franchise," he said.

"And here's to winning the Cup again next season," Cam said.

We *should* have won it that next season. But we didn't.

Coda

"That's it, guys, time for dinner," I yelled as I walked down the plywood ramp leading from the mudroom door to our backyard rink. It was a few minutes after sunset and I could see the constellation Orion rising in the southeast sky looking like a cosmic goalie clomping out of his dressing room for the next period.

"One more shot," Luc said to Jackie, who was crouched in front of the official NHL goal, one of the gifts the Bruins gave me when I retired eight years ago.

"One shot for the championship of the universe," Jackie said. "Dad, watch this."

Luc was six years old and Jackie eight. It was February school vacation. They'd been playing all afternoon on the sixty-five-by-thirty-five-foot rink I'd made out of plywood boards on a flat patch of ground behind our house in Vermont. In December I'd put a plastic liner in the rink and flooded it with a garden hose. We could skate from about Christmas into early March as long as I kept the rink free of snow.

"Here he comes!" yelled Luc, stickhandling the puck and picking up speed as he skated counterclockwise in front of me before wheeling up ice and skating full bore on Jackie. In the tradition of kids everywhere Luc had to do the play-by-play: "Savard sweeping behind his own goal . . . breaks down the right wing . . . past one defenseman . . . he's in alone . . ."

Jackie stood at what would have been the top of the crease,

giving Luc not much more than the five hole and a sliver of space in the top left corner.

"He cuts for the net . . . goes high . . . and he . . ." but as Luc started to yell "SCOOOORES," Jackie's blocker flashed up to tip the puck over the goal and into the garden fencing I'd nailed above the boards to keep pucks in play. Luc retrieved the puck as it came off the fencing, held it behind the net for a second, faked coming out to his right just long enough to move Jackie to that post; then Luc cut to the opposite post and tucked the puck into the net. "He SCOOOORES . . . on the wrap-around!" Luc yelled lifting his stick in the air and dancing on his skates.

"We said ONE shot, you moron. That was TWO shots!" Jackie yelled.

"I still scored. Look at it, it's in the net," Luc said, pointing to the puck. That's when Jackie threw the goalie gloves on the ice and ripped off the goalie mask, letting her long auburn hair fall onto her padded shoulders. "I'm going to kill you, Luc," she said, grabbing her brother by the V-neck of his hockey shirt with her left hand and hauling back her right for what might've been a pretty good shot to Luc's helmeted head.

"HEY!" I yelled, freezing Jackie's would-be punch at the top of her windup. "Don't hit a guy wearing a helmet and visor. You'll hurt your hand."

"Ah, now there's good fatherly advice to a daughter," said a voice behind me. Faith had just gotten home from work.

"Mom. They said I didn't score but I did. It's still in the net. Look at it," said Luc, skating backward away from his sister and pointing at the puck.

"We said ONE shot. That was TWO shots," Jackie said, holding up two fingers.

"Picked up some Chinese for dinner," said Faith, switching to a subject that had everyone's approval.

"You guys have so much energy, grab a shovel and help me clean the ice. I'm going to resurface."

Faith headed for the house while Jackie, Luc, and I tilted the heavy metal goal over the low boards and off of the ice; then we each grabbed one of the three plastic snow shovels I keep near the rink and began scraping the ice and flipping the shovels full of snow over the boards. When we finished, the kids walked up the plywood runway to the mudroom to take off their skates and hockey equipment in the warmth of the house. I opened the metal bulkhead doors to the cellar, grabbed a bottle of Molson Canadian from the cellar fridge, then hauled up the garden hose and screwed it onto the water faucet protruding from the basement wall. I had to pour a pitcher of warm water over the faucet to thaw it out. The hose hissed and shuddered like a snake as water surged through it. Setting the brass nozzle on a hard spray and stepping over the boards, I walked to the far end of the rink and—a beer in one hand, the hose in the other—began sending a spray of water over the ice. Resurfacing is a healing act, like forgiveness. The water rushes into the cracks and skate cuts, melting what ice chips escaped the shovels and producing a perfect uncut surface. It makes the ice new again.

Cam, Tamara, Lindsey, and Caitlin would be visiting for the weekend and I wanted the ice to be as good as it could be. Cam is a senior partner of Carter & Peabody and an alternate governor of the Bruins, which his father still owns. When Cam joined the company he founded the Sports & Gaming Fund, a mutual fund investing in the stocks of sports equipment makers, publicly traded European soccer teams, and casinos. It returned 33 percent in its first year and has earned double digits every year since, pleasantly shocking his father. "If you'd have asked me I would've said Cam was just keeping the goddamn chair warm for Lindsey," Cam's dad said.

I signed on as a volunteer goalie coach for Vermont. I go to most afternoon practices but I'm home in time for dinner. It's a nice life.

"Dad, dinner in twenty minutes," Jackie yelled from the mudroom door.

"OK," I said.

It took me about fifteen minutes to finish the ice and the beer. I coiled the hose, threw it down the bulkhead stairs, and dragged it onto the floor of the unfinished portion of our basement. About a pint of water gushed from the hose over the basement floor, where it would quickly dry in the heat from the furnace. I closed the bulkhead doors, left my boots near the hose, and took the empty beer bottle into the finished portion of the basement— "the Man Room" as Faith calls it—to store it in a case of other empty bottles.

That Man Room was my idea. It has a wet bar, a half bath, a hundred-bottle wine rack, a working fireplace, a plasma TV equipped for hi-def, and some great framed hockey photos. There's a print of Bill Barilko scoring in overtime to win the 1951 Stanley Cup for the Toronto Maple Leafs, and the picture of an airborne Bobby Orr after he scored the goal that won the 1970 Cup for Boston. There are shots of Cam and me from our playing days with the Bruins including a great shot of Cam knocking Serge "the Weasel" Balon through the door to our team's bench in my first year back in Boston. We could've won the Cup that year. But we didn't. Cam missed seven weeks with a broken foot; I missed twenty games with a groin I kept pulling; Taki missed the whole season with his knee injury; and Rinky Higgins wrote his ticket to Providence by going 4–16 and three times being replaced by Rudy Evanston. The next season, my last, was better.

"It's on the table, hon," Faith called down the stairs. I started toward the staircase but couldn't stop looking at the pictures. There were photos of Rudy and I working together at practice . . . Cam on his special night when the team gave him the seat from the penalty box after he'd racked up 211 minutes in penalties in his final year . . . Kevin Quigley on one knee giving a fist pump after he'd scored the goal that eliminated Ottawa in the quarterfinals.

Then I stared at the photo I always stare at, the one over the fireplace. It was a hurry-up thing our team photographer put together on the night Cam and I played our final game. We were in various stages of undress when the photographer called for us to get together in the middle of the room. Players only. There was no posing. Some guys stood, some knelt, a few sat on the floor. There was Quigley, bare-chested, his hockey pants held up by an old-fashioned suspender looped over his right shoulder; Flipside Palmer still dripping from the shower, a towel wrapped around his waist; Taki, who'd come back after missing a year, still in uniform and smoking a cigar; Cam sitting on the floor staring straight at the camera, exhausted. And, beside Cam, me, in my long underwear, hair sweat-matted onto my forehead, and grinning ear to floppy ear, my skinny welted arms wrapped around that big silver Cup.

I closed the door and went upstairs.

R.I.P. 9/14/2008

Globe
9/15/08

MISCELLANY

Hockey writer Falla dies of heart failure

Jack Falla, a former hockey writer at Sports Illustrated before becoming a communications professor at Boston University, died of heart failure in Maine. The Natick resident was the author of a number of books on hockey, including "Open Ice: Reflections and Confessions of a Hockey Lifer," that is to be released this month...

FALLA John M. Of Natick, suddenly, September 14, 2008. Beloved husband of Barbara (Baldwin) Falla. Devoted father of Brian D. Falla and his wife Kimberley Davis of Hudson, Tracey A. Falla and her husband Maurice H. Fontaine III of Cumberland, ME. Loving grandfather of Demetre J. and Ella R. Fontaine, both of Cumberland, ME. Brother of Patrick Falla and his wife Jane of Conway, MA, and Elizabeth (Falla) Verrill of Hampstead, NH. Nephew of Mary J. Sweeney of Manchester, NH. Uncle of Emily Verrill-Ballard of Conway, MA, Ami Verrill of Philadelphia, PA, Liam and Alden Falla both of Conway, MA, Stephen and Mark Reynolds both of Natick, Patricia (Reynolds) Ferrotti of Chicago, IL. And Kathryn (Reynolds) Maloney of PA. Brother in law of Raymond and Mary Reynolds of Wellesley, and Harriet Holich of Northampton, MA. Funeral from the George F. Doherty & Sons Funeral Home 477 Washington St. (RT 16) WELLESLEY, Thursday at 9 AM. Funeral Mass in St. Patrick Church Natick at 10 AM. Visiting hours Wed. 4-8 PM. Relatives and friends kindly invited. Interment private. John received his master's degree in communications from Boston University. He was a professor at Boston University, and a sports writer and most recently published several books on hockey, life, and love. In lieu of flowers donations in John's memory may be made to Food Pantry C/O Natick Service Council, 11 Pond St. Natick, MA 01760. For directions and guestbook www.gfdoherty.com.

George F. Doherty and Sons
Wellesley 781 235 4100